CW00433948

SOMEONE'S THERE

C. J. GRAYSON

First published in print format by the method of self-publishing via Amazon (Kindle Direct Publishing) in 2019. This is the third edition of this novel (updated in Sep 2022). I have made improvements. The narrative remains the same.

Text Copyright © C. J. Grayson in 2019 (2022)

Cover design © C. J. Grayson

C. J. Grayson asserts the moral right to be identified as the author of this novel. No part of this book may be reproduced, or stored in a retrieval system, or transmitted in any form or by any means, electronic, mechanical, photocopying, recording, or otherwise, without express written permission by the author, C. J. Grayson.

This novel is entirely the work of fiction. The names, characters, and incidents portrayed throughout the novel are the work of the author's imagination. Any resemblance to actual persons, living or dead, or events is coincidental, and has not been intended by the author. There are several locations which the author has used, mainly in the areas of Toddington, Luton, Hemel Hempstead in the south of England, as the setting for this novel, but the reader should know the events that happen in these particular locations are subject totally on the work of fiction and imagination and not the actual opinion of that particular location.

ISBN: 9781699669471
Version: Revised updated Edition Sep 2022

C. J. Grayson

Books by C. J. Grayson

Standalones –
Someone's There

DI Max Byrd and DI Orion Tanzy –
That Night (Book 1)
Never Came Home (Book 2)
No One's Safe (Book 3)

For my wife, Becky, and my three boys. Without your support, patience, and belief that one day I'd finally finish this, none of this would have been possible.

Thank you.

1

14/07/1983

On Monday, just after five in the afternoon, the glass doors of Watford General Hospital Casualty swung open. Hot summer air blasted through the threshold, along with a flying trolley being pushed by two tall, thin paramedics. They took a right and dashed along the wide corridor, one on either side.

A bright light shone down from the low ceiling onto the polished grey linoleum floor. The revolving wheels of the trolley squeaked as the paramedics wasted no time. Their footsteps pounded on the floor with urgency, echoing inside the aging hallway, where the smell of disinfectant and hospital food lingered in the air. They passed the busy waiting area occupied by small crowds of people waiting to be seen. A father, sitting with his son, glanced up at the two paramedics as they whizzed by.

'Just hold on, please,' said one of the paramedics, his wide eyes glaring down on the unconscious teenager below him.

'She'll make it, Jim, don't worry, she'll make it,' panted his colleague on the other side of the gurney.

Jim gave him a weak smile and looked forward.

The teenager was in a bad way, unconscious with heavy blood loss from a crushed, twisted leg. Her face was covered in blood and was bruised, covered in cuts and tears which made you wince.

Along the wide corridor, after hearing the chaos, a doctor came out of his small office and stared at the trolley hurtling towards him. He gulped hard. He'd heard about the accident and the A+E doctors were readying themselves for emergency surgery.

'This way!' he urged, waving frantically.

The two hunched-over paramedics nodded twice, picked up their already-impressive pace. The wheels of the gurney screeched even louder, rotating like burning Catherine wheels on a cold November night.

Metal clicked and clonked.

Sweat poured from their tired skin and their arms were in agony, their legs feeling the burning of lactic acid building up. When they reached the end of the corridor, they took a left then an immediate sharp right through the open doorway of room 106. The doctor followed them in and, seconds later was joined by three more, who all fixed their attention on the girl on the gurney.

The room was alive and busy.

Brilliant light shone down on every nook and cranny. The floor was polished, the walls were white. Multiple footsteps caused a hectic pitter-patter. One nurse grabbed a metal tray full of clean instruments while another collected the defibrillator, and placed it by the doctor's side.

The room suddenly fell silent.

'What do we have?' asked the doctor, his voice loud and clear.

The closest nurse appeared by his side with a clipboard containing notes.

'Severe RTA,' she declared. 'Collision with a tree at high speed. Heavy bleeding from her right thigh, likely damage to the femoral artery. No sign of life since the incident.'

'Is she alone?' the doctor asked, not taking his eyes off the blood in front of him. He rolled up his white sleeves like he'd done so many times before.

'According to a passer-by who witnessed the crash, there was a man, but he ran away. No sign of him.'

The doctors surrounded the unresponsive teenager and went to work.

'Will she make it?' the young nurse asked innocently – it was her second shift as a trainee nurse.

'Hard to say,' the doctor replied with his back to her.

The young nurse with the clipboard offered a sad smile and stepped back, allowing the doctors the precious space they need. She returned along the corridor to a small room to examine a patient who was waiting.

Later the young nurse heard the good news: the teenager had been revived and was now breathing. There was a full report on the incident the next day. Signed by the doctor himself, he dated it: 14/7/1983.

The doctor needed to speak to the victim about something that bothered him. Her crash injuries were obvious; they were fresh, easily noticeable. But the bruising on her throat and arms was not: shades of green and yellow covered the skin. The stage of bruising appeared between six to ten days after whatever caused it.

Someone may have tried to strangle her at some point days before the crash.

2

Wednesday Night (August 2015)
Toddington

The Deacon brothers dashed over the dry, hard ground. Their lungs burned for a desperate breath of air in the summer humidity. Blood raced through every vein in their trembling bodies as they headed for the tall trees in front of them.

Time was against them.

They were both running for their lives.

Leon Deacon, the bigger of the two, winced from the bullet wound to his bloody calf. His blue jeans were ripped, moist flesh draped over the wet twisted fabric. Every stride was an agonising blow. He wanted to stop, needed to, but he knew what would happen if he did.

'Fuck!' Leon shouted. His head was fuzzy, twirling with dizziness, his vision blurry with tears fuelled by both pain and anger.

His brother, Baret, smaller and thinner, clutched his own arm to stop the explosion of blood forcing its way from the open flesh of his ripped bicep.

'Keep... going,' Baret managed, but it was so quiet and weak, it was almost inaudible. 'Come on.' Side by side, they closed in on the large cluster of trees.

The meeting with Alexander Hunt hadn't gone to plan. The Deacons didn't think Hunt would find out they'd screwed him over, but they were terribly wrong.

Hunt wasn't stupid.

He'd been in the game long enough to figure these things out. He had connections all over the place. He was an old dog with years under his belt, someone who'd seen it all. Screwing Hunt would be their final and, very costly, mistake.

The meeting had been arranged close by. When the brothers had turned up, they had no idea of Hunt's plans, assuming it would be a routine meet, to arrange the transport of more weapons and drugs. They'd been in business with Hunt for months. Everything ran like clockwork.

Until now.

Until they got greedy.

Hunt's men were snapping at the heels of the injured brothers. His right-hand man, Phil, a 6 foot, four mountain of a man, guided the adrenaline-fuelled wave like a pack of hungry wolves.

Leon Deacon, with blood pouring from his leg, somehow managed to take the lead, his muscular legs motoring on as he ducked under the low awkward branches. For a moment, the aging greenery blocked the glare of the setting sun which gave them clear vision - a split second to decide where to go.

Where to escape.

Baret levelled with Leon and passed him, still clutching his arm. 'Come on, go over there!' Baret shouted, noticing a small gap ahead. He changed his direction darting forward, but seconds later, he stopped when he heard the loud, hard crunch behind him. His heart sank into his stomach.

Hunt's men had caught them up.

Phil had smashed Leon round the back of his head with a baseball bat, the powerful blow echoing through the warm, evening air. Leon now unconscious, collapsed to the ground. Blood oozed from the open gash at the back of his mangled head. Phil lifted the baseball bat to the sky again, and threw it down with everything he had into Leon's face. The crunch of wood hitting bone was sickening.

Phil, without hesitation, charged toward Baret, swinging the baseball bat. He walloped the broken flesh on his arm, the slap forcing Baret to wail almost inhumanly as he fell clumsily to his knees, screaming in pain.

Leon was dead. A pool of crimson disperses around his body. Baret wriggled like a worm on his back and, with his eyes clamped shut, he clasped onto his drenched arm.

Phil's large figure stood over the beaten brothers as the rest of Hunt's men finally catch up. All dressed in black, they slowly surrounded them.

In his long brown coat, Alexander Hunt slowly approached the commotion. He glared down at the two men and laughed at the sight of Leon who, now, was almost unrecognisable: half of his face torn away from the hefty blows.

'Did you really think you could rip me off?' he asked Baret in a very calm manner. Baret didn't comprehend Hunt's words, instead, he focused on the pain of his own arm. Hunt paused, allowing the evening air to soak up the wails of Baret. 'No one rips me off.'

Hunt reached inside his long brown coat with his right hand and pulled out his gun. He leaned over the body of

Leon Deacon and shot him in the back. Leon's body shuddered an inch from the impact of the bullet, but it made no difference; he was already dead.

Baret, forcing the warm air in and out of his nostrils, squinted at Hunt.

Hunt glanced back and smiled. His sparkling white teeth reflected the dim glare of the falling sun.

'Just fucking do it,' Baret shouted, his eyes almost closed, beyond the point of giving up.

Hunt shot him in the face an inch below his right eye: his cheek ripped away from his face, parts of bloody flesh splattered on the ground behind him.

Little did Alexander Hunt know, someone nearby was watching.

3

Toddington
JACK

I glared at my wife from across the bedroom, feeling my face grow warm and my pulse getting faster.

'Well?' she said. Her wide eyes stared back at me as she placed both hands on her slender hips.

I hated that look - a look of disappointment.

'Listen,' I said, trying to keep calm, 'I only do what I think is right. There's nothing wrong with caring for my own daughter. I-'

'Jack, for God's sake,' she interrupted, dropping her hands by her side. She moved around the suitcase to the foot of the bed. 'Listen, I was young once, I know how things are.' She pointed a finger towards my feet, emphasising her point. 'But I also know she needs her space. She's sixteen now, she's left school...' Her finger lowered by her side along with her volume. 'She isn't a child anymore. Is she?'

I shrugged in the silence of my own answer, reached up with my left hand, and pulled my reading glasses up off my face.

'Exactly. Just - just give her the space she needs.'

The tension in the air could have been sliced with a knife.

'I – I just want to know what's going on,' I informed her. 'I know what the world is like, I know what people are like…'

She raised a palm in the air and I trailed off into silence.

'Lucy spoke to me two nights ago. You want to know what she said to me?'

I shook my head and waited.

'She told me she feels trapped. Said she was annoyed at you for ringing and texting her all the time when she was out.'

'I-'

'No, listen! You need to know this! When she was out with her friends, she was embarrassed. They made fun of her for it. They said-'

'Embarrassed of what, of me-'

'Yes, of you!' she screamed.

I stared at her, stunned.

She brought a clenched fist up and slammed the humid air in front of her to vent her frustration. The rage in her eyes met mine and I sighed heavily. I knew I wouldn't win this debate. Sometimes it was pointless arguing with Joanne. She was strong-willed, stubborn, and usually *never* wrong. And when she was wrong, it was never her fault.

'She was not a child anymore,' Joanne said, 'so even though you don't feel like you're treating her like one, *she* feels like you are. So please, just give her some space. If we, as her parents, need to know something or something is bothering her, she'll tell us.'

I nodded, decided I'd had enough, and walked out of the bedroom.

End of conversation.

Later, I stood in the kitchen lost in a gaze, and, through the window, I watched the birds flutter away from the drooping branches on a tree at the bottom of our long garden. They seemed so happy and chirpy, coming and going as they pleased, communicating with each other in a language only they understood.

I checked my watch. Nearly 10 p.m. Lucy wasn't home yet. I'd be lying if I said I wasn't starting to worry.

I replayed the earlier conversation with Joanne in my head.

She was embarrassed.

You're embarrassing her.

I felt awful she feels this way. She could tell her mother but not me. Did she feel she couldn't open up to me? That I'd be offended? I assumed that's what parents did. Cared for their children – to know where they were and what time they'd be back.

Lucy was over the fields capturing shots of the sunset with her new black Nikon camera, taking advantage of the heatwave that had hit the south of England. She started her A-levels in Photography, Media, and Art Design at Luton sixth form – it was so far so good, she told me-

My phone buzzed in my pocket.

I stopped watching the birds in the garden and took out my phone, unlocked it with a swipe, and entered the four digits. I hoped it was Lucy.

It wasn't her.

It was Ray, a colleague from work. I briefly read the message and sighed, then closed my eyes briefly. The work-related matter could be dealt with sometime tomorrow, although tomorrow wasn't ideal either. That was the joy of being the Financial Director of a bank: you had responsibility.

And I'll tell you, it was amazing the amount of issues employees bring to you; pointless, trivial things which if I'm being honest, didn't interest me. I don't say that to be nasty, inconsiderate, or unsupportive of my staff, but taking the day off work because someone's goldfish died just didn't cut it in the banking world. The text from Ray was about helping him finalising the accounts for July, kindly asked me if I would look over them when it was convenient.

Where the hell was Lucy?

I walked out through the open door onto the decking, the warm air gently rubbed my forearms where I'd rolled up my sleeves. I hadn't changed yet, still wearing the shirt and trousers from work. I even managed to add a little bolognese sauce for effect.

Across the fields, the sun dipped quickly. The vast open space of natural greenery pleasantly presented itself but my mind searched for an explanation for my daughter's whereabouts. The birds on the tree branches had vanished, presumably taking a higher position where they'd already diligently built their nests for their young.

In the distance, a very low hum of M1 traffic tinkered in the air. So far away, it was almost silent. Usually, the silence was nice and comforting. Right now, it allowed my mind to wander about Lucy.

I took the phone back out of my pocket and found her number.

No, don't, Jack. Joanne's words hung over me like a dark cloud.

I locked it and put it back into my trousers.

Joanne was still in the bedroom upstairs packing her suitcase for the two days away in Barcelona. My cousin, Joseph, was getting married and, being regular visitors of Spain, we inclined it would be over there.

I observed the fields out the back, taking it all in. It was beautiful. I scanned along the fence, which separated our land from the nature surrounding us. The small lake in the distance looked calm and still and above and beyond, the sun dipped gently in the sky, sliding over the lip of the earth's curvature, forcing small shadows that crept slowly across the decking towards my feet.

Another check of my watch-

The sound of the front door buzzer hissed sharply from the speaker in the kitchen.

Lucy was finally home. As I returned to the kitchen, I heard the quick sounds of her trainers slapping the wood flooring in the hallway before I saw her at the kitchen door. Her cheeks were red and her breathing was heavy. The black Nikon camera swung from her neck.

'Hey, you okay?' I said. I closed the door and locked it.

'I'm fine, Dad,' she replied without looking at me.

Lucy took off her coat, and hung it on the wooden hook on the wall to her right then, using both hands, she tucked her long blonde hair behind her ears, then sighed.

'What's up, Lucy?'

'Nothing,' she said sharply. 'I'm fine.'

She wasn't fine – she was fidgety, something was bothering her. She pulled the camera over her head, placed it on the large wooden circular table in the centre of the kitchen. From her jeans pocket, she grabbed her phone and unlocked it. The glow from the phone dimly lit her bright blue eyes as she peered over it.

Her hands and forearms trembled.

'Did you get some good shots? There's a lovely sunset out the back,' I said, watching her unsteady hands curiously.

'Yeah.' She kept her eyes on her phone. Her thumbs frantically tapped the phone screen. Without looking up, she said, 'Why aren't you working?'

'I have been. Just finished. Going to double-check that we've got everything for tomorrow. Have you packed your case?'

A one-worded response: 'No.'

'Why are you shaking, Lucy?'

She glanced up at me with nervous eyes. 'I'm not!'

'Lucy, look, your hands are shaking.' I took a step towards her-

'Don't, Dad, just… I'm, I'm fine, okay?' She backed away, increasing the space between us.

'Okay, right.' I held both palms up in surrender, then angled my body towards the table. I extended my arm for her camera. 'Let me have a look-'

'No, Dad!' she bellowed, charging forward, snatching the camera from the table, holding it close to her chest.

I frowned with my arm still extended in mid-air. 'Lucy, what-'

'Don't…. I need… I need to edit them,' she explained. 'I'll show you when I'm finished.'

I let the frown on my face fade away and moved back a little. I could see her eyes were glassy. She'd been crying over something.

'Okay?' she said. The phone in her hands beeped. A message. She looked down.

'Okay, no problem.' I nodded my head and retired backward to give her some space. 'Well, let me know when you've done them, I'd love to have a look.'

I smiled but it wasn't returned.

'Yeah,' she agreed. Whatever she was doing on her phone had priority over speaking with me, so to give her the freedom Joanne had told me to, I said good night and walked past her towards the hallway.

'We're setting off early, so don't be up late,' I said, leaving the kitchen. 'Oh, and turn on the house alarm okay?'

'Yeah, okay. Night, Dad.'

'Good night, Lucy.'

I climbed the stairs, knowing I should've pushed her to tell me what was going on. But in the wise words of my wife: if we need to know something or something is bothering her, she'll tell us.

This time, I wasn't too sure.

4

Toddington

Phil stood on the grass verge at the side of the road waiting for Derek and Stuart to catch up.

A niggling stitch stabbed between his ribs, but his slow, deep breathing encouraged the pain to fade. Tall and wide, a mountain of a man, his dark thick eyebrows sat above his well-trimmed goatee to compliment his tanned features.

He was man who did what's asked of him.

And a man who did it well.

Little to his knowledge, his boss, Alexander Hunt, made the right choice not killing him a few years ago. Phil turned out to be valuable to Hunt, there's no question about it.

Phil heard the heavy, clumsy footsteps on the dry grass behind him, accompanied with the exhaustive gasps of Derek and Stuart who finally appeared by his side. Stuart's hands were on his hips as he gasped for air. Derek was barely holding himself up, almost doubled over like a dog on all fours.

Phil turned and shook his head at them.

When they gathered themselves, the three men stood at the side of the road behind the six-foot tall concrete pillar which supported the heavy, wide black gate. On the other side of the open gate, there was another pillar, supporting the symmetrical joining gate. Phil peered along the road, noticing the brick wall running the whole length of the property parallel with the road.

Using his eyes, he followed the winding, gravel-filled driveway until he met the front of the house.

It was an impressive, extravagant looking house. Not co-lossal in size, but large enough to stand out. In its isolation, the nearest property was at least half a mile away in a small place called Toddington, which respectably was made up of a few streets. Phil knew that's too far for the boy and girl to run. He knew his own fitness ability and could almost guarantee they didn't reach that far.

'They must be here,' said Derek, looking at the house.

Phil nodded. 'Yes.'

In the sky, the sun faded fast, allowing the darkness to settle in. Phil spotted a security light above the front door which could pose a risk if they got too close. Two cars – a Volvo XC90 and a BMW 330d - were parked on the gravel in front of the house.

Probably man and wife, Phil thought, but he knew not to assume, because assumptions could be the mother of all fuck ups in this line of business.

To Phil's right, a car engine roared, disturbing the quiet ambience.

Dazzling head lights illuminated the rural road.

Moving fast.

'Quick, move now!' Phil urged.

They shuffled across the gravel, along the width of the gate, around the edge, and backed on themselves to hide behind the opposite side of the same pillar.

The car approached, the tires rotating quickly, the hot rubber against the cold tarmac.

A flash of brilliance whizzed by the opening of the drive-way and, moments later, the sound of the engine faded into the darkness behind them.

'Listen, Derek,' Phil said, 'you need to go around the side of the house – go to the left, keep a distance in case a light sensor picks you up. I couldn't see any from here, but we don't know. Stay off the gravel otherwise you'll be heard.'

Derek nodded.

'You go around to the right Stu – keep a distance,' Phil told Stuart. 'We don't know who's here. Two cars parked up. Could be two people, could be ten. It was a big house.'

'Okay, Phil.'

Phil liked Stuart or 'Stu' – more so than Derek. Stuart could get aggressive and did as he was told. Phil watched his slim, wiry frame go to the right.

Derek angled left.

Phil stayed behind the concrete pillar, using it as a good vantage point to see the front and left side of the house simultaneously. His men crept away from him.

In one of the windows upstairs at the front of the house, a light flashed on. Phil saw the curves of a woman through the glass. She passed the left window, then passed the right carrying something in her arms. Piled items of clothing. She lowered herself in front of the window and, with her back to the glass, the shape of her buttocks tested the tight flexible material of her well-fitting leggings. Phil blinked to focus, allowing the creative side of his imagination to develop a fictional fantasy. It wasn't long before the show was over and the woman stood up.

The woman disappeared from both windows, then the room plunged into darkness.

Stuart kept clear of the sensor above the front door as he rounded the rear of the cars. To his right, he saw the long brick wall, running along the side of a freshly cut lawn, disappearing around the side of the house. The space between the side of the house and the high wall was joined by a sturdy fence of similar height.

'Shit.'

Stu was stuck now, unsure where to go. He approached the side lawn with limited options. He couldn't see a way around the side of the house.

Something in the dark caught his eye. Something reflecting the light. Something metal. As he peered closer, he saw the handle of a gate a few metres along the fence. Creeping slowly and, not to make a noise, he stayed off the gravel the best he could until he reached the gate. Next to the gate, four overly-filled bin bags were lined up against the fence, causing the smell of fresh-cut grass to waft up to his nose.

He glanced left at the house.

In the shadows, he saw the front door. Made of solid pine, varnished in a layer of creamy white protection, with a small, clear, rectangular glass plane installed at eye level. Either side of the door, two narrow, tall, crystalized glass planes stood proudly like bouncers standing at the door of a nightclub. A very dim light soaked through the glass. Right of the door, he saw a square window. Lightly as he could, he crept across the gravel and peered through the glass into the dimness of the room but saw nothing. A wave of panic washed over him - he needed to find them quickly.

The boy and girl.

At the gate, he grabbed the handle and, using his thumb, very cautiously pressed downwards.

The gate edged open with a creak.

'Shit,' he whispered.

He froze, keeping hold of the gate until the sound vanished into the hushed darkness.

After inhaling a deep breath, Stuart slowly stepped through the gate.

On the opposite side of the house, Derek distanced himself, carefully making his way along. He stopped, crouched down on the grass, his back against the cool brick wall. It was evident the house is fairly new, the sharp edges of its outer shell, the deep, dense colour of each red brick, the almost perfect jointing lines of the craftmanship. The light had almost gone, giving him a vague cover of stealth.

To his right at the end of the driveway he saw Phil's outline standing at the pillar. To his left there was a fence running along from the wall he was leaning against to the side of the garage. The gap between the garage and the house was maybe a metre or so, filled with a gate which, Derek assumed, led to a rear garden.

He scanned across the three visible windows of the house.

It seemed quiet, no one-

A figure moved across the left window. A man wearing black trousers and a white shirt. Thin and tall. Not noticeably tall but he'd hold his own in a crowded room.

'Who's this?' Derek muttered to himself.

The man moved towards the back of what seemed like a kitchen, out of his view.

An unusual sound caught Derek's attention from somewhere above. He craned his neck, glanced up, squinting into the dark sky.

He saw movement. 'What's that?'

It looked like a ladder. He heard the noise again. A metallic rattle. Another one.

'What the…'

The cause of the noise was now obvious.

Someone was climbing a ladder, pulling themselves upwards, rung by rung, dissolving into the night up to a small balcony.

He focused hard.

'Who the hell is that?' he whispered.

Judging by the man's figure, Derek wondered if it could be Phil but, as he glanced to the right, Phil was exactly where he was before: by the pillar at the front gate. Derek returned his attention to the sound, watching the man curiously. The man was dressed in a grey tracksuit and, as he reached the top, he watched him climb over onto the balcony and out of sight.

Stuart closed the gate slowly but didn't allow the lock to catch, preventing the click he was certain it would cause. He scanned through the darkness at the length of the house, noticed it didn't go very far until the brickwork hit a corner.

He rounded the corner slowly. A bright light shone from a wide, rectangular window towards the end of the house. The two windows he'd passed were in darkness.

He stood a metre from the window where the light was, slowly leaned across and peered inside. The kitchen.

A large wooden table rested in the centre of it. To the right there was a U-shaped spacious area filled with white cupboards above and below, separated by a standard gap with black granite worktop which sat on top of the lower cupboards. A large set of knives caught his eye near the sink.

On the opposite side of the kitchen, a door was open to what seemed like a platform of decking space.

Moments later, he witnessed a man enter through the door, his shirt sleeves rolled up, dark trousers hanging over his bare feet.

Stu backed off into the shadows, knowing if the man glanced his way, he would be seen. The man's mouth opened and moved as if he was talking, but the sounds were muffled by the window. The man closed the door, locked it, and turned to face whoever he was speaking to.

Stu angled his head around the edge of the window.

It was the girl they were looking for.

Long blonde hair, camera hanging from her neck under a red, tired face. He watched them through the window. Stuart observed the man, who he assumed was the girl's father, reaching for the camera she'd placed on the table but she grabbed it before he did. Then after some words the man disappeared, leaving the girl alone.

Once her father was out of sight she picked up the camera and stared at it for a long moment. She then ambled to the back door where there was a square keypad fixed to the wall. She punched in a few digits, then glanced up to her right. Stuart, watching through the window, followed her gaze, noticing the sensor in the top corner of the kitchen flashing.

System alarm active.

The girl turned, killed the light, and left the dark kitchen with the camera in her hand.

A while later, the night was in total darkness. Cars passed every so often along the rural road in front of the house. Headlights cut the air like neon arrows of blinding brilliance. Engines approached then vanished, passing quickly without knowing he was hiding there.

Stu and Derek returned to the pillar at the front of the driveway. Stuart told them both about the girl in the kitchen speaking with her father.

'Does she have the camera?' asked Phil.

'She does.' He nodded. 'Her father tried grabbed it-'

'Shit,' Phil said.

'…but she got there first,' Stu added quickly.

'Okay. Good.'

'Another thing…' said Derek.

They both glanced at him.

'I saw someone climbing a ladder at the side of the house. He was tall, dressed in a grey tracksuit.'

Phil mulled over his words before he said, 'Okay.' He thought a moment longer. 'So, we know there's at least four people in there. Think it would be easy to kick the door in. You up for it?'

Derek glimpsed at Stuart, unsure.

'I would be,' said Stu, 'but the girl just turned on the house alarm. However we enter, we'll set it off. We don't know how long we'll have before we have to get back out.'

Stu's words lingered in the air and neither Derek nor Phil responded. Shoving his hand into his pocket, Phil plucked out his phone, punched in a number, and put it to his ear.

'Boss, we're here,' he said, then listened.

'Did you see the girl?' asked Hunt.

'Yes, we did. We think the boy climbed an outside ladder to get into the attic.'

'The attic? The fucks he doin' up there?'

'God knew.'

'Have you been inside the house yet, Phil?' Hunt asked.

Silence.

'Phil, have you-'

'We haven't yet, no.'

'What are you waiting for? An invitation?' Hunt shouted.

Phil didn't answer.

'Go in and get the fucking camera.'

'They've just turned on the house alarm. We'll set it off,' Phil explained.

Alexander Hunt absorbed Phil's words in silence.

'Boss?'

'Okay, Phil, we don't want to draw attention to ourselves.'

Phil waited for Hunt to said more, then said, 'We should find out who lives here. There's two cars but plenty of lights on.'

'Leave it with me, I'll speak to Johnson,' Hunt told him.

'Okay.'

'We'll re-group, go back early morning, take them by surprise.'

Phil ended the call, placed the phone back in his pocket.

'What's the plan, Phil?' asked Stuart.

Before Phil could answer, a noise of a loud motor startled them coming from a small box located at the base of the gates. The gates started to close.

'Go now!' Phil gasped.

One by one, they darted along the length of the moving gate, rounded it, and managed to squeeze out before they fully closed. On the grass verge, Phil turned to the men. 'The plan is to come back early in the morning with more men.' He pointed at the house. 'Doesn't matter if there's four or forty in there, we're getting that camera, no matter what.'

5

Thursday Morning
Toddington
JACK

I returned to the bedroom holding a mug of coffee and a plate of toast. It was early, the bedside clock told me it was 6.04 a.m.

Joanne was on her knees sorting her suitcase, re-folding her clothing. She had already been down for breakfast and was dressed. Black jeggings under a loosely fitting light green top. A scent of her favourite perfume wafted through the bedroom.

I sat down on the edge of the bed, watching her whilst I eat. My mind was going over the conversation we had last night about Lucy.

You're embarrassing her…

I watched her thin face, her prominent cheekbones, her full pink lips, and her straight dark brown hair as she folded her favourite black dress delicately.

'You're gorgeous, you know that?' I said.

She paused to look at me. Oh, and her eyes. Have I mentioned her eyes? Them perfectly shaped, brown hazel eyes which lured you in?

'You're not too shabby yourself, Mr Haynes.' She smiled. Tiny dimples formed in both cheeks.

I returned the grin as she looked away and focused back on her suitcase.

Joanne and I didn't really spend much time together. I worked back late and often brought my work – and concerns - home with me, then spent endless hours of my evenings with a gallon of coffee in the study staring into the monotonous glare of my laptop.

Part of the parcel, I guess.

She didn't mind though – it gave her time to do what she liked. The gym for one. Out with her friended another, whether it be coffee at an overpriced cafe, or round one of her friend's houses for a girl's night in, filled with glasses of prosecco and mouths full of gossip.

Joanne wasn't working at present. Her previous job at a small florist sadly came to an end. The twenty-six-year family-run business, after a steady decline, finally crumbled, forcing them to let the handful of employees go. Shame because she loved that job.

I looked behind me. 6.31 on the clock. I'm dressed and ready. Dark blue jeans with a black t-shirt on top. I'll top it off with my thin grey jacket which I've left near the door downstairs, so I don't forget it.

Through the large bay window, the world was calm and quiet, the early sun rising through the clear, blue sky, igniting the vast green countryside at the front of our house. The landscape seemed limitless, stretching under the humidity of another fine summer morning filled with warmth and dancing birds hovering across the distant skyline.

The plan was to set off to Luton airport at half-seven. Meet the family at eight, exchange the usual oh-I-haven't-seen-you-in-ages pleasantries, and grabbed a coffee before we board for Barcelona.

'We've got half an hour,' I said, tapping my watch.

'Yes, I know,' she said sharply, clearly flustered with her current suitcase arrangement.

'Okay,' I said.

I entered the small space between our bedroom and the bathroom. Approximately ten feet long, five feet wide. We called it the 'through-room'. Sliding doors neatly conceal built-in wardrobes on either side. I went to the right, slid the wooden door along the runner until it hit the end. I kept my best suits in there and other personal things. There was a safe at the bottom where-

I froze. A noise downstairs grabbed my attention.

'Jo?' I said facing the bedroom.

'Yeah?' Her voice was close, near the bed.

'You hear that? Downstairs?'

'Yeah,' she replied.

I walked back to the bedroom, looked at Joanne. 'What was it?'

'Maybe Lucy is up?'

'Maybe…'

I went to the side of the bed, lowered to my packed suitcase. Next to it, I unzipped the front pouch of my Nike rucksack and dug my hand in.

Passports. Tickets. Money - some English but mostly Euro currency.

Another noise stole my attention coming from downstairs – what is it?

'Can't believe she's already downstairs,' I said.

'Not as useless as you seem to think,' Joanne countered.

'I know she isn't useless…' I trailed off, avoiding another debate. I couldn't be bothered with it right now.

Joanne smiled to herself, happy with her suitcase.

'Sorted?' I asked.

'Yup.'

'Good.'

She rose to her feet after dramatically zipping it up, then checked the tag making sure they contain the relevant information. 'Name and number – that's what we write on these, isn't it?'

I nodded.

From my wardrobe inside the through-room, I grabbed a bottle of aftershave and sprayed it on my throat three times. I looked down at my watch. It was 7.10 a.m.

'You ready to go?' I said, closing the wardrobe.

'Yeah – two seconds.'

'I'll check on Lucy.' I went to our bedroom door, shouted out onto the landing: 'You ready, Lucy?'

'Yeah, I won't be long,' her distant voice replied.

Strange.

Her voice came from above. Not below.

I stepped back into our room, passed through the through-room, and reached the en-suite. I brushed my teeth thoroughly, allowing the electric toothbrush to do the hard work. I turned it off and the house suddenly fell silent for a moment.

Until I heard a noise.

Upstairs this time. Footsteps moving frantically.

Toward the bedroom, I stopped in the closet in the through-room, leaned to the left, and slid my door open again.

Inside the bottom of my cupboard was a safe.

My safe.

I'm the only one who knew the combination. I glanced at the bedroom doorway quickly. No sign of Joanne but I heard her huffing about something in her case. I lowered to my knees, pulled open the small cupboard door, tapped my fingers on the digital safe number lock and the door popped open, making an almost inaudible click.

There it was.

My little secret.

I smiled at the contents of the safe. The little voice in the back of my head warned me to be careful.

Don't push it, Jack.

Still hidden. Still safe.

Without a sound, Joanne startled me when she appeared in the doorway. She held up a dress against her body. 'Do you think this would be nice for Saturday night?'

As I gently pushed the door of the safe ajar, I watched her sway left to right as if she was standing at the end of a cat-walk.

I smiled and nodded. 'Looked lovely.'

'What you getting from inside there – you bought me another present?' Her eyes narrowed in wonder.

'It was a secret,' I said. 'Top secret special agent stuff. Above your pay grade anyway.'

She smiled and backed into the bedroom.

My heart pounded through my chest – I realised I was pushing it. 'Jesus,' I whispered under my breath.

'You got your phone, Jack?' she asked from the bedroom.

'Yeah, just getting it now.' Which is the truth because my work phone was in the drawer just above the safe. 'You got your phone?' I asked her. She took her time answering. I figure she'd be checking her pockets, searching around the room unable to find it. This wasn't the first time – it happened most days.

'No... I - I couldn't find it,' she moaned.

'I'll ring it,' I offered.

Still kneeling at the barely open safe door, I plucked my phone from my jeans pocket, dialled her number, and put it to my ear.

'It's ringing, Jo.' I said. 'Can you hear it?'

'No,' she shouted.

Then I remembered, I knew where her phone was. I saw it when I was downstairs earlier after I'd turned the alarm system off and made breakfast in the kitchen. It was on the table. When-

I froze.

The hairs on the back of my neck stood on end. Icy fingers crawled up my spine and a chill shot through my body when her phone was answered.

'Hello?' the voice said.

It was a deep voice. A man's voice. Coarse and harsh.

I could hear other voices, but they lacked clarity: a background of inaudible humming. I opened my mouth to speak but the words got stuck in my throat.

I rose to my feet, rushed to the doorway of our bedroom, and glared at Joanne. She looked up, seeing the horror on my face.

I pulled the phone away from my mouth and covered it with my hand.

'Joanne, there are people in our house,' I whispered.

6

Toddington
JACK

Joanne glared at me. 'What?'

'Joanne, there are people downstairs in our fucking house.' This time, my voice was louder than a whisper.

She brought her hands up to her mouth. 'There's some-one in the house?'

'Yes! Downstairs in the kitchen.' I raised the phone back to my ear.

'Hello?' said the man. He was louder this time and impa-tience filled his voice.

I ended the call immediately and glared down at my phone in confusion, wondering what the hell was going on. I clicked on the call list.

'Is this a wind up, Jo?'

She shook her head, stood up, and edged towards me.

I listened carefully in the silence of the house. Lucy had stopped jumping around upstairs. I tip-toed through our bedroom door out onto our wide square-shaped landing. Joanne followed me closely, I could feel her breathing on my neck.

We stopped at the thick, varnished bannister above the stairs. I rested my hands on the wooden railing. Joanne and I locked eyes, but we didn't say anything. My pulse bounced through my body as if being pumped mechani-cally. Waves of heat captivated me – I felt like I might be sick. I lowered my head over the bannister, looked down onto the floor of the hallway. Nothing but a polished reflection from the sun's glare came in through the glass on either side of the front door.

I closed my eyes to enhance my hearing, but all I could hear was the solid thumping in my chest.

The house was still—

A noise from the kitchen made me jump back.

'Maybe it is Lucy?' Joanne whispered in my ear.

'She was upstairs. She was literally upstairs just a second ago.'

'Maybe it was Lucy who answered it – I don't hear her upstairs anymore. Maybe she was joking around?'

For a long moment, I thought hard about that possibility.

She may be right. Lucy may have gone down so quietly, we didn't hear her. I don't hear her up there anymore. But with almost certainty, I was sure she was still up there. Seeing Joanne's phone on the kitchen table was so vivid in my mind.

'Go see if she was upstairs, Jack – maybe I left my phone upstairs.' Joanne's grip tightened. 'I was up in her room before. She was probably messing about putting on a silly voice. You know how she likes to mess around.'

The strange thing was that Lucy didn't like to mess around. She wasn't that type of person. So, Joanne's words didn't resonate or offer any logical reasoning.

'Your phone is downstairs – I remember seeing it.'

We both waited, hanging our heads as far as possible over the bannister without toppling over and tumbling down the stairs. My pulse was off the charts, my body growing hotter with anticipation.

It was the longest minute I've ever endured. Seconds felt like hours. We heard nothing from anywhere, not even up in Lucy's room. As if someone had switched the whole house into *mute* mode.

Joanne pinched my arm when there was a sudden sound upstairs. Then another.

Lucy *was* up there.

Which only meant one thing: there was definitely someone downstairs.

'Should I go downstairs?' I whispered.

'Wait, just wait, please.'

Sweat built up on my trembling body and her grip made me feel claustrophobic. I couldn't think straight. The hot air suffocated me so much that I couldn't control my breathing. I'd never had one, but it felt like the start of a panic attack. I steadied myself.

I grabbed her hand, leaned over the bannister again, and stared down onto the hallway floor.

Another sound.

Coming from the kitchen.

Then Lucy moved upstairs.

'Shit,' I said.

I felt a vibration in my pocket: my phone started ringing. The ringtone echoed on the landing. 'Fuck' I murmured harshly.

Joanne panicked, flapping her arms like a crazed bird, hitting me with her frantic palms. 'Shh, turn it off, turn it off.'

'Joanne, get off me!' I said, fumbling with the Samsung. I silenced the call and let it ring out. I looked down at the phone display.

Joanne calling. Answer – YES or NO?

'Should I—'

'No, you shouldn't - don't answer it, for God's sake!' Joanne grabbed my wrist to stop me from raising the phone to my ear again. 'Don't, Jack, please.'

I shrugged her off and, using my finger, I tapped YES and raised it to my ear. I listened very, very carefully.

'Hello,' the voice said. The accent was local. I remained quiet, waited, and locked eyes with Joanne. In all the years we've been married, I'd never seen this look in her eyes.

'Who is this?' the man said.

I didn't reply.

I heard the man say something, but it was faint as if he covered the mouthpiece of the phone to speak to someone else.

Joanne frowned at me in horror, desperate for an update. I shook my head, watching the thick film of fear suffocate her body. She couldn't stop shaking.

I wondered what Lucy was doing upstairs.

I pressed my ear closer to the phone, loosening my hand from the railing to wipe my hand onto my jeans from the sweat that was pouring out of me. Joanne was rosy-cheeked and warm. A mixed scent of fear and perfume radiated from her. Her eyes were wide and completely lost.

'Who is this?' the man said again. His next words were loud and firm: 'We will hurt you when we find you.'

I wanted to gasp but I kept silent, not reacting to his words. I stayed level-headed, listening, and hoping for something in my head to tell me what to do. I took my eyes off the stairs below, and focused on the door of the stairs leading to Lucy's room. The door was open a few inches.

Loud, clumsy sounds were coming from the kitchen now. Cupboards opening and closing, people shuffling around.

Please, Lucy, stay up there. Don't make a noise.

I needed to tell her. If I could just shout up and –

'What is it?' Joanne asked me, seeing an idea circulating around my head.

'We need to tell Lucy to be quiet.'

Joanne gripped hard on my arm.

'Jo – my arm,' I said, shaking her off. 'I'll text her.' I lowered my phone, opened a new text message, and started typing:

Lucy, I'm being very serious here. This is not a joke. There are people in the house and I need you to-

As if on cue, Lucy's voice echoed through the house: 'I'm coming, two minutes, Dad!'

I clamped my eyes shut and the silence that followed was deafening. Shit. I threw a wide-eyed glare at Joanne.

The voice from the kitchen said, 'They're upstairs, fucking get them.'

7

Toddington
JACK

Pounding thuds on the tiled kitchen floor spilled out into the hallway, echoing through the whole house.

I froze. I tried to move but fear glued me to the carpet. We needed to get to Lucy.

Now.

'Lucy,' I whispered out of desperation, staring at the doorway leading to her room. 'Quick, head for her door!' I grabbed Joanne, shoved her towards the door. She yelped in sudden pain. 'Fucking go!' I shouted.

Being quiet didn't matter anymore.

A voice from downstairs screamed, 'Find them. And bring them here when you do!'

'Jack!' Joanne scolded me for digging my palm into her back.

'Joanne – fucking move it!'

She seriously needed to speed things up. We jumped onto the other side of the landing, turned our bodies left, and rushed for Lucy's door.

'Jo, hurry up!' I screamed.

I jerked my head quickly at the base of the stairs. Three men. The first, sliding on the wooden floor, grabbed the post of the stairs with a gloved hand and propelled himself upwards. He was dressed in black, a dark-coloured masked concealing his face. Holes were just big enough for me to see the evil in his dark eyes. In a flash, his physique grew closer. He was frighteningly quick.

Jesus, hurry up, Jo!

I shoved Joanne's back again. 'Come on!'

'Jack, you're hurt-'

'Jo!' I begged her.

'Fucking come here!' the man roared.

The thuds on the staircase vibrated through our bodies, amplifying our anxiety.

Who were these men?

I didn't know - I didn't want to find out either. It was obvious they hadn't come here for tea and biscuits.

Joanne threw her arms forward into Lucy's door. It swung back on the hinges and slammed into the wall. She jumped up to the first step then the second. The door bounced back knocking me off balance as it collided with my shoulder. I slapped it open again, seeing Joanne gallop up the stairs out of sight. I closed the door shut, shoved my foot to the base, forcing my whole weight against it.

A pulse pounded in my neck as the sounds on the landing grew louder.

A heavy pitter-patter of anger, rage, adrenaline, and desire.

'Lucy!' I yelled.

'Lucy!' Joanne shouted, entering her room above me. 'She's here, Jack, she's okay!' They both appeared at the top of the stairs, Joanne's arm wrapped around Lucy.

'Dad, what the hell-'

'Just stay up there!' I ordered them. Through gritted teeth, I braced myself for the door to be knocked through any second.

They were getting closer.

'Dad... Dad, the lock!' Lucy shouted. 'Lock it. Lock the door!'

For a split second, I had no idea there was a lock on the door. I'd never put one on. I blinked to focus - I couldn't think straight. Adrenaline pounded through my body causing a whirl of dizziness.

'Dad! At the top and bottom!' she screamed.

Using the weight behind my left shoulder, I flicked both locks across.

'Upstairs now!' I shouted. 'Go.' Spittle was thrown from my mouth onto the carpet as I gasped in panic.

'Dad-'

'Go now, Jo, go! Take her to the room!'

The door rattled as one of the men bounced off it, but my weight and the flimsy locks somehow managed to hold it. My heart pumped blood so fast it felt like it was beating out of my neck. An adrenaline-fuelled blur. The door rattled again. This time more. The screws holding the locks were now loose. Shit.

'Open the door now!' a voice screamed against the other side of the closed door.

I remembered seeing three of them at the bottom of the stairs. But there could be more. This door wasn't going to hold much longer.

'Open it now, Jack!'

Shit, how'd they know-

'Have you got them yet?' another voice said behind the door.

'Not yet, boss. He's locked the door, he's behind it-'

Footsteps reached the other side of the door, then stopped. Eerie anticipation followed. The pressure on the door disappeared for a moment.

I heard a voice on the landing. 'Move, let me see.'

I firmly planted my right foot on the first step of Lucy's stairs, force my shoulder against the wood, and tensed my body.

'Jack Haynes. Let me in please.'

His voice was deep, croaky, and oozed an air of authority.

'Jack, open the door. We know you're there,' the man said. 'If you don't, I'll shoot you and your family.'

I swallowed hard, nearly choking on my saliva. I knew the door wouldn't hold for long.

'What do you want?' I finally said, my voice weak.

'I need the photos, Jack. My boss needs them.'

'Photos…'

'Yes. Photos.'

'What photos?' I said.

'You know what photos, don't play silly bastards with me.'

He said something else, but it was quiet as if he was talking to someone behind him on the landing. 'Check the main bedroom, see if there's a safe somewhere. There'll be in there.' His voice was now louder, facing back to the door. 'We need the photos or the camera, Jack. The boss won't be happy with us if we go back with nothing.'

'What fucking photos or camera?' I shouted in frustration.

'You three, check the other rooms. Be thorough,' he said, again quieter, ignoring my question, speaking with others behind him.

Check the main bedroom…

You three, check the other rooms…

One man speaking…

There were at least five of them.

'You know which photos, Jack. I'm gonna give you to the count of five, then I'm gonna blow this door off its fucking hinges with this shotgun. Five… four… three-'

I breathed hard, propelled myself away from the door, jumped up the stairs two at a time to reach the top, turned left, and pushed open the door into Lucy's room. Jo and Lucy both screamed when they see me.

'Just me.'

I shut Lucy's door firmly and checked for locks.

'Get in the corner!' I ordered them, my finger stabbing the air.

Lucy cowered into Joanne's arms kneeling on the floor. They watched me drag Lucy's bed across her light blue carpet and placed it against the door. It was a heavy bed, but I found a new lease of strength fuelled by adrenaline and fear.

The door at the bottom of the stairs smashed open. The wood door frame shattered, cracking sounds of the pine wood sheering up through the house. Heavy thuds pounded the stairs.

'This door isn't going to hold either. We need to get out of here.'

Joanne and Lucy both stared at me, searching for an answer, in desperate need of guidance.

'Open the cupboard. Get inside,' I whispered harshly, wafting my hand at them. 'Go!'

I was last inside the cupboard in the corner of her bedroom. I pulled the small door inwards using the circular knob handle. We had to be careful to stay on the joists as the floor wasn't boarded beneath our feet.

It was dark inside, but there was enough to see the outlines of my wife and daughter. I turned around to face them.

We weren't alone.

Behind them, there was someone there.

8

Hemel Hempstead

Alexander Hunt, sunken in his dark brown leather chair watching the fire crackle in front of him, heard his phone vibrate on the small marble table next to him. He picked it up, put it to his ear.

'Yes?'

'Hey, boss—'

'Have you got the photos?' he said impatiently.

'Not yet, boss,' Phil said, then cleared his throat. 'They've run upstairs to the attic. We've got through the first door, but they've locked themselves in the attic room.'

Alexander took a slow sip of his whiskey then lowered his arm, and rested the glass down on the arm of the leather chair, leaving Phil to wait for his response.

'Boss?'

'Yes, I'm here. You do know how important these photos are don't you, Phil?'

Phil hesitated, then said, 'Yeah, of course. Don't worry. If—'

'I'm not worrying, Phil.'

'You're... not?' Phil was confused.

'No,' Hunt said, 'I'll get them one way or another. If you can't get them, then I'll send someone who can.'

'There's no need for that, we'll—'

'You better do.'

'—we'll get it done,' Phil added. 'They're upstairs – and they're not going anywhere.'

Alexander Hunt made it clear when he sent his men to do a job, he wanted it done. Whatever it took. If they messed up he'd be forced to send someone who could get it done. A man he could rely on: Pollock.

Pollock was a highly trained operative previously involved with black ops for government operations. A hit record of one hundred percent. He didn't miss a target or fail a mission. However, obtaining Pollock's services came at a costly price. Pollock had no family, no friends, no ties, and, with that, no weaknesses. Nothing Alexander Hunt could ever gain leverage from if he needed to. It was wise having him on his side.

Because of his high-skill set, Pollock named the price.

Phil knew if Alexander needed Pollock for *this* simple task, that would be it – his last chance gone. His family wouldn't be safe anymore. Alexander Hunt was ruthless and evil. Phil couldn't risk that.

He needed the photos.

'Are you sure we don't need Pollock for this?' said Hunt. 'I mean Jack Haynes works at a bank, and his wife, well his wife Joanne, she stays at home cooking. They're not exactly Mr and Mrs Smith are they? Get it done. Get the photos, Phil. It isn't difficult.'

He devoured another sip of whiskey. The taste of the thick, smoky, peaky flavour soothed his throat as he watched the flames rise above the crackling coals.

'Yes, boss.'

'Tick, tock.' Hunt hung up the phone.

Toddington

Phil stood on the landing for a few seconds before he lowered his phone and sighed deeply, struggling to control his adrenaline. He put his phone back into his coat, watched Andy and Jacob climb the stairs up to the attic. He knew the importance of getting this done, and it didn't stop playing on his mind like a pounding headache.

'One more time, and your gone, Phil!'

No more mistakes.

Another chance to live.

'Get those fucking photos!' Phil screamed to no one in particular. His anger ripped through the house, echoing in every room. His men received the message loud and clear. He tapped his gun off the outside of his thigh and turned his body away from the shattered doorframe. 'Found anything in the bedrooms?'

'Not yet, Phil,' replied Stuart faintly from the Haynes bedroom, flipping the two suitcases open onto the floor. Stuart was Phil's right-hand man - or so the others said. The others were Andy, Jacob, Derek, and Terry.

Phil had known Stuart the longest and was his most reliable asset who he trusted the most.

'Derek, Terry… found anything?' he yelled towards the other bedrooms.

Derek's round face appeared from one of the rooms. 'Not yet, Phil, nothing in here. Just a bed and wardrobe. Fuck all in the wardrobes.' Derek disappeared back into the room.

Terry was in the other room, next to the Haynes' bedroom. 'No, nothing yet.'

'Any safes or anything, lads?' Phil shouted.

'No, nothing.'

'Fuck all, mate.'

'No, Phil.'

'Keep looking,' Phil said.

Phil gave another beaten sigh. He needed to find these photos, or at least the camera which the photos were taken on. They would save his life. The photos were the only thing in this whole world that could put Alexander Hunt behind bars.

Phil knew he'll be included in the photos, so not only was he protecting his boss, but himself and his family. If Hunt is caught, Phil knew he'd take him down with him.

Hunt's men continued to search the bedrooms while Phil headed for the stairs up to the attic. He stepped through the broken door which Jacob has smashed through, taking the stairs two at a time and, taking a left at the top, he met Andy and Jacob at the closed door.

'Are you not inside yet?' said Phil, showing his disappointment.

Andy shrugged. Jacob did nothing. Phil held back his rising temper.

'They say anything?'

'No,' said Andy.

Phil moved past them, chapping his knuckles firmly on the wooden door three times.

'Hey, Mr Haynes. Let us in. We mean no harm to you or your wife. We just need the photos.'

Silence answered him back.

'Mr Haynes, I'd rather do this the nice way. We mean no harm to you. Or your wife. Just open the fucking door.'

Still no response from Lucy's room.

'We just need to speak to your daughter!' Phil barked.

He glared at Andy and Jacob after another long silence. 'Smash the door off its fucking hinges.'

9

Toddington
JACK

Lucy's bedroom door was destroyed, the door frame split and cracked. The door collided with the single bed I'd put up against it. Another hard kick shoved her bed further into the room, the four legs vibrated off the floor as it juddered across the carpet. The door came away from the frame, held on barely by the top hinge.

Lucy shook as Joanne held her tightly, both lost in a realm of confusion and fear. What was more confusing was the figure a few feet behind them. I tensed up to brace for an adrenaline-raged fight, but soon realised that Lucy knew him - Joanne didn't seem too fazed by his presence either. I noticed how comfortable they felt around him. I stared at the stranger with caution and anger, who met my stare, but I saw an apology in his expression.

I turned my body back towards the door, tightened my grip on the small knob, and pulled it towards me. Knowing the men would easily get through the door into Lucy's room, I needed to use my head to divert their focus away from the small cupboard in the corner of her room, making it appear we've gone through the double glass doors onto the small balcony.

Before I got into the cupboard, I'd opened the glass doors, stepped onto the balcony to unclip the latch of the emergency ladders – installed for the unlikely case of fire - but they'd already been extended. Staring down the aluminium rungs, I'd calculated our descent time – there wouldn't be enough time for us to escape down the ladder. On the floor below, I didn't know who, or what was waiting for us. Inside the small cupboard and area of the void, spider webs drooped from the angled roof from the right to the vertical bricked wall on the left. The space below was filled with wooden joists travelling from left to right, spread out a foot apart, the space between them crammed with yellow, itchy insulation.

The young man behind Lucy and Joanne watched me carefully.

My first thought was what was his involvement? Had he broken in with these thugs? But when Lucy called him Carl, a wave of relief washed over me. From the ladders being extended on her balcony, it was obvious Lucy had let them down last night after she'd got home, allowing Carl to climb up and stop over the night.

In my daughter's bed. Oh, God, I'm not ready for this.

I shushed them when I heard voices inside the room.

'They must have gone outside!' I heard someone say.

Heavy footsteps bounced across Lucy's floor.

'Could you see them?' asked another man.

His words downstairs played over and over in my head. *The photos. The camera. Where are the photos?*

'The photos, we need them,' said a firm voice.

I heard someone go out onto the balcony.

'They're not out here, Phil-'

'Check the roof, check everywhere!'

'Okay, boss.'

More pounding thuds across her floor.

I was confused. 'The photos, what photos?' I whispered, facing the small cupboard door.

What photos are they talking about?

A whisper behind me: 'Dad?'

I turned my head, nearly catching my forehead off the diagonal beam. I locked eyes with Lucy barely seeing her gaze under the dim conditions.

'Yeah?'

'Did they say *photos*?' she whispered.

'Yeah. They asked for them downstairs.'

In the dark I noticed Lucy raise her hands to her mouth.

'What photos, Luce?'

She sheepishly turned back to face Carl.

A sliver of light sliced through the thin gap around the cupboard's outline, allowing my eyes to gauge Carl's reaction. The 'photos' meant something to them.

'Shit, what have we done?' Carl said.

'What *have you* done?' I asked wearily.

'Dad, you know the woodland near the pub?' she said weakly, just loud enough to be audible in the musty silence. I nodded. It was the only pub for miles. 'Me and Carl were shooting scenery –'

'Scenery?' I said.

'Let her talk, Jack,' said Joanne, placing a hand on my back. 'Listen to her.'

I maintained my grip on the cupboard handle in front of me but kept my body twisted to focus on my daughter.

'Go on,' I said.

'We got loads of great shots, didn't we?' She looked at Carl for a nervous confirmation, who bobbed his head.

'We heard shouting in the woods and-'

'Any luck boys?' shouted a voice in the bedroom, silencing Lucy. I turned back to the small door, ensuring my grip on the door handle, and pulled it towards me, the door tightly up against its small, thin frame.

One factor was against us: the door couldn't be locked from the inside, so it could be easily opened from the bedroom side. It was a waiting game before they saw us piled in here like sardines in a tin.

'Ahh, Phil. Over here,' shouted one of them. 'Some photos here.'

Footsteps faded to allow silence to flood the stuffy air.

Whatever photos they are looking for, Lucy hadn't had the chance to tell me.

I knew one thing: we had to get out, the air was getting too hot in this cramped, painful confinement. Sweat fell off my face and my saturated body soaked my t-shirt.

Down by my side near my right sock, something caught my eye in the insulation.

I couldn't quite make it out. Was it a corner of a small box? I wasn't sure.

A noise from the other side of the door startled me.

I turned, looked beyond Carl, further into the void. A rectangular space with a solid brick wall on the left and a slanted roof pitch on the right.

But I saw something: the wall on the left side wasn't solid all the way along. At the end, there was a gap. A gaping hole of unknown darkness, playing hide and seek with my limited vision.

'Hey, listen,' I said, keeping my voice barely a whisper, 'have you rang the police yet?'

'I tried but I couldn't get any signal,' Lucy explained.

'Me neither, they have my phone,' added Joanne.

'Shit,' I said. 'Hey, we need to get down there, away from this door.'

Pointing past them with my left hand, I almost lost my balance on the narrow beam. Joanne gasped until I managed to balance myself. They all turned in the confined space to follow the direction of my finger.

'You see down there. It seemed there's a space on the left. We need to get there now.' I lowered my finger towards the floor. 'Careful on the floor, stay on the beams.' Carl was in front. 'Carl, you go first-'

'Hey Phil, there's a cupboard here,' said a voice on the other side of the small door.

10

Toddington

'Open it then - what are you waiting for?' Phil said, glaring at Jacob standing in the corner near the cupboard. 'Open it!'

Jacob nodded, lowered to his knees, and pulled the cupboard open towards him.

Phil turned to Andy currently scanning through the photos in front of Lucy's wide, low desk. The right side of the desk accommodated a laptop with plenty of space underneath for a desk chair, although Phil couldn't see one. On the left side, sheets of paper with the title 'Art Design' lay next to a handful of single photographs displayed in no particular order. Phil picked them up, scanned through them one by one.

Sunsets.

'Shit,' he commented.

Fields.

'Shit.'

Rivers.

'More shit.'

One photo was of Lucy herself. She was standing in a field with the gentle glare of a dipping sun simmering behind her.

'Bonny-looking thing this one.' Phil angled the photo towards Andy, who looked his way briefly to see the photo, pouted his lips.

'Very nice.'

A trio of drawers was stacked vertically within the desk unit on the left-hand side. Phil opened the top drawer, finding hundreds of photos inside, many clustered in elastic bands depending on size. Six by fours. Seven by fives. He grabbed a handful and placed them on the surface in front of him.

'Anything?' Phil asked Andy, keeping his eyes on the photos in his own hand.

'Nothing yet,' replied Andy, who opened the middle drawer, where he found more photos.

'Keep checking them.'

Moments later, Andy put the photos back, then pulled open the bottom drawer and, in there, he found it crammed to the brim with colourful underwear and socks. He picked up some pink thongs, raised them to his nose, and sniffed them.

'What on earth are you doing?' Phil asked in disgust. 'What the fuck is wrong with you - just find the photos, nothing more!'

After he had checked all the photos in his hands, Phil focused his attention on the laptop resting on the desk surface. He opened the lid, pressed the 'on' button. A light flashed, followed by a gentle hum. He angled his head towards the corner where Jacob was still kneeling, peering into the darkness.

'Anything Jacob?'

'Erm, don't think so – it's so dark in there.'

Phil sighed hopelessly and went over to the cupboard, lowering himself to have a look. Horizontal joists ran from left to right with insulation between them. A brick wall was to the left. A slanted roof ran from the top of the left wall and slanted down to the right. The lonely dust in the air hadn't moved in a long time.

'Boss, what d'ya think?'

Phil looked at Jacob. 'Me and Andy would keep looking in here. You go inside, have a look-'

'But it was empty.' Jacob pointed inside. 'We can see, there's - there's no one there.'

'Just please check it, please. We need to make sure, okay?'

Jacob wasn't keen on tight spaces but nodded. Phil got up and headed back over to Andy. Jacob gingerly poked his head through the threshold, holding his weight on his palms over the horizontal beams. As he found his unsteady feet, he positioned his weight across two parallel joists. He stepped over the third joist onto the fourth, waving away the hanging spider webs. The natural light coming from Lucy's room allowed him to see there were at least fifteen joists until it reached a brick wall at the back of the void.

He turned his body back to the small, narrow hole.

'Phil, there's nothing here, man,' he said. He was uncomfortable. Sweat started to pour from his body under his black leathers.

'Keep looking!' Phil shouted from the bedroom.

He swivelled in the cramped space, seeing something he had missed down near his feet; something poking through the top of the insulation.

A small rectangular box.

'Ah, what's this?' he muttered.

Holding onto one of the angled beams with his right hand to steady himself he bent down and grabbed the box with his left hand. The box wasn't necessarily heavy, but whatever was inside, it rattled. He placed it down on the same joist he was standing on and plucked his phone from his pocket to use the torch function to aid his ability to see. A beam of brilliance brought the space to life and he wondered to himself why he had only just thought of it.

The box was black, wrapped in a skin of aging leather, the corners and edges both wearing thin. The back of the box had two small, thick brass hinges. He rotated the box slowly to look at the front. A latch secured the top and bottom together tightly. Above the brass latch, there was a keyhole.

It was locked.

'Bastard.'

He rattled it back and forth near his ear. Dull metallic clunks. Nothing of importance he decided; not compared to the camera they desperately needed to find. And the camera certainly wouldn't fit inside the box.

'No, nothing in here, Phil,' Jacob shouted, glancing back to the open door leading to the bedroom.

And that's when he heard it.

A sound came from the far end behind him. He swivelled on the beam, the phone light rotating with him. Placing the old box on one of the joists near his feet, he shone the light on the brick wall at the end of the void. Frozen, he watched the dense brick wall stare back in absolute silence, the only noise coming from his thumping chest.

After ten seconds, Jacob was satisfied there was nothing there, so turned back to the bedroom, picking up the box on his way out.

'Anything?' asked Phil, watching Jacob uncomfortably stand to his feet.

'Just this box. And air and fucking spiders… you found anything?'

'Not yet – what's that box?'

'Some old box from years ago,' Jacob said.

'Pass it here.' Jacob handed it to him. Phil rattled it and tried prizing it open but failed, then, in anger, tossed it against the wall just above Lucy's desk, dropping down the back of it. 'The photos here are full of scenery shit. Nothing useful at all.' Phil explained to Jacob. He turned his focus on Andy. 'Andy, look outside on the balcony again.'

'Already have-'

'Just do it, mate,' Phil said persuasively.

Andy dropped the last couple of photos carelessly on the desk and headed for the balcony. His skin felt the warmth of the morning heat as he used his palm to shield his eyes from the sun. On the balcony, he looked right and left, knowing he had already checked it. It isn't as if—

'Ah, what's that?'

How had he missed that?

He leaned carefully over the balcony, noticing the extended ladder which gave some form of access to a smaller balcony below. The smaller balcony had a glass door, leading to one of the rooms on the first floor.

'Phil. There's a ladder here,' he shouted.

Phil appeared quickly, shielding his eyes with a handful of photos from Lucy's desk.

'There's a what?'

'Look.'

They both leaned over to observe the ladder.

'Fuck, fuck, fuck!' Phil slapped his palm off his tanned forehead several times and sighed. 'They're long gone by now. Let's go see the others. See what they've found.'

Phil headed for the broken bedroom door, annoyed, frustrated, and angry. He kicked the remainder of the shattered wood off the frame on his way past and, on his descent to the first floor, terrible thoughts crept into his mind. The repercussions of messing up again.

'Found anything?' he shouted, standing on the landing. 'Stuart, Derek, Terry. Found anything?' His deep voice echoed from the floor to the high ceiling.

'In here, boss.'

'Who said that? That you, Stu?'

'Yeah. In here. Their bedroom, one at the front,' replied Stuart. He took his volume up a notch. 'All of you, in here now.'

Phil heard the change in his voice and dashed into the front bedroom.

'Where are you, Stu?' asked Phil, standing in the large room with two windows, two fancy wardrobes, a large kingside bed, and two empty suitcases with an assortment of crumpled clothes spread across the carpet.

'In here, the en-suite.' The voice came from the right.

Phil stepped over clothing, inhaling the womanly scent of perfume, and headed around to the right. His men followed like sheep.

Stuart was on his knees leaning inside an open wardrobe. 'Boys, come and see this here. There's a safe.'

'Photos?' Phil asked, hopeful.

'No. Something else.' Stu smiled.

Phil threw him a confused gaze. 'What is it?'

'Have a look,' offers Stu.

Phil darted over, lowered to his knees. 'Let me see.'

There was a black titanium safe staring back at him. The other men huddled excitedly at the door.

Phil's wide eyes glared into the safe. 'Jesus Christ.'

'What is it?' asked Jacob, standing at the door.

'What?' asked Andy. 'What is it - Jewellery?'

Phil looked up, his square jaw cracking half a smile. 'There must be half a million pounds in here.'

11

Toddington
JACK

We waited silently under the layers of yellow insulation, keeping perfectly still. Loud noises underneath us were coming from our bedroom. Glass smashing. Doors slamming. It wasn't long until the noises stopped. They either found what they were looking for, or they gave up and left, leaving the house to fall quiet.

An hour passed. It felt like six.

'Dad,' Lucy whispered, scratching her skin furiously. 'Could we get out? This stuff is itching like hell.'

'Yeah, I think so,' I replied.

'Good, it was bloody awful,' moaned Joanne, positioned on the other side of Lucy.

At the end of the void, I was right in thinking there was a gap. I was the last to turn the corner just before the cupboard had opened and slithered through the gap into a space of roughly ten feet by ten feet.

We carefully lifted the insulation up, the space between the joists just wide enough to squeeze into which I knew was a risk, but as long as we spread our weight evenly, we wouldn't fall through to the floor below.

After we'd positioned ourselves, we pulled the insulation over us and waited. Someone was there inside the void. The beams creaked quietly.

Lucy coughed into the palm of her hand.

My pulse raced as we all froze.

Towards the slit in the brickwork, I saw a light pierce the back wall. *Oh shit.* I held my breath, watching through the gap at the opening of where we were, thinking that at any moment, we'd be found.

But then the light finally disappeared, and his quiet footsteps faded back across the beams into Lucy's bedroom.

It was safe now. We got up carefully and I let out a relieved sigh as I made my way to Lucy's room and stood up, my back feeling like it was in knots. I noticed the balcony door was open, allowing warm air to enter her bedroom. Her room was a mess. Photos, underwear, clothes, her college work, dirty footprints everywhere.

'Dad, have they gone?' asked Lucy, who pressed her hands on the top of her head, absorbing the state of her room. 'Look at my fucking room!'

'Lucy!' Joanne scolded. 'Watch your language!' Joanne glared at the room too. 'Jesus, what's happened here.' She paused, looked at me. 'Jack, what is going on?'

'You tell me.'

'Sorry, mum,' Lucy apologised for her language. 'Look at the state of the door.'

Carl was last out of the void. He stood up uncomfortably and scanned Lucy's room. I noticed he was taller than me. And wider. His hair was short and black. The bottom half of his face was lined with a short beard making him appear in his mid-twenties.

'We don't know where they are,' I said, 'just keep it quiet for now. They could still be downstairs.'

I took another look at the room. The bastards.

'Hey, listen, you two.' I pointed my finger at Lucy and Carl. 'You two need to tell us what's going on – first we need to make sure they're gone. Carl, come with me.' I pointed back to Jo. 'You and Lucy, stay up here. Wait for us to come back up, okay.'

Standing together, they both nodded. Carl sheepishly approached me, obviously feeling awkward about meeting like this.

'Okay, let's go,' I said. He nodded.

We headed for the door, stepped through the broken frame. The dark smudges on the stairs' carpet infuriated me as I descended them.

With caution, we passed over the smashed wood of the first door onto the landing. I stopped, turned my head to listen. Carl wasn't watching me and stepped on the back of my ankle. It was agonising.

'Carl, what are you – be careful!'

He shuddered backward, holding his palms up in a sudden apology.

Across the landing, further smudges on the carpet boiled my anger. It was a total disregard for someone's property. A smell of masculinity and sweat still lingered in the air.

'Carl,' I said quietly as I turned to face him. 'Check the rooms there.'

He followed my finger pointing at the three spare bedrooms. He nodded and moved away.

'I'll check our bedroom and check downstairs. Okay?'

Carl nodded.

I stepped into our bedroom. 'Jesus!' I gasped.

It was a bombsight: clothes everywhere, two empty suitcases near the window, stained footprints on our new carpet. Joanne's vanity unit was sideways on the floor. The television was barely hanging on the wall. I went to my bedside drawer. My possessions were gone: my Breitling watch; Gucci bracelet; gold-plated pen. In the through-room, both wardrobes were open. The rail of clothing had been shoved from side to side, most of the clothes in a heap at the foot of it. Smashed bottles of aftershave pooled on the top shelf of the wardrobe and dripped down onto the carpet. The mixture of smells almost made me gag.

I looked down. *The safe.*

'Jack!' Carl shouted, stopping me dead. 'Jack!'

I left the bedroom and yelled his name on the wide landing.

'Jack, down here!' his voice echoed loudly.

I dashed down the stairs.

'Jack, in here.'

'Carl, I told you to stay up here - where are you?'

'Kitchen.'

'I asked you to wait, didn't I?' I said, entering the kitchen, giving him a cold stare. 'What if they were still here?'

He shrugged. 'They're not.' He was on his knees looking at the broken lock of the back door. 'The lock was drilled. That's how they must have got in.'

I took a closer look, my shoulder almost touching his, my nose picking up the scent of the teenage sweat oozing from him.

'You see this,' he said, pointing to the lock. 'They inserted the drill bit in here.' I leaned closer and nodded in understanding. 'The lock would have become slack, and then pop.'

I eyed him wearily.

'Seen it done, you know. On the television.' He smiled but avoided eye contact.

'Did you check the other rooms?' I asked, meaning the rest of the rooms downstairs.

'Yeah, quickly. No one there. They're gone.'

I nodded. 'I'll get my wife and daughter down – then you two could tell us why the hell they were here in the first place.' Without replying, he stood up, unsure what to do with himself.

At the bottom of the stairs, I shouted up, 'Joanne. Lucy. Come down, it's okay.'

Joanne looked sheepish and Lucy looked horrified at the mess of the carpets on their way down. I waved my arm in the direction of the kitchen.

'In there, please.'

They made their way to the kitchen, and I followed.

'Right, we need to know what's happened here,' I said. 'You and Carl could enlighten us.'

'Dad…'

'Yeah?'

'Where's Carl?' Lucy asked, her eyes darting around.

'He was here a second ago,' I said.

Carl had gone.

Lucy noticed a piece of paper on the kitchen table with a blue pen resting beside it. She cautiously went over, picked it up, and read it. 'Dad, dad. Look.'

My eyes widened as I absorbed the words:

If you tell the police what your daughter saw last night, we'll come back and kill you all.

12

Previous night
Wednesday
The woods, Toddington

After Alexander Hunt killed the second brother, Baret, he took a lung full of air, held it for a few seconds then exhaled heavily. Then he smiled into the sky.

Silence set in whilst his men waited for his next instruction.

He savoured the moment like he had done many times before.

'Put them in the van, you guys know the drill,' he told them.

Out of the six men, three went towards Baret, the other three went to Leon. Hunt stood watching the masterpiece he had created: the human flesh of dead bodies soaked in crimson pools of blood seeping into the woodland soil. The red and browns. The earth swallowing the blood of another victim. Beautiful.

That was when he noticed something.

A flash.

He shot a look to his right. His eyes met a low-level row of thick bushes. He focused hard with unnerving cold eyes. It wasn't long before a man's head rose above the tip of the bush, and locked eyes with Hunt's.

Hunt didn't panic, nor was he afraid. He simply smiled at him.

The man's head dropped like a lead balloon out of sight below the bush line. The realisation of the flash being a camera swiftly dawned on Hunt. A sheet of anger engulfed his body. *How fucking dare, he?*

In the dipping sun whilst his men deal with the bodies Hunt swivelled his full body towards the bush after feeling a longing strain in his neck.

He watched.

He waited.

The man's head crept over the tip of the bush again. Next to the man, Hunt saw blonde hair rise cautiously revealing the young face of an attractive teenage girl. Frozen with eyes as wide as bin lids, they both watched Hunt.

Hunt raised his gun at them. The girl let out a scream. Hunt's men all froze and glared in the direction of the shriek.

'Gentlemen, we have a problem,' Hunt said loud and clear.

The pair sunk behind the bush again.

'What's that noise?' Phil shouted, staring in a vague direction of the bush.

'Someone's there,' Hunt said, raising a pointed finger.

'Was that a flash?' Phil said.

'Yes, it was,' confirmed Hunt.

In a blink of an eye, the pair jumped up to a crouching position behind the greenery and, with the top halves of their heads now visible, they scurried to the left keeping as low as possible.

'Get them, now!' Hunt ordered his men.

Phil, Stuart, and Derek dart off in pursuit. The others stay with Hunt to make sure the bloodied bodies of the brothers were dealt with, and that all evidence of them ever being there was erased.

Hunt was sure of one thing as he watched them flee: he had to get his hands on the camera hanging around the blonde girl's neck.

Lucy and Carl dashed along the winding dirt track towards Park Road avoiding the potholes and lengthy tufts of uncut grass. Their footsteps were quick, dull slaps on the dry ground as they disturbed the evening silence. The sounds of chasing men on their heels only increased their panic.

Every step for Lucy was torturous, the camera swinging in a circular motion bouncing off her chest as she ran, causing throbbing, dull pain. With her right hand, she clutched the camera, holding it out in front of her as much as the strap allowed, but her off-balance technique slowed her movement.

Carl glanced back. Lucy was nearly ten metres behind him, the gap only increasing.

'Lucy. Come on!' he screamed.

The head start had been valuable but, as the seconds ticked by, Hunt's men were closing in the distance. Lucy panted hard and frantically, her burning lungs desperate for oxygen, her blonde hair flicking side to side across her petrified face. Carl looked beyond Lucy. He guessed the men were forty metres behind, which wasn't a lot when they were sprinting. A single trip or fall would allow the men to catch them in seconds.

'Quickly, Luce. Come on, keep up!' he begged her. Carl slowed his pace and turned, waiting for her. 'Give me the camera, here, give it!'

As she pulled it over her head, the small clip on the strap caught in her hair yanking her head forward. She cried out in pain and used her other hand to help free the strap and passed the camera to Carl like a baton.

'Right, fucking come on!' Carl glanced beyond her towards the chasing men. Twenty-five metres now.

A minute later, they arrived at Park Road, both panting, both in physical pain. Impressively, they'd covered half a mile in just over two minutes. Carl peeked back.

'Shit!'

'What – what is it?' panted Lucy.

'They're close. Come on.'

They took a quick right and crossed the noiseless road onto the grass verge opposite. Lucy eyed the tarmac beyond her, feeling like it would take forever before they reached home and it pained her. It felt like a million miles away.

The rural road was quiet. Lucy prayed to see a car, prayed to see anyone. Someone they could ask for help. But the only help was the lonely silence of the dwindling summer night cushioning the sun's descent to their right as dusk settled in. When cramp shot through her right calf, she halted and cried out in pain.

'Lucy!'

'Cramp, cramp!' She almost stopped.

'Lucy, come on, we—'

'I'm fucking trying!' she screamed at him through gritted teeth whilst clutching at her calf.

Behind them, the men reached the road, their heavy feet pounded the tarmac like a set of drums, banging to the beat of cat and mouse.

'Stop! Wait!' shouted one of the men.

Out of nowhere, an engine roared behind them. Getting louder by the second, Carl nervously looked behind him. A black van approached fast, the headlights growing brighter and bigger.

'Shit, shit.'

'What, what is—'

'Come on,' begged Carl, interrupting her. 'Faster!'

Lucy cried in pain, losing all hope as she struggled for air. Carl saw a pub up on the left which gave him a slither of hope. A place where other people were – a place to get help.

The van's engine quietened behind them. The frightening brilliance of the headlights faded on the dark road beside them. It stopped to pick up the three men chasing them. Within seconds, Lucy and Carl gained valuable time. Sixty metres now. Maybe seventy.

But the men now had a van. A huge game changer.

Lucy and Carl took a sharp left into the pub car park and, behind them, they heard the frantic screech of spinning tyres and the rising thunder of the van's engine, ripping through the evening breeze.

'The pub,' Phil said, pointing. 'They've gone to the pub. Come on, come on.'

'I see it,' said Jacob, behind the wheel, guiding the black van around the slight bend in the road. Within seconds, he slowed, turned into the car park. Phil, Jacob, Stuart, and Derek, all cramped in the front of the van, scanned the car park desperately.

Phil counted eleven cars. Seven of them were standard saloons, three of them larger SUV.

The eleventh was a police car. An Astra parked in the corner.

'Shit,' whispered Phil.

Jacob came to a swift halt. 'Phil?'

Phil's mind went into overdrive.

'Phil, what we gonna do?' asked Derek, squashed against him, shoulder to shoulder. The smell of sweat from Derek's overweight body overpowered the small space in the front of the van. The rotting smell of the Deacon brothers in the back wasn't helping either.

'Get out, Stu, Derek,' Phil said. 'Jacob, take the van back to Hunt's place. The last thing we want to do is draw attention to ourselves here with them two dead fuckers in the back. He pointed towards the police car, poking the stuffy air in front of him. 'With them pigs here.'

'Okay.' Jacob nodded.

'You could pick us up later.'

Terry had driven Hunt away in a different vehicle. Hunt had faith that Phil and his men would catch them and all would be resolved. In Hunt's mind, they'd get the camera, then all evidence of the killing would be destroyed.

The three men got out slowly. They looked calm, but their hearts beat like drums, the rush of the chase still very present. They were about to enter the pub when Phil stopped. Derek and Stuart came to a halt behind him.

'Boss?' said Stuart.

'Listen, you two wait here. We can't go in dressed like this. Hey,' he said, pointing at Derek, 'you go around the side. Stuart,' he lowered his arm, 'You wait here, I might miss them.'

Both men nodded at their instructions and parted ways.

Phil removed his leather gloves, shoved them in his right pocket, reached for the handle of the brown glass door, and went inside. It was an old traditional pub with low ceilings and exposed dark brown wooden beams that had matured over the years. The place was full, considering its rural location and lack of cars parked outside, the hum of happiness and scent of spilled beer pleasantly hit Phil as he walked into the bar area.

An elderly man, dressed as if it was December, was perched on a high bar stool, sipping on a pint of ale. The man slowly turned and smiled at Phil, then returned his attention to his frothy drink. Phil ignored him and walked on.

'Ignorant prick,' muttered the man under his breath.

Couples were seated opposite each other on the wooden tables. There were a few families, several with toddlers dotted around, pens in their hands over colouring books.

No sign of the boy and girl they were looking for.

He remembered what they are wearing: the boy, a grey-coloured tracksuit; the girl, light blue jeans and a thin blue hoody. After no sign of them, the next obvious choice was the toilets. There was nothing in the men's apart from dim spotlights above three urinals, a cubicle with an open door, and a cherry scent hanging in the air from an automatic air freshener on the wall.

He came out and walked straight into the Women's. No sign of the girl in there either.

As he left the women's toilet, a voice stalled him.

'Excuse me, sir?'

Phil span around quickly, eyed the policemen staring at him. A good-looking man, six feet, tanned.

'Yes?'

'You do know you're meant to use these toilets?' said the man in uniform, pointing to his left.

'Got mixed up, won't happen again.' Phil forced a smile, knowing valuable time was being wasted.

The man nodded. 'You have a good night, sir.'

Phil smiled, dipped his head, and left.

'Anything out here?' he asked Stu and Derek, stepping outside.

Both men shook their heads.

'For fuck sake. We need that camera.'

An elderly couple opened the door of the pub, stepped outside, and looked at them wearily before slowly heading for their car. They looked back several times. Phil wanted to tell them to mind their business but thought better of it.

Phil planted his hands on the top of his head, taking in a lung full of warm air. Wondering what to do next, he trotted towards the line of cars that made up the limited space and glared over the fields.

'What's that?' Phil's eyes narrowed.

'Huh?' mumbled Derek.

'Over there.' He pointed. 'Look, there they are. Going towards that house.'

Derek and Stuart turned to the open fields behind them. It was dark, but two small figures could be seen.

'Come on,' Phil said, heading after them.

'Nearly there, Lucy. Hold on,' Carl said. 'Nearly there.'

Lucy let out a small smile filled with both relief and sadness as they arrived at the back of the large-detached house. They took a moment to catch a breath. Carl turned, looked beyond Lucy across the long field near the pub, seeing nothing but small lights in the darkening distance.

'Here's your camera,' Carl said, handing it to her.

'You wait here, I'll go in first… make sure the coast is clear and let you up the ladders.'

She kissed him, opened the side gate into the driveway, and headed around to the front of the house.

13

Thursday Morning
JACK

In the kitchen, Joanne read the note:
If you tell the police what your daughter saw last night, we'll come back and kill you all.

'Oh, my God,' she said, throwing her hands over her mouth.

'Carl?' I said, spinning in search of him.

'Dad, where's Carl, where-'

'I told him to stay here.'

I swung open the back door, darted out onto the decking, and made a visor with my hands to shield my sight from the morning glare. The only sound I heard was the birds tweeting on the tree at the back of the garden. I stepped off the decking onto the path, took a left at the end of it, and headed around to the rear of the double garage. I reached the side gate which led to the open fields.

'Bastard,' I shouted.

I returned to the kitchen.

'Where the fuck is he?' I said.

'Jack – your language!' Joanne scolded.

Lucy glared at me in disbelief.

'Lucy. Where?'

'I - I don't know where he is. I don't know why he would leave,' she explained, shrugging her small shoulders.

'Jack!' Joanne said, 'would you just calm down? Being angry isn't going to help anything here is it?' She was right as usual. Joanne usually saw everything rationally. 'I'm sure he has a good reason for leaving.'

'He must have one hell of a reason.'

'Lucy, sit down, please. Talk us through this.' I took a seat at the kitchen table and pulled my chair in. Lucy was hesitant but joined the table, sitting opposite me. Joanne sat next to her.

'Okay, Lucy,' I said, placing my elbows on the table. I interlocked my fingers and dropped the weight of my chin on the bridge of my curved hands. 'Tell us – me and your mum - why they were asking for the photos and camera. What photos?' I leaned forward a little.

Lucy's eyes became glassy. 'I, I…we—'

'It was okay, Lucy,' I said, 'whatever it is, just tell us.'

'Jack, she is,' Joanne said matter-of-factly.

I held up an apologetic palm.

'Me and Carl were walking—'

I couldn't help myself: 'And who the hell is this Carl—'

'Jack… would you be quiet for one second? Let her speak!' Jo shouted, ramming the side of her fist onto the table, the thud echoing around the large kitchen. Her language and actions startled both Lucy and I, but she continued: 'What's the point in asking her to explain? You just keep interfering.' Joanne shook her head at me and returned her focus to Lucy. 'I'm very sorry for my language, Lucy, that isn't like me at all. Please, go on.'

I kept silent.

'Me and Carl were walking over the fields where we normally go - well, where *I* normally go. We took some shots – Carl takes photos too. That's how I met him…' Lucy paused, feeling the heat of my burning glare. 'We got some good ones. We were walking back past the woods. You know, just off the road.'

I bobbed my head. I knew where she meant although I hadn't been down there in a while.

'We walked past the woods when we heard shouting. We stopped, then heard a loud scream. Carl said we should check it out. I said no, I wanted to go home.'

'When was this, Lucy?' I said calmly.

'Erm, around nine.'

'Okay, go on,' I encouraged her.

'So… Carl persuaded me to get closer. We kept low and went into the woods. After so far in, we saw a group of men. Most of them dressed in black – like in leather, I think. But there was one man with a long brown coat who was standing in front of two men on their knees. The two on the floor weren't a part of the group – I could tell. One of them was on the floor quiet and the other was screaming in pain. Then we saw the blood.'

I heard Joanne gasp quietly, but I kept my attention focused on Lucy, who paused to take a breath and mentally collected her thoughts.

'The man in the brown coat put his hand inside his pocket—'

She paused and began to tremble. Tears ran down her cheeks, her eyes fall to the table, her blonde hair hangs forward.

Joanne leans closer to her and rubs her back gently.

'Hey, it was okay, Lucy,' Joanne said. 'Take your time.' Jo flicked her eyes at me. 'She could take as long as she needs, right?'

'Yeah, of course.' I nodded sincerely.

Lucy smiled sadly at her mother. She was appreciative of the comfort but I could tell it made her uncomfortable. 'I'm okay, Mum.' Joanne gave a half smile and eased back a fraction.

'And then he pulled out a gun, pointed it at the men on the ground. I heard Carl taking pictures. His fingers tapped the button over and over. Then… the man fired a shot, then another. There was a flash. Carl must have turned the flash button on by accident. They all looked at us. The man in the coat pointed his finger toward us. He told the others to get us. That's when we got up and ran. Along the road, across the field. I came in shaken up.'

No wonder she seemed different when she got in last night.

'And then when I went upstairs, I let down my ladder, and Carl climbed up,' Lucy said awkwardly, knowing I'd disapprove that he'd stayed over.

In my daughter's room.

In her bed.

'Did you know about this?' I asked Joanne with disappointed eyes.

She sighed as if it was no big deal. 'Not about last night, but, I know about Carl, yes.'

I shook my head, then clapped my hands together, applauding her for not being open with me.

'Jack, she was eighteen,' Joanne explained. 'Fucking grow up, for God's sake.'

'Yes, I know she is - she was my daughter. I know when she was born. I know her date of birth,' I said. 'We had a party for her, didn't we?'

'Stop being ridiculous, Jack. She's an adult now.' She angled her head back to Lucy. 'Go on Lucy, it was okay.'

I bit my tongue.

Lucy kept her eyes low on the table, struggling to make eye contact with either of us, no doubt feeling the burden of responsibility.

'So... maybe they followed you home then?' Joanne asked.

Lucy shrugged. 'Yeah, must've done.'

'Why didn't they come last night?' Jo asked.

Lucy shrugged again.

I looked up at the red rectangular clock on the large wall to my left. It was just past 10 a.m. - Jesus, where's the time gone? We missed the check-in and the flight. We won't be making the wedding.

'I'll ring work. Let them know what's happened – I'll give Ray a ring. Tell him about it. Still take the two days off. Give us time to sort this out.'

Joanne agreed.

'Could I sleep in one of the spare bedrooms tonight?' asked Lucy.

'Of course, sleep anywhere you want,' replied Jo. 'We'll need to ring the police. Jack, could you do that?'

I nodded as I stood up.

'Did they take anything?' she asked me.

'Unfortunately, yeah - my other watch. A little money from the bed drawer. Apart from that, I don't know. Carl and I... we didn't look thoroughly. Anyway, while we're all here, why not tell me about this Carl?'

She swallowed. 'I met him on Facebook. He posted some pictures on a photography page. We got talking—'

'How long have you been seeing each other? If that's what this is?'

'Two months nearly.'

I shook my head at Jo. 'And you knew about this?'

Joanne bobbed her head but didn't care I was angry with her. 'We didn't tell you because we know what you're like.'

'What do you mean?' I couldn't help but frown at her.

'Well… judgemental could be one word,' Joanne said. 'He seemed okay. And I approve of him.'

'Each to their own opinion, and I would certainly have mine,' I replied. 'But first of all, where are the photos? They on your camera, Lucy?'

Lucy bowed her head. 'Should I show you?'

'Yeah, you need to. Where's your camera?'

'I hid it, Dad. I normally put it in my drawer in my room. Good job I didn't. But I knew the pictures were important. I hid it in the cupboard.'

'Cupboard?' I scowled.

'The cupboard we hid in.'

'Up in your room?'

She nodded, rose to her feet, disappeared from the kitchen, and went upstairs.

'I'll get my phone, ring the police, then Joe, then Ray at work.'

Reaching the top of the stairs, I picked out my phone from my pocket. There was a text from Joseph: *You set off yet? Looking forward to seeing you all x.*

It was followed by three missed calls and a further two texts:

Jack, we're in the food court having a coffee, see us in there x.

And:

Jack, you're gonna be late, they're calling us through soon. Hurry up x.

After reading it, I stepped into our bedroom, and headed for the en suite. Then I remembered something.

The safe.

I dropped to my knees, my heart sinking into my stomach. The safe door was open an inch.

'Shit.'

Using my hand, I pulled the door open fully. I clamped my eyes shut and sighed in disbelief. I wanted to cry.

The money was gone.

'Hey,' Joanne said, startling me from the door of the en-suite. 'Anything missing in there?'

I raised my hand to the safe door and edged it closed.

'No, nothing missing, Jo.'

She didn't know about the money.

She could never know about the money.

14

Hemel Hempstead

'Alexander?' said a short, stocky woman who stood in the doorway of the large living room.

The room was spacious, airy, and rectangular, approximately twenty feet wide by forty feet long. Large oak bookcases filled the far wall, jammed with an endless list of novels. All different genres, the majority made up of crimes and thrillers. Mainly fiction, some non-fiction. There were two large bay windows to the left, where miles and miles of land could be seen. A long rectangular table rested against the wall in the space between the windows reflecting a dull shine in the morning light. A sofa, capable of seating three people, sat in the centre of the room facing the fireplace on the right side of the room. Hunt sat in a single leather chair next to the sofa watching the coals crackle in the burning fire.

Hunt leaned forward, cocked his head to glance at the woman.

'Yes, Ann?'

'Phil and the boys are back. Should I send Phil up?'

'Please, Ann, yeah send him up,' Hunt said. After he smiled, he sank back into the comfort of the brown leather to watch the orange flames sizzle.

'Okay.'

Ann had worked for Alexander Hunt for six years. As his personal assistant, she advised him on matters which he requested. And sometimes, matters which he didn't. She voiced her opinion and, above all, she was honest. Even if it upset him. He didn't like it, but he respected her for it. He needed someone to be straight with him, to keep him on the ball.

Ann was small but feisty and had broad shoulders. Nearly as wide as she was tall. She didn't hesitate to give any of Hunt's men a slap if needed.

Hunt's stare was lost in the fire. He finished the remaining drop of whiskey in his glass and lowered it to the table beside him. The room smelled of burning coal and warm leather. Warm air seeped in through the windows behind them.

Regardless of the weather outside, Hunt always had the fire on. The novelty had never worn off over the years, reminding him of when he was a small child with his parents around the fire, cuddling together, hiding from the cold outside.

One of his men – one of his previous men – had commented on the fire being on during summer, and said he was sweating because of the heat. Hunt drove a six-inch blade through his throat and smiled when he dropped to the floor like a used toothpick. Stuart and Phil didn't know where to look.

Hunt's parents were killed at the age of ten. Three-masked men broke into their house with machetes. Hunt and his father were tied up with rope against the front of the bed. Two of the men raped his mother in front of them while the third man held Hunt's head forcing him to watch. Hunt clamped his eyes closed blocking out the horrendous scene before him, but he heard the screams of his mother. His own urine soaked his pyjama bottoms. When they were done they stabbed his mother through the chest with a knife. His father screamed and received the same fate minutes later.

Hunt was left tied to the bed. He was found two days later covered in faeces and urine, and almost unconscious from dehydration.

That was the birth of the real Alexander Hunt. Long gone was the sweet boy playing with his toy trains in front of the warm coal fire.

He moved from home to home, terrorising every foster parent who had the kindness to take him in. But all he had was a broken angry heart. They weren't his real parents. Every carer handed him back - they couldn't do it anymore. He attacked their children and stole money and their possessions from them.

At sixteen, the government ran out of options - fostering options anyway. His old man had a cousin living in North London, and social services had persuaded the uncle to take him in. But he couldn't cope with him either, not long term anyway.

'Boss?' Phil said, knocking on the door. The sound echoed around the large, warm, stuffy room.

'I'm hoping you have good news, Phil?' Hunt didn't move, his eyes remained on the crackling fire.

Phil swallowed nervously, stepped through the threshold into the room, feeling the heat of the fire against his face.

'Erm… we couldn't find the photos or the camera, boss. But we did find—'

'Phillip, Phillip.' Hunt sighed and closed his eyes. 'Is it situations like this where I have to ring Pollock?'

Phil knew the question was rhetorical, and to answer him back would only fuel his anger, so he kept silent, hoping Hunt didn't ask again. Phil edged a little closer and cleared his throat. 'We found something else for you, which I think you'll like,' he said softly.

'Oh, yes?'

Hunt leaned forward, rose to his feet, turned, and locked eyes with Phil. He was much smaller than Phil who had six or seven inches on him, but Phil didn't feel the bigger man, not when rage fuelled Hunt's personality – he was very unpredictable. In his prime, Hunt was a very good boxer. Now fifty-seven, he could still throw a knockout punch or enough to rattle a few jaws.

Hunt stepped across the red rug, stopping dead before Phil.

'Are you hot, Phil?'

Phil glanced to his left, noticing the window was cracked open a touch. 'Just nice,' he lied.

'So, what's this thing that you have for me?'

At first, Hunt didn't see the black bag Phil was holding in his hand. As Phil held out his arm, Hunt watched him carefully.

'Have a look, boss.'

Hunt it, pulled apart the rim of the bag, dug his thick hand in deep. Hunt peered up at Phil. A small grin lined his face, then he lowered his eyes inside the bag again.

'There must be half a mill in there,' Phil informed him. 'What you think?'

His boss nodded. 'Maybe. Where was it?'

'In Jack Haynes' safe. When we were checking the house, Stuart looked in the en-suite in their bedroom. Found a safe inside a cupboard – it was open. Just sitting there.'

Hunt absorbed Phil's words instead of thanking him. 'Photos?'

Phil shook his head slowly.

Hunt continued, 'I have money. What I need… are the photos. Because their photos,' he raised a finger, 'if in the wrong hands could put us away. *Us both* away.'

Hunt's face changed as an idea washed over him.

'What are you thinking?' asked Phil.

'We could use it as leverage,' said Hunt. 'We've got his money. He has a camera with the photos. No doubt by now, he'll have spoken to the police about it. They'll be looking at the mess you've done. You can't go back round, not right now. It's too risky.' Hunt fell back in deep thought.

'We know who he is,' Phil said. 'You got that information from Johnson last night.' He ploughed his hand inside his leather jacket, pulled out a Breitling watch.

'You keep the watch. Don't tell the other guys.'

Phil smiled and nodded, then put the watch on his wrist.

'I'll get hold of Detective Johnson, tell him to do more digging.'

'Ok. What do you want us to do now?'

'We'll need Johnson to visit Mr Haynes, persuade him to find the photos. If not, at least we could use him as leverage with his money.'

Detective Johnson was the man Hunt had on the force - his inside man, his ticket to freedom. A man that Hunt went to with problems he couldn't handle with brute force. Where a more delicate approach was needed. Johnson, although dirty, was an intelligent man. Gained his Master's in Criminology at university and studied for a second degree in Forensic Science. He'd been a detective for years, but it didn't take him long to realise where he could make better money. He had helped Hunt on many occasions: misplaced evidence, made-up stories, and God knew whatever else to defend him under the radar of policing ethics and morals.

Everything had a price. Johnson had told Hunt what it would cost and, after Hunt accepted the terms, Johnson happily joined the payroll.

'For now,' said Hunt, 'you guys arrange the stuff for the Manco deal. You know how much we need?'

'Yeah.' Phil gave a firm nodded.

'Good.' Hunt turned away from him, stared back into the fire.

By Hunt's change in tone and body posture, Phil knew it was the end of the conversation and edged back. 'I'll leave you to it, boss.' He turned, left the living room, happy to feel the cool air in the long, wide corridor.

Hunt dropped the bag of money on the floor and sunk back into his chair. His dark eyes focused on the last burning coals in the small, simmering fire.

He picked up his phone, scrolled through the phone book, pressed CALL, and put it to his ear.

The phone was answered. 'Alexander Hunt?'

'We have a problem, Pollock.'

15

Toddington
JACK

I ended the call, placed my black Samsung on the kitchen table. I scanned the threatening note. Suddenly, a sick feeling filled my stomach and I became dizzy.

'The police?' Joanne asked.

I managed a nod.

'They'll be here when they can, they said,' I replied. 'Where's Lucy?'

'Lucy would be down soon with the camera. We'll see what happened.' She leaned into me, put her arms around my back and took a heavy breath which I felt against my chest. 'Jack, I'm just glad we're okay.'

I glanced at the note on the table. 'For now, maybe.'

She followed my eyes to the note. I felt her grip tighten. 'Wait till the police come,' she said, 'they'll sort it.' She leaned back and, with both hands, bowed my head forward and kissed my forehead.

If you tell the police about what your daughter saw, we'll come back, and kill you all.

My pulse quickened as I absorbed the words again. I sighed, pulled away, not able to hold it together, and headed towards the kettle. I needed to get away from her. I needed space. I felt like her arms were claws that were squeezing the life out of me. I felt myself get hot as I reached the worktop.

'Coffee?' I asked, trying to take my mind off it.

She half-smiled.

Whilst standing at the kettle, a searing pain formed at my temples. I clamped my eyes shut to block it out, but the roar of the boiling kettle irritated me almost to the point I wanted to scream. Joanne wandered to the back door, stepped outside onto the decking. The kitchen appeared smaller than it used to be. The four walls crept in inch by inch. If only I could go back a few life chapters to do it differently, I'd make better choices.

'One sugar,' Joanne called from the decking.

I didn't reply. Instead, using the flats of my sweating palms, I held the weight of my body on the black granite worktop. My right knee almost buckled as I nearly fell into a complete mess, but I stayed upright, giving myself a mental shake.

Focus, Jack.

Lucy would be down soon. Joanne and I would see the photos, see exactly what had happened and we'd fix this problem like we did any other problem. For a moment, I thought about my father, John, and how I needed him right now. He'd know what to do. Smiling at the memory of him, I made the coffees.

John passed away four years ago from lung cancer. Years of consistent heavy smoking. We – my mother, brother, and sister – warned him over and over about it after he developed COPD in 2008. He ignored us; he ignored the doctors. He allowed himself to slip into a steady decline; it was only a matter of time before it took him from us. I was angry at him. Told him he was being selfish. 'You do know you're going to die and leave us behind, don't you?' I used to say to him. He told me he could die by being hit by a bus anytime so would it matter?

Yes, John, it did matter. Right now, I needed him and his guidance.

On the decking, I handed Jo her coffee. A distant hum of traffic from the M1 brushed over the garden. The rush of commuters and travellers being directed where ever they were going. The mid-morning brought the world to life: bees buzz back and forth to flowers, and birds sang and danced in the trees. The blistering heat radiating from the rising sun.

'You spoke to Joe?' Joanne asked.

I shook my head. 'I'll ring him now.' After taking a sip of my coffee, I placed it down on the handrail of the decking and pulled my phone out. Joanne returned to the kitchen when Lucy appeared nervously at the door. I held up a finger in their direction as I spoke with my cousin, indicating I'd be a minute.

'I know mate, I couldn't believe it myself,' I said, towards the end of the call.

'Hey, get things sorted on your end,' he said. 'Find the bastards that did it.'

'Sorry again, Joe,' I said softly. 'Have a great wedding.'

'Speak soon,' Joe said and with that, hangs up.

I dropped the phone back into my jeans. I never mentioned to him the note that was left. I needed to understand what was on that camera first. At the kitchen table, I found Lucy shoulder to shoulder with Joanne focusing on the contents of her camera. Their eyes narrowed in concentration at the images before them. As I appear behind they parted to leave enough space for me to lean in between them.

Silence hung in the kitchen as we scrolled through them one by one, carefully studying each shot for a few seconds. Some were a little blurry, offering no more than vague outlined shapes of men. But others were crystal clear. Clear enough to see what was happening in the woods last night.

'How many is there?' Jo asked, referring to the pictures that Carl had taken.

Lucy shrugged. 'Twenty-five, maybe.'

The man in the long brown coat hid his face well. There wasn't a clear view of him. Noticeably, he had a bald head and tanned skin. Broad shoulders packed the width of the long coat he wore. Other shots showed good facial definitions of the other men. One man, standing next to the man in the brown coat, was tall and wide. He had a goatee and his face was bronzed, either from extreme sunbed use or foreign parentage. All the men wore black, singling out the man in the brown coat.

After a while, it was obvious we didn't recognise any of the men.

'Lucy, are these photos just on here? This camera?' I asked. 'Nowhere else?'

'Yeah… but…'

I pulled back and frown at her. 'Lucy?'

She turned, glanced at me. 'I uploaded them to my laptop, too.'

'Delete them please,' I told her.

'Do what?' said Jo, glaring at me, her dark fringe smothering her forehead.

'Delete them please,' I repeated. 'These photos – getting caught taking these photos has caused this trouble,' I said. I know my words upset Lucy, although it was not my intention. 'They need to be gone as soon as possible. Whoever this guy is…' I scrolled along, stopped at the clearest shot of the man in the brown coat aiming his gun toward the two men lying on the floor. I pointed my finger at him, stabbing the air. 'He had sent these men over to make sure the photos disappear. Or we disappear before we have the chance to do anything with them. You saw the note.'

I tapped the piece of paper to the left of me. Joanne and Lucy followed my finger.

If you tell the police what your daughter saw last night, we'll come back and kill you all.

'So, I'm going to delete them from your camera, Lucy. And I suggest you delete them from your laptop, too. Before anybody else sees them. Okay?'

She responded with a slow, painful nod.

'We should show the police the photos, Jack,' Joanne suggested.

I stabbed the note again with my finger. 'Could you not read?'

She frowned at me.

'Listen,' I explained, 'we need to pretend it never happened. If the police get wind about this, then it'll be on the news. If that happens, it was game over – they'll be back for sure.'

'They might come back anyway – what's stopping them?' Lucy had a point.

The secret money they stole from my safe which no one knew about, maybe? They know I won't say anything because I'll do everything in my power to get that back. I'm going to keep the photos, find out who this man is, and get my money back. Jesus, if anyone finds out about that money and where it came from-

A loud knock at the door startled us all.

16

1972
Luton

The early evening sun beat down on the street outside the small window. The occasional neighbour walked by every so often. The boy waited a long time until he saw someone. The glass he was looking through was dirty and hadn't been cleaned in a long time. Just like his bedroom. Discarded food packets and drinks had been left, and unwashed plates with scraps of food lined with mould sat on the old carpet near his bed. The piles of clothes hadn't been washed in weeks. He took them downstairs, left them at the washing machine, and realised they were still there days later. He decided to start washing them himself in the bathroom sink but they still reeked. The food stains were still visible.

In the room next to his was his sister's. She too faced the same daily struggles.

Neglect.

Alone in this world.

It wasn't their mother's fault. No, she did her best; she too, also felt their pain. More so than they did.

It was their father's fault.

He was a bastard. A lying, cheating bastard, who took his anger out on their mother. A horrible bastard of a father.

He winced at the sound of it. Another beating. Their poor mother downstairs, being constantly whipped with a battered old belt over and over and over again.

'You deserve it, you do!' her father shouted, the anger in his voice finding its way upstairs. The boy slowly got up, passed the room where his sister sat scared in the corner. Their sad eyes met for a second.

'I'll go see what he had doing to mum.'

The little girl, two years younger than him, nodded, then placed her hands over her ears again to block out the sounds.

Downstairs in the kitchen, he found his mother and father. 'Go upstairs, you don't need to see this,' he told him. His mother's face was pinned to the surface of the worktop with his father's strong hand. 'Go on, fuck off upstairs.'

He saw the look on his mother's face. Fear. Helplessness. His father grabbed the belt from the side and hits her with it a few times, the slap of the leather hitting her bare skin made the boy cower.

His father stopped, scowled at him. 'Go upstairs, she deserves this.'

The boy dropped his head and returned upstairs. He stepped into his sister's room, and sat down next to her, putting his arm around her and holding her tight.

Upstairs, they heard the screams rip through the house. There was a loud smash, sounding like glass on the tiled floor in the kitchen. Another scream.

'Look what you've made me do!' their father screamed.

The small girl started to cry again.

Like she had done many times before.

'It won't be forever. Okay?' the boy whispered.

She nodded, feeling comfort in his chest.

17

Toddington
JACK

I opened the front door slowly, peered cautiously around the side of it. Bright light flooded in and the sound of idle conversation came to a halt.

A broad-shouldered man, dressed in a black jacket and trousers, introduced himself as DCI Matthew Clarke of Bedfordshire police. He was of average height but with a good posture. His thick mousy-brown hair was styled well, combed over to the side of his forehead. He had a nicely trimmed goatee, a shade lighter than the hair on his head. I noticed his light blue eyes were the focus of his face, hypnotising anything they looked into.

He turned to the man to his right, who was dressed similarly, but his coat was dark blue. 'This is DS James Horton.'

They showed their IDs in unison as if practised over and over through years of working together. Horton was a little smaller and thinner, more withdrawn, his posture not as upright as Clarke, and he was younger. His hair was dark and curly, his face clean-shaven, most likely from this morning judging by the faint rash. He wasn't a contender for winning the front cover of Men's health, but he wasn't ugly.

I nodded at them both. 'Hi.'

'You've had a break-in?' DCI Clarke asked.

'Yeah, that's right. Please come in.' I stepped back, opening the door further. I led them through to the kitchen where Joanne and Lucy wait nervously at the table. An expression of relief washed over both of their faces.

'Keen photographer?' DCI Clarke noticed the black Nikon camera sitting on the windowsill to his left. Not only good-looking and charming but observant too.

Shit. Why haven't I moved that camera?

'This is my wife, Joanne. My daughter, Lucy,' I said, stopping at the table.

'Hello, you two,' said Clarke, who stole a look at my wife longer than he should have.

Once I stole their attention back, I showed the detectives the damage to the back door.

'Think they broke the lock here.' My finger pointed to the broken keyhole.

DS Horton took the lead, bending at the knee to have a look. Joanne and Lucy stood side by side watching next to the table. DS Horton nodded in agreement from past experience.

'Okay.' Horton said. 'Looked like it was been drilled. Then popped open. I'm not an expert but I've seen it done before. So… they broke in, then what happened?'

I filled them in over the next few minutes. Joanne and Lucy occasionally nodded at different parts of the story as the detectives glanced their way.

'So, where's your phone?' Clarke asked Joanne.

Joanne shook her head. 'I haven't seen it.'

'They've probably taken that too.' I sighed hopelessly.

The detectives looked at me, waiting for more. Without telling them about the murder that Lucy had witnessed, the pictures she'd taken, the missing half a million from my safe which no one knew about, that's it.

'Could you show us upstairs?' Horton said.

'No problem,' I replied. 'This way.' They follow me.

'Terrible mess on the carpets,' Clarke commented.

'Insurance would cover that,' countered Horton. 'Don't worry.'

After I showed them the first broken door, I took them higher, showing them the damage in Lucy's room. I pointed to the cupboard where we hid.

The detectives popped their heads into the void one at a time.

'Cosy in here.' Horton looked up, sympathetically.

'It wasn't ideal,' I agreed.

DS Horton pulled out his notepad to make some brief notes. DCI Clarke seemed very meticulous in the way he moved around the room, his eyes scanning everything methodically. He noticed the photos on the desk against the wall.

'Keen photographer, your daughter?'

'Yes. She was been doing it a while now – there are some great shots there.' I nodded towards the pile of photos in a way of an invitation if he felt like perusing.

'Quite professional, some of them.' Clarke was very careful not to touch anything that could possibly contain fingerprints, although we all knew the men would have been wearing some type of gloves.

I smiled at the feeling of pride growing inside of me.

'What's out here?' Horton looked away from the notepad and glanced up over the top of his glasses towards the double doors.

'A small balcony - have a look.' I opened the door, and let it gently swing open in the morning breeze. Both detectives passed me, and a whiff of aftershave wafted from Clarke's neck. They looked along the rooftop and up at the sun, then down at the ladder protruding over the tip of the balcony perimeter.

'You think they assumed you escaped down the ladder?' asked Clarke.

'I think so,' I said, stepping out to join them.

'Where does it lead?'

'Down to the spare bedroom to another double door.'

Horton nodded behind Clarke as further notes are jotted down. Clarke turned to his partner. 'James, we need to check every room, see if we could see anything.' He looked back at me. 'You okay with us checking the other rooms?'

'Fine by me.'

'Anything taken from your safe?' Clarke asked, peering into it.

'I don't think so,' I lied.

They searched the rest of the rooms upstairs thoroughly, but it wasn't long before we were back in the kitchen where the scent of coffee lingered in the air.

Joanne stood at the kettle. 'Coffee?'

'Please, strong, milk, no sugar,' Clarke said with a smile.

'Same, please, Mrs Haynes,' added Horton.

She smiled. 'Please, Joanne is fine.'

Both detectives nodded in understanding. They settled around the kitchen table for a moment to gather their thoughts. 'So, you didn't see the men? There's nothing you could tell us about them?'

We all shook our heads at different times.

'Just their voices,' Joanne said.

'Do you guys have any security cameras?' DCI Clarke asked.

'Just a standard motion detector system.' I pointed up to the top corner of the room.

'It wasn't triggered?'

'I was down before they broke in, turned it off before I made breakfast.'

At the table, we lost Lucy's attention to her phone. Joanne brought the coffees over.

'Thanks,' they both said.

I took the seat next to Joanne, opposite the detectives.

'Do you feel safe?' Clarke asked. His stare switched between us.

'No,' Jo said, shaking her head.

Her reply lingered in the growing silence. Lucy looked up from her phone, shaking her head in agreement with Joanne.

'There is a company who we work with – they set surveillance around the house,' Horton explained. 'Placed where people may try to enter the property.'

Clarke added, 'This company if we ring them now, would come here today. We would say it was an emergency and schedule it as urgent. All we could do is take back the notes that we've made and get someone here for fingerprints and footprints. Your best bet, in my opinion, is this company. They'll cover you for the future and in the meantime, we'll do what we could, but if the prints come back with no match, we don't have much we could use as evidence.'

He fell silent for a moment, focusing on Joanne again. Their eyes met for another moment too long. He looked back at me. 'The firm is called Vision Security.'

Lucy placed her phone down on the table, looked up, her blonde hair tickling the side of her cheeks. 'Could we not have a police car outside of our house?'

Horton grinned. 'Unfortunately, Lucy, we couldn't arrange that as a long-term solution. We could have someone watch the house for today until you decide your options.'

'Yeah, okay,' I said.

'Should we think about it?' said Joanne, sceptical. 'What if it was too expensive?'

'We need to feel safe,' I reminded her. 'You and Lucy need to be safe. Doesn't matter about the cost. Couldn't put a price on it.' I nodded at both detectives. 'Give them a ring. When could they get here – you said today?'

'If we ring now. Say it was urgent. Within the hour usually. They're really good,' explained Horton. 'We'll get a team over to get some prints first, hopefully, give us something we could go on. I noticed the stairs and carpets are marked but there didn't look like there's a solid footprint.'

'Okay, get it done,' I said firmly.

DCI Clarke nodded. 'Of course.'

Then he suggested we have a quick look around the outside of the house, get a good idea of where we'd want the cameras before the Vision Security engineers turned up. Clarke pulled out his phone, tapped a few buttons, and put it to his ear. Within two minutes, he'd told Vision Security all they need to know and ended the call. 'Yeah, within the hour.'

I thanked the detectives and led them outside. I offered them another coffee until the security firm turned up, but they gratefully declined and said they'd wait in their car. They needed to submit a formal report which went back to the station to update them on what was happening.

Back in the kitchen, I found Lucy and Joanne still at the table. 'Personally, I think we need it. Even if it was expensive, we could afford it. Rather feel safe – especially now anyway.'

'Sounds good,' Joanne said. 'You're right, Jack, sorry I questioned you.'

I leaned down and kissed her forehead.

'Or I could go out and tell them what I saw?' suggested Lucy.

18

Thursday afternoon
Toddington
JACK

DCI Clarke knocked on the door and told me they had to leave. He reassured me forensics were en route and the engineers from Vision Security were on their way too. Leaving with a smile, he crunched across the gravel back to his car, turned on the engine then disappeared through the gates.

Shortly after, there was a knock at the door. I opened it to a small man wearing a grin, carrying a small briefcase in his right hand. He told me he was here for the prints. I showed him the back door and the damage upstairs. He surprisingly wasn't here for very long, then said someone would be in touch with any findings or further developments.

Minutes later, there was another knock at the door.

'Security?' the man said. He was small and thin, sporting a light beard and brown eyes. He told me his name was John. I smiled at the familiar name, being the same as my father. In his hand, there was a small, plastic box with a heavy-duty handle.

'Yes, please come in.' I moved out of his way, allowing him room to enter. 'Did you walk here?' I asked him, not seeing a vehicle on the gravel.

'Parked it round the side,' he explained.

'Oh, okay.' I smiled at him. 'Tea, coffee?'

'I'm fine, thank you.' He beamed, showing his perfect white teeth. He glanced around the hallway, absorbing everything from floor to ceiling.

'I've been around the outside with the detectives,' I told him, 'to see the best locations for the cameras. You want me to show you?'

'Not just yet, I need to have a look inside first, mainly at the windows if that's okay. I need to see what a camera would see if it was placed at a high point. So, if I stand at each window, I could see what the camera would cover – then I could make a better decision. You okay with that?'

I nodded.

'You sure you don't want a drink before you start?'

'Honestly, I'm fine, but thank you all the same.' He grinned, took his shoes off, and started in the living room. I left him to it, returning to the kitchen to find Joanne and Lucy. It wasn't long before he appeared in the kitchen.

'Downstairs is pretty much done, just going upstairs.'

I nodded. Then watched his slight frame vanish out of view as he climbed the stairs with the small box in his hand. Lucy got, went to the cupboards, grabbed some food to make a sandwich, and asked if we wanted one, which we both declined.

'What you up to on there?' I asked Jo.

She looked up from her tablet. 'Messaging the girls – told them what's happened.'

'What they say?'

'Alison said: oh, my effin' God! That's horrendous. I'll ring you in five minutes on the house phone - the others haven't replied yet.'

Alison Lewes was Joanne's best friend. They'd first met at the age of twelve at school and hit it off on the first day. They'd been best friends ever since. They often bickered over some trivial things, but I guess that's what it was like being close to someone. She worked as a vet in Luton, in a street close to where she and Joanne grew up together.

Three years ago, Alison faced something awful: her husband, Peter, was found dead in a field with stab wounds to his stomach and chest. The police informed Alison he'd left a nightclub, got into a taxi, and was dropped off near the park where he was found. According to the records, the taxi driver dropped him off and continued his shift for another three hours. The findings on the autopsy about the time of death and, the route which the taxi driver had taken, ruled out the driver's involvement. To this day, she couldn't fathom why he would ask to be dropped off where he did or what the hell had happened. The police were still no further forward with closing the case or finding the persons responsible.

The other two friends she messaged were Jane and Natalie. They too were in the same class as Joanne and Alison. They often liked to meet up and go for coffee, go shopping, go out drinking, and in general, have good gossip about the world and the people in it.

The sound of John's footsteps was heard above, going back and forth to different rooms.

'What's he doing up there?' Joanne said.

'Said he had looked out the windows to gauge a better angle, so he knows where exactly to position the cameras,' I explained.

'You wanna go up, see what he's doing?' she asked with a concerned frown.

I stand up. 'Okay.' As I left the table, quiet footsteps descended the stairs. I stood still in the kitchen doorway and, as he turned right at the bottom of the stairs, I watched him put his shoes back on.

'Okay, I have a good idea of what's needed. I need to go outside.' He paused in thought, then pointed to the back door. 'I'll go through that door. I need to see where is best.'

'Okay, sure,' I said. My eyes followed him onto the decking.

Joanne mouthed silently, 'He is weird!'

I was about to sit down at the table when we heard a loud knock at the front door. Lucy jumped. Joanne's face grew with worry.

'Who the hell is this?' she said.

'Wait here,' I said.

I opened the front door to find a man dressed in dark blue work trousers and a green t-shirt with a bright yellow logo on it. He introduced himself as Paul, the Vision Security engineer.

I frown at him.

'Everything okay?' he asked, noticing my confusion.

'I don't - I don't understand,' I said. A sick feeling grew in the pit of my stomach.

Paul gave me an awkward smile. 'You called us to set up new security?'

I managed a painful, confused nod. 'I don't understand – one of your guys is already here,' I explained.

He tilted his head and narrowed his eyes. 'Jeff and I,' — he turned and pointed to the bright green van behind him where a man sat in the passenger seat, leaning forward over a clipboard with a pen in his hand —'were sent by my manager.'

Jeff smiled at us through the slanted window of the van.

'There's someone already here,' I said.

'Did he say he was from Vision?'

'I…' I paused. I'm not actually sure. I just assumed. 'I don't know.'

Paul's face flashed a serious stare. 'If what you're saying is true, the man in your house is not from our company. I can assure you of that because they wouldn't make that mistake.'

Where were Joanne and Lucy I wondered?

'Shit. Wait here,' I told him.

He nodded in understanding. I turned quickly and closed the door. I dashed down the hallway into the kitchen to find Joanne at the table, hunched over, looking at her tablet.

'Jo, where's Lucy?' I shouted, searching the kitchen with darting eyes.

'What...' she glanced up.

'Where is Lucy?' I screamed.

'Jack, what... what's the matter?' She moved back, rose to her feet, and stiffened with worry.

'The man here for security isn't with the company we asked for!'

'Who... is he?' Her palms raised to her open mouth as she dropped the tablet on the table.

I burst out of the back door onto the decking, my feet pounding the wooden boards causing a racket. In the garden, all I found were plants, sunshine, and a long stretch of grass that led to the back fence.

'Where the fuck is he?'

My chest thumped so fast, it almost hurt.

Where was Lucy?

Where was John?

As I reached the end of the garage I rounded the corner in my socks, my eyes scurried across everything in the search for the stranger. The side gate was ajar. I threw a palm to barge it open. As I passed the gate, I heard the whirring of fast-spinning tyres kick up the gravel and watched a little white van rush down the driveway.

I came to a halt.

There was nothing but two thick wheel marks left on the gravel and the distant sound of a vanishing engine.

Whoever he was, he had gone.

19

Toddington
JACK

'Could I please see some ID?' I said to Paul, back on the doorstep.

He'd heard and seen the van speed away moments before, realising I was being serious when I told him the situation. He pulled some identification from his pocket and raised it close to my face, long enough for me to see the details.

I studied it carefully. 'Thanks.'

'There's a number at the top if you need to ring, check our credentials,' he suggested. 'Put your mind at ease.'

I pondered the offer. 'You wouldn't mind?'

'Not at all – after what you've been through this morning. Please, go ahead.'

I called the number.

Paul stepped back and returned to the van while I kept hold of his ID card. A confident, soothing female voice told me the names of the two men that should be here. She also told me the colour of the van and registration plate. I asked her if there was anyone who worked at the firm with the name John.

She said there was, but not one of the installers.

At the front door, I waved him back and apologise profusely for checking. He told me not to worry. We walked around the outside of the house to see possible camera positions. There would be eight cameras he informed me. I filled him in with a detailed account of what happened this morning as we moved across the gravel. He reassured me with these cameras, no one would get anywhere near without being seen. After we agreed on the best positions for the cameras, he closed his notepad and returned to the van to get his tools and equipment.

'Where's Lucy?' I asked Joanne, sitting on the sofa in the living room watching television.

She cocked her head towards me. 'Upstairs.'

I pressed the fob in the hallway to lock the gates and placed it down on the small table near the bottom of the stairs. From my pocket, I took my phone out and made a call to DCI Clarke, who'd left me his personal card earlier. He advised me to secure the house, stay vigilant and allow the engineers to install the system as planned. He said he'll send a car here to watch over us until the system was up and working. I thanked him and ended the call.

Through the living room window, I gazed out onto the world. Nothing seemed suspicious, but these days, nothing ever did.

I turned, noticing the time on the wall clock. 'Jesus! Is that the time?'

'Twenty to four,' Joanne confirmed, peering down at her watch. 'Have you told work about what's happened?'

I shook my head, padded across the soft carpet towards the door. 'I'll do it now.' For the next conversation, I needed privacy. A place where no one could hear what was going to be said. I pulled my phone from my pocket as I entered our bedroom and pushed the door closed, leaving a slither of a gap so I could hear if anyone approached from the landing. I tapped on Ray's number and pressed CALL.

Ray was a work colleague. I'd known him a while and, although I was his boss, I considered him a friend.

'Hey, Jack.'

'Ray. Listen, we have a big problem,' I said, matter-of-factly.

'What is it?'

I kept my voice low. 'The money.'

'What about the money?' I heard his tone change.

'We've been burgled.' I paused, then, 'It's gone, all of it.'

'Even my half?' he asked.

'Yeah, all of it.'

20

Hemel Hempstead

Alexander Hunt had asked Stuart to count the money in the bag found at the Haynes' house. He trusted him. He was a loyal dog. Speaking of loyalty, he could also count on Phil. The other men were just numbers. Replaceable pieces of meat.

Hunt sat in his chair, watching the remaining fire fizzle out. The scent of burning charcoal overpowered the large, low-ceilinged room.

Stuart approached Hunt. 'Boss?'

'How much is there?' Hunt turned his head.

'There's six-hundred and twenty thousand pounds.'

'Wow.' Hunt raised his eyebrows for a second. 'Thank you, Stuart.' Hunt returned his gaze to the fireplace while Stuart remained silent by his side. 'Pass me the bag, please.'

Stuart did as he was asked.

Hunt dipped his hand inside, pulled out a wad of notes. 'How much in each?'

'Ten thousand in each block.'

Hunt's eyes narrowed in thought. He nodded to himself and extended an arm towards Stuart. 'You take this.'

Stuart froze. 'Boss, I—'

'You take this!' Hunt's tone suggested it wasn't a request. 'I know what troubles you've been going through. Phil has told me about your wife. The cancer she's got.' Hunt fell quiet and offered him a sympathetic smile. The room fell deadpan silent. 'Take this, treat her.'

Slowly, and cautiously, Stuart accepted the money Hunt placed in his hand.

'In fact,' Hunt said, dipping his thick hand in once again, 'take another.'

'Boss…'

Hunt looked him dead in the eye. 'You take this, you treat her well, okay? Do not mention it to anyone, including Phil. You keep this to yourself, and you enjoy what time you have left with her. You're a good man, Stuart. A loyal man.'

'Thank you so much.' Tears formed in his eyes.

Hunt waved the thanks away as if it was nothing. Stuart smiled gratefully and left the room with twenty thousand zipped up in his jacket pocket.

Moments later, Ann entered the room.

'Alex - William is here if you need some time with him?'

Hunt mulled over her words. 'Not today, I'm sore.'

'You need to keep active,' Ann told him, walking around the back of him to the far end of the room. She opened the black cabinet, grabbed a worn black A5-sized file. 'Well, he'll be here for a while if you change your mind,' she said before she left.

William had worked for him for seven years. Tall, thin, and full of domesticated knowledge: plumbing, electrics, joinery, gardening, you name it. He also did boxing at championship level in his earlier days, so Hunt occasionally sparred with him to keep himself in the game. The past couple of months, however, had proven difficult for Hunt. Sore niggles in his right hip, as well as a constant aching shoulder hindering his flexibility. Although Hunt was very capable of getting rough, he knew his scrapping days are slowly and painfully dissolving into his past.

Hunt's phone rang on the small table next to him, the vibrations interrupting the peace of the warm room. He leaned over to see the caller.

'Shit,' he whispered before answering. He accepted the call. 'Red?'

'Alexander. How are you on this fine afternoon?' the female voice said, carrying the usual confidence.

'Can't stop laughing. How are you?'

'I'm good. Are we ready with the Manco deal?'

'Yes, we are, Red.' Hunt paused, then: 'You don't need to ring me. I'm aware of our arrangement.'

'Don't be like that, Alexander,' Red said. 'You know everyone who deals in the South needs to do what they're told. It was a simple fact of living in this modern-day world.'

Hunt swallowed. 'I'm aware.'

'So how much are you selling and what'll be your profits?'

'I've already told you this, it was the same —'

'How much Alexander?'

Hunt thought about lying. He had tried that in the past and it hadn't worked out so well, so he won't be making the same mistake again. One of his men had had his throat slit because of his mistake. Personally, he didn't care much for the man, but he couldn't afford to lose men if he could help it.

Red had people everywhere.

The police.

The government.

Overseas.

She was a very dangerous individual. The name Red apparently came from a vibrant hairstyle she sported in her earlier years. Her hair was no longer red, it was black but the name had stuck.

'Fifty kilos. Half a mill in total.'

'Not a bad price, Alex. But... you could be making more money?'

'I know, but I like to keep business going, keep the customers happy. The better the price, the more likely they'll come back. I'm sure a woman of your business knowledge would agree?' Alexander gritted his teeth. 'Twenty percent for your well-deserved cut...'

Ann's short, stumpy figure entered the living room. Hunt rose to his feet, turned, and raised a hand. Ann bowed her head, knowing who he was speaking with.

'You all set then?' Red asked.

'Yes, got my best men on it. I'll be supervising from a distance.'

'Good to know. I know the Manco's well. Dangerous people. But so were the Deacon Brothers. They had connections in the right places and… what I hear is that the Deacons are no longer with us.'

'I hear that too, Red.' He knew she was aware of what happened to them last night. Nothing got by her. But he played along anyway, keeping his cards close to his chest.

'Be in touch, Alexander.' Red ended the call.

He put the phone back into his pocket.

'Her again,' Hunt said, rolling his eyes.

'Should I ring Phil, and see how things are going?' asked Ann.

Hunt held up his thick palm. 'It's fine, Ann. Thank you. I'll speak with them later. Phil knows what the plan is.'

'If you're sure—'

'I am.'

Ann screwed her face and vanished from the doorway.

He was aware of the Manco's. The violent stories, the fierce reputation. Three of them, all kickboxers, are highly motivated and dangerous.

Hunt stood up, his hip causing a niggling pain but eased when he was upright. He wandered over to the window, gazed out on his property. The perfectly cut grass stretching to the base of the high stone wall surrounding the impressive land made him smile. The sun descended, falling behind the high walls, causing the air to carry a slight chill as it seeped through the open window to his right.

Not a moment's remorse ever came over him when he looked back on his life. About the people he had killed, the lives he had damaged. The few people out there who went up against him have been dealt with quickly.

The murder of the Deacon Brothers would be doing the rounds soon. News always travelled fast in this game. They tried to fiddle Hunt out of money and, in return, were now dead.

Regardless of how tough someone thought they are, they all fear someone.

Someone more dangerous.

Red.

No one had ever seen her. She has no trace, no leads, no ties.

Nothing.

She hired the most loyal, lethal assassins available. These hired professionals were the best at what they did. It was clear to everyone that no one crossed her.

Unknown to the police, unknown to many.

An untraceable ghost with eyes and ears everywhere.

21

Near Toddington

DCI Clarke and DS Horton were cruising down the A5120 back to the station after leaving the Haynes' house. Clarke, behind the wheel, focused on the road ahead. Horton's attention was down on his phone in the passenger seat.

'Scary shit, eh?' Clarke muttered.

Horton looked up at him. 'What is?'

'What they've been through this morning,' said Clarke. 'Must have been scared. I certainly know I would be.'

Clarke slowed the Astra as they approached a bend, then smoothly guided it around the bend. 'Yeah,' Horton agreed and returned to his phone.

'How's Julia?' Clarke asked.

'She's okay. Just, just getting on with things.' Horton dropped his phone and sighed, glancing in Clarke's direction. 'It was hard for Courtney, you know. She does her best, but – but she wants to be out with her friends. Doing what her friends are doing. But when I'm working, she has to be there for her Mum.'

Horton's wife, Julia, was told months earlier she had breast cancer. After three months of chemo, she wasn't looking her best. Horton's daughter, Courtney, cared for her when she was not at work. But she struggled with it. She hated seeing her mother like that.

'It must be hard for her,' said Clarke softly.

'Yeah, it is. She was doing well, though - they both are. I'm really proud of them – really, I am.' Horton wiped away a small tear that crept from his eye. Clarke noticed. He told him Julia was a strong woman and he had no doubt she would pull through.

'Thanks, mate.'

They approached a junction where a red light signalled them to stop. Clarke lowered his window, allowing warm air to seep in, but it was so warm, it made no difference.

'How's Mandy doing?' asked Horton.

'Okay.'

'You don't… sound sure?' Horton commented.

'Not good – well, she's okay, but I mean *we're* not good.' Clarke set the car into first gear, edged it forward when the light turned green. 'We're trying to sort it out, but it isn't working. Too much shit has happened. Plus, she was a fucking lunatic anyway, so – I just know I'm better off without her.' Clarke has been seeing Mandy for a few months. From day one, she had been trouble, constantly getting drunk and making a scene everywhere they went. The trouble was, when she was sober, she was a perfect match for Clarke.

'Maybe you'll find someone else? You're good-looking chap.'

Clarke sighed. 'Maybe. It's hard work, you know—'

'Hard work?' said Horton cutting him off. 'Shagging anything that moves at 3 am on a night out. I'd swap shoes with you in a heartbeat for a random Saturday night on the town, let me tell you!'

They both laughed. Clarke knew he was only joking.

The Astra pulled into Bedfordshire Police station and came to rest in one of the available parking bays. Clarke removed the key and rested the set of keys on his thigh.

'Mrs Haynes is nice, ey?' Horton said. 'Noticed the mutual eye contact between you two.'

Clarke grinned. 'When we entered their house, I felt like I'd seen her somewhere before. Then it clicked. She was out last weekend in the city with a few friends.'

'You speak to her?' Horton enquired, his palm gripping the handle of the passenger door, readying himself to get out.

'No. I noticed her though.' Clarke fell silent, but Horton felt like he wanted to say more.

'What is it?'

'I don't think Joanne Haynes is being totally honest with her husband, Jack.'

22

Toddington
JACK

'What the hell do you mean, Jack?' Ray shouted in my ear.

'The money. They came in and… it was gone, Ray,' I said, keeping my voice as low as possible.

'It's gone?'

I glanced at the bedroom door, checking it was closed enough. I took a seat on the edge of the bed, pushed my free hand hard against the side of my head to suppress an oncoming headache.

'Who did it?' Ray asked. 'Who the fuck took our money?'

'I … I don't know. They broke in the back door, came upstairs, and asked for the photos. They smashed the house up, then chased us upstairs. Didn't find us because we hid in the attic.' I paused, grabbing a breath. 'When we came out, they'd gone. I thought they were going to kill us, Ray. We checked the house—'

'I thought you had a secure safe, Jack? That's why I let you look after the money in the first place.'

'Yeah, I do. I put it in the safe. We were just about to leave for the wedding in Spain when we heard them downstairs. I must have left the safe open by mistake, Ray.'

Ray didn't reply.

'I'm - I'm so sorry,' I added.

'You're sorry? Half of that money is mine, Jack. You do know how long it took us to plan it? I mean—'

'Ray… I know.' I didn't need reminding. I dropped my head, closed my eyes, and allowed my chin to meet my chest.

I opened my eyes, seeing somebody standing in the bedroom doorway. Joanne.

I froze, watching her, keeping the phone to my ear.

She locked eyes with me for a second and sauntered across the white carpet towards her wardrobe. She had already tidied up the heaps of clothing and moved the suitcases which were left earlier in the day.

'Who's on the phone?' she asked, rustling through the clothes on the rail.

I wondered how much of the conversation she'd heard.

'It was Ray,' I told her.

'How they doing with the security?'

'Okay, I think. Just noise really. A lot of drilling.' Joanne flung her arms up hopelessly at carpet stains before leaving the bedroom. Then I heard her light footsteps fade as she made her way back downstairs.

I stood up, went to the window, peered out onto the bright afternoon. My vacant stare fell on a tree in the distance. It was surrounded by green fields and a simmering horizon.

'Are you there, Jack? Jack?' shouted Ray in my ear.

'Yes Ray, I'm here. I was talking to Joanne. Calm down.'

'Calm down? Half of that money is mine. That's over three hundred thousand pounds. How do I know you're not just saying it's gone to keep it for yourself?'

'Don't be ridiculous, Ray. I'd never do that. How would I get away with it? You know where it came from. You'd just tell the bank - or the police?'

I heard his mind tick over in his silent response, then, 'Yeah but I was in on it, Jack, I'd be setting myself up. I'd be cutting my nose off to spite my face. Wouldn't I?'

'Listen, Ray, we're in this together. A promise is a promise. We both know how the money went missing from the bank. If one of us fucked off with it, that'd be stupid. Think about it, Ray. My money has gone as well.'

'I have to go,' he barked. 'I'll ring you later. You could count on that!'

The line went dead.

I mulled over the biggest question in my life right now: would he say anything?

'Shit!' I shouted but the four walls of the bedroom answered me with a pitiful silence. I threw my phone on the bed, dropped my heavy face into my sweaty palms.

Ray had worked for Hembridge Bank for ten years as a financial analyst. He was the best we had. He knew the system inside out. I'd known Ray for three years, the same length of time I'd been at Hembridge. Previously, I was at Barclays as their finance manager before I took the same role here before being promoted five months ago to the Finance Director. My predecessor, Keith, had retired, which opened up the spot for me to step into.

I shouldn't have taken it. I didn't deserve it, not after what Ray and I had done.

My mind went back nine months ago to the cold, wet Friday night. A handful of us, including Ray and I, had prearranged a night out in London. We'd been dropped off at Harlington station and rode the Thameslink to St Pancras where we met the others. It didn't take too long. Horizontal rain pelted the train windows and the cold passengers sported that I-just-want-to-get-home look all over their tired faces.

The winter night ticked on. The rain had stopped but moisture lingered in the air as we shivered from bar to bar. A few of the group had called taxis or headed for the nearest underground links, making their way home as midnight had come and gone. Ray and I were left in a corner booth of a busy, dimly lit bar. We sank jaegers and sambucas like it was going out of fashion until our heads got dizzy.

The next morning, I sat on the edge of my bed battling with a head that felt like it was filled with glue. I vaguely remembered the night before. The foggy images of beautiful women, heavily scented perfumes, flashing lights, and stale beer.

Ray text me: *I think we should go through with it.*

I re-read the message over and over, and that's when it hit me.

We had a conversation about robbing the bank.

Over the following month, Ray's idea buried itself inside my head. 'But we know everything about it, Jack... We won't have to do it, we'll get someone else to do it...we'll be wealthy, we'll pay them enough to keep quiet... it'll be fine,' he said.

It would be fine...

We worked it out, running through different scenarios. We knew almost everything about the bank: the security, the staff, the location of the money, and more importantly, how it could be done. We hired only professionals.

Shortly after, the bank was a million pounds lighter. Police investigations were non-stop for weeks, followed by daily board meetings jammed with questions fired from all directions. But no one could shed any light on what happened.

During the time of the robbery, I'd conveniently put a week's holiday in, soaking up the sun on the Greek island, Rhodes, with Joanne and Lucy. How convenient.

And Ray, well Ray had taken sick leave. He had stomach pains and the shits – he informed me he'd downed a bottle of laxatives and purposely embarrassed himself at work to make it look legit.

So, *neither* of us knew anything about it, according to the police report anyway.

Every few months, Ray and I had come to the agreement that I'd give him ten thousand pounds in an envelope, a secure way of filtering it to him without causing too much fuss. I'd bring it into the bank, hand it to him when it is safe to do so, quite often in the car park out of sight. If anyone asked, we'd agree it was a personal loan from a caring friend.

Ray trusted me well enough for me to keep hold of it locked up in my safe. He didn't want it in his house; he was afraid his son would find it. Rumour has it that his son was into drugs, so I understood why. Ray also had said there's a policeman living next door to him who'd heard about the robbery, who'd already questioned him about his knowledge on the matter, as he knew Ray worked at Hembridge.

I sighed into my hands.

I thought about Ray.

I thought about Joanne.

I thought about Lucy.

About Carl.

The photos.

The money.

The mess of the house.

The men who broke in – when they'd be back.

I closed my eyes, leaned back onto the bed. My eyes were so heavy, I let them close.

I just wanted to go to sleep. Forever.

A sound woke me as I jolt up from the bed.

'Jack!' Joanne shouted.

23

Toddington
JACK

I dashed down the stairs and locked eyes with Joanne who waited at the bottom with the Vision Security engineers standing behind her. The smell of drilled brick and dust filled the air.

'What's the matter?' I asked with wide eyes.

'They're finished now,' she said with a smile. 'They'd like to show you how it works...' she frowns, 'have you been sleeping?'

'Maybe drifted off for a second,' I admitted.

'Come, they'll show you.'

Paul, the engineer I showed around the house earlier, beamed at me and wiped the beads of sweat off his forehead with the back of his hand.

'This way, we've set it up in the study for you,' he said.

I followed Paul into the study. On the large, oak desk in the far corner of my high-ceilinged room, there was an extra monitor placed to the left of my computer screen. Above the two monitors, there was a thin black wire fixed to the wall with small clips running vertically until it reached a circular box twelve inches from the ceiling.

'What's the box for?' I said. He followed my eyes.

'It links all the cameras wirelessly,' he said. 'You're probably wondering why I've put it up there?' I nodded. 'It works best at a height – we've found when located in a similar height, or close as possible to the cameras themselves, we get a better, more reliable connection.'

On the additional screen, there were four small screens, each one showing four separate camera angles around the exterior of the house. Paul leaned forward, picked up the remote from the desk, and pressed a button that changed the screen to the alternative four screens.

'Eight camera angles in total.'

Eights screens to keep my family safe.

'Here - have a look,' he said, handing me the remote.

I fiddled with the buttons looking at the various angles around our house. I felt happy it covered what we need.

'Also remember – the screens would record twenty-four seven,' he said. 'They are linked to our head office. We won't be monitoring them continuously, but they'll be saved to our hard drive if you ever need to look over them in case you lose your data.' He paused. 'And also, it's all linked to your computer, which Joanne said was okay.' He turned to Joanne, who nodded.

Paul continued. 'You could replay the files in slow-mo, and in real-time, or however quickly you need to. I've installed a program for you to do that.'

'Okay,' I said.

'There's a step-to-step guide when you open it, but it was pretty self-explanatory. If there's an emergency, you can press the red button.' He pointed to the top of the remote. 'There. And by pressing that, it would flag up on our system that something is wrong. Someone would ring you straight away so only press it if it was absolutely necessary.'

The whole package sounded great. His explanation satisfied me.

Paul and I set the payment method up and agreed on a continuous monthly payment. After a few minutes, they left. Job done.

Shortly after they'd gone, there was a knock at the door. I opened it to find my brother looking up at me from the gravel.

'Hey, Markos! How are you doing?' I leaned forward, shook his firm hand then hugged him.

'Hey, Jackal! I'm good. Sorry to hear about the break-in. Them fuckers come back yet? I could do with punching someone's head in.'

'Well lucky for them, they haven't,' I said, smiling. 'Come in guys.'

Mark passed me. I looked down at my sister-in-law, Elaine, who glanced up with a sad smile and stepped up through the door. At the base of the stairs next to the small waist-high table, Joanne appeared. Mark padded across the wooden floor, wrapped his big arms around her, and hugged her tightly.

'You okay, Jo?' he asked her.

'We're okay, we're okay,' Jo replied, tears filling her eyes.

Elaine embraced Joanne for a hug once Mark had let her go. 'Hey,' she said softly.

'Who were they? These men?' Mark asked.

'No idea,' I said, 'they were asked for photos or a camera, that's all I heard really.'

'Show me upstairs,' he said.

Mark followed me up the stairs two at a time.

'Look at the carpets!' he commented, shaking his head.

'Tell me about it. We only got them new last week.'

'Bastards,' he muttered when he stepped up onto the landing and saw the broken doorway ahead of us.

I told him exactly what had happened. I showed him Lucy's room and the small cupboard in the corner where we had hidden.

'Who's this Carl?' Mark asked. 'Couldn't have my niece shacking up with any Tom, Dick, and Harry.' Anger spread across his face.

'Joanne knew about it, too. Never said a word.'

After a few minutes of looking around Lucy's room, he said, 'Where're the photos?

'I deleted them.'

'Why would you —'

'I'll show you the note then you'll know why.'

Back in the kitchen, the air wafted in through the back door. It was getting colder, the sun pulling away for the day.

'So, what time are you setting off?' I grabbed four mugs from a cupboard and, two at a time, place them down near the boiling kettle. It wasn't long before we were sitting at the table with a plate of biscuits and the satisfying smell of coffee lingering between us.

'In an hour,' he said. 'Bags are packed in the car. We're back early Saturday though. Elaine has an important business meeting. I've told her to miss it, but you know what she was like.'

'Business is business,' she said with a serious look.

'Of course, it is,' Mark replied sarcastically. He stood up, pulled out a pack of cigarettes from his pocket, and walked outside. After he lit his cigarette, I watched the swirls of blue smoke rise above his head before they dispersed in the gentle breeze. He appeared taller than usual standing on the decking. His arms and chest looked solid. I recalled him mentioning he was starting back at the gym a month or two ago.

I looked back at Elaine. She worked for a prestigious property firm based in North London. They dealt with high-priced properties. Occasionally, she met celebrities, helping them find the right home. The rest of her clients were vain, patronising individuals with plenty of money, most of their wealth, from rich parents. But she soaked up their arrogance and got on with it.

'Where's Lucy?' Elaine asked.

'Living room. Come, we'll go see her.' Joanne stood. 'We'll go sit in there. Let the men talk football.' Elaine rose too and they dissolve into the hallway.

Mark and I sat for a little while, discussing the recent poor run of Manchester United, including their latest game where they held on for a measly draw against a poor side. Then we spoke a little about the work he was getting done at his home. 'Elaine's idea – obviously,' he explained with a shrug.

'It always is.' I smiled at him and took a sip of hot coffee, then placed it back down on the table. 'You seen much of mum?'

'Not in a few days, I haven't. Maybe a week actually.' I noticed a pang of guilt wash over his face. 'You?'

'Three days ago. Spotty the cleaner was there doing her bit.'

Mark couldn't help but smile. Our mum, Kathy, had a nickname for almost everyone. For any passing person, she'd mutter something under her breath. It wasn't anything malicious by any means, always only in jest. But her cleaner, Janet, who's been cleaning her bungalow for nearly two years on the same three days every week, had an issue with facial spots. Whatever she'd tried didn't work. Kathy even had nicknames for me and Mark. To Mark, she referred to me as 'Beard', and to me, she referred to Mark as 'Eyebrows'. His eyebrows were slightly thicker, but nothing noticeably different from anyone else's eyebrows.

I stood up. 'Follow me,' I said. 'You'll like this.' I led the way to the study.

'I'll just say Hi to Lucy.' He popped his head into the living room. 'There's my favourite girl. Wow, you're getting big now.'

Lucy's eyes narrowed in his direction then she grinned at him.

'Not as in big, big.' Mark used his hands to motion a large ball in front of his stomach imitating someone overweight. 'I mean grown-up, big.'

Lucy smiled knowingly at him before he backed out and joined me in the study.

'One-hundred and fifty pounds a month?' Mark said, his mouth making a small 'o'.

I shrugged. 'I feel safer.'

'You have too much money,' he told me as he played around with the remote, changing the camera angles on the screens. He was like a child with a new toy. 'That red button is clever stuff isn't it?'

'Hopefully, we won't need it,' I said.

Without a sound, I felt someone standing behind me. I turned to see Elaine standing there.

'Oh hey. I'm just showing Mark the new security. Joanne has probably mentioned it anyway.'

She nodded.

'Have a look.' I moved to my right, motioned her forward. She slipped between us. She took the remote from Mark and fiddled with the screen.

'Impressive stuff. It covers almost everything,' she said, glancing at me approvingly.

'My main concern is the back door,' I said. 'Over the decking. That's where they came in today.'

'Maybe you could—'

'I'm happy with it,' I said, cutting her short. I felt the silent tension build. The study became dead quiet. She could be the argumentative type, so I avoided her eye contact. There could be tension in the air when she was around.

'Okay, that's good,' she said, handing back the remote. 'Mark, we should be setting off very soon. We need to check in by seven.'

Mark sighed, checking his watch, then agreed with a nod. Elaine left the study and Mark gave me a knowing look, almost as if apologising on her behalf.

'Well, it has been a pleasure, brother.' Mark wrapped his big arms around me and squeezed. He then whispered in my ear, 'Let me know if anyone comes back, I really do feel like smashing someone's face in today.'

24

Friday Morning
Toddington
JACK

The clock near my head told me it was 5.32. The faint neon glow reflected on the wooden surface of the bedside table as my tired eyes slowly opened.

I rolled onto my back, stared at the ceiling for a moment before I close my eyes, hoping sleep would pull me back under but, after five minutes, I realised it wasn't going to. The bedroom was waking up, bright light peeking around the edges of the long dark curtains at the windows. I shoved the covers off without a sound, got out of bed, and made my way through the through-room to the en-suite. I washed my face and beard in the sink, then dabbed them dry with a towel from the rail near the sink.

Mark had helped me secure the back door before they left last night, screwing random pieces of wood we'd found in the garage across the top, middle, and bottom of the door. I hadn't slept well, waking several times but I hadn't heard anything loud enough to wake me.

The joiner was coming early today to fix the broken doors and frames. Lucy had slept in the spare bedroom next to ours. She'd left her bedroom for Joanne to clean because she couldn't face it. Plus, she felt safer closer to us.

Thinking about her room reminded me of the space in the attic where we hid. My heart beat increased remembering the anger in their voices, the frantic desire to find the photos. I then remembered seeing that small box hiding in the yellow insulation.

The box I'd never seen before.

I made my way using the balls of my feet, quietly along the short narrow hallway leading to the large square landing. The door on my left – Lucy's temporary bedroom - was closed. I walked lightly along the landing towards the broken door at the top of the stairs, climbed the stained carpets in the dark, turned, and entered Lucy's large bedroom. The morning light flooded in through her double doors.

At the small cupboard in the corner, I kneeled and opened the door. I leaned in and rummaged through where I had seen it. It wasn't there. I backed out, frowning, then found my feet, and I scanned around Lucy's room. It didn't take long to notice something on the floor behind her desk.

How did it get there? I bent down and picked it up. The box rattled. Bits of metal or something hard inside, although it wasn't heavy. A rectangular shape, six inches wide, four high, and four deep. There was a lock on the front keeping it tightly shut. Solid corner braces and two firm hinges at the back.

'What the hell is this?'

I tried prizing it open with my bare hands but failed miserably. I placed the box down on Lucy's desk. I'll ask Lucy about it later. Maybe she knew what was in it. I went over to the double door, unlocked it, and stepped out into the fresh summer air. A vast array of greenery stood before me as the smell of nearby farms tinkered in the wind.

It wasn't long before I was downstairs in the kitchen. I made coffee and toast and ate them at the table. Then, I spent the next ten minutes in the study reviewing the whole night of camera activity on fast forward.

Clear as a whistle.

The men hadn't come back.

25

Luton

John, the man who posed as the security engineer at the Haynes house, made his way downstairs in his dressing gown after a quick shower, carrying a cup of lukewarm coffee in his hand. In the dark living room where the curtains were still drawn, he took a seat at his computer desk located in the corner, placing his mug right of the monitor. He switched the computer on, listened to the whirl as it hummed to life.

He was tired, he hadn't slept. His eyes were sore, and his head felt heavy as if there was a weight balanced on top of it.

He had been out all night sitting in a small white van almost four hundred metres from the Haynes house where he'd escaped once the real security engineers had arrived. Remembering he'd passed a gated dirt road, which seemingly led to an old unused farm, he returned later to cut the lock and parked a few metres down the dirt track out of sight.

It had been a long night but eventful. As the morning arrived, the sun started peeping over the horizon and his heavy eyes closed gradually.

A drum of quick knocks on his window woke him up.

Opening his eyes, he saw a farmer peering in through the glass, eyeing up him and the equipment positioned on the dashboard: a laptop; a speaker; a small rectangular expensive-looking box; an antenna.

John turned on the ignition and lowered his window.

'And why you parked 'ere then?' said the farmer, in an accent of someone living closer to Devon or Cornwall.

'Erm, I'm working with the police.'

'Doing what exactly?' The farmer asked, screwing his face up in interest.

'Surveillance.'

'Hmmmm. Well, if you could just move out my way son, I need to be through.'

'No problem.' John nodded and checked his watch. Just after seven. He started the van, edged out of the open gate, and drove down the road in the direction of his home.

He took a sip of coffee and, on the screen in front of him, he manoeuvred his mouse cursor to a folder named HAYNES, then he double-clicked. The folder showed four files labelled one to four. He clicked on the first one and an audio app opened up on the screen.

The time frame was between 4 p.m. to 7 a.m. In silence, he leaned back in his chair, listening with his eyes closed for a few minutes. File 'one' was from a device positioned under the Haynes' bed. He'd glanced along the recording bar where it displayed the whole-time frame before he closed his eyes knowing that very soon, a sound would be detected and would be indicated by a raised chunk of heightened waves along the sound bar at the bottom of the screen. The flat-line silence in the audio recording was disturbed when someone entered the Haynes' bedroom. Jack made a phone call, spoken with a person called Ray about the money that had been stolen. The sound of multiple springs compressing came through loud and clear on the recording, John presuming Jack had sat down on the bed.

Soon after, more footsteps were heard, then: 'Who's on the phone?' It was his sexy, dark-haired wife. She left the room soon after and Jack continued with the call.

John knew from planting the devices, he'd have approximately sixteen hours' worth of recording before the devices failed. It was the norm. As long he was within five hundred metres of where he planted them, he could listen until they burnt out. Although, that was cut short by an hour when the farmer knocked on his van's window.

Through the clear microphone, John heard what he'd picked up last night.

'Yeah, I guess – listen, Ray, we're in this together. A promise is a promise. We both know how the money went missing from the bank. If one of us fucked off with it, that'd be stupid. Think about it, Ray.'

John sat back and smiled. He rewound the last fifteen seconds: 'We both know how the money went missing from the bank. If one of us fucked off with it, that'd be stupid. Think about it, Ray.'

'Jack, Jack, Jack, you silly man,' John said, laughing to himself hysterically. He picked up his phone to ring the person who'd sent him to the Haynes' house in the first place.

26

Toddington
JACK

At 9 a.m., there was a knock on the door. I cautiously opened it to find the joiner standing there in black overalls wrapped with an old brown leather belt around his waist. He smiled. Wrinkles formed at the corners of his mouth; crow's feet lined the edges of his aging eyes.

'Come in, Matthew,' I said, with a warm smile.

'Thanks. Long time, no see,' he said, stepping up from the gravel. 'Them doors still hanging?' he asked, referring to the new doors he'd fitted upstairs last year. Joanne had this great idea that she wanted four panel wooden doors instead of the six-panel ones which were already here when we moved in. They looked classier, she'd said.

'Still hanging,' I said, moving aside to let him into the hallway.

'Good.' As he walked, his movements seemed slower than they were last year. A slight imbalance at his core. Maybe a hip issue with his old age. He had been retired for over three years, only doing this as a hobby to keep himself busy.

'You want a tea? Coffee?' I asked.

He mulled over the question, his right hand running through his thin grey hair. 'I think I will.' Further silence followed as he thought long and hard about what would probably be his most important decision of the day. Finally, he said, 'Coffee, milk, no sugar.'

In the kitchen, I asked Joanne to make the coffee. I briefly told Matthew the events of yesterday whilst we wandered upstairs to see the damage he was here to fix.

I left Matthew with his coffee and tools, returning to my study where I phoned Jerry, one of the bank's board members to inform him what'd happened.

'When would you return to work?' he said, without asking if my family were okay.

'Monday.'

'Okay, see you Monday. Let me know if it was sooner,' he said before he hung up.

'Thanks for your sympathy,' I said into the disconnected phone.

On the wide sofa in the living room sitting opposite Lucy, I lowered my eyes to my tablet, absorbing the daily news. Usual rubbish, although one story did catch my eye: two teenage boys abducted a toddler in the west midlands area. They wanted a new pair of trainers before they gave him back to the parents.

The world had gone mad.

'Daaaad,' Lucy said, purposefully drawing the length of the word out to catch my attention.

I glanced up. 'Yeah?'

'Should I go in today?' She was referring to afternoon college classes.

'I don't think it's a good idea, Lucy. Not with what happened yesterday.'

She nodded and returned her focus to her phone.

'I have plenty of books in the study if you want to do something useful?'

She frowned and curled her lip. 'Books about what?'

'Well, fictional stories – I have plenty. Linwood Barclay, Peter James, Lee Child. The list goes on.'

Her frown deepened.

'Other non-fiction stuff on engineering or finance. There's even a book about the world.' I smiled, already knowing her answer. She hated reading, always had. Anything to do with books – reading or writing - knocked her to the realms of boredom, unless it contained the latest celebrity gossip crammed in a glossy magazine lined with fake pictures of false people only out there to make a few quid.

'You spoke to Carl yet?' I asked. 'I need to speak with him.'

'No, Dad. I haven't heard from him – I tried ringing, but he didn't answer.'

'Okay. Let me know if-'

A loud knock on the door echoed through the hallway.

I paused for a moment, stood up, leaving Lucy in the living room, and wandered to the door. On the gravel outside stood a heavy-set man with an overhanging stomach covered by a dark coat, zipped up to his chest leaving a thin gap where I caught a glimpse of a blue tie squashed between a white collar, similar to the one DCI Clarke and DS Horton wore yesterday. Small aging lines appeared around his narrow, dark brown eyes as he smiled.

'Can I help you?' I asked, wearily.

'Jack Haynes?'

'Yes?'

He showed me some identification. 'I'm Detective Inspector Andrew Johnson of Bedfordshire Police.' I looked down, briefly studying his card before he put it away. 'I'm following up on the events that happened here yesterday. May I come in?'

'Err, yeah. Sure, come in… detective.' I closed the door once he was inside, then lead him to the kitchen and offered him a drink, which he declined with a palm. 'Please, have a seat,' I said.

'I read up briefly this morning on the events of yesterday, so you may have to educate me a little if you don't mind?' He sported a thick moustache over his lip, reminding me of Magnum PI.

'Sure,' I said.

'We have so much going on at the station. My boss asked me to check up on things. Mainly to see how you are doing and—'

The sound of drilling into wood whirled above our heads, stealing his attention for a moment.

'We're getting the doorframes fixed up,' I explained.

'I see,' he said with a genuine sad smile. 'So, they broke in, you guys hid in the attic?'

'Yeah, pretty much.'

'Did they ask for anything? Say why they were here?'

'No – they answered my wife's phone and asked me where I was.' I leaned back a little. 'To be honest, I wasn't waiting around to find out.'

He nodded in understanding, tapping the surface of the kitchen table several times with a fingernail. 'You did the right thing. Did they say anything about photos?'

'Your colleagues yesterday advised us on a security system.' My face grew warm, knowing I'd ignored his question. 'They came and installed a new system. I'll admit we're still shaken from what happened, but we feel much safer now.'

He leaned forward with intrigue. 'Can I have a look?'

'You can… if you like. Just in the study. Follow me.'

I stood up and led him to the spacious study room just off the hallway.

Silence captivated the air while he played with the remote, flicking across the screens, analysing the angles of the cameras. The awkward silence became deafening.

I coughed on purpose. 'What are you looking for, Detective Johnson?'

My words almost startled him, as if he'd forgotten I was there. 'Oh…erm… Just checking that the cameras cover everywhere. You don't want this kind of thing happening again.'

I shook my head. 'No.'

Johnson placed the remote down on the desk, and turned slowly towards me. 'So why don't you tell me where the photos are?'

His words grew on me like icy fingers crawling up my spine. 'I'm sorry?'

'I saw it yesterday in the report,' he explained. 'I've just asked you in the kitchen, yet, you ignored the question.'

I raised my right hand to my face to scratch my beard. 'I thought you said you saw the report this morning?'

His thinking clogs were doing overtime. 'I heard someone mention it at the station,' he corrected himself. 'I *read* it this morning.'

I wasn't sure about this guy. There was something… something not quite right.

'They asked for photos, yes,' I finally said.

'What photos?'

'I honestly don't know. They kept saying it over and over. I think they may have us mixed up with someone else.'

'Is your daughter at home?' he asked, glancing up to the ceiling.

'My daughter?'

'Yes. Your daughter.'

'She's—'

'She's a photographer, right?'

'Not yet. She's at college doing Photography, along with Art and Design.'

'What's she into?'

'Hmmm?'

'What photography is she into?' His eyes narrowed.

'Sunsets, that type of thing.'

'Has she taken any other photos?' he said, tilting his head back. 'Photos she… maybe took last night?'

'Afraid not, I'd have seen them if she had. She always shows me them when she comes home – she was proud of them.'

'Could I see them?' he probed.

I remember I'd deleted the photos that Lucy took. 'Yeah, of course. Wait here.' I left the room.

The camera was hidden inside the cupboard above the kettle. Within twenty seconds, I was back in the study. DI Johnson was studying the monitor carefully, mentally absorbing the different camera angles, nodding his head as he processed it.

'Here,' I said, handing him the Nikon.

He held the camera with both hands close to his face, slowly clicking through the photos. I stood next to him, peering over him as he flicked from shot to shot. Beautiful shots of green scenery complimented by a falling sun. Other shots included a small-secluded river, winding as it progressed downstream, beams of bright sunlight stabbing the air above it as it sneaked through gaps in the trees.

His breathing quickened in what seemed like frustration.

'What are you looking for?' I asked. After he reached photo seventy-two, it restarted back to photo one.

He passed the camera back to me. 'Some good shots on there.'

'Yeah, she's good.'

He turned to face me showing me his full width. He probably had two to three stones on me, but he was of similar height.

He smiled. 'You've deleted them, haven't you?' Leaning forward, he closed the gap between our faces to six inches.

'I'm sorry?'

'You heard me, Jack, don't play silly bastards with me.' He edged even closer with a stern expression. The tip of his moustache inches from my mouth. I could feel the heat of his horrible breath on my face. As my heart pumped faster, I felt myself succumbing to a surge of rising adrenaline.

'Your daughter took pictures of something she witnessed on Wednesday night in the woods. She was there with a boy. She saw what she saw because she didn't mind her own business. She was brought this on herself.'

'Listen, detective whoever-you-are.' I glanced away for a second then return his hard gaze. 'How dare you have the audacity to—'

'The audacity?' he interrupted me. 'I'll do whatever I please, Jack Haynes. So, listen up, and you listen well. If the photos have been deleted, then that's fine.'

'I'm ringing DCI Clarke about this.' I turn away from him, taking a step away toward the hallway. 'Your job is to serve and protect the—'

He grabbed my wrist with a fierce tug, pulling me with a jolt so hard, he almost yanked me over. The strength of the man shocked me. Then, he burst into frightening laughter, whilst maintaining his vice-like grip, his fingernails digging into my skin.

The electricity of fear ran through me with this man in my house.

Near my daughter.

My wife.

'Get the fuck off me?' I said harshly, wriggling, but he overpowered me, keeping my arm trapped in his vice-like grip.

'Listen!' He leaned in close again, his mouth an inch from my ear. 'Whether the photos have been deleted or not,' he whispered, 'if you decide to speak to Clarke or Horton about me, or about what your daughter saw last night, I want to tell you a little story I heard: over a million pounds was stolen from the bank you work at. I know it was you who arranged it. I have recorded proof of it, so just bare that in mind.' He pulled his face back and, with a deep glare and a smirk, his big dark brown eyes sucked me into a world of helplessness. 'Understand?'

'I understand,' I whispered through a clogged throat.

He released his grip and patted the side of my bicep. 'Good.' He stepped around me, heading for the hallway. 'I'll be in touch,' he said. His broad shape disappeared through the doorway, then he stopped and turned. 'Nice house by the way.'

Cautiously, I followed him into the hallway, watched him open the front door, and step out into the sunlight. I dashed across the wooden floor, closed the door, and locked it.

'Shit,' I said to myself.

27

Toddington

Lucy was upstairs in the room she'd slept in the previous night, lying on her stomach on the king-sized bed, looking down at her phone, scrolling through the endless unimportant posts on social media, carrying the sole purpose of collecting as many 'likes' as they could. It was a popularity contest among our younger generation and, unfortunately, they relished it.

Lucy sighed, dropped her phone and used her elbows to turn herself over, and stared at the blank ceiling.

Why did she let Carl take the photos?

Why didn't she just trust her gut and mind her own business?

Lucy closed her eyes in the quiet room. The image of the man in the brown coat came to her in vivid waves as he stood there pointing the gun at the men on the ground, drenched in blood.

The echo of the gunshots went off in her head. She flinched, clamped her eyes shut for a moment. She opened them, now feeling the cool breeze coming in through the window.

Her phone buzzed. It was Carl.

She answered. 'Carl?'

'Hey, Lucy,' he said.

She propped herself up with excitement, swung her legs across the bed, and planted her feet on the grey carpet.

'You okay?'

'Yeah – hey, tell your dad I'm sorry for leaving yesterday. He told me to wait, but I had to go.'

'He was pretty pissed about that. Where did you go?'

'My dad phoned me, needed me home straight away. He didn't say why, so I had to leave.'

Lucy smiled to herself. 'I was pretty pissed about that too…' Although said in jest, she expected some form of apology or some humorous excuse, but instead, he remained silent. Lucy pulled the phone away from her ear to check if Carl was still connected. 'What you up to?'

'I'm just sat with my dad. Going to help him with something soon. He needs something building.'

'Like something from Ikea?' she said.

'Yeah… something like that.'

Lucy thought for a moment. 'Have I done anything wrong?'

'What do you mean?'

'You're being off with me, I can tell.'

'Lucy,' he said, 'I promise you that you haven't done anything wrong.'

Sitting on the edge of the bed, Lucy dipped her head and thought about the reasoning behind his weird mood.

'Listen, Carl, you need to delete the photos.'

'I need to what?'

'You need to delete the photos,' she repeated.

When they returned to the Haynes house on the night Hunt had killed the Italian brothers, she uploaded the photos she'd taken onto her laptop, storing them in a folder ten deep of 'My Documents', making it almost impossible to find. Then Carl had emailed them to himself, so he also had a copy in case they got lost.

'They committed a crime – bloody murder, Lucy!' Carl's voice barked through the phone. 'They can't get away with that.'

'Yeah – but I've spoken to my mum and dad about it. Taking photos is the reason we're in this mess. They followed us to my house, Carl. They know where we live. My dad deleted the photos from the camera so there's no trace here. But we need to get rid of everything that links us to it.' Lucy takes a breath, then: 'They left a note saying they'd come back and kill us if we tell anyone – this is serious.'

'What if one day we need to use it as evidence? If we delete them, then we'll have nothing?'

'Please, Carl, if there are no photos then nothing could be used against us?' Agitated, she rose from the bed, moved in small circles in the bedroom. 'Carl, please?'

'Yeah, I guess…'

'You haven't told anyone about the photos have you - your dad, or mum or anything?' she asked.

'No, I haven't.'

'Good. These men are dangerous – you saw what they did to the house. They might come back but my Dad has had a security system installed. Covers all the exits, and the windows. We feel a little safer – but they might still come back.'

'Covers all the exits?' Carl asked.

'Yeah…why?' Lucy asked suspiciously.

'Then I won't be able to sneak up to your room anymore without your dad seeing me on the cameras, will I?'

'Well, you'll have to be sneakier, then won't you?' Lucy felt naughty at the thought of it.

'Sounds like a challenge… I like challenges,' whispered Carl. Lucy released a childish giggle. 'I'll delete those photos, Lucy, I promise,' he added, then he ended the call.

Lucy smiled as she locked her phone, headed for the doorway but froze at the sound of an incoming text message. It was from Harry:

Hey Lucy. Hope you're okay. Haven't spoken in a few days. I'll put some photos on later – let me know what you think x.

She'd met Harry on Facebook four months ago. According to his pictures, he was a good-looking lad, who was a year older. He'd finished Luton Sixth form after studying photography at A-level. They'd never met physically but knew the same people and were both members of several photography groups where they commented on each other's shots.

'Is it serious?' Harry had asked her when she mentioned she was seeing someone.

He wanted more. Lucy knew that. It made her feel good. But as things start to get more serious with Carl, she ignored his messages, and, after looking at his Facebook page, she realised he wasn't as popular as he made out. He didn't have any mutual friends, which she thought was very, very strange, as he lived in Luton and had attended the same school.

Lucy locked her phone screen, once again ignoring him, put her phone in her pocket, and went downstairs.

Carl delicately placed the phone onto the kitchen table where he was sitting with his Dad. Carl looked at him. 'She wants me to delete the photos. Said it would be in the interest of their safety. Apparently, these men are dangerous.'

'I do not doubt that,' his dad said.

'What should we do, Dad?'

'We're going to use the photos against the Haynes.'

'How?'

'In such a way that Jack Haynes would deeply regret ever fucking with me.'

28

Toddington

Detective Johnson got back into the police car outside the Haynes' house and closed the door, wearing a smile on his face. He turned the engine on, set the gear in first, and accelerated away along Park Road against the warm morning breeze. At the junction, he took a left in the direction of Luton.

He had one thing on his mind: he needed to update Hunt on the situation, who'd made it clear he wanted Johnson to either get the photos or make sure they were gone.

According to Haynes, they'd been deleted. Johnson believed him. Jack Haynes now knew what was at stake, first-hand witnessing what Hunt's men did and, what scared Haynes more, is what they'd be willing to do to him. Adding the fact that Johnson mentioned the bank money, had not only put Haynes on the back foot but down on one knee, low enough to grovel.

Johnson slowed the police car outside Alexander Hunt's house, the tyres crunching before they came to a halt on the gravel before the steps leading to the wide front door. To his right, he enviously eyed the Bentley continental, following the shape of the impressive exterior.

He stepped out into the warmth, closed the car door, and glanced around at the vast expanse of land surrounding him: pristine gardens as fine as golf greens. As he stepped up towards the magnificent front door, the gentle continuous flow of running water from the fountain on his left grabbed his attention. The small naked, metal green lady, wrapped in a shawl standing near the top of it. She seemed to watch him as he passed. Once he was on the large step he wrapped his knuckles on the thick door. The sound echoed around the quiet estate but was gobbled up by the silence.

It wasn't long before Ann answered the door with a smile, wearing a white apron with a tight belt that cut into her midsection.

'Come in,' she said, making way for him. 'Tea? Coffee?'

'No, thank you, Ann.' Johnson entered the house, stepped into the monstrous hallway with a high ceiling with light, brown-coloured walls and expensive paintings. 'I'm not stopping for long, just need to see Mr Hunt.'

'He's in the living room,' she said, before disappearing back into the kitchen. The smell of chicken captivated the warm air, reminding his rumbling stomach he'd missed breakfast. Johnson made his way through the familiar, long hallway lined with a red carpet, extravagant ornaments, and golden-patterned flowered wallpaper. The smell of chicken faded into a growing scent of lavender.

Johnson knocked on the open door.

Hunt's aging face was illuminated by the laptop screen resting on his lap. The fire before him crackled and spat, and the coals shuffled and sunk deeper into the dark, dirty, ashy pit at the bottom.

'Mr Hunt,' Johnson said, stepping inside the room.

'Come in, come in.'

Hunt folded his laptop carefully, edged forward with a slight struggle, and placed the laptop on the small table to his left. He stood up to face Detective Johnson.

'What could you tell me, Detective?'

'His security system is very good. It'll be hard to go back without being seen. It's linked to the security system's mainframe. It was the company we advise people if they need protection. They're good - almost too good.'

'And what of the photos?'

'Said he had spoken with his daughter. He's deleted them,' Johnson explained.

'You believe him?'

'Yeah, I do.'

Hunt thought for a moment. 'You mention the money my boys found in his safe?'

'Yes.'

Hunt slumped back down in his chair. He picked up his half-filled mug of coffee and took a long sip. Johnson swivelled his body, dropped down on the sofa next to Hunt's chair.

'So, if the photos are now gone,' Hunt said, 'he has nothing on me anymore?'

'That's correct.'

Hunt stood up; a niggle pained in his hip. He struggled across the room to the window near the bookcase, watched two birds flutter back and forth from a small tree down near the gravel.

'I hope you're right, detective. Because if I go down, don't think I won't mention your name in all this too.'

Johnson's eyes widened as he scowled at Hunt, who was still looking out the window.

29

1975
Luton

The sounds coming from their parent's room were horrible.

Sitting in the corner of the boy's small bedroom on the worn carpet against a wall with fraying wallpaper, the girl dropped her face between her knees, covered her ears with her trembling palms, attempting to block out the sounds of violence.

Her mother screamed again. This time her brother winced too. Another loud thud followed, the sound of it breaking through the thin wall between the two bedrooms.

'Don't ever fucking tell me I can't go out and have a good time!' her father shouted.

Then a loud slap, followed by a helpless yelp again from her mother.

They wanted it to end, they couldn't take it anymore. Seeing their mother black and blue every day, slowly moving around the house in a fragile, battered state. The only peace they got was when their father left for work.

Usually, it was nine hours of bliss, but recently, it has been filled with tears and sobbing; their mother's sobbing.

Sobbing of hopelessness and fear, dreading the time he'd come home with his bad temper, or even worse when he was drunk.

Moments ago, their mother had told their father she didn't want him coming home drunk and begging for rough sex anymore. She'd claimed she wasn't an object that he could use whenever he felt like it. In the drunken state he'd come home minutes ago, he punched her straight in the mouth, which dropped her like a stone to the floor, before she scurried away to the corner of their bedroom and curled herself into a ball. He then stood over her, pulled out his penis, and slapped it several times on the top of her head with it.

'Go on then!' he shouted, 'put it in your mouth!'

With his free hand, he grabbed her hair, pulled her towards him until she put up a good enough fight for him to let her go, allowing her to sink back onto the floor in a heap of terror, flooding herself with tears and low self-worth.

He smacked the side of her face hard and walked away, muttering under his breath, 'Pathetic.'

The little girl and boy couldn't help but listen to what had happened through the closed door. When it went quiet, the boy raised his head towards his door, anticipating the day his father would open it, barge in, and relieve his anger on him and his sister, too. Luckily, that day hadn't arrived yet.

When they heard the heavy footsteps of their father descend the stairs, they opened the door carefully, tiptoed into the dark bedroom where they saw their mother lying on the floor in the corner, sobbing and trembling.

Blood ran down the side of her face.

This had to end.

30

Toddington
JACK

My phone buzzed in my pocket. On the sofa, I leaned to my left, dug my hand inside, and pulled it out.

It was Ray – this was all I needed.

'Ray,' I said, not hiding the disappointment in my voice. I rose, leaving Joanne in the living room, and climbed the stairs for privacy.

'How are you my dear friend?' he asked.

'Surviving,' I said, stepping onto the landing, then I turned towards our bedroom. 'The joiner is here now fixing the doors that were broken.'

'Aww that's nice, isn't it? Hope they're new and shiny in no time.' Sarcasm wasn't his usual approach. It didn't suit him. I heard a loud hammer bang several times above me as I went to the window and peered outside.

'What are you ringing for?' I asked.

'We're friends, Jack, aren't we? You've had a break-in. I'm ringing to see how you are – how your family is. What did the police say?'

I didn't reply. Then through the bedroom window, I noticed a black van pass the front of the house slowly. The man inside peered up at me, held my distant gaze, then smiled at me before the van disappeared to the right.

'You know,' Ray said, reminding me he was still there, 'I've been thinking.'

'About?'

I leaned left trying to catch the registration plate of the van, but it was gone. I hit the ledge of the window sill in frustration.

'I believe what you said about the money.'

I sighed in relief. 'Ray, I don't expect anything less to be honest - we're in this together.' I moved away from the window and took a seat on the bed. 'A detective came earlier.'

'Okay…?'

'Different to the detectives who came yesterday. He came on his own, said he knew about the bank being robbed and knew that I had the money in my safe and now that it was missing.'

'How - how could he know that?' There was a knot in Ray's throat.

'I don't know, he's a detective I suppose.' The slight humour didn't go far.

'What did he say about the money?'

'Said there was a robbery at Hembridge bank. Said I was in on it. He also asked me about the photos.'

'Are they deleted?' Ray asked.

'Yes, they're gone.'

The silence grew between us.

'Listen, Jack, I'm giving you seven days, pal.'

'Seven days? Seven days for what?'

'Seven days.'

'I'm not following?' I frowned.

'You owe me three hundred thousand pounds – I'm giving you seven days to get it back to me.'

'Ray, you can't be serio—'

'Seven days, mate.' He hung up the phone.

I threw my phone onto the bed and, with a heavy sigh, I dropped my face into my palms.

'Everything okay, Jack?' I heard a voice say.

I turned to see Joanne standing in the doorway of the bedroom.

31

Hemel Hempstead

Phil dabbed the brakes on the new Land Rover, bringing the vehicle to a halt outside of Hunt's mansion.

'You got the bag?' he asked Stuart.

Stuart nodded, stepped out onto the gravel and met Phil at the front grill of the vehicle, then handed him the bag of money. It wasn't full to the brim, but half a million does have a healthy weight which certainly brought a smile to your face. The other men climbed out of the 4x4.

Phil tucked the bag under his thick arm and told the men to wait by the car. Hunt didn't want six or seven men inside his home to invade his privacy. One man made that mistake once. He'd walked into his living room uninvited and left with a broken jaw. Hunt had unleashed on him, giving him several blows to the face. Stories suggest the man had moved away somewhere up north in fear of his life. Other stories claim he'd already been killed.

Knowing Hunt, the latter wouldn't be surprising.

'I won't be long,' Phil told them. He moved through the titanic house, ignoring the flamboyant familiar pictures which lined the walls. He made his way down several hallways until he reached the living room and rapped twice on the door.

'Come in, Phil. Have a seat, mate.'

Phil wandered over to the sofa near Hunt and lowered into it, staring at the dancing flames of the fire. The heat was almost unbearable on his skin.

'That for me?' Hunt asked, eyeing the contents in Phil's right hand.

'Who else, Boss?' Phil laughed.

'Things go as planned with the deal?'

'Yeah. No problems at all. Handed over the gear, and they gave us the money. Usual business.'

Hunt let out a silent sigh of relief. He wasn't sure how the Manco's would take the news of the Deacon brothers. They knew their deaths had been Hunt's doing; they were aware of the business arrangement they had. What Hunt had feared was the possibility of a previous alliance between the Deacon's and Manco's, but so far, so good.

Hunt used his fingertips to open the top of the bag, then a sharp loud melodic buzz stopped him, coming from his phone on the small table. He knew who it was.

'This fucking idiot,' Hunt shouted.

Phil, being polite, asked if he should leave. Hunt shook his head indicating for Phil to stay. 'I'll ring her back shortly. She's probably looking for an update on the Manco deal. She'll be wanting her cut. As fucking usual.'

Phil, unsure what to say, remained silent.

'I'll ring her back soon. She can wait.'

Hunt looked away from his phone and focused back on Phil. 'So, the Manco's were happy – did they mention anything about the future?'

'They said they would be happy to. I said I'd speak with you first.'

'Good man. I've been thinking… we could get a constant supply coming in.' Hunt fell silent in thought. 'Be good for business.'

Phil agreed with a confident nod.

Hunt's phone rang again. He glared down at the glowing screen once more.

'I wish she'd just fuck off!' he screamed, his anger disturbing the serenity of the warm living room. Phil tensed a little.

Hunt stood abruptly. 'Do you know what I'm gonna do?'

'What's that?' Phil remained tense, unsure what Hunt was going to say.

'I'm going to ring Pollock, remove her from this world. I've had enough of her shit.'

Hunt's words ran over Phil like a cold shiver. He couldn't contemplate what he just heard. Red? No one knew who she was. How could Hunt pull this one off?

'I'm sick of that stupid bitch ringing me whenever she wants,' Hunt continued. 'Wanting a percentage of my money. Well, she could think again. She could fuck off.'

Phil's heard vicious stories about Red and what she was capable of. She was a force not to be reckoned with.

'What you think, Phil?'

'I… I think you should do what you feel is right, boss.' Phil half-turned on the sofa, keeping his focus on Hunt, who was still at the window. Hunt turned to face him. The top three buttons of his silk shirt were open, revealing a hairy chest filmed with an artificial sun tan. As Phil locked eyes with Hunt, he saw the face of an uncertain, anxious man. He had never seen that in Hunt before.

Hunt wandered back to his chair, winced at the pain coming from his hip as he drops into it.

'What's the latest on the Haynes situation, boss?' Phil asked.

'Johnson went to the house to speak to him. Told him he knew about the money in his safe; the same money that went missing from the bank. He told them if the police get wind about what I'd done, the source of the robbery would be made known.' Hunt paused to take a breath. 'And not to mention the fact that I'll personally kill them myself and burn their bodies. Speaking of which, Phil, has Stuart emptied the incinerator yet?'

'It was been taken care of,' Phil said.

The bodies of the Deacon brothers had been tossed inside of Hunt's incinerator on Wednesday night after he gunned them down in the woods. The flames of the furnace had burnt the brothers to ash within minutes. It was down in the basement with enough filtered ventilation not to cause a stir.

Hunt thanked Phil for bringing him the money from the Manco deal and placed several envelopes into his palm. One package for each of the men waiting outside next to the Land Rover.

'Get yourselves home. Thank the lads. See you Monday morning.'

Phil accepted the envelopes with a nod, turned, and left Hunt to be alone.

Hunt grabbed his phone, tapped on Red's number, pressed CALL, and put it to his ear. He took several deep breaths.

'Mr Hunt, when I ring you, I need to hear your voice. That's what usually happens when you phone somebody. You expect to be able to speak to them.' She allowed the disappointment to reach him through her silence. Then, said, 'Do you understand me?'

In his better judgement, he held back his growing rage. In a falsified calm manner, he said, 'My apologies. I was busy with something. What's up?'

'What's up is that I haven't had my cut yet from the Manco deal.'

'I've just received the money myself.'

'What has taken so long?' she asked.

'The deal was a little later than we thought,' Hunt explained again in a calm manner, although gritting his teeth. 'It would be sent later first thing in the morning. Does that suit you?'

Her silence caused the hairs on Hunt's neck to stand on end.

'Yes, Alex, that's fine.'

'Good.'

'Well, I'll let you handle your business - oh, by the way,' Red said, 'I'm loving the new Land Rover your little minions are driving around in.'

Red hung up. The line went dead.

Hunt exhaled in relief that the phone call was over. After thirty seconds of thinking, he made a firm decision. He tapped a few buttons on his phone and put it to his ear.

'Yes,' said the voice.

'It's Alexander Hunt. I need your services.'

'For when?'

'As soon as possible,' Hunt said.

Pollock smiled on the other end of the phone.

32

Toddington
JACK

'Is everything okay?' Joanne asked, standing in the doorway of the bedroom wearing a pale complexion across her face.

How much did she hear from my phone call with Ray?

'Jack - is everything okay?' She stepped closer. I realises I was staring through her with a blank gaze and suddenly snapped out of it.

'Yeah... just a problem at work, nothing major,' I lied through a thin smile, hoping it seemed genuine.

'Who was on the phone, Jack?' Nervously, she moved toward me. I could see an 'I-don't-really-believe-you' expression on her face.

'It was Ray,' I said.

She moved to her wardrobe, and bent down to grab something from her bag. 'Well, whoever it was, I'm sure they're capable of handling it.' She stood up with a purse in her hand. 'They know what's happened here, surely they could give you a little time to get things sorted.'

I nodded, agreeing with Joanne. 'Yeah... Ray would sort it out, I'm sure.'

As Joanne left the room, I rose, walked to the window, and peered outside. The day was hot and sticky, the sparse clouds lonely against the deep blue skies. I cracked the small window open and took a deep breath of warm, stagnant air.

Suddenly, I felt sick. My stomach was in knots. Twisting like the flames of a fire, I dashed around the foot of the bed towards the en-suite, lowered to my knees at the toilet, lifted the seat, and emptied the contents of my stomach into the pan. A burning taste clung to the back of my throat from the rising bile. I tried hard to swallow. I heard footsteps enter the room. I looked towards the door and saw a concerned Joanne.

'Jack? Is…' she paused and winced, '…everything okay?'

'Yeah,' I whispered. 'Just a second.' I wiped my mouth with the back of my hand and felt embarrassed when I stood up. I ran the basin tap and stared at the man in the small circular mirror who had a red, blotchy face and bloodshot eyes. I looked exhausted.

'You okay?' Joanne asked softly.

'Yeah, I'll be okay.'

'Why were you sick?'

'Just came out I guess.' I shrugged without offering more. If I told her everything that was going on, I couldn't imagine the shit storm that would follow. With her morals, goodness, and natural ability to not take any shit from anyone, she'd drive me to the police station herself.

'You want a drink? Coffee or something, maybe water?'

I said to her I'd like a coffee – I always wanted coffee. I followed her out of the bedroom, trailed her down the stairs where we met Lucy standing in the hallway.

'When would he be finished?' she said, pointing upstairs, referring to Matthew, the joiner.

'I don't know, Lucy.'

'I want my room back,' she said impatiently.

'I'll ask him when I see him.'

She nodded and headed toward the kitchen. Joanne and I followed.

'You don't look very good,' Joanne said to me, making her way to the kettle while I took a seat at the round table opposite Lucy. I felt shaky. I could feel a thick headache forming behind my eyes. The noise upstairs continued, but the house seemed to absorb it well through its solid structure.

'You've gone white,' added Lucy.

'I'll be fine,' I said.

Joanne placed a cup of coffee in front of me. 'Thanks, Jo. Could I have water too?'

She returned to the sink and ran the tap. The smell of coffee hit my nose and it was normally something I loved, but I found myself gagging and stopping myself from being sick. In the centre of the table, my Samsung tablet screen lit up. I grabbed it, and checked the list of notifications.

There was an email to my work email address.

Sender: D.Morton@hembridgebank.co.uk -
Jack,
Sorry to hear about what happened at home. Hope your family is all okay – you too of course. Hope you get things sorted. See you when you're back… take care.
Deb.

Debra's been my PA since I took the role of finance director. She sat in a small office joined to mine, separated by a door that she used regularly.

She had been at the bank for over sixteen years and, in that time, had been the PA to every finance director. She was experienced, knew her job well, and had a kind, professional face to go with it.

I continued looking at the news on my tablet. Lucy, sitting opposite me, giggled. I glanced up at her. 'What's funny, Luce?'

'What?' Her eyes met mine.

'You're smiling?'

'Am I not allowed to?' I watched the frown form on her face. I'd hit a nerve, which wasn't my intent.

Joanne pondered over. 'Leave her alone, Jack. She's in love.' A smell of chicken wafted through the kitchen. On the worktop there was a pile of veg next to a sharp knife, waiting to be cut. Lucy glared up with warm, pink cheeks and let out a nervous grin. Joanne turned to me and rubbed my shoulders for a moment before she dropped into the seat to my right. 'How's the coffee?'.

'Coffee's good.' I sat for a moment, then, said, 'Listen, you two.'

Joanne looked at me, but Lucy's head was forward, her bright blonde hair running down either side of her face, her piercing blue eyes concentrating on her phone.

'Lucy.'

'What?' Her focus remained on her phone.

'I need your attention,' I said.

Lucy heard the serious tone in my voice and reluctantly placed her phone on the table, then look up with a forced closed-lipped smile.

'I need to make sure that the photos are gone,' I said. I felt my cheeks warm as Joanne frowned. I needed to be sure. 'I know I've deleted them from your camera, but I really hope there aren't any copies. A detective came over – I don't mean Clarke and Horton, someone else. His name's Johnson.' I paused. 'He told me to get rid of the photos and said there would be consequences if they weren't deleted. I asked him who he worked for, but he didn't say. He made it obvious that it would be in our best interest.'

Lucy mulled over my words. 'You saw for yourself. They're deleted.'

'You sure?' Joanne asked her.

'Jesus Christ! I've told you! How many times do I have to say it?'

I held up an apologetic palm and watched her face redden.

'It's done, okay!' Her anger filled the kitchen as she stood up, knocked the chair back with the hind of her knees, grabbed her phone, and left. We heard her footsteps thud on the stairs as she climbed them.

Lucy entered the spare bedroom she'd slept in the night before and closed the door quickly. It rattles off the wooden door frame before it came to rest.

She plucked her phone from her pocket, found the number, and pressed CALL. 'Come on, pick up pick up.' Then it was answered.

'Yeah...'

'Hey, you okay?' she said.

'Yeah fine. You?' replied Carl.

'Yes. Listen, Carl, I need to make sure you have deleted those photos – I know you said you have, but it's important.'

'You've already asked me this and my answer is the same as it was before. Yes, they're deleted. I've told you.' Carl was annoyed.

'I know, I know. It was just a policeman who came over yesterday, threatening my dad about it. Saying if the photos are not deleted then it would get nasty for us. And I'm guessing by what happened yesterday morning with the break-in – he means worse. More serious... I don't know. They'll probably come back round. No idea but I'd rather not find out, and neither would my dad, so I'm sorry for repeating the same question but they need to be gone —'

'And they are. Simple,' Carl grunted. There was a pause for a while. 'I need to go. Talk later.' He hung up.

Lucy sighed on the bed, tried to ignore the drilling above her. Her phone beeped. A text message.

From Harry.

JACK

I checked work emails on my tablet when Matthew courteously knocked on the kitchen door. His tool belt hung from his thin waist.

'All done upstairs,' he said. 'Now for the door in here.'

I nodded in appreciation, then asked him if he wanted any help, which he answered the way I thought he would. What help could I possibly offer when I couldn't put up a picture frame?

'I wouldn't mind a coffee, if there's one going?' he said, making his way towards the back door. He stared in concentration, ran a palm through his grey, thinning hair. I noticed it was the second time he had done that. I told him it was fine and headed over to the kettle.

Earlier, I'd asked Joanne what she fancied for tea. She told me she wasn't cooking. She just didn't have the energy for it. Lucy had suggested a takeaway. Joanne and I both agreed.

I made Matthew a coffee, left it on the long window sill next to him. He thanked me, then said, 'I wouldn't mind a biscuit if there's one going?'

I nodded and grabbed the biscuit tin from one of the lower cupboards, opened it, and left it on the table. 'Help yourself.'

'Thanks.'

In the living room, Joanne and Lucy were fixed on the television. That Kardashian program was on. Great. I took a seat next to Joanne.

'How's he doing?' she asked.

'Last door. Shouldn't be too much longer.' I turned away from Jo and faced Lucy. 'You ordered the food?'

She nodded, in such a way that suggested I was interrupting her focus on the television.

The old woman on the screen reminded me of my mother. A pang of guilt washed over me as I realised I hadn't spoken with her today. I always liked to see how she was doing and made the effort to see her a few times a week. I stood and stepped out of the room, grabbed my phone, and called her.

'Hello, son,' Kathy said.

'Hey, Mum, how you doing?' I ambled up the stairs away from the sounds coming from the joiner in the kitchen.

'I'm okay, my back is playing up though,' she said. I heard the struggle in her voice. She had been on tablets to soothe the pain, but some days, like today, the pills didn't quite mask the pain.

I knew she probably had, but I had to ask. 'Taken your tablets?'

'You know I have, seven in the morning, one just after dinner, and seven in the evening - you always ask me, and I always have, Jack. Really, there's no need to remind me.' She fell silent for a moment. I smiled through the phone - she always took them precisely at the times. Not a minute earlier or later.

'That's good. Listen, sorry I haven't had the chance to see you recently. Something happened here.'

'What happened – oh, wait for a second, this bit is good, I'll pause it,' she said. I imagined her sitting on her chair in front of the television with a tattered red blanket - which she'd had for as long as I could remember - draped over her legs and the television remote glued to her hand. The background fuzz disappeared. 'What's happened, son?'

I filled her in, missing the parts where Lucy witnessed a murder, the stolen bank money was taken from my safe, and about Detective Johnson with the overgrown moustache threatening me.

'Oh, my sweet Jesus, Jack! Is everyone okay?'

'Yeah, we'll be okay,' I said. 'We have a security system now.'

I heard her sigh.

'Jack, I told you about this, didn't I?'

'Told me about what, Mum?'

'Living alone. No houses around you. Anything could happen, and no one would know. I read a statistic about bad things happening in rural areas, Jack.' Kathy, herself, loved being around people. Neighbours she could speak to daily to find out what's going on. Being a part of a small community lightened the feeling of loneliness; many of the others feel the same.

I shook my head. 'Mum, we'll be fine, okay? I'll pop through and see you tomorrow if you'd like?'

'Yes. I'll get the kettle on.'

We arranged a time, said our goodbyes and I let her hang up first. I drifted along the landing and headed up to Lucy's room to admire the work Matthew has done on the first door. Very neat. The new timber stood perfectly straight, firm, and square. I opened and closed the door a few times. The scent of fresh pine hit my nose. I did the same up in Lucy's room and, again, a brilliant job. It wasn't rocket science to hang a door, but I'd tried it before and, once I'd finished it, I tried closing the door, but it wouldn't close, so to avoid embarrassment, I left these jobs to the people who can actually do them.

I stepped through Lucy's doors onto her balcony. The sun was still high in the clear blue sky. The gentle westerly breeze blowing across the fields felt good on my face.

A buzz came from inside my pocket.

A text message.

I read it: *I want £100,000 in cash or the photos your daughter took go to the police. I'll be in touch with further information. Do not reply to this message.*

I brought my hands to my face, absorbing the heavy breaths in my palms. My whole body tingled with fear, anger, and the whirring of absolute helplessness.

'I don't fucking believe it,' I whispered.

When I lowered my hands and opened my eyes, I saw something.

A black van was parked at the side of the road opposite the house.

There were two men inside.

They stared up at me. The driver smiled.

I heard a loud knocking sound.

A familiar sound. Like someone was knocking at the front door.

33

Friday Late Afternoon
Police Station

'I can't stand his attitude sometimes,' DCI Clarke said, sitting down at his computer. He shook his mouse to awaken the sleeping monitor screen.

DS Horton, peering over small glasses, engaged in a report, glanced up from the opposite side of the large desk. He had been waiting for Clarke for ten minutes. 'Hmmm?'

'Come on, for God's sake!' Clarke told the monitor as if it understood his frustration.

Horton dropped his concentration on the report of a burglary and placed it down on the desk. The desk was wide and deep, and had plenty of room but today it didn't. If Chief Superintendent Connor saw it, she wouldn't be happy at all. Too cluttered.

'Who's attitude?' Horton asked, leaning forward, removing his glasses.

'Hmm?'

'You said you can't stand his attitude sometimes.'

'Johnson,' said Clarke. 'That prick.' He pointed towards the door.

Horton nodded, knowing who he meant. 'What's he done now?'

'It was what he *hasn't* done that's the problem.' Clarke paused. 'Not filing the reports in on time. Everyone here,' Clarke raised a palm, circled it in the air, indicating the people within the office, 'know what needs to be done and when it needs to be done. It isn't difficult.'

'What did you say to him?'

'I reminded him that he needs to up his game. That Connor is watching us all. To be honest, I've had enough of him – he told me to mind my own business and fuck off.'

'Charming,' Horton said, smiling.

Clarke's office space was generous. Three metres by almost four. The door was positioned in the middle of the longest side. Inside the office, the desk sat in the centre and, behind that, were certificates and a few photos on the wall. Before Clarke had stepped into the office, Horton admired the photo of Clarke and his sister taken nearly twelve years ago on holiday.

On either side of the wall of certificates and photos, were two filing cabinets, filled with metallic drawers stacked on top of each other. A window was located to Horton's left, where he could see nothing but blue skies.

Clarke said, 'So, what do we—'

There was a sharp knock at the door.

Dressed in a suit tailored made to fit his tall muscular frame was superintendent Ian Thompson. 'Quick word?' he said, stepping in. He was younger than Horton and Clarke but carried himself impeccably well. With a master's degree in criminology, he had deserved every promotion he had received. Some colleagues treat him with a false sense of recognition laced with jealousy, but others, like Horton and Clarke, genuinely respected him and supported him when he needed them to.

He pulled out the seat on the opposite side of the desk and sat down. In his hand, they saw a thin, black A4-sized file. Clarke remained silent and waited, knowing what was inside. Often, unsolved cases were handed out and, every so often, Connor sent Thompson around delegating these cases to keep her little minions busy. As if they were sitting there with their feet up on the desk and drinking coffee.

'Got a good one here,' Thompson started, opening the page where a thin pink tab was stuck to. Horton noticed another seven or eight tabs inside the folder. Thompson rested the file on the desk and started to skim-read it, as a reminder. Clarke knew it wouldn't be long before he mentioned the mess on the desk.

'What is it?' Clarke asked.

'This… is one from 2012. Murder of Peter Lewes.' Clarke and Horton vaguely remembered the name but waited in silence as Thompson read on. 'The victim was found dead in a park by an early morning jogger. Multiple stab wounds to his stomach and chest.'

Horton winced as Thompson shows them the photo.

'The officers on the case'—Thompson narrowed his eyes, looking towards the bottom of the report—'had minimal leads and came up with nothing in the end.' He smiled. 'Hence why, I'm handing it to you guys. You two could work as a team on this.'

He handed the file to Clarke, who accepted it with a professional nod.

'Okay, gentlemen, enjoy the rest of your day.' Thompson stood. 'I'm popping out, so if you need me, ring my mobile.'

'Okay,' Clarke said.

'Clean this desk,' he said, then disappeared through the open door.

Clarke rested the file on his computer keyboard and started reading. Six pages in total, which was light compared to other murder enquires. No wonder it came back as unsolved. There wasn't much information. But here they were, fighting the good fight, keeping busy, as Connor wanted.

'Interesting,' Clarke said, after ten minutes of reading.

'What's that?'

'Witness statements from the night he was murdered.' Clarke readjusted himself in his chair. 'Alison Lewes, his wife, claims she was on a night out the same night he went missing. Any idea who was in their company that night?'

Horton shook his head.

'Jack and Joanne Haynes.'

'Small world isn't it?'

34

Toddington
JACK

As I slouched on the sofa with a plate on my knee, half filled with pizza, chips, and a dollop of garlic sauce, my appetite seemed to slip away. I was hungry, but I knew I'd physically throw up if I had any more. Joanne and Lucy finished theirs and had gone back to the kitchen for seconds. The smell of donner meat, garlic sauce, and warm pizza dough hung in the air, overpowering the plug-in scents near the door. It niggled at my senses, twisting the knots in my stomach tighter.

I glanced at the window before I stood up and padded over to it. Through the glass, I saw the black van. I could make out the van's roof over the brick wall. Standing on the balcony earlier, I'd sprinted downstairs when I heard the knock at the door, beating Joanne to it, who glared at me as if I was out of my mind. Turned out it was a spotty teenager in a red t-shirt, a name badge on his chest that told me his name was Jenk. Probably a nickname. Or a surname. I thanked him and watched him leave.

I had noticed the front gates were wide open. When Jenk had passed through, I used the fob to close them and watched them until they did to make sure.

The van hadn't moved in what seemed like the longest hour of my life.

Joanne and Lucy didn't know it was parked out there because I hadn't told them.

I didn't want them to worry. If the gates were closed and the security system was working, we'd be fine. But maybe Johnson had informed them about the security system? Yes, that would make sense. They were keeping their distance, sitting out there, making it obvious they were parked there but there were no rules against parking up on the side of a public road, unless it was on double yellow lines.

I heard Lucy's voice get louder as she walked along the hallway. I reached up, pulled the curtains across, and did the same with the other window. Lucy entered the darkness.

'Bit early for that, isn't it?'

'Hmm,' I said, sitting back in my seat.

'It was not even dark.'

I ignored her and zoned out, thinking about the text I received about the money. One hundred thousand pounds.

I felt restless, I couldn't keep still. I was agitated. Even the way the cushion supported my back which wasn't perfectly square made me angry.

Joanne eyed my half-filled plate. 'Not hungry?'

Shaking my head, I patted my stomach, indicating I was full. She smiled and turned away. My head was swimming. I stood up abruptly and left the room, almost staggering a little as the pain behind my eyes took over. I needed to get out.

'Jack?' she said. I stopped at the door and turned around. 'You want to watch a film?'

'You choose, I won't be long.'

Back up in Lucy's room, I stepped out into the warmth of the day, peered down at the stationary van. The driver noticed me, cocked his head up, and smiled. He had a round, overweight face.

The van's engine came to life. It slowly set off and dropped onto the road. The driver adjusted his hand in the shape of a gun and pulled the trigger toward me. My heart raced. A pocket of air got stuck in my throat as they disappeared along the road out of sight.

I waited for five minutes to see if they returned. They didn't. In my pocket, I felt something against my leg. I pulled it out. DCI Clarke's card with his number on it. I scanned the number carefully, found myself in two minds about whether to ring him or not. Tell him what really happened. About Johnson. About what Lucy saw, about –'

No. No, I couldn't do that. What if he and Horton were working with Johnson?

Who could I actually trust? I didn't know. Johnson knew about the bank – he had pieced that together. Maybe Horton and Clarke knew too.

I returned downstairs, entered the darkness of the living room. Joanne commented on the curtains being closed but I explained I had a headache and the light was making it worse. She told me they'd found a film to watch.

And for the next two hours, that's what we did.

I didn't see the end of it as I reached the land of nod. Joanne woke me with a gentle shove to my arm. I turned the lights off and double-checked the windows and doors before we all went upstairs, I glanced through the living room window at the gates. They were locked. I climbed into bed, closed my tired eyes, and succumbed to the power of sleep.

I woke up. The clock next to me told me it was 3 a.m. I tried to go back off, but soon realised I was wide awake. Rubbing my eyes and finally accepting it, I got up, moved lightly into the en-suite, and sat down on the toilet. To my right, I picked up Linwood Barclay's Never Look Away. I loved reading. I loved thrillers. I could reel off a list of my favourite authors, but it would get boring.

Folding the corner of chapter thirty-six, I placed it on the side unit near the sink and stood up. From the back of the bedroom door, I grabbed my dressing gown and quietly descended the stairs. I could already see the transition from night to day down in the hallway, the dim light creeping in through the gaps. When I turned at the bottom of the stairs, I froze.

There was a glowing light coming from the study.

Frantically, I searched my brain for logical reasoning. I didn't remember leaving the curtains open in there. Or did I? I squinted at the thought, starting to doubt myself.

It took me a few moments to realise it wasn't the sun. Very slowly, I made my way along the wooden floor, my eyes focused on the open doorway laced in the very dim green glow.

A hazy green flare softly lit up the room as I entered. Turned out to be the glow from the security monitor. I took a seat on the black swivel desk chair, scanned the monitor closely, flicking from each camera angle. Everything seemed okay. The men won't try anything, they wouldn't be—

Something caught my eye on the screen in the bottom left corner.

Two men emerged from the distance at the front of the house. I saw a set of ladders leaning against the brick wall, the top of them peering over the top of the wall. They were heading towards the front door. Two heavy-set figures grew bigger with each step they took.

Towards the camera.

Towards the house.

Towards me, my family.

'Shit,' I whispered.

Both were dressed in black. I double-clicked on the small screen, expanding it to fill the whole monitor, the camera above the front door watching them. They stopped at the Volvo, one on either side, and peered in through the windows with torches.

I held my breath.

There was a flashing camera icon on the right bottom part of the screen, which meant it was recording, as I recalled Paul, the security engineer, telling me.

I also recalled him telling me about the red button – if you needed to press it, do so, and we'll contact the police who'll dispatch their services as soon as possible. I gripped the security remote, my thumb hovering above the red button.

I waited, glaring at them through the screen. The pounding in my body had reached my throat now. I raised a trembling hand, held it against my chin, contemplating pressing the button.

'Shit,' I said, my mouth open. Both men looked up at the camera, smiling at me. They turned to each other and both gave a knowing nod, then headed towards the front door.

I jabbed the red button and waited. Nothing happened. I hit it again. And again. My thumb tapped wildly.

A message came up on the monitor: The Emergency Services had been—

The screen went black. I couldn't see them anymore.

'Shit,' I said, staring blankly at the screen. 'What the fuck.'

I heard a rattle at the front door. Sounded like the door handle. I started to tremble, couldn't handle the warm adrenaline building in my body. I heard the door open. Shit, it wasn't locked. Why was it not locked?

'Oh, God…'

I slid back on the chair, turned one-eighty to face the door to the hallway, noticed changes in the lighting in the hall, shadows dancing slowly on the wooden floor against the growing daylight.

I heard another voice. A female voice. I—

'Jack!' the voice said, 'Wake up, Jack. Jack.' I felt a shove on my upper back, a small grip rocked my body back and forth. 'Jack.' The person saying my name was concerned, but their voice was soft and caring. It was Joanne. I opened my eyes. They flickered, adjusting to the light around the bedroom. I cocked my head and saw Joanne's worried face.

'Hey,' she said. Her dark hair was messy, hanging loosely over her smooth, thin face. Her deep, brown eyes hypnotised me, almost pulling my heart from my chest. In them, I saw everything; I felt everything. She was more beautiful than she was on the day I met her.

I propped myself up, found my bearings. My back was saturated through severe sweating.

'You okay?' she asked.

I nodded a few times, but still wasn't fully alert.

'You shouted: they're in the house, they're in the house – I had to look around the bedroom to check, but when I realised our door was closed, and when no one was here, I knew you were dreaming.'

'Two men were looking in the cars, Jo. They looked up at the camera and smiled at me – I was watching them from the study. The screen went black and I heard the handle of the front door go. Then I heard them come inside, into the hallway…' I trailed off.

In silence, she didn't reply.

'Jo,' I said.

'Yeah?'

'I need to tell you something.'

I felt the weight of her body turn onto her side and face me, using her left arm to prop herself up.

'Someone sent me a text last night – they want one-hundred-dred thousand pounds, or the photos go to the police.'

She gave me a plain, bold stare.

'We're in trouble,' I added.

'But you deleted the photos?'

'Unless there are other copies?' I said.

'Lucy said there wasn't…'

'That's what she said.' I shrugged. 'But… she must have sent them to someone else – we need to ask her.'

Jo didn't agree or argue. 'She wouldn't lie to us, would she?'

I replied with another shrug, genuinely unsure.

Joanne looked away and glared up in thought, searching for an answer somewhere on the ceiling.

'I think it could be Carl,' I said. 'It must be—'

Joanne raised a palm in protest, but I continued: 'We'll speak to Lucy when she wakes up. I'm not bothered if she lied, I just want to know the truth. There's too much shit going on right now.'

Jo nodded in understanding, feeling the same frustration. 'Is there anything else the matter, Jack?'

'What do you mean?' I said, giving her a quizzical frown.

'You mentioned other things in your sleep.'

I didn't like the sound of this. 'What did I say?'

'You said: I can't keep doing this anymore, it's not fair on my wife.'

Joanne stood up, ambled to the en-suite, and closed the door behind her without looking back.

35

Sunday
Hemel Hempstead

Ann entered the kitchen, seeing Hunt leaning forward over the table reading yesterday's newspaper.

'Good morning, Alexander.' She passed him, heading for the kettle.

'Morning,' he grunted, distracted by the contents on the page in front of him.

'How are you this morning?'

Hunt, sitting at the large rectangular wooden table from Barker & Stonehouse, didn't answer straight away. He finished the article about the probable petition to stop building work in a nearby area.

'I'm good, Ann,' he finally said. He averted his attention away from the story, cocked his head towards her. The kettle started to bubble and rattle. 'I know I've said it, but thanks for coming in again. I know it was a Sunday and—'

'It's fine, Alex. Not a problem,' she said. She then raised a finger. 'I'm going to the park with the little ones this afternoon, so I won't be here all day. Don't be asking every Sunday, either,' she added.

Hunt smiled at her tenacity. 'It'll take maybe an hour – two at the most. And don't worry, I won't.'

Ann asked Hunt if he wanted a coffee. He nodded, turning over the next page of the paper. She placed the mugs on the counter and made coffee.

'So, did you speak with Pollock last night?'

The question, along with the smell of strong coffee, lingered in the big space.

'Yeah. I did,' Hunt said quietly, his focus still down at the paper.

'Okay... and?'

'And what?' Hunt jerked his neck up, turned his upper body towards Ann, his eyes piercing her with anger.

'Answer the question, Alexander.' Ann folded her arms, matching his stare. 'Don't play fucking games. You spoke to Pollock... what for? What's happening?'

After a long moment, Ann turned back to the counter to stir the coffees. Hunt maintained his stare, focusing on her back. He inhaled deeply, suppressing his anger. 'Make sure there's sugar in there, Ann.'

'Don't change the topic, Alex. You want to say something, don't you? I can feel your eyes burning the back of my head. Don't be shy, come on, speak up.'

Hunt sighed like red flames were coming from his nose. She had big balls, metaphorically speaking. 'Yeah I spoke with Pollock,' he said. 'We need to get rid of her, Ann, she's getting in the way of everything.'

'Please don't tell me you're speaking about Red? Just – please tell me you're not serious.' She stopped stirring the coffee, turned slowly, and winced at him.

'Ann…. She's getting in the way. She—'

'Jesus, Alex. Do you know what she'll do to you?'

'Ann… listen, she wants a cut from every deal. Not just me. Fucking everyone. She speaks to me like shit – like I'm nothing. She hasn't a clue who I am.' Hunt grew louder in agitation.

'Okay. Just calm down, Alex,' she said softly, which seemed to soothe the situation.

'Calm down?'

'Alex, yes, calm down.' She casually brought the coffees over to the table, placing a mug next to the paper he was reading. Steam rose and twirled from the surface. Placing the other cup next to him, she pulled back a chair and took a seat. 'You've spoken to Pollock about getting rid of Red. No one knows who she is. She's a ghost. A ghost that knows everything and can be anywhere, at any time – I could be her and you wouldn't even know.'

She watched the terrifying thought wash over him and saw Hunt absorb her words in silence.

Maybe she had a point?

Ann put her mug back on the table, cupped it with both hands, and looked up at him. 'What exactly did you say to Pollock?'

'I told him to get rid of her. He wants two hundred thousand. I said yes,' he explained with a shrug.

Ann closed her eyes and took a long, deep, thoughtful breath whilst Hunt brought the coffee to his mouth and sipped it. 'What?'

'Alex, don't you think she'll know about this? You can't sneeze without her knowing.'

Hunt waved it away. 'Don't worry about it, we'll be okay.'

'I'm more worried about you.' An ongoing joke behind Hunt's back was that Ann was like a mother to him. She was firm, and kept him right. If a man like Hunt went off on his own, the police would have a very busy few weeks before he was more than likely gunned down.

'It'll be fine, Ann.' He tried to reassure her with a smile. 'When has Pollock ever failed? When as he never hit his target?' He waited for an answer. Ann stares mutely. 'Exactly.'

'Well, I hope you're right, Alex. I really do.' She stood up, put the chair back under the table, and picked up her coffee. 'I'll do this paperwork, Alex. Let me know if you need anything.' Ann left the kitchen, her short footsteps fading along the corridor.

Hunt sighed heavily, dropped his face into his thick hands for a few seconds. He ran his right palm over his balding head and remained still for five minutes, before the silence became too much to bear. He stood up fast, knocking the chair back with the hind of his knees, leaving the kitchen, and paced down the corridor with clenched fists to the warmth of the living room.

'Fuck.' He stared through the wide window out over his land, his hands shoved deep into the pockets of his grey trousers.

In quiet, he let the tranquillity pacify him. The fire crackled and, for a second, he forget everything. He turned, moved over to the chair in front of the fire, and dropped into the leather. His safe place. A place he went to think, to relax, to remember his younger life. Without the violence, without the hate. A place of naïve hope.

He let his eyes close.

A noise woke him up. The fire had burnt out, and the mustiness of sizzling coal and warm leather drifted around the room. He shuddered in confusion, feeling something moving by the side of his leg. It didn't take him long to realise it was his phone. A phone call. Digging his hand in, he pulled it out.

'Shit,' he muttered to himself.

It was Red.

His heart started to pound so strong, he felt something beating out of his neck. Does she know about him sending Pollock to kill her? He stood up, steadying himself. After thoughtful hesitation, he answered.

'Hello.'

'Alexander Hunt. I won't keep you long… I'll be quick to save wasting any more time. You want me dead. You tried it. It didn't work. It will never work.' Her voice was calm as if she was a teacher offering sound advice to a very young student. 'Pollock has been the most loyal soldier of all and, to be honest, Alex, you should know better.'

Hunt swallowed but kept the phone to her ear.

'Stop acting like a child and don't try anything like that again. The rate has gone up to twenty-five percent. Have a fine day, Alexander Hunt.'

She hung up.

The line went dead.

Hunt dropped his phone on the carpet and turned to face the window. The skies had become darker, pillows of grey casting an eeriness across his gardens. He ran a palm over his mouth and whispered, 'Fuck.'

After a moment, he gave himself a shake, mentally telling himself to shape up and get on with it. Shifting to his left, his hip suddenly caused discomfort. At the large bookshelf on the far wall, he leaned down, grabbed an old black folder, and pulled it out. The fraying, rounded corners indicated its age.

He returned to his chair, sat down, and opened it carefully to see the newspaper article.

Hemel Gazette - dated 14/7/1983. The title of the piece: Teenager survives an almost fatal car crash. He read over what happened like he had done so many times before. His eyes widened when he saw the name of the teenager involved.

Lorraine Headley.

36

Toddington

Sunday afternoon turned grey above Park road. Lucy used her forearms to support her weight as she leaned on the concrete wall enclosing her small balcony. Tapping fingers on her phone, she searched through her college emails. After scrolling past all the junk mail, she came across one from her tutor.

She smiled at the feedback about a recent exam, then reread it, feeling a sense of pride overwhelming her. Her hard work had paid off.

Her phone beeped. A message appeared at the top of the screen.

From Harry.

Hi Lucy, hope you're well. You haven't put any new pics on the Facebook page recently. Are things okay?

'Does he ever give in?' Lucy whispered.

She returned to her room. A wave of heat came from the tall column radiator to her left. At her dressing table, she sat down.

She noticed something on the left-hand side of the desk. 'What's this?'

An old box.

She frowned and picked it up. After careful examination of the box, she used her hands to try and prize it open. It didn't budge. It was solid. She had never seen this box before, had no clue how it got there. She rattled it. Although it wasn't heavy, something inside moved. Something metallic.

Downstairs she found Joanne in the kitchen preparing dinner, placing a tray of chicken in the warm, whirring oven. The light from the inside of the oven gently illuminated her mother's face. There was an array of vegetables cut on the worktop beside her.

'Mum?'

Joanne closed the oven door and turned to her. 'Hey, Luce.' She saw something in her daughter's hand. 'What's that you have there?'

'I… I don't know. I found it on my dresser upstairs.' She rattled it and scowled.

'Let me have a look,' Joanne said, stepping forward. Joanne shook it. 'Hmmm?'

'Yeah, weird eh,' said Lucy. 'I'll see dad, he might know.' Lucy held her hand out.

'No, it was okay, he was in the study doing work. Don't disturb him. I'll ask him when I see him.'

Lucy nodded, returned upstairs to her bedroom, closed the door, and stepped out onto the balcony where the air was cooler than before. She glanced up at the grey skies.

She received another text from Harry. She read it and sighed. Then, with her hand in her pocket, she pulled out something she really shouldn't have in her possession. Something she knew she'd get into big trouble for.

She exchanged several texts with Harry until the next text he sent surprised her.

Really surprised her.

JACK

There was a pounding in my head and a belting pain behind my eyes. The tablets I'd taken earlier were either taking their time to kick in or as pointless as shovelling snow when it was snowing. I used to get migraines before I wore glasses, which the optician had told me, had been the reason.

It wasn't the reason today, though.

Somebody had the photos. That person is threatening to go to the police if I didn't come up with one hundred thousand pounds. I found my face in my palms, the pounding inside my head viciously coming and going. In the hallway, I heard Lucy walk past the closed door, then moments later, back again.

I looked away from my computer and stared through the French doors out onto the gravel, finding myself zone out for a few seconds then I snapped out of it. To my right, my phone sat next to the keyboard. I grabbed it, unlocked it, and stared at the text message from the number demanding the money.

I pressed CALL.

To my surprise, it rang.

A male voice answered, 'Mr Haynes. What a surprise.'

I stood up suddenly, knocking the chair back.

'Who is this?' I asked quickly.

'It doesn't matter. What's important is what I have, which is very important to you and your family. And if it finds its way to the police, along with a note telling them it was from you… well, let's just say you'd be in trouble. Not just you. Your daughter, Lucy. Your wife, Joanne. You seem to have a lot on the line here, Jack Haynes.'

'Who the hell is this?'

'It doesn't matter,' the voice said calmly. 'As I said, it was what I have that's important.'

I wandered around the study, my free hand pressing hard on the top of my head. I stayed silent, waiting for him to speak. He didn't.

'What do you want?' I said.

'You know what I want,' he said.

'I can't just come up with that sort of money.'

'Well, you'll just have to find a way, won't you? If you don't, I'll send the police the photos. They'll wonder why you held back the information and suspect you of something. And not only that, I'll send it to the person who killed the two brothers along with a note informing him what you've done. And let's just say you don't want that to happen, do you? Come on, Jack Haynes, you're the financial director of a bank. You're intelligent, resourceful, you know what needs to be done to get the things you want.' He paused a beat. 'You have five days to get me the money. I'll text you on Wednesday evening with a time and place to meet on Thursday. Rule number one here, Jack. Don't fuck with me. It's the last thing you want to do.'

He hung up.

I placed my phone back into my pocket, opened the door of my study, took a left, and found Joanne in the kitchen chopping carrots. Her long dark hair flicked from side to side.

'Hey,' I said, approaching her from behind, and placing my hands on her slender hips.

'Hey,' she said.

'I've just spoken to the man wanting the money.'

The chopping stopped. The kitchen became silent. She turned to face me. 'What?'

'He told me he'd send them to the man who Lucy saw shoot the two men in the woods if he doesn't get the money.'

'Jesus. What are we going to do, Jack?'

I shook my head. 'I don't know, Jo. I really don't.'

She sighed, leaning into me. We embraced each other for a moment. I watched the potatoes simmer in a pan behind her, heard the fan above the hob whirl, and felt the beating of her thumping heart against mine.

I broke away slowly. 'What's Lucy up to?' I asked.

'In her room I think, getting ready.'

'We need to see her. We need to ask her what she's done with the photos.'

Jo nodded, then a tear fell from her eye.

'Hey, come on, we'll fix this,' I said, wiping the tear away with a soft thumb. Her forced smile told me she didn't believe me.

'I'll go see Lucy. You watch the potatoes,' she said.

'You want a drink – coffee?'

'What I really need is a vodka.' She smiled and rubbed her eyes. 'But a coffee will do for the moment.' I watched her move along the hall and disappear up the stairs.

'Lucy? You up here?' Joanne stepped onto the attic's landing. Strange. There was no music playing, no humming, no movement whatsoever. In the bedroom, she glanced at the small cupboard in the corner. A sick feeling grew in her stomach as her mind flooded with the events that happened a few days ago. The room was quiet. Too quiet. The French doors to the balcony were open an inch.

No sign of Lucy.

'Lucy?'

The kettle boiled and clicked off. I made the coffees and stirred them.

'Jack!'

I turned. Joanne was standing in the kitchen doorway, out of breath.

'Jack. She was gone,' she gasped, 'Lucy's gone.'

37

1975
Luton

The small girl cried in her bed. Her loud sobs shook her body under the old blanket lined with holes. Her brother stepped into her bedroom, lowered down by her side, and rubbed her back lovingly.

'I can't take this anymore,' she cried.

He felt a tear form in the corner of his eye and wiped it away before it fell down his face. He had to be strong. Had to be the one to look after her.

'I know. Dad's at work and will be until five.'

'Where's mum?'

She was in there—

Their mother stepped into the room. The boy and girl froze.

'Mum,' said the boy, absorbing the pain on her face. Her left eye was black and blue, nearly bulging from the socket.

'Are you two okay?'

The boy nodded, then stood up and hugged her, leaving his sister on the bed. The boy started to sob uncontrollably.

'Hey, hey,' their mother said, 'don't be upset.' She saw her daughter looking toward them with teary eyes. 'Hey, come here.' The little girl got off the bed and went over. The three of them shared a long silent hug.

It was the most love the children had felt in months.

38

Dunstable

Harry sat in front of the computer screen looking at pictures on Google. The phone on the desk vibrated. It was a text from Lucy.

Yes, I'm well. R U Okay?

Harry found a suitable picture, right clicked on it, then saved it. A reply to Lucy informed her some pictures would be soon uploaded on the Facebook page, *Scenic Beauty*, and that he would value her opinions on them.

Lucy responded: *Yes okay. I'll let you know what I think x*

Harry found another suitable picture of a stream dissecting two steep sides laced with flowers with the sun creeping through staggered trees in the background.

'Yes, beautiful,' Harry said out loud. The pictures didn't belong to Harry. None of them posted to the page under his name belonged to him. He searched the internet, usually typing and searching words like 'scenery shots' or 'amazing scenery', and chose the most suitable he could claim as his own.

Harry didn't even like photography. It was boring.

Harry clicked on Lucy's Facebook page, scanned through her photos. Not just her photography images, but her personal pics – family occasions, that type of thing. He noticed her dad, Jack, and her mother, Joanne, had their own Facebook pages too.

Harry clicked on Jack Haynes' profile. On his pictures, there was a photo folder named 'Greece 2015'.

'Aww look,' Harry said, seeing Lucy's smiling tanned face. My God, she was beautiful. 'Happy with mammy and daddy on holiday.' Harry continued looking for the signs that would give it away – he knew it was coming. Lucy had been to Greece six months ago – a small place called Kiotari, located several miles from Lindos on the Island of Rhodes.

'Yes, there it is,' Harry said, noticing an expensive watch on Jack's wrist. Lucy's mother was wearing a thick chain around her neck, very flattering to the eye. Harry stared at Lucy's mother in envy, admiring her beauty. Thin, full-chested. Like a model from a glossy magazine.

The admiration turned to hate within a fraction of a second.

What Harry was looking for was proof. Proof that Lucy's mother and father had money. Harry was confident about asking Lucy the right questions to get the right answers, but that would come in time.

A noise from downstairs startled Harry's silence. After logging out of Facebook and quickly turning the computer off, Harry stood up—

'Hey mammy,' said the little voice at the door. A small boy around the age of eight. 'Could you make me something to eat, mammy? I'm really hungry.'

The woman, standing at the computer, posing as a young man called Harry, felt her cheeks warm. She smiled at her son and said, 'Of course, I will.' She tapped her boy on the head, meeting him at the door, encouraging him to turn and leave. The boy went downstairs, but before the woman followed, she double-checked that 'Harry' was logged out and the computer was turned off.

39

Toddington
JACK

'Where the hell is she?' I shouted, galloping up the stairs two at a time, using the handrail to propel myself upwards. Joanne trailed behind me.

It didn't take long to realise that Lucy's room was empty. The only sound I heard was from the thumping heart in my chest. Joanne entered the room seconds later, breathing heavily.

'Where is she?' I said, throwing my palms up hopelessly.

She slowly shrugged. 'She came up here before. I – I don't know.'

'Jesus.' I sniffed the warm air. 'Can you smell that?'

'Smell what?'

'It smells like burning. Like something's on fire,' I said.

I descended the stairs, stopped on the first floor to check all the bedrooms and bathrooms. I found nothing, only the disappointment of not finding her. I started to panic. My mind imagined the worst.

'Where the fuck is she?' I dashed down the stairs and checked the living room. The television was off. No one was there. In the study, my computer hummed almost silently.

'Fuck.' I decided to check outside. 'Lucy! I shouted, my voice echoing in the quiet kitchen.

'Lucy,' Joanne shouted, arriving at the base of the stairs. 'Jack, I don't like this one bit.'

'You're not the only one.'

I could still smell the burning, even outside on the decking. I scanned the garden as I walked down the footpath. Angling left, I headed towards the side gate near the garage, unlocked it, and pushed it open. All I saw were the closed gates at the front of the house and the gravel leading to it.

No Lucy.

I saw Joanne charge out onto the decking as I ran back up the footpath. 'Did you see her?' she asked.

I quickly shook my head. Then a simple thought washed over me. 'Have you rang her?'

Joanne sighed. 'My God, why haven't we tried ringing her?'

I took my phone from my pocket, found Lucy's number, and pressed CALL. Joanne watched me closely. After each ring, my heart beat faster, my brain raced through so many possibilities. It rang through to her voicemail. I tried again.

'I'm checking every room again.' I shoved the phone back in my pocket, went back inside, and heard Joanne say she'd try calling her. In the hallway, I heard a ringtone, coming from somewhere above me.

I heard footsteps on the stairs. I stopped in midstride and listened. My eyes widened. I knew someone was there, a few feet to my left. The footsteps halted and everything went silent. And that's when I saw her.

'Lucy!' I said. 'Where the hell have you been?'

She turned at the bottom of the stairs and frowned. 'What?'

'Where the hell have you been?' I said again, this time louder.

Joanne came behind me from the kitchen. I saw the worry on her face. 'She's here,' I informed her.

'Lucy!' Jo gasped. 'Where the hell have you been?' Jo shoved past me, stopping in front of Lucy.

'What's going on, Mum... Dad?' Her confused stare flicked between us.

'Don't 'what's going on' me, Lucy. Where have you been?'

Lucy, hearing the panic in her mother's voice, didn't respond.

'Lucy, answer your mother,' I demanded.

'Upstairs in my room – I...' she trailed off.

As I got closer, a strong smell of smoke hit my nose. Then it clicked. 'You've been on the balcony, haven't you? You've been smoking?'

A look of guilt arched across her face.

'Is this true, Lucy?' Joanne said, sniffing the rancid aroma oozing from her daughter.

'Yes.' Her face reddened with embarrassment.

'If you want to smoke, you can smoke,' I said, 'but you can fund it yourself. Without a job, you'll struggle – you know how expensive cigarettes are?' I took a short breath to pause. 'With what's happened recently... we need to know where you are—'

'Well now you know,' she bit back. 'Now you know I was on my balcony smoking.'

'Lucy – don't speak to your father like that,' Jo said. 'Apologise now.'

Lucy glared in defiance.

I held a hand up to Joanne, indicating it didn't matter. I inhaled and exhaled slowly, keeping my eyes on my daughter. 'As long as you're fine, that's all that matters. With what's happened, I need to know where you guys are, until things settle anyway. Smoking is bad, Lucy, you must know that. I don't agree with it, but you're an adult and you can make your own choice.'

Joanne knew about the text asking for the money and gave me a knowing look. Lucy was none the wiser with a blank look on her face.

'Ok, sorry,' she said quietly. She turned and went back upstairs.

'Wash your hands, too. You stink!' Joanne shouted before she headed back into the kitchen.

Sitting at the kitchen table looking down at my laptop, I heard footsteps sheepishly enter the kitchen. Lucy, with her head bowed, appeared by my side. She leaned down and kissed my cheek.

'Sorry, Dad,' she said softly.

I smiled. 'Don't worry about it.'

A voice behind Lucy. 'Sit down, Lucy.' Joanne entered the kitchen. 'We need to talk.' Joanne took a seat. 'Come on.' Lucy considered it for a second and agreed to take a seat. Joanne looked at me. 'Tell her about the text.'

I told her.

A large 'O' formed at Lucy's lips. 'What – what we going to do?' Her worried gaze switched between us.

I gave her a reserved shrug. I didn't have an answer right now, so I lied: 'I'll sort it out, don't worry.' Joanne nodded and smiled at her reassuringly, but I noticed her expression suggested otherwise – she could hear the doubt in my voice.

A smile formed on her face, but I could see her glassy eyes fighting the tears. She got up slowly and left the kitchen. Joanne watched her go, then turned to me. 'What we gonna do?'

'I have no idea, Jo.'

Dunstable

I pulled up outside of my mother's house, put the gear into neutral, and turned off the Volvo's engine. As I hadn't seen her in a while, a sudden wave of guilt washed over me. I walked up the path towards her red front door.

I knocked twice before I opened the door, and —

It was locked.

I stepped back and frowned. I knocked again and waited. Strange – it was always open. Especially as she knew I was coming. Unless she forgot, which was unlikely, but possible I suppose.

I moved to the right, looked through the living room window. The television in the nearest corner was off. I returned to the door and leaned close; my head turned in an attempt to hear anything behind it. Silence.

I pulled my phone out, tapped her number, and pressed CALL.

It went straight to answerphone.

'Where are you, Mum?' I whispered towards the front door.

A voice behind me startled me. 'Hi, Jack!'

I turned suddenly, seeing the dark brown eyes of Mrs Beagle, the elderly lady who lived next door, standing at my mother's front gate, most of her weight supported by a black shiny walking stick.

'Oh, hi,' I said, with a courteous smile. 'How are you doing?'

She told me she was good and what she was been doing earlier that morning. She then told me about how the council had not filled the potholes on the road, which didn't concern her because she didn't have a car, and also how the bin men were refusing to take pizza boxes with the cardboard, because it was, apparently, considered too dirty to be recycled. She went on to comment about how she didn't get takeaways, so it didn't affect her.

When she paused, I interrupt her: 'Have you seen my mum? You know if she's in?'

Mrs Beagle shrugged, smiled, and walked on. 'Off to the shop now to see Larry. Bye Jonah.'

'You take care.' I watched her go, smiling. She'd always called me Jonah – I'm past the point of reminding her otherwise.

I knocked on the door a further three times. Still no answer. I heard a car engine roar behind me. I turned to see a teenage boy behind the wheel. Music was blaring out the open windows and a low drone was coming from an exhaust which has clearly been modified.

I rang my mother again – straight to voicemail.

'Jesus, Mum, where are you?' I shouted into the phone.

'Jack? is that you?' I heard a voice behind me.

I turned to see my mum, walking slowly through her gate, a pint of milk in one hand, her walking stick in the other.

'Mum! There you are.'

I met her halfway down the short path, kissed her cheek, and wrapped my arms around her. 'Where've you been?'

She held the milk up in the air and shook it. 'The shop. I knew you'll want a cup of coffee – you love coffee,' she said. 'I had no milk. You can't have coffee without milk, Jack.' She beamed at me. I moved off the path, allowing her to pass. She unlocked the door, opened it and we both entered.

An hour later, after kissing my mother goodbye, I stepped outside. She closed the door, excited about getting back to the television. The air outside was cooler, even though it was still in the low twenties. I smiled as I get into the Volvo, my head filled with childhood memories. When dad was here, we used to look forward to a Friday night when we'd go to the shop to buy hotdogs and cheap popcorn, then spend the night on the sofa watching channel four. Life was simple back then. We appreciated the smallest of things.

Along the road, the bright sun hit my eyes. Pulling down the visor to block the vicious glare, I noticed there wasn't a cloud in sight as I approach the oncoming junction when my phone rings through the Volvo's hands-free system. I checked the caller. It was my brother. I accepted the call.

'Hello.'

'Jackal!'

'Hey Markos, how you doing?'

We exchanged pleasantries. He told me about the wedding and I told him about the text and phone call about the money. We spoke for a few minutes and he told me something very important.

'Are you sure?' I asked him.

'Yes, I'm sure.' He hung up the phone.

I found Joanne's number and pressed CALL.

'Jack.' Her voice sounded weird through the car speakers.

I told her about what Mark had said.

'Really?' she said in surprise.

'Yeah, he'll be round in twenty minutes.'

I put my foot down and headed home with a hopeful smile growing on my face.

40

Toddington

Mark and Elaine, in their red Vauxhall Insignia, headed east towards Jack's house. It was quiet on the narrow winding road, the sun starting to descend somewhere behind them, leaving dusk to creep in.

They drove in silence: no radio, no talking. The whirring sound of the wheels rotating against the dry tarmac trickled up through the vents.

Jack needed their help. Badly.

'What's the situation with your brother, they gonna be okay?' Elaine asked, her eyes down on her phone, navigating through an endless list of work-related emails.

'Hopefully. We'll find out soon,' Mark said. 'Just up here.'

Elaine looked up as Mark dabbed the brakes slightly, seeing his brother's house in the distance. Marks slowed, took the turn, and stopped at the closed gates. He beeped the horn twice and a moment later, the gates swung open. The Insignia crawled forward, crunching on the gravel as it snaked towards the front of the house. Mark parked next to Joanne's blue BMW.

He opened his door and behind him, he heard the sound of the gates ticking closed.

Elaine stepped out. 'You see it?' She glared towards the front gates.

'I did,' said Mark.

'Strange place to park up, isn't it?'

Mark nodded before they both headed for the front door.

Elaine stalled for a second and turned again. Through the gates, she saw a black van. The driver was glaring in her direction. She smiled at him.

JACK

There was a knock on the door.

I opened it to find Mark standing there. He smiled and stepped up, hugging me. 'How are you doing?'

'I'm good. Come in.' I moved out of his way. 'I like that jacket.' He was wearing a dark blue Ralph Lauren number. Easy on the eyes.

'Please don't mention that jacket, he'll never take it off now,' Elaine said, smiling as she entered.

'Not my fault I have style.' Mark wandered off to the living room to see Joanne and Lucy.

We made eye contact. 'How are you doing, Elaine?'

'I'm good – more importantly, how are you? How are things? Have they come back?'

Assuming she was referring to the men who broke in on Thursday morning, I said, 'No, they haven't.' Pausing for a moment, I could hear Mark speaking with Jo and Lucy in the background. 'Has Mark told you about the phone call?'

'He has,' she said. 'He has an idea. Or so he told me.'

I offered them both a drink. They said yes: one coffee, the other tea. Elaine then disappeared into the living room.

In the hallway, as I turned for the kitchen, Mark grabbed my forearm.

'How much is the security?' he asked.

I frowned, unsure what he meant. 'You've noticed the cameras?'

'No,' he said, frowning. 'The black van outside.'

I felt a white heat run across the top of my shoulders. 'What?'

'The van outside, Jack – has this got anything to do with what happened?'

I looked beyond him towards the door. 'I don't know, maybe. They were here yesterday too.' I kept my voice low so Joanne and Lucy didn't hear. 'I was on Lucy's balcony and they were parked there, watching me. The driver made a gun with his hand'—I imitate a gun with my hand—'and he shot me with it.'

'You got a baseball bat?'

'Mark, why would I have a baseball bat? I don't play base-ball.'

'Because me and you are going out there to see who it is—'

'We're going to do what?'

'Listen, Jack. You're not taking this shit anymore. I'm not having these dickheads hanging around here. It's obvious they're watching your house. I assumed they were the se-curity – I've seen the cameras you have set up and thought you had them as an extra.' Anger built up inside him – it was rare to hear it in his voice. 'Have you got some kind of weapon?'

I told him I didn't.

'Jack, we're going out there,' he said, matter-of-factly.

I threw my palms up. 'Listen… we should ring the police. They—'

'The police will do nothing. A van can park wherever it likes. In the eyes of the law, it's doing nothing wrong. Come on, we'll go out and have a word with them. See what they're up to.'

My heart missed a beat at the thought of it.

'Mark, it's dangerous.'

'That's why I'm asking if you have a baseball bat?' He paused to cock his head. 'Come on, brother. Remember when we were at school that time?'

It took a second to recollect the memory. Two boys bullied me for nearly a year before Mark told me to go over and face my fears. Mark could have ended it there and then, but he wanted me to do it – for me to stand up for myself. I ended up fighting with the two boys and beat them both. It was the last time they said a bad word to me.

'That was different – we're not thirteen anymore, Mark.'

He stepped closer. 'Would you get a fucking grip here. This is your family. Your wife. Your daughter. Your home. Step your game up and go out there. I'm coming with you.'

I stayed silent, feeling the adrenaline fill my body.

'Let's go.'

'Joanne?' I shouted.

Her voice from the living room: 'Yeah?'

'Just showing Mark something on the car. Two seconds.' She didn't reply. I put my trainers on, tied the laces tight. Mark took his dark blue jacket off, hung it on the post at the bottom of the stairs.

The gravel crunched beneath our feet as we headed towards the closed front gates. I used the fob in my pocket to open them. The motor started to whir, persuading the mechanical device to separate the tall metal gates.

I took a deep breath and swallowed.

As we passed the concrete pillars and angled right, my body started to shake when I saw the van parked on the opposite side of the road, the front end facing us.

When the driver glanced up and saw us, he grabbed the other man's attention and pointed. I let Mark walk a little in front. There was a thumping in my neck, surging adrenaline of not knowing what was coming next.

'Keep calm, Jack. I'll handle this,' Mark whispered.

The driver opened his car door and stepped out onto the grass verge.

Here we go.

41

Toddington
JACK

The driver was tall and thin, built like a pencil. He was wearing a black leather jacket. His face was gaunt and angry. He closed the driver's door, ambled along the long grass towards us, stopping beside the front grill of the black van.

Mark reached the grass verge on the other side of the road and stepped up. I followed his lead.

'Could we help you, gentlemen?' Mark said very calmly.

The driver shook his head slowly. His friend, a smaller, fatter excuse of a man, stepped down from the passenger side onto the road. He waddled around to join his friend at the front of the van.

The fatter one said, 'Help us with what?'

Mark closed in on them until he was three feet away. I was two feet behind, consciously remembering *he* was the one doing the talking.

As I stopped, I tripped on something in the grass, stumbling forward a few inches.

'Oh… watch yourself there!' shouted the fat one, laughing. His head was like a bowling ball and his double chin annoyed me so much.

The thin one cracked a small smile at my hiccup. His focus bounced between us until it settled on Mark.

'You're parked up here,' said Mark, 'watching my brother's house. I want to know why?' His jaw tightened.

'What's it to you?' the driver asked.

'Because you have no right to be here. What's your business?' Mark raised his voice now. I had to hand it to Mark – he had balls. The driver and passenger stared at him in awe. The passenger then moved to our right, went to the van, opened the door, and grabbed something.

I froze.

He stepped away from the van with a gun by his side. I didn't know the type. It was black and metal, and that's all I'm really bothered about.

The driver smiled at the short, fat passenger, then returned his focus to us. 'Like I said, what's it to you?'

I gulped, finally finding the courage to speak: 'Hey listen, we don't—'

'Jack, I'll handle this!' Mark cut me off quickly. He didn't take his eyes off the thin driver who was only a few feet in front of him. 'You're the men at my brother's house a few days ago? You smashed it up?'

The thin man curled his bottom lip and shrugged without a care in the world. 'Maybe.'

'Think you're big and tough with a weapon, do you?' Mark said to the chubby one. 'I'd love to see me and you go toe to toe, you fat little shit.'

Slowly and smoothly, the driver used his left hand to lift the back of his leather jacket and his right hand to pull a gun from the back of his dark jeans. He brought his hands back in front of him and tapped the tip of the gun off his right thigh.

'Big mouth, eh?' said the driver.

'I don't see his gun,' laughed the fat one. 'Do you?'

The driver turned at an angle to his friend. 'No, they must—'

Mark, ready on his toes, took his chance. He leaped forward, landed a head butt to the side of the man's face. With the man already turned and off-balance, the force of the blow knocked him down like a lead balloon. He grunted in pain as he crashed to the ground. He dropped his gun which landed a few feet to Mark's left.

'You stupid fucking idiot!' he shouted at Mark, holding a palm up to his temple. A river of blood flows through his fingers. Mark jumped back a little, ready on his toes, ready for what was coming next. Mark reaches behind him, pulled a flick-knife from the back pocket of his jeans, and opened the blade. Leaning forward, close to the driver who was still on the floor, he pointed it at him, the tip of the blade inches from his face.

'Mark – what are you doing with that?' I shouted.

To his right, the driver noticed the gun a few feet from him. It was too far for him to grab it without Mark getting to it first.

The fat passenger panicked and aimed his gun at Mark. 'Oi, oi, get – get back now!'

Mark backed off in surrender, switching focus between them both.

'Stuart, you okay?' the fat man said, glaring down at the man who we now know is named Stuart. 'Get back. Look what you've done!'

Mark backed away slowly, flicking the blade away. A knife wouldn't beat a bullet under normal circumstances. He put the knife back in his pocket, then raises his hands in surrender.

I didn't know what he was doing. 'Mark, what—'

There was a hum of an engine approaching us.

Stuart, with his face pouring with blood, crawled over to the gun, grabbing it quickly. He jumped up, eyeing Mark with fury, then forced a painful smile. 'You're fucked now, aren't you?'

I'm thinking the same. Now we have no chance.

Until the small, overweight passenger turned and sees the oncoming car.

'Stuart, put that fucking gun away now!'

'What?' Stuart frowned at him.

'Hide that fucking gun!' The fat man shouted, retreating to the van and climbing in. He dipped his head down for a moment, presumably hiding his weapon in the glove box.

It was a police car.

It slowed beside us. The driver scowled at the scene before him. He looked familiar. Then I realised who it is.

Johnson. The dirty fucking copper.

He turned off the engine. We fall into an awkward silence and watched him step across the quiet road, the only sound are his shoes lightly tapping on the tarmac. 'Good evening, gentlemen.'

'Good evening,' said Mark.

'What have we got ere then?' said Johnson.

I glared at him but said nothing. He met my eye.

'Mr Haynes.' The tash on his lip appeared more ridiculous than it had when I first met him. 'What a pleasant surprise,' he said.

'I wish I could said the same.'

He gave me a half-smile for my humour.

'These men had an issue with their van,' Mark informed him. 'It's all fixed though.'

Johnson turned to Stuart, who was still holding his hand firmly against his face to stop the blood. 'That true?'

Stuart without hesitation, nodded quickly. 'Yes. We needed some coolant, and these guys,' he pointed at me and Mark, 'sorted it for us – thank you, gentleman.'

'What happened to your face?' Johnson asked him.

'Oh, this?' He removed his hand as if it was nothing. 'Caught it on the underside of the bonnet. Silly really.' His hand was plastered with blood.

Johnson smiled. 'Cool story, that.' Then he turned to us.

'I suggest you two return to the house, let me have a quiet word with these two. They won't bother you again.'

'Okay,' I said. 'Mark - let's go.' He nodded but didn't move. His stare was fixed on Stuart. 'Mark – let's go!'

'Make sure you get that nasty cut fixed up, ey?' he told Stuart.

Stuart glared at him.

We stepped off the grass verge and walked across the road through the gates. I could feel their eyes burning the back of our heads. Using the fob in my pocket, I closed the gates once we were inside.

Johnson got closer to Stuart and examined the cut on his face. 'Nasty that one, ey?'

'Tell me about it.' He winced in pain. 'The bigger one, his fucking brother. Hurt like hell. Solid headbutt – knocked me on my arse.'

'Well it was your own stupid fault really, isn't it?'

Stuart grimaced.

'Why are you here?' asked Johnson.

'We don't answer to you, we answer to the guy who pays us,' said Stuart, matter-of-factly.

Johnson gives him a 'fair enough' shrug.

'And that's the same guy who pays you,' Stuart added. 'So, the question is: what are *you* doing here?'

42

Toddington
JACK

When we returned to the house, I closed and locked the door. In the living room, I heard Joanne and Lucy entertaining Elaine, laughing at something that had happened on one of the shows they waste so much time watching. Their cheery voices faded as we moved into the kitchen.

'Fucking hell, Mark.'

'Good headbutt though, wasn't it?' He smirked, pulled the chair out at the table then took a seat. He maintained his grin as if replaying the moment in his own head.

'Mark…' I stepped forward, keeping my volume to a whisper, 'they could have killed us. They—'

'But they never killed us. Now stop being a fanny and get the kettle on.'

I opened my mouth to speak but didn't say anything. Instead, I turned towards the kettle, flicked it on, and waited for it to boil. I grabbed the cups from the cupboard above the worktop and placed them on the surface in front of me. I felt myself shaking. Mark could see it too, but he didn't comment.

'So, what's the problem, Jack?' He casually drummed the table with his fingertips.

'The problem? The problem is me and you have—'

His palm stopped me. 'No – forget what's just happened outside. The problem is why I'm here. We need to discuss a way to get you the money you need.'

I made the coffees and drifted over to the table. I placed them down, took a seat opposite him. Over the following few minutes, I ran through everything with him.

Everything. Some of it, he knew. Much of it, he didn't.

The break in.

The photos Lucy took.

The police detective threatening us – the same detective we'd just seen outside.

The man on the phone wanting one hundred thousand.

Then finally, the three-hundred thousand that Ray wanted.

And more importantly, why he wanted it.

Mark leaned back in his chair, gave me a heavy sigh, but managed to maintain eye contact. The shape of his mouth indicated he was about to say something, but he didn't, as if he was thinking carefully about what to say.

'Jesus, Jack,' he finally said.

A wave of embarrassment washed over me.

'Jack, what are you playing at?'

I shrugged and forced my lips together, fighting back my emotions. I felt so stupid and irresponsible for putting my family in this situation.

'What would Dad say if he was alive?' He let the question hang in the air, which made me feel even worse. He got up abruptly, knocking the chair back, and stared at me with wide eyes. 'You… should know better. I need some fucking air,' he snapped, then opened the back door open and stepped out onto the dark decking.

I heard a rustle, then a spark, then the smell of smoke drifted into the kitchen. I hung my head, and stared at the table until I heard footsteps at the hall doorway.

'Is everything okay, Jack?'

It was Elaine.

Mark finished his cigarette and stepped back inside. He padded over to the table and took a seat, avoiding any eye contact.

'Go on then… tell her how much of a useless, thoughtless, piece of shit you've been.' He dropped his face into his palms and sighed loudly.

Just what I needed.

For a second, I didn't say anything.

'Jack,' said Mark through his hands, 'Fucking tell her.'

Elaine quietly took a seat next to Mark and I told her the same as I had told him.

She tilted her head right, then left, like a dog that was unsure what it was looking at.

Suddenly I felt sick to the pit of my stomach. I stood up, went to the sink, and threw up. Mark and Elaine both wince at. Then I splashed my face with water.

'This gangster, the one who killed the two men, what Lucy saw. What's his name?' asked Mark.

'I have no idea. No idea at all.'

'I think I have a plan,' said Mark, 'I'm confident this will work.' Elaine looked at him intrigued. 'I have about eighty grand saved up… there's a poker tournament in Hemel Hempstead tomorrow night. Fifty grand buy-in. I've been invited to play.'

Elaine, not hiding the disgust on her face, shook. 'No way, Mark.'

Mark ignored her. 'Originally, I said no, but I could make a phone call and get back in—'

'How much could you win?' I asked.

'Winner walks home with half a mill – it's a one-off jack-pot.'

I curled my lip. 'Wow.'

'Yeah.'

'Can you play poker, Mark?' I asked.

Mark, as if it was the most ridiculous thing he had ever been asked, laughed. 'Jack, there's no one better. I'll make the call. I'll put the fifty grand in and get you that money.'

I held my palm up.

'Don't be daft, you're not putting in anything. It was my problem so I'll give you the fifty grand for the buy in. Well, if you lose it then—'

'I won't lose it, I've played in them before,' Mark informed me. 'For smaller amounts of course. This is a one-off occasion, but I know how it works.' Elaine glared at him, burning the skin on the side of his face. 'It's easy money – if you know what you're doing—'

'And do you know what you're doing?' Elaine snapped.

He gave her a firm nod whilst she continued to shake her head, then finally looked away in disgust.

Collecting myself, I picked up my mug and drained the remaining coffee before I placed it back down on the table. 'I'll get you the fifty grand.'

'There's one problem though, Jack?' Mark said.

'What is it?'

'When you go to these things, you need to take someone – a woman, a partner, or wife.' He glanced in Elaine's direction. She didn't accommodate his idea. She got up abruptly and left the kitchen. Mark watched her go then tilted his head back to me. 'Which is what I thought would happen. Do you think Joanne would go with me?'

'But she doesn't know about the bank money—'

'She doesn't have to know about the bank money, does she?'

'What bank money?' Jo asked, standing in the kitchen doorway.

43

Toddington
JACK

Joanne slapped my face. The sound echoed around the kitchen. Although my face was on fire, I didn't raise a palm to soothe it. I accepted it as I deserved it because I did.

Mark sat like a statue at the table.

'Jo, I …' I stopped myself.

Tears welled up in her eyes and her lower lip quivered. She maintained hard eye contact. I saw so much emotion and anger in her glossy eyes. She looked like a different person.

She moved towards me, but instead of another slap, she rammed her shoulder into mine, knocking me off balance. 'Fuck off, Jack,' she screamed, her anger bouncing off the walls.

I turned and watched her yank a chair out at the table, the legs scraping loudly across the tiles, and she sat down. Her red face dropped into her hands and she started to cry.

I sighed hopelessly. Then heard a duo of quick footsteps coming from the hallway.

'What's going on?' Lucy shouted. Elaine was a step behind her.

I looked at them with a shameful, sad smile.

'Mum, what's the matter?' Lucy lowered to one knee next to Joanne and put an arm around her. 'Mum – what's happened?'

'You better asked your stupid fucking dad!'

All eyes were on me for an explanation. I looked away and sighed heavily. I wanted the ground to swallow me up. Elaine stared at me with hard eyes as she lowered herself to the table, on a seat near Joanne.

Lucy remained standing, glaring. 'Well, Dad?'

I explained to Lucy everything while Joanne sobbed into Elaine's shoulder. Mark shook his head several times and shuffled occasionally on his chair as he heard the story for the second time. After I finished, Lucy gave me the most disgusting look I'd ever seen. 'I don't believe this. Dad – tell me this isn't true?'

I answered her with silence.

The kitchen fell dead quiet for what seemed like forever. The only thing I could hear was the thumping in my chest and Joanne sniffling away her tears.

'I think… there's a way we could fix this,' I said.

Lucy shot me a stare. 'We…? Dad, are you for real? I think you've done enough, don't you? This is all *your* doing. *We* are not the ones who stole money from a bank. Dad, that's prison time, you know?'

I didn't need a reminder.

'*I* may have a way of fixing this.' I stared at Mark, gave him a nod, hoping he'd speak up. 'With the help of Mark,' I added.

Mark's expression was sour, almost as if he had changed his mind because of the way I had hurt my family.

'Mark?' I begged.

He scowled for a few seconds, then finally, and obviously reluctantly, nodded.

I told Lucy and Joanne about the tournament in Hemel Hempstead. I added that Mark would need a partner to go with him. I glanced at Elaine, who shook her head slowly. 'I've told you – you're on your own, Jack.'

'Jo?'

'I can't believe what you've done!' she screamed. 'What were you thinking?' She slammed the bottom of her clenched fists down onto the wooden table. The dense low thud rattled the wood and echoed through the house. Lucy edged back an inch. I could see the pain on her face. She had never seen her mum so upset.

And it was all my fault.

'He obviously wasn't thinking,' commented Elaine.

Oh, for God's sake. Here we go.

'Jo, would you go with—'

Her sudden movement cut me off as she got up and wiped her eyes. A moment later, she left the kitchen. We all watched her go. Lucy rose and followed her.

'Lucy,' I said, 'Lucy, where are you going?'

'Shut up, Dad. This is all your fault!' she shouted, disappearing in the hallway, her heavy feet pounding the wooden floor.

If Mark played in the poker tournament tomorrow night – and won – then we might find a way out of this one. The whole problem could disappear.

Joanne stormed out of the house, dragging Lucy with her. In the darkness, the engine of the BMW revved, then a rush of tires skidded on the gravel until we didn't hear them anymore.

'What am I going to do, Mark?' I asked.

'You seem to have all the answers, Jack. You tell us,' said Elaine.

'Listen, Elaine, I don't need your shit right now.'

She stood up fast, knocking her chair back a little. '*My* shit?'

'Let's just calm it down, shall we?' suggested Mark.

'Elaine, please,' I said, 'would you go with Mark tomorrow, we need—'

'You're on your own.' She turned away from me and stormed out the front door.

44

Toddington
JACK

I sat at the kitchen table alone after Mark and Elaine left. The silence in the house overwhelmed me.

I picked up the glass of Amaretto, took a long sip, felt the sweet, amber liquid soothe my throat. It wasn't long before I was in bed. The clock on the bedside table told me it was only 10 p.m. I felt exhausted, my eyes were desperate to close. I rang Joanne, but it went straight to her voicemail. As I listened to her pre-recorded message, her voice reminded me of what I'd done and how much she was hurt.

'She'll ring me when she was ready,' I whispered. She was probably at Alison's house – her best friend.

I thought about watching some television, but the thought of crawling across the bed to get the remote was too much, so, instead, I stared at the ceiling in silence and, for the first time since Mark and Elaine left, I felt relaxed.

I turned the lamp off, the room around me succumbed to darkness. Usually, I was asleep in seconds, but not tonight.

My mind went back eighteen months ago when I walked into the office of Keith Grey, who, at the time, was the Financial Director of Hembridge bank. His face was a picture. He panicked and started clicking like crazy at the monitor in front of him.

'What you doing, Keith?' I'd asked.

The screen in front of him froze, and he stared at the screen in horror, hoping I hadn't seen it. I had seen it.

He did not attempt to stop me from reading what was on the screen. He knew I wasn't stupid. He'd been taking money from personal accounts and buying stocks and shares with them daily, then selling them on when the prices shot up. He then transferred the money he'd stolen back to their accounts and kept the profits.

How had he done it without the account holder seeing it on their statement?

Good question – he was a very clever man. Not clever enough on that day though, because he'd been caught.

He confessed everything to me. He'd been keeping tabs on the high-value accounts and when a large transaction had been made, he would add another line to the transaction history with the exact same transaction. Once he'd used the money to buy stocks and shares and made a profit, he would transfer it back. For example, the account holder would notice a transaction from Morrison's for their weekly shop, then another line of the same amount is taken out too, but then underneath that, he'd add another line with the money being returned, as if Morrison's had made an innocent mistake and had corrected it on their part. At the end of the day, the account balance would be the same. Rarely did the account holder ever really question it, because the money was how it should have been. In addition, he found a way to hide account numbers and sort codes, processing them as normal card payments. How he did that went beyond my knowledge.

He had been doing it for years, he confessed. I couldn't believe it. Not only small amounts but similar amounts to what you'd spend on car purchases or house renovations. You name it, he'd done them all.

'How much have you made, Keith?' I'd asked.

I remember him dipping his head in shame, staring at the monitor in front of him. 'Thousands.' He'd stood up and closed the door. 'Listen, Jack, I'm sixty-four, I don't have long left. Do you know about my wife? Her cancer? We haven't got long left together. I'll stay until we get our bonus, then I'll retire. You could have this position because let me tell you, you're the best financial manager that's ever worked under me.'

At the time, I knew the bonus was coming within a few months. I told him I'd think about it. I knew what he was doing was illegal, and most of all, it was immoral. But if he could put in a good word with the MD, recommending my promotion, then maybe, turning a blind eye to what he'd done might not be such a bad idea after all.

So, that's what I did: I said nothing.

There was talk around the bank of Keith retiring. A few names of others had been mentioned for the likely promotion. I said nothing and bided my time. Then, out of nowhere, I was the face of the financial division. I'd like to say my MBA (Master's in Business Administration) played a part in that, and it may well have, but I knew deep down the real reason why I was promoted.

45

Monday
Toddington
JACK

When I opened my eyes, I felt sick. It was so painful, I forced my hands on my gut trying to soothe it but, if anything, it made it worse.

I rolled over to my right. The covers were flat, the pillow empty. My heart sank into my twisted stomach.

Joanne hadn't come back.

In the silent loneliness, I struggled up, swung my legs onto the carpet, and sat for a moment. I ran through the events from last night and recollected Mark's option to play poker later tonight. He needed a partner, which, at the moment, wasn't looking likely.

I'd speak with Joanne to apologise profusely.

I told Mark, before he left last night, that I'd get him the money for the buy-in. Last night, I made a call to the bank, and spoken with our chief cashier, Susan, to arrange it.

I pulled myself out of a daze and noticed the time was nearly seven. The last thing I wanted to do was to go back to work. I wasn't sure I could face it. Hibernating under a quiet rock sounded much more appealing.

In the en-suite, I washed my face in the sink, then a thought came to my head.

Where was the box? The one I had seen in the attic? I was meaning to ask Lucy about it. I'm sure I left it on her desk.

I reminded myself about the dream I had. It was so vivid, so real. In the dream, I'd found the box in Lucy's cupboard, placed it on the table, and opened it. But my eyes were blurry and I couldn't focus on the rattling contents. That's when I woke up. I hadn't seen what was inside. I closed my eyes, trying to visualize it. Silver, metal…

I left the bedroom, walked along the landing, and climbed the stairs to Lucy's room. Pushing the door open, I stepped inside. The dressing table contained many items, but I soon realised there was no box. I felt bad about doing it, but I opened the drawer.

Underwear.

I closed it quickly.

I checked the other drawers. Photos. Make-up. Leaflets. Everything but the box I was looking for. I'll ask her later I decided.

Back in our bedroom, I got dressed, adjusted my tie in the mirror and threw wax on my hair, used my fingers to spread it evenly.

I descended the stairs, stepped down into the painfully quiet hallway. There were no sounds. No television in the living room. No kettle boiling in the kitchen. No smell of early coffee or burnt toast lingering down the hallway. No idle chatter coming from the two people in the world that I loved the most.

I froze in the hall, trying to imagine it, forcing myself to hear their laughter, their joy. But the harsh silence hit me hard in the face with no remorse. In the kitchen, I made coffee and toast. I struggled to eat it and threw the half-eaten slice back down on my plate and washed it down with coffee.

I pulled out my phone and checked it. Nothing.

Joanne hadn't returned the calls which I made last night after Mark and Elaine had gone. I sent three text messages and left four voicemails. I didn't even know where they were. I assumed they'd gone to her best friend's house. But I hadn't made the effort to ring Alison because I would have been given an ear full.

There was a noise.

The front door. The key turned and the lock clicked open.

I stood up and looked down the hall. Lucy walked towards me and stopped in front of me.

'I'm sorry for shouting at you last night, Dad.' She leaned forward and hugged me half-heartedly as if she had been told to.

'It's okay,' I said.

She turned.

'Hey,' I said, stopping her. 'Did you see a small box in your bedroom a few days ago, when the joiner was here?'

She bit her lip softly. 'I gave it to mum.'

'Okay, thanks.'

She padded back towards the base of the stairs and climbed them. Standing in the kitchen doorway was Joanne. Her eyes were red as if she'd been crying.

'Hi, Jack.'

'Hey, Jo.'

We stood in silence for what felt like a month. Breaking the silence, she said, 'I'm sorry I left, I shouldn't have left you. Not like that anyway.' She stepped forward, clutching her black handbag nervously as if we were two strangers. 'I was so angry about what you did. I – I, just don't understand, Jack. Why you felt the need to do something like that? But, I am sorry for leaving you.'

I dipped my head. 'It's okay. Sorry I kept ringing and texting. I was going to text Alison, but I didn't want to bother her.' I moved closer. 'You… did stay at Alison's?'

She nodded, went to the table, and pulled out a chair. She glanced up to her left, noticed the time on the wall on the black clock above the back door.

'Are you going to work?'

'Yeah,' I said, glancing down at my shirt and tie. 'I don't want to, believe me.'

'Don't go like that, you don't have any shoes on.' A smile crept across her face, and my heart warmed at her humour.

'What I want is an explanation, Jack,' she said. 'Come here, tell me what the hell was going through your stupid mind when you did it.'

I hated this.

We didn't argue about anything.

'Come on, sit down, Jack.'

I went over, pulled a chair out and sat down, then turned towards her. She waited. I then explain why I did it. Pure greed. That's all it boiled down to.

'And that money has been in the house all this time. A few feet away from where we sleep?'

I nodded slowly, re-adjusting myself on the seat.

I waited for her to speak but, instead, she tilted her head left in deep thought. Then she stood up fast, grabbed the empty mug I had earlier, and threw it. I flinched, throwing my palms up in defence, and turned away, not sure if it was coming in my direction.

The mug smashed onto the floor.

I jumped up from the table. 'Jo…'

The sound was so loud, it wasn't long before Lucy dashed down the stairs to investigate.

'Mum, what the hell?' said Lucy, charging in. 'What's happened, Dad… what have—'

I waved it away. 'Don't worry about it, I'll clean it.'

Lucy stood next to her mum, watching with concern as she sat back down. 'Mum, are you okay?' Joanne nodded in her direction but Lucy could see her shaking. For a second, I thought she was going to have a panic attack. Years ago, when I first met her, she used to get them frequently. Something that seem to happen out of her control, she told me.

I cleaned up the shattered pieces with a dustpan and brush, opened the bin lid, and dropped them in. I glanced at the time on my watch. Joanne hadn't moved, her gaze somewhere at the back of the kitchen.

'Hey,' I said. Her face remained still, but her eyes flicked up at me. 'I am so sorry, Jo. If I could turn the clock back, I'd do it in a heartbeat. I need you to know that.'

She dropped her arm from under her chin, her hand reached out to me. I stepped forward, grabbed it, and squeezed it softly. She pulled me in close for a kiss.

I sat down again. 'How's Alison doing?'

'She's okay,' she said. 'Keeping well.'

'I haven't seen in her in… God knows how long. She still talks about Peter?'

Joanne nodded. 'All the time. She had a few glasses of wine before Lucy and I got there. We spoke about things in the past and she got upset when we mentioned the holiday we went on years ago. Remember that?'

'I do.' We went for a weekend away in Benidorm, I recalled. 'Must be awful being alone.'

'Yeah.' Joanne zoned out, staring past me deep in thought.

'Listen,' I said, glancing up at the clock, 'if Mark wins this poker thing tonight…'

She looked my way. 'You mean you want me to go with him?'

I nodded. 'Yes, I do.'

'I want you to know that I'm not doing it for you, I'm doing it for our safety. Mine and Lucy's. What you did, Jack is almost unforgiveable. Behind our backs makes it worse.' She broke eye contact. Her expression told me she was still appalled at what I'd done.

'Okay, I'll let Mark know, okay.' I tried to smile at her, but she was having none of it. 'You're my darling, you know that?'

'If we don't win tonight, Jack, we're leaving.' The blatant lack of humour in her voice told me she was dead serious. Her words stung me. I watched her stand up, edge back her chair, and walk out of the kitchen.

46

Toddington

At the window, Joanne watched Jack pass through the gates in his Volvo. He took a left and accelerated along Park Road, out of sight.

Joanne stepped back, turned, and sat on the edge of the bed, sighing heavily. Could Mark really pull this off tonight? Could they get the money they needed and make all of this go away? With her hands on her thighs, a single question developed in her mind: Why won't Elaine go?

Above her head, towards the back of the house, she heard Lucy padding around, back and forth. Lucy's college schedule was light this morning. Nothing until 1 p.m.. She'd be at home for a little while longer.

Joanne rose to her feet, went back over to the window, and checked on the gravel outside. No sign of Jack. She observed the cars passing the house for a few minutes, paying attention to every driver, seeing if anyone looked up in her direction.

They didn't.

She decided to take a shower and it wasn't long before she was back in the bedroom, wrapped in a towel. In the full-length mirror, she allowed the towel to drop to the floor, and, using her eyes, she followed the shape of her tanned, naked body.

'Not bad for fifty,' she said. She twisted her, admiring the profile of her behind, legs, and calves. On the back of her thigh, she noticed the long scar – it was almost as thin as a pin but seven inches long. She stared at it for a long time until it became itchy. The doctor said that that might happen. Because of the healing process, the skin would scar and the skin tissue could become irritated from time to time.

When she felt stressed or had things on her mind. Things that her husband or daughter didn't know.

Lucy entered the kitchen carrying her rucksack on her back. She dropped it on the table with a thud.

Joanne glanced up. 'What's in there, Lucy? A bowling ball?'

'Feels like it.' Lucy laughed. 'We have to take our Art textbook in. Jodie asked – one of the girls on the course – why we couldn't share, but the teacher made it clear.' Lucy leaned forward pointing a finger and, with a deep voice, she said, 'That you must have your own textbook.'

Joanne smiled, then looked back down at her iPad that she held in both hands. 'Rules are rules. You want a lift?'

'Lisa's picking me up. Thank you, though.'

'Where does Lisa live, I thought she lives—'

'She does, but she offered,' Lucy explained. 'I already said yes.'

'Fair enough,' said Joanne. 'Time you back later?'

Lucy thought for a moment. 'Last lesson finishes at three. Probably half three, depending on traffic. Or depends if Lisa wants a pitstop at McDonald's on the way back.'

'I'll be seeing you *after* half three then,' Joanne mused.

The sound of a car outside on the gravel grabbed Lucy's attention. Her phone beeped inside her pocket. 'Lisa's here.'

Joanne frowned. 'The gates are locked. How did she get in?'

'I opened them with the fob when I came downstairs.'

'Lucy, we need to be more careful. Anyone could have walked in. Or drove in…'

Lucy rolled her eyes as she grabbed her heavy bag and disappeared into the hallway.

'Study hard. Love you,' said Jo, watching her daughter's blonde hair bounce.

Lucy turned and smiled at her. 'See you *after* half three.'

At the bay window in the living room, Joanne watched the blue Astra leave, then used the fob to close the gates. On her way back to the kitchen she stopped at the under-stairs cup-board, pulled the door open, and leaned inside to grab a coat. She placed the coat flat on the kitchen table and, after locating the hidden pocket, she pushed her hand in.

'Ah, there it is,' she said.

A cheap mobile phone – something you'd buy as a spare if you were waiting for a next-day replacement.

She powered it up. It didn't take long for the phone to beep. A text message.

Her eyes sparkled at the words.

I'll be round at one x x

47

1975
Luton

'I can't take it anymore. I can't,' said the little girl, cowering on the floor in her bedroom.

'Hey, come here.' The boy lowered and wrapped his arms around her. 'This won't be forever.'

'You need to do something.'

They both fell silent as their mother cried in the next room. It wasn't long before they heard their father step out onto the landing and slam the bedroom door. 'And get that fucking mess cleaned up, you whore!' He locked the door, then stormed downstairs then out the front door.

The boy stood up.

'Where are you going?'

'Checking on mum. Wait here.' He slowly walked out onto the small landing and glared at the lock on his parent's bedroom door. His little heart sank. At the door, he took a breath, pushed the bolt across, then edged the door open cautiously.

'Mum?'

Nothing.

He crept inside.

The room was in total darkness.

'Don't come in here,' said a weak voice.

'Mum, I—'

'I said don't come in here!'

Ignoring her, the boy stepped inside and turned the light on. The room came alive. What he saw he couldn't comprehend or understand.

On the bed, his mum was naked from the waist down. Blood covered her groin and most of the bed.

The boy was confused and started to cry.

His mum bolted up and fumbled with the bloody sheets to cover herself. Her eyes were red and sore. Her right cheek was purple with fresh bruising. 'I said don't come in here! Please leave.'

Crying, the boy turned away slowly and left.

'What happened?' the little girl asked when he returned to her room.

He shrugged, then cried into her arms. After he stopped, he looked at his sister, with tears streaming down his red face.

She saw something in his face, something in his eyes.

'I'm taking no more of this,' he said.

48

Toddington

She stared at herself in her vanity mirror, feeling a wave of guilt wash over her. The woman staring back held a strong glare and, suddenly, the guilt subsided. It was replaced with both anger and frustration.

After knowing what Jack had done, she didn't feel bad.

The time had come she could finally say she had had enough. Staying back and working late wasn't going to cut it anymore. Jesus, when he was home, he was either in the office or playing football with his friends.

God, he barely even wanted sex anymore.

'Look at me,' she whispered in the mirror. 'There's nothing wrong with me.'

Now she knew of the bank robbery, it made sense now why Jack had been different. Carrying the burden of such a lie would niggle away at anyone.

Joanne smiled at the woman in the mirror. As she stood, excitement tingled through her body. Soon, there'd be a knock at the door. At Jack's side of the bed, she opened the top drawer, searched for the mints he kept there – he took one before they had sex, whenever that was. The last time was last week, but before then, she couldn't even remember. A few months maybe?

Rummaging through the drawer, she realised the mints were not there, but she did see something unusual.

A white envelope.

Her eyebrows furrowed as she picked it out. 'What's this?' It was thick, padded. She turned it over, noticed it wasn't sealed, and used her fingers to open the flap.

Money.

She froze. 'What is this, Jack?' she whispered.

After taking the money out of the envelope, she counted it. Two-thousand pounds, exactly.

'Why is this money in here?'

She heard a sound downstairs – it was a knock at the door. She glanced at her watch. Ten to one.

'He's early.'

She'd literally just opened the front gate for his arrival.

She picked up the empty envelope off the carpet, put the money back in, and put it back where she found it. Then she went downstairs.

Joanne had asked Lucy earlier about her lessons planned for today, but it was all a show. She'd already looked in her bag last night to see her academic timetable. She knew she'd have three hours free on her own – the whole house to herself.

There were more knocks on the door. 'Okay, I'm coming,' she said, skipping down the hall. In her short white summer dress, just long enough to cover her bum, she turned the key and opened the door.

It wasn't who she was expecting.

Instead, a petite woman stood there on the gravel, looking up at her with a small crying baby in her arms.

49

Hembridge Bank
JACK

Inside my office, I put my briefcase on the desk and sighed. The little red light on the phone set indicated there were new voicemail messages. Deciding I wanted a coffee, I stood and navigated through the busy corridors without too much interaction and fuss.

Back in the office, the air was stuffy and stagnant. The sun burned through the window, the bright morning light pierced the grey Venetian blinds, projecting thin horizontal lines on my office wall. I slumped into my black swivel chair, turned on my computer, and listened to it whir to life.

Debra walked in, stopped at the corner of my large oak desk, and scowled at me.

I glanced up. 'Morning.'

She folded her arms.

'Good. Morning,' I said again, this time slower.

'Morning,' she said reluctantly. 'Where is it?' she asked.

'Where's what?'

'You know what, don't play games with me.'

'Close the door, please, Debra.' We both knew this conversation was only for us. No one could hear this. She did as I asked.

'It's here.' I reached down, grabbed the handle of my briefcase, and placed it on the desk. I entered the number code and opened it. The item I was looking for was not there. I stared blankly inside.

'What's the matter?' Her eyes narrowed.

'I don't have it,' I said, shrugging.

'Why? I wanted it on Friday, Jack. I'm counting on it.'

'Well, I don't —'

There was a knock on the door. Then it slowly swung open.

'Morning…' Ian said, unsure if the door was closed for a reason. 'You okay for a chat?'

'Just give me a minute, Ian. I'll ring your desk when Debra and I are finished, okay?'

'Yes okay. Just there's someone who wants to speak with you, waiting at the desk.'

I held a finger up. He nodded and closed the door.

Debra looked back at me. 'I want my money, Jack.' She folded her arms again.

'Well, I don't have it. I left it at home. I'll bring it tomorrow. If that's okay with you?'

'Yeah, whatever, don't forget it, because you're giving me that for a reason. I don't need to remind you, do I?'

I exaggerated a shake of my head.

'Don't take the piss, Jack,' she muttered before she turned, opened the door, and left.

Two-thousand pounds a month I gave Debra every month for her silence. It was blackmail, plain and simple.

Silence about our seedy little affair a few months ago.

50

Dunstable

'Where's the house?' DS Horton asked DCI Clarke, slowing the car to round the bend of Favell Drive.

Clarke looked up from a report. He glanced through the front windscreen. 'On the right up here, number forty-seven.' He focused back down to his lap.

Horton nodded and started searching for the house numbers on the right-hand side of the street. The odd numbers. He dabbed the brake when they were level with number forty-one and guided the car up the shallow grass verge outside of forty-seven. Usually, Clarke drove, but he needed time to read over the report of a stabbing that happened yesterday. Some poor old man let an energy consultant inside his home and, unfortunately, it didn't take him long to realise the man was, in fact, a fraud. He pulled a knife and asked for money. When the elderly man claimed to have nothing, the fraudster stabbed him in the stomach and fled the scene, leaving the elderly man fighting for his life in a pool of blood.

'All of that for nothing,' said Clarke, shaking his head in disgust.

Horton was already familiar with the report and nodded. He put the gear into neutral, applied the handbrake firmly, turned the key, and listened to the engine fade into silence.

'You got the report for this?' Clarke asked, pointing to number forty-seven.

'Yeah.' Horton leaned over and reached down for the thin black file near Clarke's feet. 'Here.'

'You read it yet?'

Horton nodded twice. 'Before we left.'

'On the ball this morning.'

'Someone needs to be…'

Clarke smiled, keeping his eye on the last few lines of the report in his hand. He sighed when he finished and placed it on the dashboard. 'Ready?'

'Let's do it,' Horton replied, opening his door.

Alison Lewes opened her white front door. She cautiously eyed Clarke and Horton.

'Good morning, sorry to bother you. I'm DCI Clarke of Bedfordshire Police.' He pointed to Horton. 'This is DS Horton. I was hoping this wasn't a bad time for us to come in and ask you a few questions?'

Alison was thin, of average height, with a flat chest. A ginger fringe covered her forehead to the top of her eyebrows. The rest of her hair was tied back in a bobble. She frowned. 'Is there something wrong? What's happened?'

'No, nothing is wrong, Alison,' Horton said, raising a settling palm. 'We understand the case about your husband, Peter Lewes, was never solved.' Horton paused for a second, thinking about the best way to phrase it. 'We've been allowed to look into the case again. Maybe we could shed a light on what happened.'

Alison gave them a blank stare.

'Could we come in?' asked Clarke, smiling politely.

'Yeah… sure. Come in.' She stepped back. 'It won't do you any good, though. The detectives on the case three years ago found nothing. I don't think you would either.'

'We understand your point of view, Mrs Lewes,' said Horton. 'But we'll do our very best, nonetheless.'

At the small square table in the kitchen, Alison placed two cups of coffee down in front of Clarke and Horton.

'Who was the one with sugar?' she asked.

Horton nodded. 'That's me, thanks.' She handed Clarke the other one.

'Thank you, Alison.'

She smiled and took a seat opposite them.

Horton sipped his hot coffee and then lowered it back to the table. 'We've read over the report earlier. We know what happened, so we won't – and don't – need to remind you. But, what we'd like to know, is if there's anything you didn't mention on your statement at the time. Something you've maybe remembered since?'

Alison bit her lower lip, deep in thought. 'Not since I went back and said about the taxi.'

'The taxi?' said Clarke, intrigued.

She nodded.

'What Taxi?' said Horton. There was no mention of a taxi in the report they had.

'The taxi that Peter got into the night he died.' She couldn't bring herself to say murdered. Many people couldn't. Murder was brutal, causing a deeper level of pain.

Clarke frowned at Horton.

'What's the matter?' she asked, seeing something tick over in Clarke's head.

'The report has no mention of him getting into a taxi that night. The list of events leading up to his death, according to your statement, and others is that he was last seen in the nightclub. The next person to see your husband was a woman who was out running later the same morning.'

Alison shook her head. 'On my original statement, I never mentioned the taxi, but a few days later, I remembered that on the night, he told me he'd phoned a taxi. I was out at the same time in the same club – Popworld I think it was called. I was with friends. He asked me if I wanted to go home with him, but I said no. I wanted to stay out to enjoy the rest of my night. It wasn't late. Maybe just before one in the morning. I remember the last thing he said to me before he kissed me.'

Clarke and Horton waited.

'That he couldn't wait till I got home and take my dress off.' A teary smile formed on her face. 'That was the last time I ever spoke to my husband.' Alison trailed off for a moment. 'By the time I got home, he wasn't there. I'd thought nothing of it at the time. I was drunk, could barely stand and, to be honest, hadn't even noticed him not in the bed. It was only when I woke up with a banging headache to the sound of a hard knock at the door. God… I'll never forget it. I answered the door to a detective who told me the dead body of my husband had been found in a park. I threw up on the doorstep.'

Horton nodded sadly.

The detectives ran through the events of the night, confirming her previous statement. She confirmed she was out with her best friend, Joanne Haynes, and a handful of others.

'Anything else you remember, Alison?' asked Clarke, with a notepad in his hand.

She tapped her chin with a finger. Then it looked like a new thought had come to her. 'Something I maybe never told the detective at the time.'

'What's that, Alison?'

'It was probably nothing.'

'What was it?'

'Across the dance floor of Popworld, I did see Peter arguing with one of his friends. Peter then pushed him. I remember that clearly.'

'Which friend was it?'

'Mark Haynes.'

Horton's eyes narrowed. 'A relative of Jack Haynes?'

Alison Lewes nodded. 'His brother.'

51

Toddington

Joanne, standing on her front doorstep, eyed the young woman holding the baby. 'Can I help you?'

'Oh, thank God you've answered,' the young woman said. 'I don't mean to be cheeky knocking on your door like this. It's the only house I could see. There's not many around here.'

'Okay…' Joanne nodded wearily.

The woman dipped her head in embarrassment, then leaned to one side to adjust the strap of her baby bag with her free hand. The bag looked heavy, weighing down on her slight frame. Joanne, for a second, recalled what having a baby was like. The items you needed to organise and carry everywhere you went were relentless. Even going to the shop sometimes wasn't worth the hassle.

The woman was attractive. Long dark hair covered the sides of her pleasant, warm face. A thin, gold necklace hung from her neck with a small, thin cross at the end of it, resting in the centre of her chest.

Joanne looked down at the baby, unsure if it was a boy or a girl.

'Could I please have some hot water for his bottle? He's starving.' As if the baby could comprehend her words, his cry deepened. The girl gently bounced him up and down to soothe him, then lowered her head to his, kissing him on the forehead. 'Please,' she begged.

Joanne was wary of the time, knowing that any minute, she was expecting a visitor. 'Do you need to ring someone?'

'No, thank you. I've got a phone,' the woman said. 'Just hot water, please. I have milk powder but no water. I was on my way home to feed him but decided, because he was in such a state, to pull over and feed him. Then I realised I had no hot water. Home is too far from here. It was a silly mistake.'

'Where's home?' Joanne's curious eyes watched her closely.

'Houghton Regis. Came from Woburn,' replied the woman. The baby's cry got louder.

'The A5 road would have been quicker,' suggested Joanne. With what had happened in the past week, Joanne was apprehensive about strangers. And rightly so. But how could she turn away a young mother with a crying baby?

'I know.' The mother dipped her head in shame. 'I'll know for next time,' she said quietly. She looked up, noticed the security camera pointing down at her, and froze for a moment. She was about to ask why it was there but decided to mind her own business.

Joanne stepped back and said, 'Okay, come on in love.'

'Thank you.' The young mother and baby followed Jo-anne to the kitchen. 'This is a lovely home, just beautiful.'

Joanne turned and gave her a polite nod. 'Come on, this way.'

In the kitchen, Joanne offered her a seat while she filled the kettle.

'Thanks.' The young mother placed her bag onto the table and, with her free hand, reached inside, pulling out a bib and a small box filled with milk powder. She glanced up, smiling at Joanne. To her left, she saw the vast area of green land out of the window. 'Wow, what a view.'

Joanne followed her gaze. 'Beautiful, isn't it?'

The sound of the kettle rumbled in the background of their idle chit chat and Joanne started to feel more comfortable with the young woman.

'What's his name?'

The mother looked down at the baby, whose cry had now quietened. He was too busy chewing on a teething toy. 'He's called Logan, this one.'

'He's lovely. How old is he?'

'Just over six months. It's flying by, it really is. And what's strange is that I can't remember my life without him.'

Joanne nodded in understanding. She knew what it was like with Lucy at that age. The long, hard sleepless nights soon passed, and life seemed to fly by. She recently read a quote somewhere. It read: the nights are long, but the years are short. And it was so true.

'Do you have children?' she asked.

'Just the one. Girl. She was eighteen.'

The young woman smiles. 'You don't look old enough for a daughter to be eighteen! How old are you… if you don't mind me asking – sorry, I'm being intrusive.'

'Don't worry about it,' Joanne said. 'I'm fifty.'

The young woman puts her palm to her mouth. 'You are not?'

Joanne nodded.

'Is she hard work at that age?'

Joanne thought for a moment. 'It's a difficult age, I suppose. But don't worry, I heard boys are easier – you'll do great.'

The woman half-smiled.

'How much water do you need – have you got a bottle to put it in?'

'Oh yeah, sorry, I should have said.' The woman grabbed an empty bottle from inside her bag and held it out for Joanne. 'Erm, fill it to the number six mark. I'm trying to cut him down with his milk. I've started him on food last week.'

Jo stepped forward and grabbed the bottle. 'And how's that going?'

'So far so good.'

'He doesn't seem hungry anymore?' Jo said, staring at the baby. 'He seemed quite content.'

The comment stiffened the woman into silence who only smiled in response. She then pulled her phone from her bag and tapped on the screen. As Joanne watched the water fill up to the number six mark, she heard tires crunch on the gravel outside.

Joanne moved over to the table with the bottle in her hand, handed it to the woman, and said, 'Just a second, there's someone at my door.'

She was expecting to see a blue Range Rover.

But as she opened the door, she realised it was not blue, nor was it a Range Rover.

It was a black van.

Parked a few feet from the door.

The two men inside the van were dressed in black. They opened their doors and stepped out onto the gravel, both giving her a cold, hard stare.

Joanne froze to the step. The fear in her eyes flicked between them.

They ran towards the front of the van and charged toward her.

52

Toddington

Joanne darted back into the house but tripped on the lip of the front door and almost toppled backward. She grabbed the handle of the door which prevented her fall and found her feet. With everything she had, she threw it closed. Before it closed, a large boot smashed into it and the door swung open fast, colliding with Joanne's hip, knocking her backward. She yelped in pain and crashed onto the wooden floor in the hallway.

A thick hand grabbed the edge of the door and opened it.

'Hello, Mrs Haynes,' said Derek, stepping through the threshold.

Conscious of the woman and baby in the kitchen, she frantically turned her head and shouted in their direction.

No reply.

Joanne, laying on her side with her right hand pressed on her throbbing hip, glared at the small, chunky figure standing in the doorway of her home. He moved closer to her.

'You're coming with us, Mrs Haynes.'

'Who – who the hell are you?' she screamed. 'Leave me alone!'

'Come on,' said Derek, 'don't be like that.' He bent toward her with eyes filled with excitement and tried to grab her but she shuffled backward out of his reach.

'No! Please get out of my house.' She angled her head to the kitchen. 'Help me! Please!'

Derek laughed loudly, pointing towards the kitchen. 'Her?' He laughed even louder. 'Who do you think told us you were alone?'

Fear rippled through Joanne's blood. She stared at Derek, now realising what was happening.

It was a setup. The little bitch had set her up.

Through the open door, her fear multiplied as a second man entered. Tall and thin, with prominent cheekbones, he had a look of determination plastered on his face. 'Oh, lovely house, indeed,' said Stuart.

The woman holding the baby walked from the kitchen into the hallway with the baby in one arm, her bag on the other. Avoiding Joanne on the floor, she stepped around her and stopped in front of Stuart. Stuart leaned forward and kissed her on the cheek.

'Thank you. I'll sort you out later,' he said, rubbing her arm gently.

The small woman let out a half-smile and nodded. Her sheepish body language indicated to Joanne the woman feared these men. Maybe she was forced to do it. The woman with the baby moved past Stuart, hurried down onto the gravel and out of sight, the sounds of the crying baby dissolving into the warm summer day.

'You fucking bitch!' Joanne cried through the open door towards her.

Stuart scowled. 'There's no need for nastiness, is there?'

Derek, only a foot away from Joanne, leaned down to grab her again. She threw a clenched fist at his chubby face. His head juddered a little, but the feeble attempt didn't inflict any pain. He laughed and tried again but she kicked him in the shin.

'You fucking little bitch!' Derek grunted.

The smell of sweat, fear, and the nearest farm filled the hallway.

'Leave me alone,' cried Joanne. She slid back towards the wall away from him. Her heart thumped through her chest like nothing she had ever felt.

'Leave me alone,' Stuart said in a high-pitched mockery.

'My husband is coming back any minute now,' Joanne shouted.

'Your husband is at work,' said Stuart, shaking his head. 'So, that's a lie. Please don't lie.'

'You wait here,' Stuart told Derek. 'I'll check the house, and make sure she is alone.' Derek nodded and watched Stuart climb the stairs two at a time, his slim frame dashing up them with ease.

Derek looked back down at Joanne, who now had her back against the wall. Her eyes were sore. Her face was wet with tears. 'Now it's my time to play,' whispered Derek. Joanne silently cried as stared down at her busty cleavage, then he lowered to her tanned, bare legs.

Derek licked his thick lips, his focus now below her stomach, imagining what was inside her white underwear.

Joanne, as if reading his thoughts, stared up at him in disgust. She wriggled along the wall to her left, fighting the pain in her hip to get away from this monster. Something vibrated in her back pocket, the ringing sound of an incoming call echoed through the silent hallway.

'Don't even bother answering that,' Derek told her.

Sitting in the passenger seat of her friend's Astra, Lucy pulled her phone away from her ear.

'She's not answering,' said Lucy. 'She must be busy.'

'We'll be late, you know?' said Lisa, conscious of the time on the dashboard. She flicked the indicator on as they approached the junction of Park road and dabbed the brake to slow the car.

'I know,' said Lucy. 'But Mr Flann said he needs this assignment in. He said not to bother turning up if you didn't have it.'

Lisa rolled her eyes, not impressed having to go back. 'You should've remembered.'

Lucy sighed. 'Don't you think I know that?' She returned her focus to her phone. 'I'll try ringing my mum again.'

The blue Astra turned into Park Road, Lisa steadily moving through the gears accelerating into the glare of the sun. In the distance, Lisa squinted at a petite woman walking on the side of the road holding a baby. 'Strange place to go for a walk.'

'Hmmm?'

'A woman walking with a baby on the grass verge. Look.'

Lucy followed her friend's finger, briefly locking eyes on the woman as they whizzed by her. 'Yeah, weird.'

Lisa slowed the car to make the turn.

Lucy looked up. 'The gates might be—' She saw the gates were fully open and frowned. 'What the?'

'What's up?' Lisa asked, showing concern.

'We keep the gates locked all the time,' Lucy explained.

Lisa went through the gates, followed the winding driveway until she suddenly broke, bringing the car to a sudden halt.

'Lucy?'

'You see that?'

Lucy nodded quickly. 'Yes.'

'Whose van is that?' Lisa asked.

The black van was parked at an angle, with both doors open. The front grill of the van was parked almost on the front doorstep. They both noticed the front door was wide open.

'I – I don't know,' Lucy said. Her face turned white and she started to tremble.

Lisa looked at Lucy with concern, opened her mouth to speak, but the sound stopped her. The scream from inside the house.

53

Toddington

Lisa watched Lucy freeze in the passenger seat of the Astra, her face a ghost-like colour between her lengthy blonde hair. Lisa's skin grew cold, the feeling of icy fingers crawling up her spine.

'Who is it?' muttered Lisa.

'I - I don't know,' Lucy stuttered.

Without hesitation, she tapped nine three times on her phone keypad and hit CALL.

'Who are you calling?'

'The police,' said Lucy. 'I need to call the police.'

Lisa frowned at her. 'Why?'

Lucy waved her question away, demanding silence as the phone started to ring in her ear. Lisa fell quiet. When the call was answered, Lucy explained there had been a break-in at her house. She gave the address and asked them to send help as fast as they could.

'What the hell is going on?' Lisa said, watching Lucy pull the phone away from her ear.

'We had a break in last week.' Lucy turned to Lisa with wide eyes. 'Men came in looking for something. They threatened us. We had the police involved. I think it's something to do with that.' Lucy looked back at the black van and the front door with wide eyes. 'Oh, Mum!'

Lisa raised her palm to her open mouth. 'God.'

Lucy leaned into the passenger door to open it—

'Where the hell are you going?' Lisa shouted, grabbing her arm to hold her back. Warm air flooded through the open passenger door, filling the front of the car with the smell of manure from a nearby farm.

Lucy threw her left hand forward. 'My mum! I can't just leave her,' she explained. 'I need to help her!'

Lisa saw a combination of helplessness, fear, anger, and love in her friend's eyes. 'Wait till the police get here. They can go in.'

Lucy dipped her head, staring at the footwell. 'I, I—'

A scream rippled from the open door of the house again.

Lisa grabbed her forearm. 'Please just wait till the pol—'

A loud crunch coming from behind the car silenced Lisa. They both glared at each other, unknown fear dancing between their terrified eyes. They twisted their necks cautiously in unison, staring through the small rear-view window.

The interior of the Astra grew dark as the large vehicle behind blocked the afternoon light which stopped a few metres behind them. Lucy saw the badge on the grill, below the lip of the bonnet. A Range Rover.

The driver's door opened.

Lisa whipped her head back to Lucy. 'Who the hell is this?'

The man was huge, well over six feet four. His muscular chest stuck out with muscle. His shoulder muscles bulged through the dark material of a thin hoody. He closed the door and stepped forward.

'I – I don't think it's the police, Lucy,' Lisa whispered, her voice unsure.

Lucy silently stared at the stranger who was standing behind them. The man had a menacing stare. He didn't move. Instead, he absorbed the scene before him: the large house to which he had been invited; an open front door; a black van parked at an angle; a blue BMW (which he knew was Joanne's); a small Astra parked in front of him with two girls inside watching him.

He narrowed his gaze at the Astra, towards Lucy and Lisa. With their heads turned towards him, he met their innocent stares, seeing the fear in their young faces. 'What the fuck is going on?' he whispered to himself.

'Lucy, I don't like this,' said Lisa. 'Not one bit.'

Lucy took a breath, mentally collecting herself, and opened the door slowly. Lucy turned to face the large man. He was wearing an almost skin-tight dark hoody, arms the size of beer kegs, and below, tight light blue jeans, and white plimsols. His face was tanned. Below his short hair, a three-day stubble lined the bottom half of his face.

Their eyes met.

'Who are you?' she said, scowling at him.

The man remained still, staring blankly, unsure. In his mind, when he turned up, her daughter would be at college, and he'd go inside, take Joanne's clothes off, finally see what her body looked like, and get the chance to do what he had been wanting to do.

'Well,' said Lucy, pulling him away from his thoughts. 'Who are you?' Lucy nudged forward a touch, her finger jabbing the air, demanding an answer.

The man raised his wrist a few inches, glanced down at his watch. He was pretty sure Joanne had told him 1 p.m. Why were there three cars here? Why all the activity? He looked past Lucy to the open front door. Something wasn't right.

Lucy let her frustration show. 'Hey, I'm talking to you!'

'I'm looking for Joanne,' the man explained, his eyes flicking back to Lucy's young face. 'Is she here?'

Lucy absorbed his words and squinted at him, but finally nodded. 'She's inside.' Her finger pointed to the door and as if on cue, they heard a scream. 'There are men inside. They've broken in. My mum needs help!'

The large man's eyes widened. A focused determination swept across his face staring at the open door. This must be Lucy, the eighteen-year-old daughter Joanne had told him about.

'You need to help her, please,' pleaded Lucy. She didn't know the man from Adam but right now, he was the closest thing to help. 'Please, she's in trouble.'

'Okay.' He nodded sternly.

Another scream came from inside the house, disturbing the silent air.

He turned quickly and dashed across the gravel to the rear of his Range Rover. He opened the boot, leaned in, and grabbed something.

Lucy stared at him with weary eyes when she saw him.

The determination on his face was comforting to Lucy, but what he was holding in his hand wasn't.

A shotgun.

54

Toddington

Stuart trotted back down the stairs and was satisfied Joanne was alone in the house. He was heavy on his feet as he descended, intently dragging his dirty boots on the white carpet. He'd noticed they'd been cleaned since he was last there with the other men last Thursday.

He stepped down onto the wooden floor of the hallway. 'Nothing up here, Derek,' he said. 'She was home alone, there's – what the fuck are you doing?'

Stuart stared at Derek in revulsion.

Derek was on top of Joanne, one of his chubby, dirty hands smothering her mouth, whilst the other, grabbed at her large breasts. She frantically kicked and flayed her arms, wriggling like a fish out of water, but his little stumpy body was too heavy for her.

'Derek!' he shouted.

Derek stopped suddenly and eased back from Joanne.

'What?' He gave Stuart a careless shrug, then focused back to Joanne, rubbing his crotch where he had become hard. A smile grew on the corner of his lips.

Stuart took a step forward, shaking his head. 'Derek, you need—'

In midstride, Stuart froze.

Something caught his eye. The hallway became a little darker. Something blocked the light coming through the front door. A huge man entered slowly, with a shotgun held out in front of him. Derek hadn't seen him, but Stuart eyed him with both curiosity and awe. He couldn't believe his size.

The man with the shotgun stopped two feet behind Derek, who was still standing over Joanne. He hadn't seen him. Stuart knew Derek wasn't tall but was shocked at how much the man dwarfed Derek. Joanne winced again when Derek lunged forward to grab her.

Joanne screamed and wriggled beneath his fat, stumpy body.

'Hey!' The deep, harsh voice echoed through the hallway. 'Get the fuck off her!'

Derek halted suddenly with wide eyes and the hallway fell dead quiet. Derek turned very slowly in the direction of the demand. The first object he saw was the end of a twin barrel shotgun inches from his face.

'Shit,' he whispered. Behind the gun, he noticed the man holding it and, for a second, a pocket of air clogged in his throat.

Joanne, lying on the floor with sore, red eyes, gasped in relief when she saw the man standing in the doorway. 'Help me, Henry, please.'

Stuart, at the base of the stairs, weighed up the situation. He was currently about eight feet from the shotgun. The man was big. Maybe that meant he'd be slow.

'Get. The. Fuck. Away. From. Her,' Henry told Derek. The authority of his demand was menacing. Stuart saw the man's arms and how big they were in the tight t-shirt he was wearing.

Stuart said, 'Okay, okay, big man, just calm it—'

'Shut the fuck up!' Henry cut him off, turning his head in Stuart's direction. Stuart raised his palms in the air in mild surrender.

'Okay, man, okay,' replied Stuart.

'Come on, fat boy, I won't ask you again.' Henry nudged the gun an inch in the direction he wanted him to move.

Derek nodded and moved towards Stuart near the stairs. Joanne let out a desperate sigh.

'Are you okay?' Henry asked Joanne. She nodded several times. Henry watched a tear fall down her cheek which only angered him further. 'What did they do to you?'

'He was feeling my boobs and trying the take my pants off!' Joanne pointed in disgust at Derek.

Henry turned the tip of the gun towards the men. 'Is that awful story true? Did you do that to her?'

Guilt washed over Derek's round chubby face and he gave a small, shameful nod.

'Come here,' said Henry.

'What?' Derek asked.

'Step forward, please. Now.'

Joanne, still on the floor, watched the scene play out, wondering what he was going to do.

Derek cocked his head, looking for guidance from Stuart, who just shrugged at him. He knew being silent was the best thing to do. Derek stared back at Henry. 'Why?'

Henry tilted his head back and sighed heavily. 'Don't make me ask you again, fat boy.'

Derek dipped his head, and moved forward with caution, taking slow steps across the wooden floor, keeping his eyes on the big man.

'Come on, that's it, don't be shy,' teased Henry, waving the gun left and right.

'Bet you're not as tough without that gun in your hand, eh?' commented Stuart.

Henry ignored Stuart's childish attempt to provoke a re-action and kept his eyes on Derek, who was two feet from him. Derek tilted his head back to look up at him, opening his mouth to speak but, before any words come out, Henry shoved the tip of the shotgun up into his chin with so much force, the loud crack made Stuart and Joanne flinch. Metal against bone. The impact was so hard, Derek almost did a cartwheel as he collided with the wooden floor and shrieked in pain.

His face was hot, soaked in warm blood pouring from the gash under his bottom lip.

Stuart moves suddenly—

'Don't even fucking think about it, mate,' advised Henry. 'Or you can... That's up to you?' He smiled at him.

Stuart remained still. 'What do you want?'

'I want you both to fuck off, and never come back here again. Do you understand?'

Stuart nodded firmly. 'Come on, let's go,' he told Derek, who was mumbling on the floor holding his chin with blood-soaked hands. The crimson liquid seeped onto the wooden floor around him. Stuart bent down and grabbed his arm. 'Get the fuck up, now!'

He helped Derek out of the house and into the passenger seat of the black van, then ran around the bonnet, jumped in the driver's door, and started the engine.

'We'll be back, you know,' Stuart said, through the open window of the driver's door to Henry.

'And I'll be waiting here with this.'

The van tires spun, kicking up gravel as it accelerated down the winding driveway towards the road. They took a right, then disappeared.

Henry lowered to Joanne and helped her up off the floor. She hugged him tightly.

'Thank you.'

After he told her that Lucy was outside she raced to the door, threw her arms around her, and cried.

Lucy asked Joanne who the man was.

'The plumber. We're getting work done,' Joanne told her.

Henry frowned, unsure how to take it but played along.

'We need to ring the police,' said Joanne.

'I already have,' Lucy informed her.

The wail of police sirens rippled through the distant air. They all looked up in the direction of the sound.

Henry quickly put the shotgun back into the boot of the Range Rover.

'Maybe a good idea if we don't mention the shotgun, okay?' he said to all of them.

55

Hembridge Bank
JACK

The clock above the door in my office told me it was 1.30 p.m. On the desk, my phone rang. It was Joanne. I picked it up and put it to my ear.

'Hello,' I said.

'Jack, you need to come home!' Her voice was full of emotion.

'What's happened?' I stopped typing on the computer, leaned back, and zoned out away from work.

She told me about the two men breaking into the house, and attacking her.

'Jesus, are you okay?' I asked, pressing a hand firmly on my head.

'Yeah,' she said, then sniffed, as if she'd been crying.

I put the phone down on my desk and sighed heavily. 'Fucking hell,' I whispered. I kicked the swivel chair back, stood up, put my jacket on, and collected my things. A minute later, I leaned into John's office to inform him I needed to go and, that if anyone needed me, they could reach me on my mobile.

He wished me well and returned to the paperwork in front of him. I made my way through the back offices and out the back door. I got into my Volvo, fired it up, and headed home.

As I slowed the XC90 down, turning into my driveway, I followed the snaking gravel until I saw more vehicles than I expected to. In addition to Joanne's blue BMW, there was a Range Rover, an Astra, and a marked police car. I stopped the Volvo behind the BMW, shut the engine off, and stepped down onto the gravel wearing a frown on my face.

Before I reached the front door, Lucy opened it, stepped out, and hugged me.

'Hey,' I said, leaning into her. 'You okay?'

She squeezed me tightly. 'Yeah.'

'Where's Mum?'

'Kitchen with the police.'

I stepped into the hallway, noticed the damage to the front door, then closed it behind me gently. My eyes picked up movement in the kitchen down the hall. My ears detected voices, some of which I recognised. I followed Lucy into the kitchen and a flood of silence erupted inside the space. All eyes were on me.

DCI Clarke and DS Horton both gave me polite smiles.

'Mr Haynes,' DCI Clarke said, by way of greeting.

'Hi,' I replied. To my left, standing at the back door, a large man half-smiled at me but I didn't recognise him.

Joanne swivelled on her chair. 'Oh God, Jack!' She got up, wrapped her arms around me, and started to sob – I felt her body shake against mine. I noticed she was wearing her best summer dress which she only wore for certain occasions because of its revealing short length.

'Hey, hey, come on,' I said, rubbing her back. 'It's okay.'

'Please could you sit down, Mr Haynes,' said DS Horton in a tone that suggested he felt awkward for breaking up the hug. I glanced at him, gave him a nod, and dropped into a seat at the table.

'What's happened?' I asked.

DCI Clarke ran through the events, starting with Joanne letting the young mother in with her child.

I turned to the large man. Our eyes met. He was muscular, good-looking, and tanned, probably from frequent use of a sunbed. Jesus, he must be six feet six. Almost as wide, too. I asked him, 'Who are you?'

With confidence, he came over from the door and leaned over, holding out his big hand. 'Hi, I'm Henry.' I adjusted my body towards him, leaning sideways to shake it. He nearly crushed my hand.

'He's a plumber,' said Joanne quickly.

I frowned at Joanne. 'Plumber – why do we need a plumber – do we have a leak?'

Henry stepped away silently, not offering an answer to my question.

'Yeah… I called him. He came to look at the bathroom,' Joanne added.

'There's nothing wrong with the bathroom – we had it done last year.' I looked away from my wife, made brief eye contact with Henry. 'Did we have a leak?'

'I wanted a new shower,' Joanne said, pulling my attention back towards her. 'I phoned him.' Joanne tilted her head towards Henry and nodded, but he didn't respond with any form of gesture to confirm or deny her claims. A look of anger took over his face.

'Listen, Jack,' Henry said, 'I need a word with you.'

I frowned at him.

'In private, please,' he added, pointing in the direction of the front door. 'Maybe outside?'

'Sure,' I said, 'we'll go outside.'

Joanne looked unsettled. 'But you need—'

'No,' Henry interrupted her with his big palm. 'I need to speak to *your* husband.'

As Henry made a move towards the kitchen door, DCI Clarke said, 'Could we have a statement from you?'

'After I've had a word with Jack,' Henry replied, walking away from them. Clarke said nothing, instead, smiled awkwardly, watching Henry duck under the top of the door-frame.

Standing up from the chair, I followed him down the hallway.

'Jack,' cried Joanne, but I ignored her.

Henry reached the front door, opened it, and stepped outside onto the gravel. As I reached the step, he turned to face me. Although I was standing on the step, we were eye to eye, six inches apart.

He spoke softly, 'Listen, Jack. I think you know the situation here. Do you know why I'm here? Obviously, I'm not a plumber.'

I slowly nodded, but I didn't want to succumb to the truth of my thoughts. This couldn't be happening.

'All I knew is that she had a daughter. I didn't know she was married,' he explained, lowering his muscular arms down by his sides. His body was none threatening.

'Did she not tell you?' I said. My stomach churned into twisted knots.

He shook his head once. 'She told me she was a single mother, living alone with her daughter.'

His words hit me like a knife to the heart. Why would my wife say that? I dipped my head and looked down near his feet. My blood started to boil, my body trembled with anger and rage. Tears formed in my eyes, but I held them back.

'Honestly?' I asked, flicking my focus back to his face.

He zoned in on me with his piercing blue eyes. 'Yes, honestly, Jack.' He paused for a few seconds. 'I didn't know your situation here with those men and the police, but I could honestly say, man to man, I didn't know she was married. I'm glad that I came here to get them thugs off her. I'm also glad I found out the truth. About you and her. So, I want to apologise for this, and I promise you won't see me again.'

I rubbed the inside of my upper lip with my tongue, then asked, 'Are you married?'

He looked away from me in embarrassment. 'Yes,' he said.

'Then you know how awful this is, don't you?' I said, finding strength in my voice again.

'My wife and I are... well, we're complicated,' he explained. 'We have so many issues, that, well, make life difficult – makes our relationship difficult. I'd have never come here if I knew she was married.'

'Where did you meet?'

'At the gym, the one on —'

'I know which gym,' I said.

His words seem genuine. He seemed genuine. But there was one question I needed him to answer before anything else.

'Have you and her...?'

He shook his head. 'No. But I'll be honest with you. I came here today to do just that. But no, we haven't.'

Relief washed over me, but my heart was broken. Whether they had or hadn't, the intent was there.

He nodded his head towards the kitchen. 'They want me to give an official statement. They know what's happened, I've already told them – they've made notes.' He paused. 'If it's okay with you, I'd rather not go back inside *your* house and see Joanne and your daughter – it feels wrong.' He held out a large hand. 'Once again, I'm sorry. I'm going to leave you to it. I hope whatever situation you're in, you fix it. You seem like a good guy.'

Staring at his gigantic hand, I pondered whether to shake it. The realisation that it wasn't his fault dawned on me – it was Joanne's fault. I took his hand and squeezed it firmly.

After he gave me a small nod he turned, made his way to his Range Rover, and climbed inside. I watched him leave until he passed through the gates. He didn't look back. No goodbye wave.

The skies above turned dark. The sun hid behind a thick, grey cloud. I took a deep breath and headed back inside.

In the kitchen, Joanne was standing at the kettle with her back to me. She heard me enter but she didn't turn. I noticed her body stiffen. Lucy was sitting at the table on her phone but looked up when I approached the table.

'Henry has gone,' I informed them.

Joanne swivelled. I gazed into her sad, glassy eyes for a moment until she turned away.

'He's gone?' Clarke asked.

I nodded.

'We didn't get a statement from him,' Horton added.

'Well he's gone,' I said firmly. 'He said you guys know what's happened. He told me was sorry about all this and said he wasn't coming back to this house ever again.'

The detectives both looked away from me, feeling the sensitivity of the situation before them. Clarke mentioned the camera system that we had installed. I nodded, stood up, and led them both into the study. Lucy and Joanne soon followed, standing behind us. Over ten minutes, we watched the events unfold, starting with the girl knocking on the door with the baby. We saw the black van pull up, but we don't see any of the registration plate. Horton didn't hide his disappointment. When the men jumped out, I paused it.

'They look familiar?' Clarke asked.

I nodded. 'Yes, they do.'

He gave me a quizzical stare.

'They were parked here the other night in a black van. Mark and I…' I saw the confusion on his face. 'Mark – my brother. We went out to speak with them to ask them what they were doing.'

'Then what?' Clarke stared with concern.

'A detective turned up to save the day.'

'Which detective?' Horton this time.

I shrugged. 'I didn't get a name.'

I know he was called Andrew Johnson, but he made it clear he knew about the bank money, so I decided not to mention the name.

'Why didn't you tell me? Joanne said, standing at the kettle.

'I didn't want to worry you.'

We continued the recording right up until Henry arrived.

Clarke squinted, leaned closer. 'He had a gun?'

'Why does he have a gun?' Horton said, to no one specifically.

'Maybe he's a farmer?' I suggested.

After the detectives inserted a memory stick into the computer, they copied the video footage of what had happened. They told me they could provide a patrol car to watch our house for the rest of the day. I agreed with the idea and thanked them.

They stood and headed for the hallway.

'Oh, before we leave,' Clarke said. He stopped and turned. 'Could we ask you a few questions about Peter Lewes?'

'Alison's husband?' Joanne asked, confused.

Clarke nodded at her, then returned his focus to me. 'Is there anything that you remember about that night? Anything at all?'

'Why are you asking this?' Joanne asked. 'He was killed three years ago – poor Alison is trying to get over this.'

Horton held up an apologetic palm. 'It's routine.'

I pondered the question. 'I gave my statement a few days after it happened. I was out that night with him. There was me, my brother, him, a few other mates—'

'Your brother?' Clarke confirmed. 'Mark Haynes?'

'Yes.' I tilted my head. 'Why are you asking me this?' I watched Clarke jot something down on his small notepad. 'Why the questions, detective?'

'We've been asked to look into something, and it's important we ask,' he explained.

I gave an unsure nod. 'Okay.'

Both detectives turned and walked out of the study towards the front door.

I watched them climb into their car and waited until they went, then pressed the fob to close the gates behind them.

On the front doorstep, I turned to Joanne, and said, 'We need to talk.'

56

Toddington
JACK

I followed Joanne into the bedroom. She sat down on the bed. I took a seat next to her. My insides hurt. My brain buzzed. I closed the door gently.

I noticed the embarrassment course through her. The way her face dipped, the way she slouched her shoulders. For a second, I imagined her up here with Henry. The door closed. His big hands around her, caressing her back, kissing her, pulling off her dress, seeing her in the flesh, *feeling* her exposed naked skin whilst he was on top of her —

I clamped my eyes closed to shake away the thoughts and suppressed my boiling anger. My profession at the bank taught me more ways than one to deal with upsetting situations or difficulties when communicating with others. Time to control my own emotions.

Her face was blank. She stared at the carpet near her feet, unsure what to say. She looked sad. And rightfully so.

'Well?'

She sniffed and gave me a half smile.

I waited.

'Jack, I'm so sorry,' she said quietly.

I nodded once.

'No, really, I am.'

'I believe you,' I said, looking away. My eyes fell on her vanity table in the centre of the wall in front of me. I looked back, watched a tear fall from her eyes onto the bed covers between us.

'Why, Jo?' I said. 'Why has it come to this – I thought we were happy?'

A small shake of the head. 'I – I don't know, Jack. We were happy – we *are* happy, it's just…'

'Just what?'

'You're never here. You're always working. And when you are home, you're still working. When I see you, I try to talk, try to have a conversation. All you do is either sit in the study, or you're out playing football with Paul, Neil and… what's he called?'

'Kev.'

'Yeah… Kev,' she said. 'And when you're not doing that, you're reading.' She looked away for a moment. 'I know people change, and life changes, but I want to feel alive. I want you to want me.'

'*I do* want you,' I said clearly.

'I need to see it, Jack, I need to feel it.' Our eyes met again. 'You know, I was looking forward to Barcelona for your cousin's wedding. Getting away from this. From work. A break, just us. Together. But even that didn't pan out the way I'd hoped.' She threw out her hands in despair for a moment then lowered them back to her bare legs.

We sat in silence for what felt like a long time before I said, 'Why him? Why Henry?'

She shrugged. 'He gave me attention – he wanted me.'

'You mean like this?' I said, grabbing her right breast and squeezing it, feeling the perfect weight of it.

She let out a sad smile.

The feeling of anger built up so much that I leaned into her and kissed her passionately. I then shoved her onto the bed, which she allowed, and found myself pushing the sides of her dress up with both hands revealing her white, thin underwear. I yanked them off, slid them down her tanned, bare legs, and throw them onto the floor. I felt myself getting hard as I stood up quickly, loosened the catch on my trousers, and let them fall to the carpet. I climbed on top of her.

It didn't last long at all, but it was the most intense, exciting encounter I'd ever had with Joanne. With anyone, in fact. Just a shame it took a situation for her to almost do it with someone else to instigate it.

With my white shirt still on, I rolled off her slowly, fell onto my back, sighing heavily. I heard her breathing heavily next to me. For a while, we didn't say anything. Then I felt her squeeze my hand.

'I'm sorry, Jack,' she said again.

'It's okay, Jo.' Maybe she was right. I'm never here for her. I've been putting work first since I was promoted. All I ever wanted to do was please the company. To be a good director of Finance, keep things ticking along, making positive changes here and there. But it was clear to me now. It had affected things at home. My marriage. The thing with Debra a few months ago was bad, if not, worse. It *was* on the tip of my tongue to tell her, but I ended up on top of her and I felt the moment had passed.

I stood up, pulled my trousers back up, and tied the catch.

'Jack,' she said.

'Yeah?'

'I found an envelope in your drawer with two-thousand pounds in it.' I felt blood starting to ring in my ears. 'What's it for?'

I pondered an answer quickly, although this would be the perfect time to tell her about Debra. About how I paid Debra every month for her silence.

'I...' I tried to think, weighing up being honest and lying '...was going to buy you something.'

She grimaced. 'Me?'

I nodded. 'Yeah. I felt with everything that had gone on, and for you putting up with me working the long hours that I do, I wanted to buy you something nice and make you smile.'

A smile swept across her face and I did my best to hide the bullshit.

'Aww,' she said. 'What were you going to buy?'

I tapped the side of my nose indicating it was a secret, although I now knew I'd have to come up with something within a few days. She smiled, got up from the bed, and opened her wardrobe, looking for something more comfortable – and suitable - to wear.

I went to the en-suite, cleaned myself up, and returned to the bedroom. 'You sure you're okay going with Mark to the poker tonight?'

She turned from the wardrobe and nodded. 'Yes. Why?'

'Just checking you're happy doing it,' I explained with a smile.

'Yeah.' She returned to the wardrobe.

'Jo,' I said. 'Did Lucy give you a box?'

Slowly, she turned again to face me with a quizzical look on her face. 'A box?'

'Yeah, I found a box upstairs.' I pointed above our heads. 'When we were hiding up there last Thursday.' I lowered my hand and, with both hands, replicate the size of the box. 'About this big. Made of old leather. Things inside rattled. It had a lock on it. Did Lucy give it to you?'

As her frown deepened, she tapped her chin. 'No, I - I don't remember her giving it to me. When did she say that?'

'This morning I think.'

'No, I don't remember, Jack.'

'Oh, okay. Maybe she made a mistake.'

Joanne smiled, returning her focus to the rail of clothes inside the wardrobe.

'I'll be downstairs,' I said, leaving.

'Okay. I won't be long.'

Joanne waited almost a minute to make sure Jack had gone. She crept across the carpet towards the door, peered silently out onto the landing. No one there. She padded lightly back across to the wardrobe, reached up to the shelf above the clothes rail, and, leaning towards the back, she lifted a dark blue folded jumper out.

The jumper wasn't important. What was important is what the jumper was covering.

She glared inside, smiling at it.

The little leather box Lucy had given her.

57

Toddington
JACK

My phone rang on the kitchen worktop. It was Mark. I picked it up and answered. The kitchen clock told me it was just before 7 p.m., and I mentally noted they had an hour until the poker game started.

I told Mark to turn the engine off and come inside to wait for Joanne. I hang up the phone and listened to the sound of the hairdryer roaring through the house.

Outside the window the clouds darkened, shades of unexpected grey hanging over the fields out the back, drawing in what felt like an early night. The stuffy air in the kitchen lingered with the smell of noodles and fairy liquid.

I sighed loudly. My head throbbed. I was nervous and scared. I didn't know what was going to happen. If we won the money, I could pay Ray back. I could pay the dickhead on the phone back, and then we were in the clear. If they didn't win, worst case scenario, is I've lost the fifty-thousand pounds. And I'm still in the same shit situation.

If only things were simple.

I heard the front door open.

'Hey, Jackos!' Mark's voice rippled down the hallway, then I heard the slapping of his polished black shoes on the tiled floor as he stepped into the kitchen. He was very smart. Black suit, white shirt with the top button undone. His appearance was smart enough, although not perfect, which carried certain confidence.

'Mr smarty pants,' I said, smiling.

'You like?'

I nodded confidently. 'I like.'

'Elaine wasn't too sure. She told me to wear something else. I told her I'll do what I want.' His defiance brought a smile to my face. He took a seat at the table. I moved over to join him.

On my dinner, earlier in the day, just before Joanne had rung about the men attacking her, I had collected fifty thousand for Mark's buy-in for tonight's game. During the morning, Ray had lingered near my office door, like a fly around shit, wanting answers and dropping subtle hints about the robbery. As if telling someone was on the tip of his tongue. But I didn't say much to Ray. I had nothing to say to him. I opened a short email he'd sent: *Any luck with what we discussed?*

After the fourth email, without me replying, he'd knocked on my door. I told him it was getting sorted and to get the fuck out of my office. He reminded me the deadline was Wednesday.

Two days.

It was getting sorted.

'Jack,' Mark said, 'why's there a police car outside your house.' He pointed in the direction of the brick wall running down the side of the driveway.

'Long story,' I said.

'We have time, Joanne isn't ready. Tell me.' He rolled his eyes above his head before he settled his focus back on me.

'A woman came today with a baby, knocked on the door,' I said. Mark nodded. 'It was a setup – two men came and attacked her.'

His eyes widened. 'Jesus.'

I let out a sad smile.

'Is she – is she okay?' He leaned forward, sliding his elbows closer to the middle of the table.

'She'll be okay,' I said. I decided to say nothing more, especially about Henry turning up and saving the day with a condom in his pocket and a shotgun under his arm.

'We'll sort this, Jack. We'll get the money and pay whatever needs paying. Then we'll all move on, okay?'

I admired his confidence. 'Sure,' I said. 'You want a quick coffee?'

He glanced down at his watch. 'Erm…'

Short footsteps echoed in the hallway. We both looked towards the kitchen door. Standing there, the most beautiful I'd ever seen her, was Joanne. A red dress – the colour of the reddest rose you have ever seen - draped tightly over her gorgeous body, leaving a v shape gap revealing a cleavage that would turn even the heads of blind men. Her dark hair was straight, swathing over her small shoulders. A small, rectangular black bag hung from her shoulder by a thin gold chain, complementing the colour of her black high heels. For a second, I was gobsmacked, taken aback by her beauty.

'Wow,' I said, my mouth open. 'You look stunning.'

I noticed Mark nod his head in agreement.

She smiled shyly. 'Are we ready to go?'

Mark nodded then stood up. 'We are.' He turned to me. 'You got the money?'

In the cupboard above the cooker, I grabbed two thick, heavy jiffy bags, A5-sized. I handed them to Mark.

'Come on,' Mark said, glancing down at his Rolex, 'let's go.'

Joanne caught my eye and smiled.

We'd both made mistakes, I realised. If we held on to things in the past, we'd always live in regret filled with destructible anger. It was time to smile back and let it go. I did. I walked them to the door and pecked Joanne on the cheek. She took my hand and squeezed it gently.

'Love you, Jack Haynes.'

'And I love you, too, Jo. Be careful, okay.'

'See you soon.' She followed Mark to the Insignia.

Lucy appeared from the living room and joined me at the front door, watching them disappear onto Park Road.

'They gonna be okay?' asked Lucy.

'Yes, they'll be fine,' I said, reassuring her. 'Mark will make sure of it.'

58

Toddington

Park Road was empty. Not a single car had passed them on their way into the small village of Toddington. At the T-junction, they took a left onto Harlington Road, heading in the direction of the M1. The poker tournament was in Hemel Hempstead. A large house surrounded by an impressive wall, bordering finely cut grass fit for a putting green.

Joanne was apprehensive, fiddling with her hands, rubbing and itching at her skin.

'Thanks for doing this, Mark,' Jo said.

'Anything I can do to help you guys.' He met her shy gaze and smiled.

'Where's the poker game?'

'A friend of mine – his house. He throws a couple every year.'

'What's he like – this friend?' enquired Joanne.

'He's a bit dodgy, but deep down, has a good heart - he means well.' Mark offered no more. He returned his focus to the road, guiding the car around a slight bend. 'It's about nineteen miles away – well, seventeen now,' he said, checking the sat nav. 'Sit back, relax, if you can. We'll be there soon.'

The house was enormous. It sat in isolation from the outside world, accompanied by perfect green gardens flat enough to play bowls on. Its secluded location attracted poker players from all over the south of England.

Once inside the gates, Joanne's previous thoughts about their own gates being impressive quickly faded. They were extravagant, to say the least. Mark angled left, followed a narrow lane, running parallel with the curvature of the wall. With the car moving slowly Joanne glared through the front windscreen at the house at the end of the curving road.

'It's a castle.'

Mark laughed. 'Wait till you see inside.'

A small rectangular area of gravel suitable for accommodating ten to twelve cars was located to the left of the building. Four cars were already parked up. Their sheen finishes and polished lines of chrome sparkled in the setting sun. A brand-new black Land Rover, a black Bentley Continental GT, a red Ferrari, and something more down to earth: an Audi RS5.

'The guy owns the Bentley,' Mark informed her.

'Who owns the red one?'

'Probably one of the poker players, maybe.' Mark applied the handbrake and turned off the engine. 'You ready?'

Joanne gave him a hesitant smile.

'You sure?' he added. 'We don't have to—'

'We have no choice, Mark,' she said quietly.

Mark nodded at her, understanding the stakes. He cocked his head towards the main door. Two men dressed in waistcoats stood on either side of the door. Both big and sturdy, which was something Mark expected. It was their job to be seen, to appear to the players if anything got out of hand, they'd be there to handle it.

Mark looked back at Joanne. She was fiddling with her small handbag. 'Jo, you ready?'

She nodded.

'Listen, when we go in, I'll show you where the other wives sit, then you'll be brought into watch us play.'

Joanne gave a slow bob of the head, absorbing as much as she could.

'Try not to be shy, Jo. I know it's something a little different, but they'll notice if either of us is acting off.' He paused in case she had a question, but she kept quiet. 'Right, come on, let's go.'

Mark opened his door, got out, adjusted his collar, and pulled the flaps of his suit together. He closed the door gently. Joanne appeared across the roof of the car, her face a shade whiter than a moment ago. Mark watched her anxiously, hoping she'd pull herself together sooner rather than later.

'We go in that way,' Marks said, pointing towards the double doors towards the side of the house. He trotted around the back of the Insignia, his shoes crunching on the gravel until they were both on the path. They walked together towards the double doors. Her heart was beating so fast, pumping the blood around her nervous body, it made her head dizzy.

'We'll be fine,' Mark whispered, walking alongside her. At the door, the man to the right held up an A4-sized clipboard.

'Name?'

'Mark Ferry,' said Mark, 'plus one.'

Joanne shifted her weight a little but remains relatively calm as the large man scanned down the list with deep, black eyes.

'Is this your wife?' the man asked.

Mark, without hesitation, said, 'Yes.'

'She's lovely,' said the man, winking at Joanne. 'In you come, have a pleasant evening.' The man then held his palm up again. 'Good luck,' he said with a smile, then turned his attention to another couple walking along the path. Mark smiled and led the way through the door, which was being held open by further security. They stepped into a small corridor where the smell of lavender and fresh paint hung in the air. It wasn't long before they were greeted by a young, confident, slender lady who was somewhere around the age of thirty. She was wearing a sharp black suit that hugged her athletic figure.

'Welcome,' she said with a warm smile. 'If you'd like to leave a jacket or anything, there's a room just in here.' She pointed to an open doorway on the left, then swivelled back. 'If not, just follow me.'

Mark imagined how many times she'd asked that same question tonight as they followed her through a door. She guided them left into a large room covered by a low ceiling, classy lighting, and idle chatter. Mark scanned the area, feeling the warmth of the room hit his face like a gentle slap, radiating from a fire to the left. The room was square. It smelt faintly of gin, burning wood, and an array of sweet perfumes. A handful of people were chatting, some in pairs, others in threes and fours, some sitting on the leather sofas, and others standing in a small group.

One man, standing near the small bar on the right, presumably with his wife, nodded toward Mark.

'You know him?' asked Jo.

Mark returned the nod. 'No, just being polite.'

The lady who walked them through told them to have a good night and disappears, leaving Mark and Joanne in the centre of the room. It isn't long before a tall, thin girl with blonde straight hair appears with a tray full of drinks.

'Anything you desire?'

Mark eyed the array of drinks and grabbed a pint of lager. The girl smiled and angled the tray towards Joanne.

'Is that gin?' Jo asked, narrowing her eyes.

The girl smiled. 'Yes. Whitley Neill, Blood Orange.'

Joanne smiled, carefully taking it, not wanting to unbalance the tray in the girl's hand. The girl gave her a complimentary smile and floated away. Joanne took a quick sip to loosen her nerves.

Soon after, the smartly dressed woman appeared again, stopping in the middle of the room. To get everyone's attention, she clapped her hands twice. The idle conversations faded and all eyes fell on her.

'If the good ladies of the evening would like to follow me, please.'

'Mark?' said Jo, worriedly.

'Don't worry. They do this. A poker expert speaks to the players about the rules. It'll take two minutes. I'll see you in the other room in a moment, okay?'

'Okay.' Joanne waited for the other ladies to move before she followed them through a door.

After the talk, the men were led to the poker room. A large, impressive table sat in the centre of it. The players nervously took their seats and got as comfortable as they could, considering they'd all put fifty thousand in for it. It was a serious business. The hum of hushed voices faded and the room filled with silence.

A few hours passed. Mark was doing very well. Joanne was sitting next to a tall, leggy blonde woman with a tanned face, who continued to comment on what was going on. The women were seated a few metres away from the men. To the woman's right, there was a television on the wall, showing the game live from a camera positioned directly above the table.

'Good move, that one,' the blonde commented.

Joanne glared in confusion but agreed with the woman. She then peered around the room. There were two people behind the bar serving complimentary drinks, a waitress near the poker table, the woman wearing the smart suit, and four men dressed in black - two of whom were watching the game unfold and, the other two, guarding the door.

A loud cheer erupted at the table. Joanne jumped a little, looking wide-eyed at the poker players.

'What's – what's happened?' Jo asked the leggy blonde next to her.

'What's happened is that your husband has just won half a million pounds.' The leggy blonde stood up and frowned at her before walking away. 'Lucky bitch.'

Joanne didn't hear the harsh comment because her head was spinning. She watched the smile on Mark's face widen when he glanced over and threw a clenched fist into the air. Overwhelmed, Joanne felt her heart beating through her slender dress. She couldn't help throwing her hands over her mouth.

She watched a man walk over to Mark and leaned over to him, whispering something in his ear. Mark gave him a small nod, then stood up. After he shook the hands of the other players, he went over to Joanne with a smile on his face.

'We need to follow him to collect the money,' Mark explained.

Joanne got up a little too quick, the gin impairing her balance slightly.

'Steady,' Mark joked as he took her soft hand, guiding her around the chair. 'This way. Let's go get the money from the boss.'

'Who's the boss?'

'Guy called Alex. You haven't seen him yet. He watches on the cameras in private.'

They left the room and followed a thin man down a wide corridor. Joanne squeezed Mark's hand several times with excitement before the front man slowed and said, 'In here.'

They entered the room and frowned. The room was rectangular. A large filing cabinet filled the space at one end. The low ceiling hung a few feet above their heads and the feeling of claustrophobia started to tingle at Joanne. The dark green concrete walls made it feel unwelcoming and cold. Mark and Joanne stood anxiously waiting for the boss.

A tall man dressed in a black leather coat stepped inside. He offered no more than a nod and waited near the door, making Joanne feel he was blocking their only way out. Silence captivated the room. Joanne was hot, beads of sweat dripped down the middle of her back. She looked at Mark, who thankfully, appeared calm.

Until three men enter the small space and the room becomes significantly smaller.

Two large men dressed in black leather followed a smaller man wearing a long brown coat, who leaned forward towards Mark to shake his hand.

'Congratulations,' he said, handing him a briefcase.

'Thank you, Alex. It has been a while.'

Mark relished the feel of half a million in his hand and tugged it up and down several times, as if checking the weight.

'It's all there - don't worry about it,' joked the man in the brown coat.

Mark smiled. 'I don't doubt it. How've you been?'

'I've been good,' he said. So, who's this?' The man asked, glancing past Mark to see Joanne.

Mark turned to Joanne. 'Joanne, meet Alexander Hunt.'

Joanne slowly looked up at him. Her heart stopped.

If the day came when Joanne saw Alexander Hunt, that day would be too soon. She started to tremble. Her eyes widened in absolute fear. It was the day she dreaded since she escaped him all those years ago.

One day, she feared she'd see him again.

Today was that day.

59

Milton Keynes

'Just here on the left,' DCI Clarke said, flicking on the indicator. He dabbed the brake, took a left onto Lower Twelfth Street, leaving Avebury Boulevard. Horton leaned forward, scanning left and right through the windscreen as the car slowed to a crawl.

'Ahh, there it is,' Horton said, pointing to the right.

The flashy colourful lights ran up two vertical columns, all the way to the roof, on either side of the entrance door. According to the dashboard, it was just after 10.30 p.m. Early for the big crowds but things were warming up in Milton Keynes.

They pulled up on the kerb, both glancing towards the club. Groups of people were dotted around on the pathway leading to the entrance. A mature couple walked side by side on the path towards the police car, most likely had been to a nearby restaurant. A small group of males, probably late teens, strutted towards them on the right-hand side. One of them made eye contact with DCI Clarke and looked away as if knowing he had been underaged. In the middle of the path, a large group of women, dressed for a hen party in short, bright tutus leaving nothing to the imagination, headed in the direction of the club.

The energetic rhythm of a quiet drum bass seeped out through the open doors behind the bouncers. The buzz in the area was good. Plenty of smiling happy people immersed in boozy, louder-than-usual conversations.

'You been here?' Horton asked, glancing at the large, impressive building.

'A while ago, yeah,' Clarke replied, turning off the engine. The club music and cheery conversations got louder and clearer as the idling engine faded.

The detectives got out and locked the car. They stepped up onto the path and walked towards the two bouncers dressed in black standing outside of the club.

The man on the right held his palm up. 'There's no underaged in here tonight.'

Clarke and Horton came to a halt in front of him. 'Well, that's good to know,' Clarke said. 'We need to speak to the manager. Is he or she in?'

The man gave Clarke a frown, lowered his palm, but eventually nodded. From the pocket of his thin black jacket, he plucked out a phone, punched in a few buttons, and put it to his ear. After ten seconds, it was answered: 'Yeah… no everything's okay, they haven't come back…' he squinted a little as if trying to block out the club's music coming from the doors behind him. 'The police are here to see you… I don't know… okay, will do.'

The man put the phone back in his pocket. He looked up. 'Yeah, go inside. Take the first left, follow the stairs up, take a right, and knock on the door.'

Clarke thanked him and led the way through the doors. Horton offered him a nod as he passed but didn't get one in return. Inside, the corridor was darker and louder. The smell of lager, perfume, and a sour tinge of fresh paint tingled their noses. They followed the directions the bouncer had given them and found themselves in a quiet, narrow corridor. Horton stepped forward, chapped on the door with a sign saying "Management".

'Come in,' they hear a voice say through the door.

Through the threshold, they entered a square room. The room was dimly lit by two lamps. One lamp shone over the desk where a smartly dressed man was sitting behind a computer screen. The other lamp was taller, positioned in the right corner. The scents of whisky and cigars and aftershave hung in the room. To the right of the desk, there was a rectangular window. No doubt used to look down on the club's dancefloor. Multi-coloured lights danced through the glass, piercing the ceiling above their heads. Clarke and Horton padded into the centre of the room, their eyes focusing on the man half hidden by the computer monitor, who tilted his head at them and frowned.

'Can I help you…?' said the man.

Clarke offered the man his hand. 'DCI Clarke, this is DS Horton.'

The man leaned over the desk and shook it. 'Jacob – Jacob Smith.'

'Could we grab two minutes of your time, Mr Smith?'

The man eyed them wearily before he answered. 'Yes. What can I do for you?'

'There was an incident three years ago. A man was murdered. We've been asked to have another look at the case. We are led to believe the people that could potentially be involved were here the night the murder took place.'

Jacob frowned and shuffled in his seat. 'When was this?'

Clarke told him the date of the night, just over three years ago.

'I see,' Jacob said, not sure where it was going.

'Is it possible to have a look at your CCTV from that night? If we could spot anything unusual, it really could help us.'

Jacob thought for a second, clamping his eyes shut. The detectives waited, watching his brain tick over. When he opened his eyes, he told them he wasn't sure if the data recorded would go back that far. 'They normally save for so long, then it automatically deletes the files to make space for another block of time,' he explained.

Clarke nodded. 'Could we have a look just in case – have you got access on there?'

He was referring to the computer on the desk. By his face, it was clear Jacob didn't want the detectives searching through his computer. But, he knew, if he declined, it might cause a stir, so reluctantly, he agreed. Clarke and Horton rounded the desk and laid eyes on the monitor, standing on either side of the man. Jacob clicked through several files until he found a folder of the date requested. In the folder, there were seven video files, presumably for seven cameras. He double-clicked on the first file anxiously, not knowing what would be on the video. After a few seconds, it flashed up on the screen. It was a shot of the dance floor. People were dancing, laughing, chatting with friends, sipping drinks. The time in the bottom right corner showed 22:57.

'Could you forward it to twelve-thirty?' Clarke asked.

'Sure.' He hovered over the time bar at the bottom of the screen and clicked at the requested time. Immediately it changed to another screen. The angle was the same, but more people were congregating on the dance floor. Clarke leaned forward and squinted – he had a good idea of what Peter Lewes looked like from the picture of him in the report, but it was difficult from the high camera angle.

'See anything?' Horton asked Clarke, focusing on the people moving under the camera.

'No, not yet. There are too many people,' Clarke told him.

Horton agreed in frustration, then turned to Jacob. 'Is there a camera outside the door?'

'Yeah, sure.' Jacob minimised the screen, clicked on video file seven. It opened, and they saw the wide pathway leading from the entrance doors to the kerb of the road. Clarke mentally noted it was where their car was currently parked. 'You want the same time again, twelve-thirty?' he added.

'Yes, please,' Horton said.

At twelve-thirty there was no car on the road outside, but the path was busy with people staggering around and hustling past each other. They watched for a few minutes, but there was no sign of a taxi.

'Go to around 1 a.m. – or just before,' Clarke said, eagerly.

Jacob nodded. He clicked to 12.57 a.m.

The crowds had thinned. Smaller groups lingered on either side of the path. At 12.58 a.m., a man, wearing a white long-sleeved shirt, walked down the centre of the path towards the road. The path ahead of him lit up by the headlights of a slowing taxi until it stopped. The man opened the door and climbed in.

'That's him,' Clarke snapped. 'Look.' He glanced at the time in the corner of the camera's screen. 'His wife said he booked a taxi for one. It must be him.'

Jacob followed the detective's finger, faking an interest then glanced down at his watch, then back to the screen. Both Clarke and Horton read the report of the clothes he'd been found in. He wore a long-sleeved white top. They continued to watch the video. After a few seconds, the taxi pulled away slowly, then suddenly it stopped. The camera picked up the rear registration and the driver's side rear wheel. After a minute, the taxi rolled forward out of view.

'Why did it stop?' Horton asked, intrigued.

'It certainly stopped for something,' replied Clarke.

'Letting some drunk across the road, maybe?' Jacob added with a shrug. It was obvious he had become impatient. 'Listen, guys, how long will this take? I've got a few things I need to do.'

Clarke smiled. 'Could we have a copy of this video to take it back to the station for analysis?'

Jacob pondered the question but said, 'Erm, sure.' He was reluctant, the detectives could tell. Horton pulled a USB memory stick from his thin black jacket and handed it to Jacob.

'Save it to this please.'

'Who hasn't come back?' Clarke asked.

'Huh?' Jacob looked up, frowning.

'When your doorman spoke to you, you asked him a question. He replied with: no, they haven't come back. Who was he referring to?'

'Just a group of lads causing a bit of bother earlier. Weekly issues,' he said, brushing it off as it was the norm.

Horton took the memory stick back, placed it safely into his jacket. 'Thanks for your time.'

'Always a pleasure,' the impatient club owner replied.

After leaving the room, they headed downstairs, reached the main corridor. They noticed the music is more upbeat. A group of women approached them, walking in through the entrance door, full of laughter. One of the women eyed DCI Clarke and winked at him but Clarke ignored her. As they stepped out into the warm night, the music droned out as they headed along the path back to the car.

Back inside the quiet car Horton turned to Clarke. 'Why did the taxi stop?'

'I don't know.' He looked through the windscreen focusing on the road ahead, thinking. 'We'll run the plate, find out who owns the taxi, and speak to them.' He turned the engine on, then edged forward, then came to a halt.

'What you doing?' Horton asked, glancing at Clarke from the passenger seat. A short moment passed until he realised what his superior was doing. Stopping roughly where the taxi did.

'Right. Why did he stop?' He scanned around him. Horton did the same, looking left and right.

'Maybe it *was* to let someone cross the road?' Horton suggested, not seeing anything obvious.

'No.' Clarke shook his head. 'It was too long for that.' He tilted his head back against the headrest for a long moment and let out a tired sigh. Then suddenly, he rocked his head forward, glancing up to the right.

'There! he shouted.

Horton frowned. 'What is it?'

Clarke pointed to the right. 'Look up there, near the window.'

Horton followed the direction of his finger.

'You see it?' asked Clarke.

'The camera?' Horton squinted into the darkness.

'Yes,' said Clarke. He turned to Horton. 'We need to see the footage from that camera three years ago.'

60

Hemel Hempstead

Mark watched the blood drain from Joanne's face and a wave of fear captivate her. Something was seriously wrong.

'Jo?' Mark said. 'What's the matter?'

She didn't reply. She kept her eyes frozen on Hunt.

'Jo?' he repeated, louder.

He watched a tear fall down her cheek. He turned back to Hunt in confusion. He couldn't help but notice the look on Hunt's face was an attentive stare. They knew each other, that much was obvious.

'I've been looking for you a long time, Lorraine. And, here you are, right here with me. Finally.' Hunt smiled at her, his wide eyes glistening under the bright light above. He turned to the biggest man behind him. 'This is her, Phil, the one who broke my heart, and not forgetting, when the little bitch give me this scar on my face.'

Mark stared blankly, his focus bouncing between them both. 'What the fuck is going on? Alex? What's the problem?' Then to Joanne: 'Lorraine? Lorraine who?'

Hunt shook his head, pointed his thick finger towards her. '*She* is my problem.'

Joanne deliberately slid behind Mark, using him as a shield.

'You can't hide from me, Lorraine,' Hunt mused.

'Lorraine…' Mark frowned. 'Alex, what's going on?'

The room was silent and still. The loudest sound was Jo's heart beating against her trembling chest as she reached a heightened state of fear. The room became smaller and the air less breathable. It felt like the bare concrete walls were starting to close in on them.

In search of an answer, Mark swivelled back to Hunt, holding his left palm up. 'Listen, Alex, whatever this is —'

His words were cut short when Hunt lunged forward, his arms outstretched aiming for Joanne. Mark nudged Joanne back a little and, rotating his body a few inches to the right, he twisted back fast, hauling the suitcase through the air, smashing Hunt in the side of his face. Hunt didn't even stumble. He simply dropped to the floor like a lead balloon, blurting out a heavy groan as he collided with the concrete floor.

It didn't take long for the man on the left to charge forward. Tall and thin, he galloped over Hunt with focused, determined eyes. With Mark's right shoulder slightly dipped forward, and his body twisted with the weight of the briefcase nestled in his right hand, he waited for the perfect time to swing it back. The man was almost within grabbing distance. Mark heaved everything he had into the swing, smashing the hard, plastic briefcase into the side of the man's face. His jaw cracked loudly. The momentum hurled him to the right, crashing into a four-tier arrangement of metal shelving. His arms flapped to grab something but, disorientated, he missed and hit the cold, hard deck below. Joanne screamed at the sight of blood spilling from a cut on the man's face.

Two down. One to go.

The problem for Mark is that Phil was not only tall, but he was also wide. Also, he didn't seem fazed that his boss or the other men are almost out cold. He padded forward with confidence, not even raising his hands to fight, already knowing what he was going to do when he reached Mark.

Mark took a heavy breath, swinging his arm back. 'Come on, then, you fucker!'

The man lunged forward a few inches and pulled back, fainted him like a boxer would in the ring against an opponent.

Mark fell for it and swung at him. The plastic box zipped through the air, unbalancing Mark, and it wasn't long before Phil rammed his fist into the side of his face, rattling his jaw. It felt like a sledgehammer. His neck cracked and his head rocked to the side. Mark dropped the money, stumbled to the right, merely missing the metal shelving unit until his legs buckled and he crashed down onto the cold, solid floor.

Joanne screamed and jumped back from the violence and lowered into the furthest corner. She cried heavily, holding her knees tight into her chest and clamped her eyes shut.

Phil straddled Mark. His weight pinned him down. His heavy fists pounded both sides of his head with relentless hefty blows. Mark blocked most of them, absorbing what he could with his hands and forearms, but a few connected, shaking his skull. They nearly knocked him for six. He felt himself fading away, losing consciousness blow by blow.

Hunt shuffled on the floor, let out a heavy, painful groan as he woke up. He brought his hand up to his face to soothe the damage Mark had done with the briefcase. He cocked his head, almost oblivious to what was going on. He blinked to focus, then saw Joanne in the corner. He smiled at her.

'Lorraine… how I've missed you dear,' he said, slowly getting to his feet. 'I love it when you're scared.' A thin line of blood ran from his temple down the side of his face. Dizzy from the blow, he staggers, but found his feet. 'Come, dear, I'll look after you.'

Joanne kicked and screamed at him as he drew nearer. Hunt shrieked in pain when the point of her stiletto collided with his shin.

'Bitch! You'll fucking pay for that.' Hunt moved forward again.

'Leave me alone!' she cried. 'Mark! Help me!'

Mark was occupied. Phil was still swinging at him like a madman, pounding away at his head. Mark's face and arms were numb and, blow by blow, he had become weaker. The sound of bone against bone was sickening, but there was a look in Mark's swollen eye, a surprising focus of composure and determination.

Someone who was going to pick his time right.

After countless blows, Phil started to tire. His punches were slower and less effective. Behind his bruised, bloody arms, Mark watched the monster on top of him and saw an opportunity.

As Phil drew back with his right hand, Mark threw a fist towards Phil's chin. It did enough to knock him off balance for Mark to scurry onto his side. Phil threw another punch, connecting with the back of Mark's head. It juddered forward, the pain coursing through his body suffered the agony. Mark opened his eyes and, through the blood, saw the suitcase next to him. He wriggled his left hand free from under Phil's leg, grabbed the handle and heaved the case up into Phil's nose. His nose popped, causing a spray of blood to cascade onto the floor as he threw his palms up to his face. He fell to his right, roaring in pain.

As he struggled up, he found his bearings within the small room. In the corner, Hunt was bent over Joanne, who screamed and kicked at him.

Mark's face was covered in blood. He struggled up and charged at Hunt with his shoulder, the momentum hurling him into the far wall, forcing Hunt's skull to crack against the brickwork. He went down like a stone and wouldn't be getting up any time soon.

'Come on, Jo,' shouted Mark, 'we need to go now!'

Joanne grabbed Mark's outstretched arm and was hauled to her feet. On their way out, Mark picked up the briefcase, then they hurried into the corridor and took a right. Gasping for air, they scurried back through the bar, where several people lingered to finish their drinks, looked up at them with wide, concerned eyes.

Joanne stumbled on the thick carpet and she felt her ankle almost give way, but Mark dragged her back up.

'Hey!' they heard a voice scream somewhere in the room. 'Stop!'

Mark crashed through the glass door at the end of the corridor. It swung back, almost catching Joanne, who was crying and yelping in agony. Her ankle throbbed as they broke out into the dark, evening air.

They ran along the path, the sounds of their frantic heels and heavy shoes slapped the floor as they approached the car. Mark pulled Joanne down onto the gravel, causing her to wail in distress from her bruised ankle.

'Jo, come on!' He tugged hard on her arm.

'I – I can't,' she pleaded.

Inches away from the car they heard the double glass entrance doors swing open, the wooden frame crashing against the rubber doorstops bolted to the floor with a loud bang. Joanne flinched. Mark opened the passenger door and pushed her inside.

'Get in!'

She did.

Mark slammed the door shut and raced around towards the driver's door with the briefcase. Down the path, he saw two men dashing towards them. Joanne glared at them from the passenger seat with mascara streaming down her face. She recognised them. It was Stuart and Derek. Her whole body shook with fear. Mark opened the driver's door and dived in.

'Come on! Come on!' Jo screamed.

Mark threw the money onto Joanne's lap, then put the key into the ignition but missed, his shaking hand stabbing the plastic slot housing. 'Fuck!' he shouted in frustration. He tried a fifth time, finally managing to insert in and turned the key. The Insignia roared to life.

As the pounding footsteps of Stuart and Derek drew close, Joanne slapped the briefcase in panicked desperation. 'Mark, hurry!'

'I am!'

He threw it into reverse and the car jolted back, kicking up gravel under the spinning wheels. He yanked at the steering wheel, put the gear in first, and pushed his foot onto the accelerator. Their heads rocked back as the Insignia hurried forward.

From the passenger window, Joanne glared at Stuart who was inches away from her door. His evil eyes glared at her. He raised a crowbar high above his head, hurled it towards the window. The loud smash ripped through the car, a shower of glass exploding onto Joanne's lap and across the dashboard. Mark winced, forcing his foot further onto the pedal. Stuart didn't keep up with the car as the Insignia sped away along the winding, narrow road along the high stone wall.

Joanne, covered in glass, cried uncontrollably in the passenger seat. Blood covered her hands and forearms. Mark's face throbbed in pain. His left eye bulged and his nose was covered in warm blood. His white shirt was ruined. The car slowed as it passes through the gates and reached the junction.

'Calm down, Jo, please, just—'

A loud bang erupted. Joanne let out a blood-curdling scream as a bullet shattered the rear windscreen.

'Jesus!' screamed Mark.

'Mark!'

'Hold on, hold on.' Mark snapped his neck back to look behind him. Across the dark field, he saw figures moving towards them. Another shot. The bullet whistled past the front of the car.

'Please, Mark, go, go!'

Mark turned right, heading towards the M1. A few minutes of terrifying silence passed.

'You okay, Jo?'

'It was him, Mark, it was him. He said if he ever found me, he'd kill me.'

'Who – who was it, Jo?'

Jo fell silent.

'Jo?'

'It was him,' she said quietly, then burst into tears again, her quivering palms covering her soaked face. Mark wanted to comfort her, find out the full story, but his priority was to get her home, back to safety. Back to Jack.

'Just hold on, we'll be home soon,' he reassured her.

A few miles north Mark eased the Insignia down to seventy, moving across from the fast lane to the middle. Joanne's tears finally stopped. The brilliance of the white headlights illuminated the tarmac as the car propelled up the M1.

Mark took a deep breath and exhaled. He checked the mirrors for any cars in the left lane, ready to flick his indicator, to ease over, but something caught his eye. Headlights getting bigger in the rear-view mirror approaching fast.

Worryingly fast.

'Shit,' said Mark.

'Shit what?' she said, glancing at him with sore eyes. 'What – what is it?'

'Behind us. Hold on.'

Joanne glared behind. A black Land Rover zipped towards them.

Mark guided the car over to the right lane, planted his foot down, forcing the Insignia to dart forward into the night.

61

M1, Luton

'Put your fucking foot down!' Hunt screamed at Phil.

Phil pushed his foot further down and the Land Rover went over a hundred miles an hour. Hunt, in the passenger seat, tapped the gun nervously off his leg.

Stuart and Derek were in the back, leaning towards the middle, looking through the space between the driver's seat and the passenger seat. The gap closed on the Insignia. Two hundred metres or so. Maybe less.

'Boss,' Phil shouted over the sound of the air whistling through the vents and the rapid rotation of the whirring tires. 'What we gonna do when we catch them?'

Hunt glances at Phil as if he was thick. 'Ram them off the road. Kill them. Get my fucking money back.'

Phil gave a small nod and looked forward.

One-hundred and ten miles an hour.

Stuart and Derek sat back nervously in their seats.

One-hundred and fifteen.

One-hundred and twenty.

'Ram them!'

'Boss, you sure?' Phil frowned at him.

'Fucking ram them,' Hunt snapped at Phil.

Phil swallowed hard, tightening his swollen hands around the steering wheel. The Insignia in front showed a burst in speed, but it wasn't enough to avoid the collision. The front grill smashed into the back of the Insignia, causing a huge shudder to both vehicles. Derek let out a gasp from the back seat.

The Land Rover slowed to a hundred. Phil couldn't help drifting over to the middle lane, narrowly missing an old Ford Focus by a hair.

'Again!' Hunt screamed. 'I want them fucking dead!' He hit the leather dashboard with the gun three times.

Phil straightened the 4x4 out and moved back over to the fast lane. The Insignia accelerated and the gap increased. Phil planted his foot, feeling the Land Rover surge forward. How the Insignia had stayed on the road after the hit amazed Phil.

'Boss, we shouldn't be doing this,' pleaded Stuart from the back. 'We'll end up fucking dead.'

'Jump out then!' barked Hunt. 'Keep your mouth fucking shut!'

Phil closed in again. The rear of the battered Insignia grew closer.

'Hit them!' Hunt shouted.

'Boss,' said Derek, 'Why don't—'

Hunt threw his head back and pointed the gun into the back of the car. 'If I hear one more fucking word from any of you, I'll fucking shoot you.'

Deadly silence wisped through the car.

Derek nodded. Stuart didn't speak. So, they either died by a bullet to the face at close range, or the car flipping at over a hundred miles an hour and they get crushed in a pile-up. Hunt turned his head, glaring back through the wind-screen.

'I want them off the road!'

Phil eased off the pedal. 'Boss, I—'

Hunt pointed the gun at Phil. 'Just fucking drive.'

Reluctantly, Phil pushed his foot down again and gripped the wheel.

The sound of the tires on the tarmac was frightening. Every little imperfection on the road's surface rattled through the suspension. Derek started to feel sick, raising a palm to his mouth, unsure he would throw up. Stuart winced at him.

Hunt loved it. The rush of it all. The chase of the near-death experience.

The Land Rover roared ahead, closing the gap once again. Both cars were in the fast lane, overtaking anything unlucky to be on the road. One-hundred and twenty-five miles-an-hour. Phil noticed the thin neon indicator climbing on the dashboard as the vibrating steering wheel shuddered in his weakened grip.

Everything's a blur. Thin streams of light whizzed by from overhead street lighting.

'Fucking idiot!' Hunt shouted at the driver of a small Renault Clio in front. The car veered over to the right, causing Phil to slow down suddenly. Hunt opened his window, the inside of the car becoming a whirlwind and, suddenly, they all gasped for breath. With the gun in his left hand, Hunt threw his arm out the window and steadied it against the zipping wind.

'Boss!' Phil shouted against the sound of the wind. 'What the hell are you doing?'

Hunt fired a shot at the Clio. The bullet hit the back passenger side tire. A low thud was heard as the Clio tilted and started to shudder across the lane at high speed until it veered over to the left. Derek and Stuart glared behind them through the rear windscreen and, within seconds, the Clio became a dot left behind.

'Jesus!' Derek gasped.

'We're going to kill someone here!' Phil shouted.

Hunt watched the Insignia move over to the middle lane. Phil kept to the right. Suddenly, the car shot back into the fast lane.

'What the fuck are they doing?' Phil said.

'I don't care, get them!' Hunt urged.

They sped up.

Phil noticed the sign for a slip road, then looked back to the tarmac, concentrating on keeping the car steady – one mistake would be catastrophic. The junction approached on the left. The insignia continued in the fast lane but, unexpectedly, at a very dangerous speed, and last possible second, shot off to the left, making the slip road by inches, the bottom of the car bouncing over the dividing shallow grass verge.

'What the…?'

Phil was too late to react and the Land Rover continued its path on the M1, northbound.

'For fuck sake, Phil!' screamed Hunt, slamming the butt of the gun into the dashboard.

62

Toddington

'Can you see them?' Joanne asked Mark.

He glared through the rear mirror with focused eyes, watching carefully. His heart nearly beat through his ribs – it was painful as if something internal was damaged. He took a deep breath, held it for a few seconds.

'I – I don't think so. They missed the turn.'

Joanne sighed heavily, wiping a tear from her eye. She brushed some of the glass off her dress onto the floor near the briefcase.

'We'll be home soon. We'll be safe,' Mark said. He looked down in the footwell of the passenger seat. 'At least we have the money.'

They drove in silence until they reached Park road. Mark slowed and made the turn

'Your car is wrecked,' Joanne said.

'That's what the insurance is for – don't worry about it.'

On their approach to the gates, Joanne plucked the phone from her handbag and rang Jack.

'Hey…. Yeah good, we're nearly home… yeah, we did… no, nothing… honestly, I'll tell you when we're inside… yeah, open the gates… okay, bye.'

'Does he think there's something off?'

'Yeah,' she said. 'He could tell.'

'Well, we're all about to find out who this guy is,' he reminded her.

Joanne dipped her head for a moment as the car stopped outside the closed gates. They heard a mechanical buzz then the gates swung open. The Insignia passes through and snaked around the winding gravel until Mark parked next to his brother's Volvo. He killed the engine and sighed.

'How's the ankle?' he asked.

'Horrendous.' Joanne glanced at him. 'How's your face?'

Mark grimaced. 'Hurts like hell, to be honest.'

She winced at the drying blood and how painful the swelling must feel.

Mark leaned over Joanne's legs, grabbed the money, careful not to catch her ankle with it as he lifted it over the gear stick onto his lap. After a moment, they stepped out of the car, and crunched across the gravel towards the front door. The security light above the door flicked on, blinding them both for a moment. They opened the door, and both tiredly stepped inside.

JACK

The front door opened. I felt a cool draft seep into the living room. I honestly couldn't believe they'd won. With a spring in my step and a grin from ear to ear, I got up and dashed into the hallway.

I froze.

My grin faded. Fast.

What the hell was going on?

I tried to speak but nothing came out. Mark gently closed the front door, placed the briefcase on the floor near his feet, and looked at me with a sad smile. His eye was almost swollen shut. He looked a mess. Blood covered most of his face and his shirt. Joanne stood next to him. One look at her and my heart broke into a million pieces.

'Jo!' I gasped.

Her face was wet from crying, thick channels of mascara running down her puffy face. Her hair was in knots. Blood covered her hands and forearms. Her red dress was ripped up the side. Her stilettos scraped the wooden floor as she sauntered over to me, digging her face into my chest. Her body shook as she broke out into a helpless wail.

At the top of the stairs, Lucy appeared with wide horrified eyes.

'Mum?'

I ignored Lucy for a moment. Mark glanced up, watching her hurdle down the stairs and stop in front of Joanne.

'Mum, what's happened?' Lucy pulled Joanne away from me and glared at her in disbelief. 'Oh, God, Mum, what the hell has happened?' She heaved her mother close, squeezing her, and then started to cry.

'Mark, what the hell is going on?' I asked my brother.

He ambled forward. 'Get the kettle on mate. We need to talk.'

I gave a silent nod and they followed me slowly into the kitchen. I flicked the light on and got four mugs out ready. With my hands trembling as I placed them on the granite worktop, I lost control of one and it smashed onto the floor tiles, separating into several pieces.

I cleaned up the mess with my bare hands quickly and noted to use a brush to get the smaller parts later. Right now I needed to find out what had happened.

They all took a seat at the table. Lucy was sitting next to Jo, rubbing her back softly, struggling to see the pain on her mother's face.

I brought four cups of steaming coffee over to the table, placed them down, and took a seat opposite Jo. I kept my eyes fixed on her for a long moment. Then I looked at Mark. 'What happened?'

Mark filled us in on what happened. From arriving at the game, the fight in the small room, the man who recognised her, then escaping.

'He knew her from the past?' I asked, confused.

'Seemed so,' said Mark, diverting his attention to Joanne, who nodded slowly to confirm. Tears dropped from her sad eyes.

'Who is he, Jo?'

'Alexander Hunt,' she said, then fell quiet.

'Who's he?' I asked.

'He's the man on the photos, Jack,' she explained, 'the ones that Lucy got pictures of.'

My eyes widened. 'What?'

'The photos that Lucy took. Him killing those two men. It was him. I saw him wearing the same brown coat. Then it clicked, it was Hunt. I don't know how I never recognised him from the photos.'

I gave her an understanding nod but I was desperate for more.

'I knew him years ago, Jack when I was young. I was sixteen, I think,' she continued. 'We were seeing each other for a few months but, things… things got scary – out of control. I didn't like the person he was.' She took a moment to catch a breath. 'At first, he was kind, sweet. Taking me out for dinner. To the movies. Walking around with me on his arm… like a trophy. He… he, he—'

'Take your time, Jo,' I said.

She looked at Lucy, who gave her a comforting smile and continued to gently rub her back.

I'd never seen her so hurt. So upset. My skin warmed, and my blood started to simmer. I didn't think I could control the growing rage but fought the urge to smash my fist into the table.

'He started to hit me,' she said. 'When I didn't do as he asked, he would—'

'What did he ask of you?' I said, feeling a searing heat behind my eyes. I felt a sharp pain in my palm, then realised I was digging my nails into my hand.

'You know, things. Sexual things… other things…'

I noticed Mark move a little, no doubt disturbed by what he had heard. I remained stone still. If I moved, I knew I'd throw something in rage and I didn't want to do that.

She continued. 'After I wouldn't do as he asked, he hit me. One time...' she trailed off for a moment and looked up to the ceiling. 'I had enough, I fought back.' She looked back at us. 'We were in his garage...and he... was asking me to do something I didn't want to... and he belted me in the mouth when I said no.' Joanne raised her palm to her red lips as if feeling the pain over again.

I interlocked my fingers together and squeezed hard, feeling the shape of the small bones in my hands crack.

'He hit me three times in the face – I can remember it like it was yesterday,' she whispered. 'The stinging pain on my skin. The first two hurt. After that, I was numb. I didn't feel the third.' She moved her palm to her cheek as if soothing it. 'His face, his ice-cold glare, his dark eyes. He knocked me back into a workbench. He...' She stopped for a second. 'I saw a knife on the side bench –

a Stanley knife. I grabbed it. I wanted to use it, Jack, I' —she shook her head and curled her bottom lip—'I couldn't, that's not me.'

'Of course, it isn't – you're not a monster,' explained Mark.

I nodded in agreement.

'So, I slipped the knife into my pocket. Then I slapped him hard in the face. I then told him I was going to the police if he didn't leave me alone. I'd show them the bruises on my body that he'd caused. He was twenty-three. He's seven years older than me. I'd always lie to people - say I'd fallen over or caught myself on something. The corner of a table. Anything to excuse what he really was. But then I started running out of excuses.' She looked back down at the table with tears in her eyes. 'He was horrible.'

I picked up my coffee with a trembling hand and sipped it, using the moment to deter my mind away from my anger. 'Then what happened?'

A part of me wanted to know what did happen to her. But I knew the other part didn't. The other part wouldn't be able to handle it.

'Before I got out, he grabbed me, put his big hands around my throat, and squeezed like hell for what felt like forever. I was choking, gasping for air until I passed out. When I woke up, he was slapping my face to bring me around. He called me pathetic. When I had the chance, I ran off in fear of my life. I thought he was going to kill me. I didn't tell anyone about it. My mum and dad were in the process of selling the house and moving and, until we did, I prayed he didn't come over. He knew where I lived, but my mum and dad didn't even know about him. I hadn't told them.'

'How come you didn't recognise him in the photos?' I said, delicately.

'I don't know. I guess it had been so long. He had changed. Got fatter, lost most of his hair. But when I saw him tonight, I knew straight away when I saw *that* look in his eyes. The brown coat – it came together. Just like when he looked at me he knew straight away. Oh God, Jack. If he's anything like he used to be, he'll do anything to stop us from showing anyone the photos. It's made things ten times worse.'

'Listen,' said Mark, interrupting her train of thought. 'We have the money.' He faced me. 'Jack, you meet that person and pay him. Then we can deal with your friend, Ray. After that, we'll deal with it. I don't know, call the police, tell them about what's going on. Whatever we need to do to sort this mess out.'

'He has people in the police. We don't know who to trust,' I explained. 'That dodgy copper that came here. What if they're all like that?'

'They're not all bad, Jack, come on,' said Mark.

'Yeah…but we don't know who is or isn't, do we? What if there's more working with him?'

Mark absorbed my words and nodded in silence.

'Okay,' Mark said, 'well your security system will come in handy for now. You couldn't take more time off work. It doesn't look very good. Tell you what, Elaine has a quiet day tomorrow. She could come by and sit with you, Jo?' He glanced her way.

She nodded. 'Thank you.'

'Then after you've paid that guy,' Mark said, now looking at me, 'we can sort the rest out.'

Taking comfort in Mark's words, Joanne smiled for a second and it melted my heart. For a second, it made everything in the world okay again.

Mark looked at Joanne with narrowed eyes. 'Who is Lorraine?'

She glared at him, frowning. 'Lorraine?'

'Yeah,' said Mark, 'I heard him call you Lorraine – Alexander Hunt called you Lorraine. Is that your middle name?'

I frowned. Then I focused on Jo.

Joanne sighed and adjusted herself, ready to tell us something she had never told anyone.

63

Toddington
JACK

'Can you remember the murders of the Hembridge Bank CEO's?' she asked.

Mark, holding a bag of peas against his swollen face, shook his head, which was no surprise. I nodded. I was familiar with the story. Several pictures of them are placed around corridors of the bank. I'd never met them because it was a long time ago. The CEO murders is a story we all know about.

'Yeah, I've heard the story,' I said.

'Well… it was us,' she confessed.

The silence that followed was deafening. Out of the corner of my eye, Mark jolted his head in shock.

She clutched her hands over her mouth, squeezing her eyes shut. I glanced at Mark, who looked equally confused. She began to shake again. 'Alexander told me he was going to make some money. I asked him how. He told me he knew these two men. But he didn't tell me who they were. I asked him how we'd get the money he was talking about. He said if he cornered them, he could threaten them with a knife. Maybe they would hand over money or arrange a way to get him money.

'At first, I said no. I wanted no part in it. I wasn't threatening anyone with a knife. I wasn't a scumbag. I was just caught up in the wrong crowd. Alexander had gotten hold of me and I was too scared to let go. To get out. To be free. Too scared to say no. I was petrified about what he would do. I agreed with *his* plan. It was a Thursday – I remember it so vividly.' A look of pain washed over her sunken face. 'He picked me up in the car around four in the afternoon. I got in – he didn't say anything to me, just drove—'

'Why did you go, Jo?' I said, my tone harsher than intended.

'Jack, I had no choice. I didn't know whether he'd hurt me, or my family, my friends. You've seen what he's capable of.'

Her point silenced me.

'He picked me up,' she went on. 'We went to the back of the bank. Parked up near the wall. He told me the back of the bank had no cameras – it was a blind spot.'

I knew where she meant. I parked there every day. Someone had told me they'd installed cameras there right after it happened.

'After ten minutes of waiting every bone in my body told me to get out of the car. To run away. But physically, I couldn't move. The two men walked out the back, both holding briefcases, joking and laughing about something. There were two flash cars in the spaces to our right. Alexander was tense, tapping his thigh, glancing around to see if we were alone – I prayed for someone to walk by and delay him, hoping he'd call it off. But no one did. The men got close. Alexander did a visual sweep around us before he jumped out with the knife. He started shouting at the men.'

As Joanne told us the story I watched her trembling hands down on the table.

'Hey Jo, it's okay. Take your time,' I said.

'I didn't see anything of it. I squeezed my eyes shut and covered my face with my hands. After a minute of shouting, Alex got back into the car with both briefcases, threw them on my lap, started the engine, and raced out of there.' She paused to catch her breath. 'I looked down. Blood covered the handles of the briefcases. He'd stabbed them both and left them to bleed out. We left the car park. Alex was driving erratically, swerving in and out of cars, not caring for anyone's life. I wanted to get out but knew I'd die if I opened the door and jumped out at that speed. We joined Furlong Lane. Oh, God, we were going so fast. I wanted it to end. Something inside – I don't know where it came from – told me to grab the Stanley knife I had in my pocket—'

'The one from his garage?' I asked.

She nodded. 'And I lashed out at him and cut his face. He veered right, then left and, when I wrestled him, he forced the car off the road, hitting a tree. I went into a coma. When I woke up three days later, I was staring at the white ceiling of a hospital. He wasn't there. I've never seen him since.'

For a long moment, no one spoke. The kitchen fell dead quiet. I dropped my face into my palms, mentally and emotionally absorbing her story. I imagined what it must have been like for her to see him again after so long. I breathed heavily through my hands and, after I lowered them, our eyes met.

'Jesus, Jo,' I said. 'You should have told me.'

'And when I woke up,' she said, 'I realised I had to make a change. My name was Lorraine Headley at the time, so I changed it. That's why when you asked me about my birth certificate and documents in the past, I'd never shown you. I'd always said I'd lost them.'

It was all coming together.

64

Tuesday
Toddington
JACK

Joanne had been asleep for three hours, which was three hours more than I'd managed. I was drained. The last thing I wanted to do was to go to work today. Lying next to her, I closed my sore eyes, hoping to drift off.

I emotionally struggled to deal with the pain Joanne had been through.

Alexander Hunt.

The car crash.

Changing her name.

Trying to put it behind her.

Then for what happened last night, igniting the thoughts she'd left in the past. Not to mention the men breaking in last Thursday and the two men attacking her.

I opened my eyes again. I watched her. Her face was peaceful. Her chest gently raised and fell in the darkness of the room. She'd been saying the name Alexander over and over.

Alex. Alex. Alex.

Sweat oozed from her skin causing her nightie to stick to her body. I wanted to wake her up, but I knew she needed sleep. She'd only worry about things when she woke up.

Before Mark left last night, I told him I was so grateful for his help. For getting her out alive. I could always count on him to come through. I told him I loved him very much, and he told me to ring if we needed him, no matter what time. Day or night.

I gently lifted the covers off me, careful not to disturb Joanne, and swung my legs onto the floor. In the en-suite, I splashed my tired face in the sink with cold water, then dabbed my face with a soft hand towel. I put on my dressing gown, edged the bedroom door open, and made my way downstairs.

The house was silent and cold.

The kitchen floor was nearly ice cold on my bare feet and made me shiver. I made coffee, went over to the table, took a seat, and took a long sip. The clock above the back door told me it was 2.30 a.m. I looked out the kitchen window, noticed the blinds were still up. All I saw was unknown darkness. Someone could be standing on the other side of the glass, and I wouldn't be able to see them. A sharp shiver rattled my body before I quickly pulled the blinds down.

In the study, I sat down at my computer. I watched the screens for nearly an hour before my eyes got heavy. I stood up, went back upstairs, and climbed into bed, hoping to finally get some sleep.

The last time I checked the time on the digital clock, it was 3.35 a.m.

I blinked, then opened my eyes fully. The room was bright. Sunlight battered the other side of the curtains so fiercely, the room felt warmer. The clock beside my head told me it was just after 7 a.m. The bed felt light, unbalanced, as if there was no one beside me. I didn't hear the gentle breathing I normally heard when she was there. I rolled slowly onto my back towards Joanne.

She wasn't there.

I frowned as I sat up, pulled the covers off me in a panic.

'Jo?' I said, peering into the en-suite. The door was open, illuminated by the morning sun crashing through the window. But there was no Joanne. I grabbed the dressing gown from the back of the bedroom door, tied the belt, and padded soundlessly along the landing.

The door to Lucy's stairs was closed. For a second, I stopped, cocked my head over the bannister of the stairs, and listened. Silence answered me back. I pulled my phone out from the deep, wide pocket of the gown. No texts or missed calls from her.

I don't know why she would but maybe she had gone out.

I hurried down the stairs and peered into the living room. The tv was off, the curtains were closed. Bright sunlight crept in through the narrow slits on either side. As I stepped into the hallway, I heard something.

A dull, quiet, scratching sound.

My ears told me it was coming from the kitchen, where I noticed the door is closed. I mentally noted that we never closed that door. Ever. I grabbed the handle of the door, the scratching sound now getting louder, and pulled it open.

The tip of the blunt knife was being jarred back and forth onto the surface of the kitchen table, scuffing and ruining the wood. Joanne's face was blank, her dark eyes staring at something beyond the table, something only she could see. She didn't even notice me standing directly in front of her as her arm rocked back and forth like a piston.

'Jo?' I said, glowering.

The knife continued digging into the tabletop. I entered, stopped on the opposite side, and saw the damage to the table. Thick notches, maybe half a centimetre deep. Two of them.

'Jo?' I said louder.

Her expression was blank, her glassy eyes gazing into space.

'Jo?' I said firmer this time.

The scratching stopped. She looked up at me. 'Yes?'

'What the fuck are you doing to the table?' I glared at the knife in her hand – it was the biggest one from the set we had near the sink. I glanced over to the set, noticed one is missing. Thick-handled and wide-bladed, something Michael Myers would use in John Carpenter's Halloween films.

'What?' she said, looking muddled. Her eyes focused on me.

I nodded towards the damage. 'The knife… on the table – what on earth are you doing?'

Her eyes fell to the knife in her hand, then down to the scratches on the wood below it. Her face changed. Abruptly she panicked, as if a snake had slithered across her hand, and hurled the knife to her right. It crashed on the tiled floor with a loud ping. She elevated from the table, knocking her chair back fast, and forced her hands over her mouth as she took a few steps back. I saw her eyes flicker left and right frantically until they seemed to zone in on me. She gave me a distant stare.

'Joanne, what's going on?' I said softly, edging forward around the table. She'd been through so much, the last thing I wanted to do was upset her.

'I – I never did that,' she whispered. Tears started to form in her eyes and fall down her cheeks.

I couldn't comprehend the three things I was seeing.

The knife damage to the table.

The fact that she hasn't realised she was even doing it.

Or the fact that she was standing in the middle of the kitchen naked with absolutely nothing on. Not even her underwear.

There was a quiet knock at the door. I opened it to find Elaine standing on the gravel looking up at me wearing a black thin, long-sleeved top, and blue jeans. A laptop bag hung from a strap looping over her shoulder. She offered me a sad, sympathetic smile as she stepped inside.

'Where is she?' she asked.

'Upstairs in bed,' I replied quietly.

Elaine stepped past me but stopped and turned. 'She has been through a lot. It must be hard.'

I nodded in understanding. 'Yeah.'

Last night, Mark had asked Elaine to come over this morning to watch over Joanne and Lucy whilst I went to work. She'd agreed to work from here on her laptop. When I'd calmed Joanne down in the kitchen earlier, I'd hugged her tightly, holding back my own tears – I had to be strong for her. I'd led her fragile, naked body upstairs to the bedroom. I turned on the shower and waited by the glass door until she was finished. She didn't say anything apart from 'I want to go to bed' when she stepped out, which I agreed was probably the best place for her to be. Lucy had come down none-the-wiser about what her mother had done with the knife, asking how she was. I told her she needed her rest and was sleeping, that she'd be down later. I'd spoken to Mark, telling him what'd happened with Joanne. He couldn't believe it, then told me Elaine wouldn't be too long by the time I hung up.

'I've never seen her like that in my life, Elaine,' I said, walking into the kitchen. 'It really scared me.'

'Understandably, Jack,' she replied, a few steps behind me. 'I'll check on her at short intervals, get her whatever she needs.' She gently swung her bag off her shoulder and placed it down on the table, then pulled out a chair, then sat down. 'Is Lucy staying home today?'

'Yeah, she was staying inside today.' I flicked the kettle on. 'Let her watch films all day in her room or smoke on her balcony, I don't care – as long as she's here with you.'

'She's smoking now?' Elaine's eyebrows raised a notch.

I nodded and sighed. I made her a coffee and checked the time. 'I need to set off – or I'll be late.'

'You go. Try to have a good day.'

I stopped at the doorway of the kitchen. 'Will you be alright all day?'

'Yeah, plenty to keep me busy here,' she said with a reassuring smile, pulling the laptop from the bag and placing it in front of her. 'And don't worry, I'll lock the front gates.'

I picked up two briefcases at the door. One was my usual, filled with work-related paperwork. The other, full of money. One hundred thousand pounds to be exact. I said bye to Lucy, closed the front door behind me, and got into the Volvo.

Hembridge Bank

I pulled up in the car park of the bank and turned off the engine. I picked up my phone, texted the person about the money; I arranged to meet them in the rear car park of Sainsbury's – it would be safer than a secluded spot. I'd love to get my hands around the throat of whoever it is, but I couldn't take the risk he wouldn't do the same to me.

After the usual morning rigmarole of entering the office and offering fake 'Good Mornings', I found myself in front of my computer when I heard a knock on the door.

Debra walked in.

'Have you got it?' she asked. She was referring to the late payment of money I pay her each month to keep silent about our recent affair.

Matching her stare, I said, 'No, I do not.'

She pointed a finger at me. 'I've warned you, Jack. I'll be telling—'

'Tell who? My wife?'

'Yes, your wife,' she countered.

'Tell her what the fuck you like – it's too late,' I said, with a grin. 'I told her last night,' I lied.

Debra stared at me blankly, thinking of something clever to say. 'Well,' she placed her right hand on her hip, 'what did she say?'

'She was a little upset, but she forgave me. Because she had done things in the past, we forgave each other, decided to move on with life. There are more important things in this to worry about.'

From the expression on her face, I could see the words hurt her.

'There'll be no more money coming your way, Debra, and if you continue to ask me, you can say goodbye to your job too.'

She stared at me, gobsmacked.

'So, if there's anything else?'

'I'm going to the police - tell them that you raped me.'

65

Hembridge Bank
JACK

That grabbed my attention. I looked up, met her eyes for a long moment. 'You are disgusting.'

'No…' she said. 'You are.'

I returned my focus to my computer and clicked a few times. I noticed after a while she was still standing there. I raised my eyes, saw the cocky smile on her face.

'Really? You would stoop that low and tell the police that I raped you even when I didn't?'

She nodded firmly. 'Yes, I would. And I will. If I don't get my two thousand by today.'

I clicked something on the desktop screen in front of me and looked up at her. 'So, even after you've blackmailed me all these months to keep quiet about our affair and because I'm not paying you anymore, you're going to tell the police I've raped you?'

'Yes,' she said firmly.

'Even when I haven't?'

'Yes.'

I smiled into the small webcam at the top of my monitor before I click the STOP RECORDING button. Debra was none the wiser that I'd been recording it via a webcam video. I opened the video file and turned up the volume.

'Even after you've blackmailed me all these months to keep quiet about our affair and because I'm not paying you anymore, you're going to tell the police I've raped you?'

'Yes,'

'Even when I haven't?'

'Yes.'

I smiled. 'You're not doing a thing,' I told her.

The smug grin vanished from her face. She slammed her hand down hard onto the desk, the sound booming around the walls of the office. Then she turned and stormed out, slamming the door behind her.

At the rear car park of Sainsbury's, I stopped next to a red fiesta, killed the engine, and sighed heavily. The dull pain behind my eyes had worsened since I was at the bank. The board told me their idea to bring in a new marketing manager to improve our current advertising strategies across the branch and surrounding area. I didn't really have much input and kept quiet throughout. My mind was on other things.

I glanced at the dashboard. Nearly 12.30 p.m. I welcomed the cool breeze on my face seeping in through the partially open window, then grabbed my phone to check for any texts. There was one from Elaine, sent an hour ago:

Hi, Jack, Jo is up and about, she has been in the shower again and I've made her toast and tea. She was still not quite herself. Said she feels shivery. We're watching some American program in the living room with Lucy. Text you soon. E x

I started to reply but my attention was interrupted by the sound of a car pulling into the car park. It was a police car. It crawled along wearily, the driver looking for a space. I took a second to mentally note the registration like I did with most cars that I passed.

When I was younger, I had an amazing ability to remember every registration plate I saw. Family cars, friends' cars, even random cars belonging to the neighbours we never spoke to. Unfortunately, when the mind reached the tender age of twenty-five, its ability went downhill, including the ability to memorize numbers or absorb new information. Apparently, the best way to preserve this mental decline was to learn a new language. I was good at Spanish at school, and my ability to pronounce the words like a Spaniard impressed even the supply teacher who was sent over on a six-month secondment from Malaga. But nowadays, I'm too busy meeting random people in car parks, giving them blackmail money, or watching surveillance around my house to stop people from breaking in to even consider brushing up on my Spanish skills.

I glared back down at the phone and re-read the message, thinking about Joanne, how she was earlier. How she didn't know what she was doing, scratching the knife into the kitchen table. The events of last night had —

I heard footsteps next to my door.

'Well, hello there, Jack,' I heard a voice say.

I nearly jumped out of my skin. I turned to see who it was. 'You?'

'Yes, me. Have you got my money?' he said.

'You're kidding me?' I said, scowling.

With a wide grin, he shook his head.

I was speechless. I stared at him, my eyes burning into his. His audacity to set this whole thing up and stand there asking me for one hundred thousand pounds astonished me. And that stupid tash above his lip still pissed me off, the way it served no purpose apart from making him look like a circus joke.

'Well?' Detective Johnson asked, his tone now impatient. 'I haven't got all day.'

For a long moment, I held his stare, but eventually, his smile faded, and he gave me a stern look.

'Where are the photos?' I said.

He smiled. Whilst maintaining eye contact with me, he reached into the large pocket of his thin black coat and pulled something out. 'I printed these out. These are the only ones.' He held them a good distance away, just out of my reach.

'If you printed them, then that means you have them on a computer, doesn't it? And you could just print them again whenever you feel like it? So, don't take me for a mug.' All the niceties and kind manners had gone now.

'I guess you'll have to take my word for it,' he said, with a wink. A rush of anger swept over me and I wanted to punch him in the face so bad. However, assaulting a detective wouldn't be the smartest move. 'Listen… you have no choice here. And plus, if I said I won't, I won't. Got that?' he added.

'That means nothing. I have no assurance whatsoever.'

'No, you don't,' Johnson said, knowingly. He had me boxed in on the edge of a cliff. 'Now, I take it that's the money in that fine-looking briefcase?'

'Yeah,' I said, unenthusiastically. 'How did you get hold of the photos?'

'I have my ways. That's all you need to know, Mr Haynes. Now hand it over. As I said, I haven't got all day.'

I leaned to my left, lifted the case, and, with reluctance, handed it to him. He was about to say something when we heard something.

'Hello,' a frail voice said. We both look towards the front of the car, where a seventy-something woman, leaning on the handlebar of a trolley full of orange bags, was smiling at him. she was standing by her car, a light blue Nissan Micra.

Detective Johnson offered her a smile. 'Hi. You okay?'

She nodded and returned the wave.

'Old nosy bag,' Johnson muttered out of her earshot. He looked back to me but, for a second, stared beyond me, as if something had caught his attention. He opened his mouth as if he was going to speak, but then he stuttered. 'Well - well, Jack… I'd love to stand here and talk all day, but I have things to do. Other business to attend to.'

I watched him dash back to the police car with the briefcase. He jumped in and closed the door. The sound of the screeching tires disturbed the quiet hustle of mid-day shoppers as he vanishes like a ghost.

Whatever the detective saw behind my car had seriously rattled him.

66

Milton Keynes

DCI Clarke and DS Horton pulled up onto the kerb outside of Milton Keynes Taxis. The sun was blazing down, the temperature soaring. They both got out, headed for the entrance door. A smell of strawberries wafted through the air from a young lad vaping on the corner to their right.

'I know this seemed pointless, but just maybe, they might know something,' Clarke said.

'No harm in trying,' agreed Horton.

As they walked through the doors of the building, it was cool. The air con doing a grand job. The woman at the front desk glanced up at them and smiled. It soon faded when she realised they were not here to order a taxi. 'Can – can I help you?'

Clarke smiled. 'Can we speak to the manager, please?'

The woman, a twenty-something attractive individual called *Natalie,* according to her name tag, looked blank. 'The manager?'

'Yes, please.' Clarke nodded.

'Erm, I—'

The phone beside her rang. She held up a palm. 'Just one second.' Clarke nodded patiently and watched her grab it. 'Hello, MK Taxi's…'

Clarke and Horton took a step back away from the desk for a moment. Clarke asked Horton about his wife and daughter, and how they were coping at home.

'Life's tough mate,' Horton confessed, 'but someone's gotta do it.'

Clarke nodded. He admired DS James Horton. His head was screwed on. He knew what real life is all about. A good detective too and, with the massive potential to go far, Clarke expected promotions to fall at his feet during the long, promising career ahead of him.

They heard the click of the phone being placed back down onto the desk.

'Sorry about that,' she said. 'How can I help you – oh the manager, you need?'

'Yes, please,' Clarke said.

'What's it regarding? Maybe I can help?' she said, leaning forward a little. The top three buttons of her white shirt were undone, leaving nothing to their imaginations.

'One of your drivers picked up a man nearly three years ago from Popworld.' Clarke pointed behind her in the direction of the club. 'It's just behind this building actually. We need to speak to the driver who picked him up.'

Natalie stared blankly at them both. 'Three years ago?'

'I know,' Clarke said, 'I'm aware it's probably a long shot.'

'You're not kidding,' she said, smiling. 'Let me see.' She readjusted herself on the swivel chair and her eyes fell to the screen on the desk. The detectives heard the mouse clicking. 'What's the date?'

Horton told her.

'What time did the driver pick the client up?'

'One a.m.,' said Clarke. 'Exact time of the pick-up was 12.58 if that helps.'

'Let me see.'

The detectives watched her blue eyes flick across the screen. 'Ah, there. The driver was Manual Corr. He picked him up at 1 a.m. at Popworld. He dropped him off at Favell Drive just before twenty past one.' She looked up at the detectives.

'Is Mr Corr still working here?' Horton asked.

'Yes, he's been a driver here for nearly ten years. He's out the back if you want him?'

Christmas had come early.

'Yes, please.'

Natalie picked up the phone and called him. Within a minute, he was standing in front of them. He was tall and slim. The thick eyebrows and wonky teeth caught Clarke's attention as he leaned forward to shake the man's hand. 'Mr Corr?'

'Yes?' A look of panic ran across his face as if he'd done something wrong. 'What's – what's this about?'

Clarke raised a palm. 'Don't worry, nothing's wrong. Can we sit down and ask you a few questions?'

The taxi driver seemed hesitant and glanced toward Natalie. She nodded at him. He moved away from the reception desk and took the detectives to the small seating area to the left.

'What's this about?' he asked, before sitting down. He seemed anxious, unsettled.

'We'll get straight to it – we know you're busy,' Clarke said. 'Three years ago, you picked up a man from Popworld at one in the morning. This man was actually found murdered a few hours later.'

'Hold on a minute, are you saying I did this?' His postures stiffened.

'Wait – can you remember?' Horton asked.

'Yes, I can. I also remember seeing it on the news the following day. He was found dead. Yes, I remember.'

'Good. What we need to know is,' Clarke edged forward, 'is why when you picked him up, did you set off, then suddenly stop for nearly a minute, before carrying on again?'

Manual tilted his head back and clamped his eyes shut. 'Oh, God. It was so long ago.'

'Anything you could remember would be great,' Horton said in encouragement. A long moment passed.

He opened his eyes suddenly. 'I remember he told me to stop for a minute. Then the woman got in. They argued for a bit then we set off.'

'*Woman*?'

'Yeah,' the driver explained, 'the lady who was with him.'

Clarke's eyes narrowed. 'Can you remember her? This lady?'

Manual winced in a small apology. 'I – I glanced at her briefly through the rear-view mirror. That was all.'

'Hair colour? Build – slim, anything?' Horton said.

'Yeah, slim, I think… she had dark hair – or was it a dark red. I don't know.'

'Can you remember what she was wearing?' Clarke asked. Horton knew they had the footage from the club. If the driver could somehow remember what she was wearing, then they could watch it again, see if they could spot something.

'I'm sorry, I can't - I can't remember,' he said, apologetically.

'Okay, that's great so far.' Clarke finished scribbling notes on the pad in his hands and glanced back up at him. 'And you dropped them off at Favell Drive in Dunstable?'

Manual Corr once again clamped his eyes shut. After reciting the memory, he said, 'No, I was meant to. But as I drove them down Watling Street, the lady said she felt sick and wanted to get out. I pulled over to let them out.'

'Where?' Horton asked.

'Furzton Lake car park.'

'Was the lady his wife?' asked Clarke. 'Did it seem they were married?'

'I think so. They were arguing about someone inside the club, but I don't remember them saying a name. It... it was a long time ago detectives. I'm sorry.'

'Thank you very much for your time, Mr Corr.' Clarke stood up and shook Manual's sweaty hand.

He nodded and disappeared around the back of the desk. The detectives thanked the receptionist, Natalie, for her help and then left, stepping out into the boiling sun.

'Furzton Lake car park,' said Horton, closing the passenger door.

'Yep, very close to where his body was found.'

'First thing, I believe we need to see the camera from the building next door – it will give us a better view of what happened. Maybe we'll find out who the woman is that got into the taxi. See if Alison Lewes was telling the truth when she said she never got in the taxi with him.'

'Yes,' Clarke agreed. 'That's exactly what we're going to do.'

67

Luton

Detective Johnson pulled up onto the curb of a quiet street. He plucked the phone from his pocket and made a call.

'Hello,' said the voice on the other end of the phone.

'Hey, Ray. Johnson here. I've just met with Jack Haynes.'

'Very good. Did he have what you asked for?'

'He certainly did. You told me if anyone could do it, it would be him – you know him well.'

'Yes, he's always found a fucking way, the resilient bastard. I'll give him that. I wonder where he's got the money from?'

'It doesn't matter, does it, Ray? He has. And that's the main thing. Have you spoken with him?'

'Not recently - I'm giving him space to get things sorted.'

Johnson looked down into the footwell of the passenger seat at the briefcase. He smiled.

'So, are you going to help me get *my* money back? As planned?' asked Ray. 'It's the least you can do for me now.'

Johnson grinned inside the car, shaking his head, lying through his teeth: 'Yes, that's what we agreed. I'm a man of my word.'

'Good. Once I get the money, you can do what you like with him,' said Ray. 'Arrest him, take him to that guy, Hunt. Whatever you need.'

'Make sure you give your son some of the money too,' Johnson added. 'If it wasn't for Carl getting the photos from his daughter, Lucy, we wouldn't have got anything.'

After saying bye, Johnson put the phone down. He pulled out onto the road and joined the steady flow of traffic. Once he parked in one of the bays at Bedfordshire police station he picked up his phone and made another call.

After four rings, it was answered. 'Johnson.'

'Alex, listen, we have a problem.'

'What's the problem, Johnson?'

'Them photos, you know, the—'

'Yes, I know what photos!' Hunt snapped. 'What of them?'

'I've just seen them – they've been sent in. We received them an hour ago.'

'That fucking stupid bastard, Jack Haynes!' shouted Hunt.

'It wasn't Jack Haynes who sent them in. It was someone else.'

'Who – who was it?' demanded Hunt.

'Guy called Ray West. He works with Jack at the bank.'

'But it still means Jack didn't delete the photos, as you asked? Were you not persuasive enough? I thought you were my guy, Johnson?'

Johnson gulped. 'Oh, I made it crystal clear, Alex. Jack was well aware of what was at stake here. I told him what would happen to him if he didn't delete the photos.'

'Shit,' grunted Hunt. 'They'll know who I am.'

'No, luckily they don't recognise you at all,' he lied. 'But my boss has his best team on it, so it won't be long. It'll be on the news tonight, or first thing tomorrow morning.'

'You need to get those photos, Johnson. Find them fucking photos – and lose them. Make them fucking disappear, because if not, I'll make you fucking disappear. Then I need to send someone round to see Jack Haynes and this fucking Ray West.'

'Don't threaten law enforcement, Alex. Do you—'

'I pay your wage!' snapped Hunt. 'You'll do exactly as I ask.'

'Okay, okay,' said Johnson.

Johnson had searched through Lucy's social media profile. That led to Carl, then he found out that Carl had a Dad, called Ray, who in fact, worked with Jack at the bank. Turned out that Ray and Johnson went to the same school together, too. Small world.

The line went quiet for a long moment.

'Alex?'

'I'm here. Just thinking,' replied Hunt. 'Okay. I know where Haynes lives – obviously – but send me an address for this Ray West. I'll send someone over.'

'Okay, I'll text you.'

'Fine work, Johnson… remember get rid of the photos. Number one priority.' Hunt hung up the phone and the line went dead. Johnson smiled to himself. He was one hundred grand up. Ray West wouldn't be the wiser that his days were coming to an end. And, as for Haynes, well he was more than likely living his last Tuesday.

Hunt received the text from Johnson with an address for Ray West. Ann popped into his study, picked up some paperwork. 'Need anything?' she asked.

'No, thank you, Ann.'

She left the room.

Hunt smiled to himself. Before Johnson had rung, Stuart had phoned to inform him that he'd just seen Johnson in Sainsbury's car park, meeting with Jack Haynes. That Jack had handed him a briefcase and, when Johnson had seen him and Derek, he panicked and fled.

He knew it was time to call Pollock. He needed this done quickly. Pollock was the man to take care of it. After five rings, Pollock picked up his phone.

'Pollock, I need your services.'

'Names?'

'Ray West – I'll forward you his address soon. Jack Haynes, which I'll do the same. And, Detective Johnson – he's becoming a liability recently.'

'Alternative rates apply, Alexander,' he said.

'That's fine – how much?'

'I would require one-hundred grand per man.'

68

Wednesday
Luton

Pollock was sitting inside his white Jaguar XF-RS at the side of the quiet road. The clock on the dashboard told him it was 6.32 a.m. The sky above was bright and blue, the soaring sun climbing in the distance, the heat already warming the ground.

He had been there for twenty-seven minutes, opposite Ray West's house. Two vehicles had passed during that time. One of them was a van, picking up a labourer, who was dressed in a fluorescent vest, a hundred metres up on the right. The other, a man dressed in a suit, driving a Volvo estate.

The house he was looking at was nice and presentable. Semi-detached, painted white, with a tidy, black-glossy finish around the sills, door, and frame.

Pollock looked down at the gun in his gloved hand, admiring it for a second. It was 6.34 a.m. People would start waking up, and going through their morning routines soon, which would mean the street would get busier.

He had to make his move now. He had to be quick.

After taking a deep breath, he exhaled slowly. He delicately dabbed his pockets: pick locking tools, a small knife, Stanley knife, and a thin flexible wire. He pushed his gun into the front of the belt and opened the door, then stepped out into the early warmth.

He glanced left and right, then walked briskly across the road. Pollock was tall, borderline six foot four. The long coat made him appear taller. He wasn't broad-shouldered, but he was laced with ripped muscle under his clothes and walked with the confidence of knowing it. The sun shone off his bald head, making his skin somehow seem bulletproof.

He stepped onto Ray's driveway, taking a small moment to admire Ray's choice of car. A white Jaguar XF. A simpler, less expensive, more economical version of his own.

'Fancy that,' he whispered.

On the doorstep, Pollock dipped his right hand deep inside his jacket pocket and pulled out his tool kit. He opened the front door lock within twenty-two seconds, then silently edged the door open.

The hallway was dark. It took only a second for his pupils to dilate. Through an open door to the kitchen, strips of light poked in through either side of the long blind covering the kitchen window at the end of the short hallway. The stairs were to his left and, to his right, two doors were both closed.

In silence, he stood for a moment. Satisfied there were no sounds, he moved to the left, pulling his gun from his belt. Without making a sound he crept up the stairs. At the top, natural light flooded in through the bathroom window.

Straight ahead, next to the bathroom, there was a door slightly ajar a few inches. It was dark inside. To the right, another door was shut, and a door to the right of that was also closed.

With his gun in his gloved hand, finger ready on the trigger, he gently opened the first door with the palm of his left hand. The door swung open on nice, oiled hinges. He raised the gun as he entered cautiously.

Carl was sound asleep, snoring lightly. The sheets were half over his naked body, one of his long, hairy legs hanging off the side of the single bed he looked far too big for. Without a sound, Pollock backed out to the landing and pulled the door closed back to how he found it. To the right, the next door was shut properly. He knew he'd have to use the handle to open it and prayed the spring of the handle mechanism stayed quiet. Using his left hand—

'The fuck are you?'

Pollock shot his head to the left.

It was Carl, standing naked at his bedroom door. Before Pollock could react, Carl jumped at him, covering the distance impressively, throwing his outstretched arms hard into Pollock's chest. Pollock fell back and went down but, somehow, using his skills and momentum, he rolled backward and was back up on his feet within no time at all.

'The hell's that?' shouted a muffled voice through the closed door of the front bedroom.

'You a fucking ninja?' Carl shouted. 'Who the fuck are you? What are you doing—'

Carl fell silent when he saw the bald man raise the gun.

'Carl, what the hell's going on?' said Ray, opening his door, and rubbing his tired eyes. He saw the gun. 'Who the hell are you?'

'Both keep calm, and I'll let your son live. Make any movement, and you would both die,' Pollock said slowly and clearly as if explaining it to a pair of four-year-olds. Pollock didn't have the ideal view he wanted. The sunlight from the bathroom hid much of Carl's face, but it did enhance his large naked outline, so seeing him move would be easier.

Carl edged forward a little. He was game, keen on using his width and size to overpower Pollock at the earliest chance he had. 'Dad, who's this prick?'

'Just calm down… calm down. I don't know who he is, or what he wants,' Ray said to his son. He turned to Pollock. 'What do you want?'

'If your gorilla of a son even looks at me the wrong way, he's getting a bullet to the face. Now I suggest you ask him nicely if he would return to his room. Then you and I can have a word.'

Ray told Carl to go back to his room.

'No, fuck him. What's he doing here?' shouted Carl, pointing a hairy arm at Pollock. 'Do you know him?'

Pollock took a step closer, aiming the gun at Carl's hanging penis. 'How about I shoot your dick off instead?'

Carl cupped both hands around himself in a panic.

'I tell you what, Ray. Take this.' Whilst Pollock kept the gun on Carl, he reached inside his tool kit, pulled out a needle. 'Ray, put this into your son's arm and inject him with it.'

'I – I will do no such fucking thing!' stuttered Ray.

'Okay, you both die—'

'Whoa, wait – what is it?' asked Ray.

'It will put him to sleep for a little while. He'll wake up with a headache. That's all.'

Pollock leaned closer to Ray, dropped the needle near Ray's feet. He was aware he had given Ray a weapon but knew he'd be wise enough to do the right thing. Ray bent over to pick it up.

'Dad, there's not a chance you're—'

'Carl, just shut up! Be quiet.' Ray took the rubber cap off the end of the needle. 'Where?'

'His arm. Outside of the bicep will do. It'll work in thirty seconds. Don't worry, big lad. You'll feel nothing.'

Ray, with Carl trying to niggle free, pushed the needle into his son's left arm, using his thumb to eject the clear, viscous liquid.

'Just go in your room, now son.' Ray locked eyes with Carl. 'Go on, I'll be okay – he just wants to talk.' Carl slowly turned, disappeared back into his room feeling drowsy. Ray closed his son's door and turned to face Pollock.

'What do you want? Money, you want money. I work at a bank, and I could get—'

'I know where you work. I know all about you. I also know that you have photos in your possession that you sent to the police.'

'Photos? Police?' said Ray, frowning. 'I have no idea what you mean. What photos?'

Pollock didn't say a word and kept the gun on Ray's bare chest.

'Who sent you here? Who are you working for?'

Pollock said nothing.

Ray mulled over what photos he meant. *Ahhh the photos that Lucy and Carl took?*

'Listen, I can get you Jack Haynes. Did he send you? How does he - no, he won't have. He wouldn't have done this—'

'What about Jack Haynes?' asked Pollock.

Ray swallowed 'Did Haynes send you? The son of a bitch.'

'I will be seeing him later, but I'm here to see you first. You're still alive because I need you to do me a favour – you have some information I require.'

'What information?'

'Apparently, there's security at Jack Haynes' house – and it won't be a problem for me at all. But it would be easier if you ring him. Tell him that he has to come here. Now.'

'Now?'

'Right now,' said Pollock.

'And say what? He won't just come here at this time.'

'Make something up. If you want to live, I'm sure you think of something. Go get your phone.' Pollock stepped forward with his arm outstretched, the gun on Ray's face, encouraging him to move. He followed him inside his bedroom, watching him grab it from the small bedside unit.

Ray tapped a few buttons and, taking a nervous breath, he put the phone to his ear.

'It's ringing,' Ray told Pollock.

69

Toddington
JACK

The sound of a phone ringing woke me up. My head was spinning. I opened my tired eyes, leaned over to see my phone dancing on the bedside table. I grabbed it, recognised the name of the caller.

'Ray?'

'Jack. Jack. It's Ray!'

I pulled the phone away from my ear to see the time in the top right-hand corner of the phone's display. 'Ray, it's half six in the morning, what the fu—'

'Listen, Jack, I need you to come here now. To my house – you've been before right? I need you to—'

'Ray, what the hell's going on? Just calm down.' I found my bearings and sat up.

'It's my son,' he said desperately. 'He's got a big problem. He—'

'Call the police then. Why are you ringing me for?'

Joanne shuffled behind me. She sat up and rubbed her tired eyes.

'Jack, who's – who's that?' she asked.

I held up a palm.

'You're a friend, Jack,' Ray said, 'I need you.'

'Oh, really? You don't blackmail friends,' I countered. 'Ring an ambulance. I'm going—'

'Wait, wait!' he shouted. There's a hush of silence, then, 'I can't phone the police or an ambulance. Not yet anyway. Listen, if you come over now, I won't say anything about the bank. You can keep the money. I don't want it. Please, Jack, this is urgent.'

I wasn't happy with him but could hear the desperation in his voice. I couldn't imagine what'd happened to his son.

'What's he done? Your son?' I'd known Ray for a few years now, but I'd never met his son, Carl.

'He's got into real trouble – with money. Only you have the power to sort it. He's been up all night crying to me. Please, Jack.'

I shook my head a few times and fell silent, mulling over what he'd said.

'Jack?'

'Yeah, I'm here, Ray… okay, I'll be over when I can.'

'Jack, thank—'

I ended the call, cutting him off. Mentally, I noted where he lived. I remembered the white house on the corner. He was right, I had been there before.

'Why the hell's he ringing at this time for?' Jo muttered.

'Something's happened.'

'Oh God,' she said. 'What?'

'With his son. He needs my help.'

'Your help? Well, you can tell him to get lost, he can't just—'

'He said if I go, he doesn't want the money. He's not bothered.'

Jo sat in silence for a while. 'What's the problem with his son?'

'Something financial apparently. That's why he needs me. I don't know – I'm the only one who could sort it.' I got up and stretched, then walked over to my drawers, pulled out some jogging bottoms and a t-shirt. After putting them on, I went to the toilet, then said bye to Joanne.

I stepped out into the warmth, made my way across the gravel towards the Volvo. Following the winding driveway, I used the fob to open the gates, then pulled out onto Park Road, heading in the direction of the bright, rising sun towards the M1 motorway.

70

Toddington

Joanne got up from the bed and put on her dressing gown. She picked up her phone and dialled Mark. 'Pick up, pick up,' she said, conscious of the time on the bedside clock: 6.43 a.m.

'Joanne?' said Mark, groggily.

'Listen, I'm sorry for ringing. I wouldn't if it wasn't important.'

'What's – what's up, Jo?' His voice was now clearer.

'Jack has just got a call from Ray – the guy who is wanting—'

'Yeah, go on,' said Mark, not needing an explanation.

Joanne took a breath. 'Well, Ray said he desperately needs Jack's help. Something to do with his son or something. Said he doesn't want the money if Jack helps him with whatever it is.'

Mark waited for more.

'I think there's more to it, Mark. He left suddenly,' she explained.

'I'll get dressed, be over ASAP.'

'Okay, see you when you're here.'

Joanne's watch told her it was 6.50 a.m. when there was a knock at the door. She opened it wearing blue jeggings and an orange t-shirt. 'Hey.'

'Morning,' said Mark, stepping inside. 'When did he leave?'

'Just before I rang you. Half six maybe.'

'Where does Ray live?'

'Luton,' said Joanne. Mark watched her nervously fiddle with her fingers.

Mark nodded. 'Okay. Go get Lucy. We'll drop her off at ours. Elaine is already up.'

'I've shouted her, she'll be down soon.'

'Do you know where in Luton?'

A thin wave of embarrassment washed over her. Mark could see her cheeks start to warm. 'I – I... please don't judge me,' Joanne said. Mark stared and gave her a slow nod before she proceeded. 'I installed an app on my phone to track the Volvo.'

She pulled out her phone and showed Mark, who stepped forward to peer over it.

Mark felt it must be a trust issue she had, but it was got nothing to do with him, so said nothing about it. It was his brother's marriage, not his. 'Where is he now?'

'Stopped on Carlton Crescent in Luton.'

Mark's eyes widened. 'Carlton Crescent isn't far from our house. We'll drop Lucy off and head straight over.'

Joanne turned, glared up the stairs. 'Lucy!'

At the top of the stairs, Lucy appeared, looking tired, heavy eyes lining her sleepy frown. She was wearing a thin masked of make-up on her face, a black creased hoody, and black leggings. 'This is ridiculous. It's like the middle of the night,' she muttered.

'I know,' agreed Jo. 'But come on, let's go.'

Jo locked the front door, went over to the car, and got in the front passenger seat of the Insignia. She was reminded of the damage caused to it after the poker game. Lucy climbed in the back and slouched in the seat. She opened her phone to check social media while Mark got in, put on his belt, turned the engine on, edged forward.

'Jo, is he still there? Carlton Crescent?' asked Mark.

Joanne looked down at her screen. 'Yeah.'

'The hell is going on mum?' a tired, sated voice said from the back seat.

'It—' Joanne paused. 'We'll tell you later, okay? We're going to drop you off at auntie Elaine's for a little bit. Don't worry, you'll be back for college.'

'Keep me off if you like,' she said, hopeful.

'No chance,' said Joanne.

A few minutes passed. Mark glanced at Joanne. 'How are you doing?'

'I'm okay, tired, but—'

'I mean… in yourself?' he said. When she never answered, he said, 'Jack told me what happened yesterday with the… erm… the knife.'

Joanne glimpsed down at her thighs. Her dark hair rocked forward, covering the side of her attractive face. Once she looked up, Mark saw her glassy eyes.

'I – I'm okay now. It just got all too much for me,' she confessed.

Mark smiled sadly and looked back at the road.

Just under fifteen minutes later Mark came to a halt outside of their house. Elaine opened the front door, waiting. Lucy opened the back door of the Insignia, climbed out, closed it gently, and headed up the inclined driveway towards Elaine.

Mark and Joanne checked the tracker. Jack was still at Carlton Crescent. He put the gear into first and set off.

71

Luton
JACK

I pulled up onto the kerb outside of Ray's house, turned off the engine, and sighed nervously. I wasn't looking forward to seeing him, not with everything that had happened. But he was desperate for my help – I couldn't turn away from him. The sticky heat outside caused clammy, sweat patches under the arms of my thin t-shirt. I looked through the windscreen at the bright morning glare and scratched my beard. I glanced to my left through the passenger window. Ray's white Jaguar was nestled in the driveway. I grabbed my phone, found his number, and called him.

It rang until I heard the automated voicemail. I hung up and tried again.

Nothing.

I stepped out into the blind, blaring heat, and pushed my door closed, waiting a moment as a small, grey van edged through the gap just enough for one car. The courteous driver gave me a half smile as he passed. I rounded the bonnet of the Volvo, stepped up onto his driveway, and made my way to his front door.

Instead of knocking, I reached for the chrome handle of the jet-black door and opened it. The hallway was cool and dimly lit, enough light protruded around the edges of the drawn kitchen blinds to notice the carpet was grey and the walls were white.

'Ray, it was Jack!' I shouted.

I moved slowly towards the kitchen after no reply. The usual kitchen appliances sat neatly on the worktop: toaster, microwave, kettle, a collection of mugs. The sink was located in the centre of the worktop, on the far wall, just below the wide window. Opposite the sink, there was a rectangular table, a bowl of fruit in the centre of it, and beside that, a thin pile of paperwork. I backed out of the kitchen and, using my palm, opened the dining room door to my left. The room loomed in the darkness. Long curtains at the far side of the room blocked out the vibrant sunlight which threatened to get in.

'Ray?' I said wearily.

There were four chairs wrapped around a wooden table at the centre of the room, a television in the corner near the curtains, and a tall, wide bookshelf in the alcove towards the right, with old classic thrillers lining the spaces. I backed out of the room and called Ray's phone again.

As the phone rings in my ear, I heard something in the house.

His ringtone.

I frowned, cock my head to listen, struggling to place it. I padded along the short hallway and, outside the closed door of the living room, it became louder. I pushed down the handle, and edged the door open, the bottom of it grazing across the carpet underneath it.

'Ray, you in here?' I said quietly.

I stepped into the darkness. A white leather sofa was ahead of me, the back of it against the wall. In front of the sofa, I saw the corner of a bright blue rug on the floor. I ran my hand across the wall to my left, trying to locate the light switch. There. The room erupted in cold, harsh light.

To the right of the rug, there was a bigger sofa, facing the fireplace.

Ray was slouched on the sofa.

I threw my hands to my open mouth, letting out a harsh, short gasp, and froze, unable to move.

In his underwear, he silently stared towards the ceiling. His mouth was open wide. His body was perfectly still. His face was drenched in blood, oozing from a gaping bullet hole in the centre of his forehead. It ran down his chest in a thick, viscous crimson line until it met the top of his underwear.

'Jesus fucking Christ!' I yelled, staggering back quickly into the wall, cracking the back of my head against it. I leaned forward, throwing my hands to the back of my head, rubbing up and down with my head until the throbbing eases.

I composed myself, built up the courage to peer around the door again toward Ray. 'What the fuck is happening?' I whispered.

My head spun. I felt sick. The churning in the pit of my stomach cartwheeled inside of me. My body threw itself violently to the left over the arm of the sofa, and I threw up until there was nothing left but sour bile, burning the back of my throat.

I wiped my mouth with the back of my palm and struggled up using the aid of the sofa arm. My legs were weak, shaky and, for a second, I feared I was going to collapse. From my pocket, I pulled out my phone, start tapping —

'Hello, Jack,' said a cool, calm voice behind me.

I froze. I turned towards the hallway. A bald, tall man was standing there, wearing a long coat. At the end of the right sleeve, I saw a gun in his hands, and I moved back quickly, stumbling back on the blue rug. I saw Ray's body in the corner of my eye but focused on the confident man entering the room.

'I think he has seen better days, hasn't he?' the man said, nodding towards Ray.

I tried to speak, but an inaudible sound came out.

He raised his right arm, pointing the gun directly at my face. My body jerked into shock and I pissed myself. It was the first time since I was five. As I felt it coming through the material of my jogging bottoms, I saw his eyes lower. Realising what I'd done, a wide smile found his lips, then he laughed hysterically. My cheeks grew hot in embarrassment.

'Who - who are you?' I said.

'It doesn't matter who I am,' the man replied. He brought his left hand up to meet his right and, with both hands on the gun, he steadied the 9mm. He took a couple of steps closer. I backed into the television stand in the corner, realized I was unable to go anywhere.

I threw my hands in the air, cowered to my knees, and clamped my eyes shut. 'Pleas—'

A loud crack rippled the silence of the room. I flinched.

After a long second of realising I was still here, I very slowly opened my eyes and squinted towards him.

A guise of pain ran across his face as he staggered, then he fell to his knees and dropped to the floor. Blood ran from a cut on the top of his head

It took me a while to figure out what happened.

Behind the bald man, I saw my brother, Mark, standing there, panting, with a hammer in his right hand. 'Jack,' he said. He glared at Ray. 'What the fuck?'

'Mark,' I cried, feeling an enormous wave of relief fill the room. He dashed over, helped me to my feet.

'Are you okay?' he said.

'I pissed myself,' I confessed, looking down at my clothes.

'Come on, let's go,' he said, holding me up. He then led me towards the door of the living room.

We stopped in the hallway when Joanne appeared, a face full of worry.

'Jack,' she screamed in a short excitement. She hugs me so tight, it hurt. 'Are you okay?'

I managed a nod.

'Come on, we need to go,' Mark urged. 'Now.'

'What the hell is happening?' she asked, moving past me into the living room. She let out a loud shriek at the sight of Ray on the sofa and the bald man on the floor, who was slowly shuffling in pain.

'I don't know – Ray's dead. He killed him.' I pointed at the bald man on the floor. 'We need to go, now!' I shouted.

Mark regained his grip on my arm and told Joanne to go first.

'What about him?' Mark said, referring to the man on the floor.

'Leave him,' I shouted, desperate to get out of here.

Joanne turned, dashed out to the hallway, took a left, and headed for the open front door. The doorway wasn't wide enough for Mark and me to go side by side, so he backed off, letting me go first. I rounded the edge of the doorframe, watched Joanne go out into the bright sunlight. Mark lost his grip on me for a moment.

I made it to the door, jumped over the lip of the frame. I suddenly stopped after I hurdled the step. I didn't hear Mark behind me. No hurried footsteps pounding down the narrow hall. 'Mark?' I gasp, struggling for air.

'Wait,' he shouted back from the living room.

I went back. 'Mark, come on, we need to get out of here.'

'What about him?' he said, pointing to the wriggling bald man still faced down on the carpet.

'Leave him!' I screamed. I watch Mark stare at him with the hammer hanging by his side, mulling over his options. 'We aren't killers, Mark, come on!'

The bald man was still on the floor, moving slowly, his arms tiredly swimming across the blue rug trying to locate the gun he'd dropped.

'Mark, come on!' I yanked at his arm.

Mark nodded towards me. We turned and left the living room. Through the open door, I saw Joanne waiting at the end of the driveway in frantic anticipation. I jumped the shallow lip of the door again down on the steps.

And that's when I hear it.

Pffftttt.

Followed by brash, clumsy thuds on the floorboards in the hallway behind me. I spun around.

Mark fumbled into the hallway, hunched over, crashing into the wall of the stairs. He collapsed to the floor in a heap. I saw blood seeping from somewhere on his back, the wet circle of crimson spreading across his t-shirt quickly. He cried out in agony.

'Mark!' I screamed.

I charged over the door step but come to a halt. Loud thuds erupted from the living room. The bald man was up on his feet - I knew he had a gun. Mark let out his final sigh and dropped his face into the carpet. The footsteps from the living room rattled the hallway. I realized I couldn't help my brother. He had gone.

I decided to turn and run.

I darted down the driveway towards the Volvo, briefly locking eyes with Joanne, who stood nervously on the pavement, glaring at me with worried, wide eyes.

'Go, now!' I shouted. 'Now!'

72

Luton
JACK

'Jo! Go, go!'

I burst down the driveway, reached the path, almost knocking Joanne over as she awkwardly stood in my way. She looked terrified. She cried in pain as I barged into her, nearly toppling her forward until I grabbed her and pushed her towards the passenger door of the Volvo.

'Come on, move, Jo!' I cried.

She was too slow.

We didn't have long. The bald man was only seconds behind. She reached the passenger door of the Volvo, heaved it open, jumped in, but slipped, scraping her shin on the lip of the door causing her to wail in agony.

I rounded the back of the car, pulled open the driver's door, dived in before it bounced back and trapped me. I heard Joanne cry as she struggled up onto the seat. She winced, holding her throbbing, bloody shin. I grabbed the keys from my right pocket and placed them into the ignition but missed the slot twice, stabbing the plastic around it. I tried to steady my hand, desperate to compose myself. Joanne pulled her door closed, the harsh slam erupting inside the car.

'Come on!' I shouted, turning the key. The Volvo obeyed and started. I wanted to ask Jo about her leg, but we needed to get out of here ASAP. I dipped the clutch, threw the gear into reverse and shot back until there was enough space to pull forward to miss the car in front. Once the gear was in first, I kicked down on the accelerator pedal. The twenty-inch wheels spun viciously on the warm road.

We both flinched when we heard the loud smash.

The bullet penetrated the back window. A shower of glass exploded over the back seats of the car, followed by a rush of warm air.

'Jesus!' I screamed.

Joanne wailed like a banshee, throwing her head down to her knees. 'Where's Mark?' she shouted.

'He's gone, Jo!' I struggled to say, my voice nearly breaking.

The Volvo continued to bounce, the high front grill merely missing the parked car in front as the wheels finally gripped the road and we were thrown back into our seats.

A second shot hit the rear passenger window, the spray of glass collapsing in sideways. Speckles of hardened, tiny blocks caught the back of my left arm like angry needles.

'Shit, shit,' Joanne muttered, panting hard. I felt her small hands squeezing my left forearm as we accelerated up the hill towards the rising sun.

Through the rear-view mirror, I watched the bald man hurry across the bright road, climb into a white Jaguar, then

I lost sight of him as the road dipped down towards a set of traffic lights, which were telling me to stop.

No chance.

From sixty-five miles per hour, I slowed down to forty-five as we crossed the junction, wincing in case there was a collision. I checked the rear-view mirror for the next minute but saw no sign of the Jaguar.

'Where are we going?' Jo asked.

'We'll go to Elaine's,' I said.

She nodded, then glared behind us through the open space where the back windscreen used to be. The glass rested on the back seat like a sea of sparkling blue diamonds as the wind hollowed behind us.

I couldn't believe what had happened to Mark. It didn't seem real. I'd just left him. But we'd be dead otherwise, no question about it. Plain and simple. I couldn't have helped him I told myself. As we approached a built-up area, I dabbed the brakes, dropping the Volvo nearer to thirty miles an hour. Tears built up in my eyes, the outside world becoming blurry for an emotional moment. I glanced at Jo-anne. She smiled sadly and squeezed my trembling hand.

'You want to pull over?' she asked, watching me lose the battle with my emotions.

I shook my head firmly. 'We need to get away from here, away from him. We need to get to Elaine's to get Lucy.'

We drove through a thirty-zone on a wide road, lined with large, semi-detached houses on either side, with drives long enough to cater for three of four cars and gardens wide enough for games of Frisbee. I was on autopilot - it all seemed a blur.

Movement in the rear-view mirror caught my eye.

'Shit!' I shouted.

Jo zipped her head in my direction. 'What - Jack, what is it?'

'Jo… he's behind us.'

The white Jaguar rapidly expanded in the rear-view mirror. I gripped the steering wheel, held my breath, expecting it to crash straight into the back of us. I pushed hard on the accelerator, feeling the Volvo surge forward but I knew we couldn't escape him. We climbed to fifty. Then sixty. He was on my bumper now. It was getting dangerous. There were too many cars moving. I found myself weaving on the opposite side of the road to go around a small red Corsa. The Jag followed me. Early-morning runners and dog walkers lined the paths, glancing up in horror as we raced past them.

In the rearview mirror, I saw him. Blood seeped down his face from the top of his head. His eyes glowed red under a determined, focused frown.

'Ahhh!' I shouted in frustration.

'Oh God,' Jo said, swinging her head back and forth. 'Jack?'

'Hold on,' I told her. A young boy was on a BMX up ahead on the left, a fluorescent newspaper bag hanging from his small shoulder. He seemed to lose his balance on his bike and veered to the right towards the middle of the road. I yanked down on the steering wheel and the whole car juddered, the back wheels sliding uncontrollably.

'Fucking Jesus!' I said, nearly clipping him.

At this speed, it would have torn him in two. I instantly felt sick at the thought.

'Jack!' Joanne screamed, throwing her palms to her face in horror.

'Calm down,' I said. 'He's fine, he's fine!'

We came to a junction, took a left and I moved up through the gears, passing a bus stop where three construction workers glared at us whizz by.

We both jerked forward suddenly. The seat belt suddenly compressed my chest as the Jaguar rammed into the back of us. No more Mr Nice Guy.

'Jack, we—'

'I know!' I screamed, feeling flustered. The only way we'd escape him is if he ran out of fuel before we did. His driving was too good. He was too quick.

I hadn't had a drink or eaten yet this morning. My stomach growled at me and my head was dizzy with dehydration and stress. I blinked hard, trying to keep some level of focus. When I lost him in the mirror for a second, relief washed over me as I thought we had finally lost him.

But in the corner of my eye to the right, I saw a flash of white. He had levelled with us, his car on the other side of the road. I matched his stone-cold glare for the longest second of my life. Time passed in slow motion. He scowled at me before raising his gun. I widened my eyes, staring into the small black hole of the suppressor tip of the 9mm in his hand. I dropped the gear to third, planted my foot firmly on the floor, the Volvo surging forward. The bullet smashed the passenger window behind me and Joanne shrieked. I recoiled, throwing my body towards the steering wheel.

An oncoming white van forced him to slow and he pulled in behind us.

'Jesus fucking Christ!' I shouted. 'Will this ever end!'

'Jack! What we gonna do?'

I didn't reply.

The car juddered again as he rammed into the back of us again. Joanne screamed once more. I changed my grip on the wheel and saw a sign for the M1 motorway approaching to turn off. I slowed the Volvo down to forty as I took the first left at the small roundabout. The car felt like it was going to tip with the momentum, but the wheels kept us on the road, and, as I straightened out, the severe rocking subsided, the car finally balancing.

The M1 was busy.

We pulled off behind a white transit van, overtaking it with ease. I sped up to eighty miles an hour. The cars in the fast lane moved over like a herd of cattle being hustled across. The air that rushed in through the broken windows took our breath away. Minute cubes of glass rattled around and danced across the leather seats.

We approached an Audi A7 doing seventy which forced me to slow down. The Jag was about a metre behind us and I didn't know how he hadn't rammed into the back of us. He was biding his time now. Hitting us at this speed could be catastrophic to everyone. I looked down at the dashboard to see my fuel. Half full. Plenty, but it wouldn't last forever.

After a few minutes, I realised this was too easy for him.

'We need country roads,' I said.

'We need what?' Jo asked, struggling to hear me from the wind rushing through the car.

I repeated myself louder.

'Why?' she shouted back.

'We'll never lose him on here,' I said. 'And I can barely breathe!'

Joanne didn't reply. Instead, she glared forward to the busy four-lane hustle of the M1 motorway. The smell of a local farm flooded in, almost knocking me sick, but it only lasted a few seconds. There was a gap in the traffic in the lane ahead. I planted my foot, approaching ninety, but I slowed down because the zipping wind was unbearable.

'Jack, slow down!' Jo gasped.

I glanced back through the open gaping hole in the back of the car. The roof of the white Jag bobbled just above the back seats – he was inches behind.

'Where we going, Jack? What about Lucy?'

'We can't get Lucy with him behind us,' I shouted. 'We need to lose him!' I took a deep breath. 'A road near us.'

'A what?'

'A road not far from us!'

Joanne couldn't hear me properly.

I looked up into the rear-view mirror.

'Jack! Watch out!' Jo shouted.

A car pulled out in front of us. I slammed the brakes suddenly, fully expecting the Jag to collide into the back of us, but he didn't. Skilfully, he swerved to the left, narrowly missing us. Jesus, he was like a formula one driver. He was in front of us in the left lane. I watched him carefully, watching his movements. We slowed down to sixty because of the dawdling car in front.

I noticed a sign for the turn-off to junction twelve, knowing we needed to take it when we could. The road I mentioned to Joanne was on Park Road, close to our house. If it was taken too quickly, it would test any driver, I don't care how good they are. I knew from first-hand experience, almost coming off a few times. I'm no rally driver but I knew the bend pretty well. And unless there was less than half a tank of fuel in that Jaguar, it was our only chance to get away from him.

I glanced over to the left lane. There was a gap. I veered the car over, slipped in behind the Jaguar. I watched his hard, cold eyes watching me like a hawk through his rear-view mirror.

We were half a mile from the turn off.

'Jack!' gasped Jo. 'What are you doing?'

'Just wait,' I said. I re-gripped the wheel, focusing on the back of the Jaguar. He slowed. We almost hit him but I reacted in time, throwing the car to the left onto the hard shoulder and we ploughed straight past him. The slip road was fast approaching, and we were now in front.

I allowed him to catch up and, leaving it till the last second, I swerved left taking the slip road. It was a struggle to keep hold of the vibrating steering wheel as the car bounced and slid. The daunting realisation I was approaching the slip road too fast made my stomach flip. My eyes widened and I gripped the wheel with white knuckles.

Shit. Far too fast. I'd misjudged this.

'Jack!' she screamed, her panic ripping through the airy car.

The car shuddered as I slammed the brakes on, approaching the sharp U-bend.

Sixty.

Fifty.

Forty.

The sharp curve was seconds away.

Thirty-five.

Joanne tensed up, her left hand gripping the inside handle of the door, her right pressed firmly on the side of her seat in preparation for a collision with the curved steel barrier straight ahead.

I pushed the brakes harder, testing their limits.

We were down to thirty.

I yanked the steering wheel as far as it went to the left. The Volvo skidded under locked wheels, shuddering at an angle, the momentum carrying it forwards instead of sideways. Joanne shrieked in terror. We were inches from the barrier when I clamped my eyes shut. I felt the warm air zipping through the car, whirling around me, as if it was trying to lift me out of the seat, to another place. I thought about Lucy and how much I loved her. How much I loved them both.

They were my life.

The twenty-inch alloys suddenly gripped the dry tarmac, throwing us to the right as the car rocked to the left. I cracked the side of my face against the window. Joanne's head crashed into my left shoulder. The pain was horrendous, sending searing waves of white, warm heat across my neck. The car tipped, the momentum wanting to flip us, but the wide frame held solid, aiding us around the U-bend.

As we straightened out after the severe bend, I felt a shooting pain pulsating at the base of my neck, as if I'd just stepped off the world's fastest rollercoaster. I slowed down as we reached the junction of Harlington Road, but I didn't stop.

In the mirror, I saw the white Jaguar.

Was there anything he couldn't do?

Blindly, I pulled out and took a right. I stayed on the road for nearly a mile before I turned right onto Park Road. I glanced at Jo. Through heavy pants, her chest contracted and expanded rapidly as she gagged for air. Her eyes met mine.

The Jaguar was on our trail.

'He's good…' I said.

'Jack, what's the plan?'

'Just watch.'

73

Toddington

Pollock beautifully guided the Jaguar XF-RS around the bend and accelerated along Park Road until he caught up with the Volvo. The 5 litre V8 had handled everything that had been asked of it with ease since leaving Carlton Crescent. Credit to Jack Haynes, although he hadn't managed to get out of his sight, he had handled the big SUV impressively.

A throbbing, shooting pain pulsated through Pollock's temples and neck every so often, causing him to wince. The effect of the hammer blow in Ray's living room seemed to be worsening, but he fought it off, maintaining his concentration to finish his mission. He stared through the smashed broken window of the SUV, seeing the fear in Jack's nervous eyes through the rear-view mirror of the Volvo.

Something on the dashboard flicks on. A warning light.

'Fuck,' muttered Pollock.

The EPAS warning light. The posh term for power steering. He knew he couldn't stop now, even though the car, nor him, were one hundred percent. He needed to finish his mission – he had never failed a target.

Not once. Not ever.

He planted his foot down and the Jaguar surged on.

JACK

We whizzed by our house which was on the right. I saw Joanne grip the handle of the passenger door and her posture stiffened. The corner I mentioned moments ago was fast approaching. Time to see if my plan worked. So far, he had matched everything I'd done.

It was our last hope.

'Hold on!' I told Joanne.

I took the corner at the last second, hoping the size of the Volvo blocked his view of the upcoming double bend. Jo straightened in the seat, forcing her feet to the base of the footwell. I tensed my arms and tightened my grip on the steering wheel. Wind rushed through from the west like tiny daggers against my arms and face.

I rounded the corner at fifty-five. We crossed the dividing white line for a moment but swung back to marginally miss an oncoming white transit van—

The ear-screeching crunch wailed in the air. Metal on metal. Like a pang of thunder. We straightened out and took the next bend just as quickly.

I glanced in the rearview. The Jaguar was hauled into the air from the collision with the oncoming Transit. I watched it. It felt like time had stopped. As if it was in slow motion. I slowed the Volvo down and heard another sickening crash.

'Jack!' shouted Jo.

I stopped dead in the middle of the road, feeling my beating heart through my chest.

I opened the door and climbed down onto the hot road. I could feel the sun as I walked back towards the bend with wide, watchful eyes. The curving road was silent apart from farm machinery, whispering somewhere in the distance to my right.

On the bend, I saw the transit. It was spun one-eighty degrees and was now facing me. The driver was hunched forward, the top of his head covered in blood, his face against the steering wheel. I didn't know if he was dead. The front windscreen had shattered from the impact and the front end was mangled. Bits of metal and pieces of plastic from the crushed headlights laid across the tarmac.

There was no sign of the Jaguar on the road.

As I stepped up onto the grass verge I peered through the gap in the hedge. The Jaguar was on its roof. From the back of the car, there was no sign of the bald man, but I didn't expect there to be.

I let out a nervous sigh and felt a pang of guilt. What had we done?

A ball of flames ignited on the bottom of the car, rising in the blistering heat, like a mirage, shimmering heat dancing up into the air.

Shit, it was going to blow.

I sprinted around the bend, climbed back in the Volvo, and slam the door shut. Joanne flinched for a second in wonder what was going on.

I planted the gear into first and charged forward.

'What happened?' she asked.

'It worked, Jo!' I said over the sound of the gushing wind. 'Come on, let's go get Lucy.' I couldn't help but smile as we passed The Red Lion pub on the right and quickly move through the gears on the straight until we slowed down, reaching the junction. I edged out and took a right in the direction of Elaine's house.

Just as we passed St. Peter's Church on Battlesden Avenue, a loud explosion erupted coming somewhere from the right.

The white Jaguar sizzled in flames.

74

Police Station

'Good morning,' said DS Horton to DCI Clarke, who was sitting down at his desk. 'You're in early?'

'I couldn't sleep, been up most of the night.' Clarke looked up at Horton with heavy, bloodshot eyes.

Horton dropped into the seat next to him, placed his coffee down on the desk. 'Sorry, did you want a coffee? I—'

Clarke raised a palm. 'Just finished one. You can get the next ones in.'

Horton smiled. 'So, what do we have?'

'I've contacted Susan Leach about the footage from three years ago. She was—'

'Susan Leach?' Horton asked with a frown, shifting his weight uncomfortably on the seat.

Clarke looked towards Horton. 'She was the manager of Mini Monsters. The place next to Popworld. Where the camera is for the footage we need from three years ago. We…' Clarke trailed off seeing no change in Horton's face. 'The taxi,' he reminded him. 'The one that stopped, remember? A woman got in with Peter Lewes. That's what the taxi driver said - we couldn't see the camera from Popworld, so we need this camera to find out who the woman is?'

Horton gave him a slow nod, but it lacked any conviction.

'James, have you been drinking last night or something?' It was Clarke's turn to frown.

'Erm… no, not last—'

'James,' said Clarke, quietly cutting him off, 'I can smell the lager on you.'

Horton's eyes widened. 'Is it that bad?'

'Yeah.' Clarke hit him with serious eyes. 'Get your head in the game. Connor will be coming around any minute, asking for an update. If you get done here, I'll be taking the shit for it. You're under my supervision. Come on, you know that.'

Horton dipped his head, his eyes finding the floor for a short moment. 'Sorry, boss. Things – things got carried away.'

'Looks like it. Let's make sure it doesn't happen on a school night anymore, okay?'

Horton nodded and gave him half a smile.

A sound came from the door. Chief Superintendent Connor entered wearing a dark blue suit, over a white blouse, a few of the buttons undone. 'Good morning, gentlemen.' She was chirpy for 8 a.m.

'Good morning, chief,' said Clarke.

She stopped at the desk, peered over both of them. 'Good morning, DS James Horton.'

Horton looked up wearily. 'Morning, Chief.' His voice was quiet, sheepish, but Connor didn't think too much into it.

'What do we have on the Peter Lewes case?' Connor moved to her left, where she grabbed a chair and dragged it over. She took a seat and stared into Clarke's tired eyes.

Clarke cleared his throat and began with the visit to see Alison Lewes. He told her about visiting the nightclub, the nightclub camera footage, then speaking with the taxi driver.

'A woman got in?' Her eyes narrow, intriguingly.

Clarke nodded. 'We're waiting on the footage from the place next door. It shouldn't be too long.'

'Then you'll see who got in the taxi?' she said.

'That's right,' replied Clarke.

'Good work, gentlemen.' Connor stood up, leaving the chair where it was. 'Keep me updated.' She left the office, the sound of her stilettoes echoing under her confident stride.

Dunstable
JACK

It took just over twenty minutes to reach Mark and Elaine's house. No doubt, the longest twenty minutes of my life. My brother was dead. We were almost dead. The only thing I wanted was to get Lucy to make sure she was okay.

When I stopped the Volvo outside of their house I grabbed my phone and rang the police. I informed them what'd happened at Carlton Crescent with Mark and Ray. They asked how I knew and my current location. I told the mature-sounding operator that I'd ring her soon when it was safer. She asked me a question, but I cut her off before she finished.

I placed my phone back into my jogging bottoms. The urine had dried and was reeking. I apologized to Joanne about it, but she rubbed my shoulder softly.

She was tired, looked pale. She nodded her head slowly and curled her lip as if she was about to cry, but she mentally shrugged and opened the door. I was surprised. We'd been through more in the last week than most people had in a lifetime. As she stepped out, I noticed tears falling from her eyes. It made me well up inside, but I fought it.

I stepped out into the warmth. The sun blaring down was hot. As much as I couldn't wait to see Lucy, I dreaded seeing Elaine. How could I even begin to tell her about Mark? That he was dead? The thought sickened me and, for a second, I bowed down beside the car, waited a few seconds to steady myself. I felt a heavy surge come up from my stomach up through my throat and lunged forward, throwing up on the road. An elderly man walking a dog glared over at me in disgust. I heard Joanne round the front of the car and appear at my side, asking me if I was okay. I held up a weak palm and wiped my mouth with the back of my hand.

'Come on, let's go see Lucy,' I said, standing. My head started to throb, waves of pain niggling somewhere behind my eyes.

'Are you okay?'

'I'll be fine,' I said, weakly I stepped up onto the path, towards their gate. Joanne followed.

I pushed down the front door handle, but it was locked, so I knocked and wait impatiently. I leaned forward, knocked a second time. A long minute passed, and there was still no answer.

'Maybe they can't hear us?' I said to Jo, who stared at me with a blank expression. I pulled my phone out, found Elaine's number, and rang her. It rang until I reached her voicemail. I tried Lucy's phone. It went straight to her voicemail.

I knocked a third time.

'Jo, what the fuck is going on?' I said.

'Maybe they're in the kitchen and they can't hear us?'

'Something's wrong,' I said, trying the handle again. 'Come on, we'll try the side gate.' I led the way along the side of the house until we reached the raised platform of decking. I stepped up and reached the back door.

'It's open,' I whispered, staring at the inch gap between the edge of the door and the frame.

'What?' Jo muttered behind me.

'Shh.'

I edged the door open slowly and stepped inside. The smell of fried food and cooled pan-fat hung in the air, knocking me sick. I moved forward, repelling a sudden gag in my throat.

'Lucy,' I said just above a whisper. 'Elaine?'

Silence answered me back as we left the kitchen into the short, narrow hallway.

'Lucy?' I said, this time louder. I waited for a response. 'Lucy?'

'Maybe they've gone out?' Joanne said, behind me.

I shook my head. 'Elaine's Mazda is parked outside – ring her again.'

Joanne grabbed her phone, clicked on Elaine's number, and raised it to her ear. 'It's ringing.'

A sound came from somewhere ahead of us, along the hallway. A ringtone. I dashed to the living room where the noise was louder.

I stopped suddenly.

There she was, lying on her front, her body slightly twisted on top of the white rug in the centre of the bright room. The sun was glaring in from the left through a wide window. She was alone.

'Help me,' she said, weakly. 'Help me.'

'Jesus!' I shouted, seeing her swollen, bloody face. One of her eyes was almost closed as she gazed up at me. I rushed over, lowered to my knees. She was semi-conscious.

'What happened, Elaine? What happened?' My voice was full of panic. I placed a palm on her back and took hold of her weak, trembling hand. 'Where's – where's Lucy?'

'Jack…' her voice was quiet. 'They've taken her…'

Her words crawled up my spine, and the skin on the back of my neck prickled.

'Lucy is gone,' she added.

Joanne let out a blood-curdling scream that ripped through the whole house.

76

Hemel Hempstead

Phil approached the black, shiny Bentley from the rear. He leaned down, pulled the door open, and climbed inside. The interior was very smart. The white leather of the luxurious seat welcomed his steady weight as he lowered into it. He scanned his surroundings, noticing the passenger door had more buttons than an airplane cockpit.

'Hey, boss,' he said, twisting his body towards Hunt, who was sitting next to him. He appeared calm and collected like he had all the time in the world. The air inside the Bentley was cool, gently circulating. The driver was silent in the seat in front of Phil, wearing a hat, staring forward, through the clear, sparkling windscreen. Phil heard the quiet hum of piano music leaking from the speaker beside him.

Hunt wore his familiar long brown coat. It was nearly thirty degrees outside under the blaring sun, but he decided it wasn't time to crack a joke about it. Instead, he focused his thoughts on why he was actually there, and that built a moment of excitement within him, so much so, a smile grew on his face. He couldn't wait to tell Hunt the news.

His boss would be happy, that's for sure.

'I received your phone call,' said Hunt. 'Got here when I could.'

'No problem… glad you're here.' Phil adjusted himself on the white leather.

'So, how did you do it?' asked Hunt.

'Well… on Monday,' explained Phil, 'when we chased them from the poker game – just before we set off, I told Jacob and Terry to take the old Beemer. To trail us – if we failed, to catch them….'

'So…?' said Hunt, wanting more.

'When they turned off the M1 – when they lost us – the man dropped the wife off at home. Boss, it was the Haynes' house! It isn't Mark's wife. It was Jack Haynes' wife!'

'What?!' Hunt snapped.

'Lorraine Headley. She must've changed her name completely since you knew her.'

Hunt's eyes widened, the crow's feet trailing off at the corners of his eyes. He couldn't believe it.

'Lorraine Headley is Joanne Haynes?' Hunt asked.

Phil nodded.

Hunt glared away in the direction of the window, falling silent for a moment. 'So, all this time, it was Lorraine Headley's daughter who got the pictures of me killing the Deacons?'

Phil bobbed his head. 'Seems so.'

'What a coincidence.' Hunt smiled. 'I hope Stuart and Derek weren't too rough with her when they went round?'

Stuart had told Phil that Derek was on top of her, smothering her with his fat, sweaty body in the hallway, but Phil missed out on telling Hunt those specific details.

'I asked Terry to follow the Insignia. It led him to a semi-detached house in Dunstable. He had been watching the house ever since Monday night.'

'That's why I haven't seen him then?' said Hunt. He was impressed.

'Yeah.' Phil let out a smile and met Hunt's eyes for a second. 'So, this morning,' Phil continued, 'when the insignia went out early, Terry rang me. I told him to wait there until it came back. And when it did, there's the Haynes daughter… what's her name?'

'Her name is Lucy,' Hunt reminded him. He remembered everything.

'Yeah, Lucy - Terry called me. I spoke to Stuart and Jacob, who got the van, picked me up, and we all went round the house.'

Hunt ran his tongue across the inside of his upper lip, patiently listening. He won't admit it, but he was impressed.

'We went around the back, picked the lock. Found the girl and a woman, who I assume is Mark's wife.' Phil held a palm to his face for a moment. 'She put up a surprisingly good fight. Give me a good slap.' He saw Hunt smile, and continued, 'We handled her. Roughed her up a little and got the girl – Lucy.'

'Did you kill her?'

'Lucy?'

'No… Mark's wife. Is she dead?'

'We left her in a bad way… I don't know. I punched her in the face so hard in the hallway, she nearly did a cartwheel into the living room. She didn't get up, put it that way.' Phil made a tight fist. Hunt lowered his eyes to the wide gold ring on Phil's middle finger.

'And Lucy?'

'She's in the van,' said Phil.

Hunt looked past Phil, towards the black van parked nearby.

'Did anyone see you?'

'Not a soul in sight, boss.'

'Good work, Phil.'

Phil smiled inside, then looked away.

'Well… let's go see her,' Hunt said, grabbing the door handle and edging it open. He stepped out into the heat and almost struggled to stand up straight, letting out a quiet un-comfortable moan. His back and hip were both sore. Early life spent boxing and fighting were finally catching up with him.

Phil led the way to the rear of the van and pulled both doors open. A terrified moan broke out into the air. Hunt smiled, peering inside. The van was almost bare. A thin layer of wood was screwed to the floor. The walls were empty, lined with the interior shell of the van's metal struc-ture. Inside, Hunt felt the warmth seep out and narrowed his gaze into the darkness.

'There you are,' Hunt said happily. 'My favourite little observer. Lucy.'

Lucy lay on her side. Her left shoulder was hard against the solid floor. A moan came from her mouth, muffled by the thick, wide duct tape wrapped around the lower half of her face. Her cheeks were red from crying, and there was a damp puddle under her face pooled with salty tears and blood. Hunt stared coldly at her. She matched his gaze, although her bright blue eyes struggled to see through the floods of tears.

'Lucy,' Hunt said quietly. 'It's nice to officially meet you.'

Lucy stayed in silent fear. Her whole body shook, her rapid breathing throwing her shoulders up and down like a set of pistons inside a diesel engine. Hunt noticed another wet patch near the top of her thighs.

'Aww, did you need to go wee-wee? Bless.' Hunt laughed. 'I can see your mother in you. You know, when she was young.' His eyes brightened, a smile rising from the corner of his mouth. 'Let's see if we can get a little get together with your mummy and daddy, ey? For old times' sake.'

Lucy mumbled loudly through the tape as Hunt turned away. Phil stepped forward and closed the door, drowning out the groans in the back of the van, isolating her in the urine-stinking darkness.

'What the hell have you done to her?' Hunt asked Phil, turning to him.

Phil shrugged, smiling. 'Thought we'd rough her up a little, that's all.'

'You're an animal,' Hunt said, breaking out into a laugh. 'There's roughing someone up. And there's doing that to them. Jack Haynes will not be a happy man when he sees what you've done to his daughter.'

Hunt plucked his phone from his pocket, found the number he needed, pressed CALL, and put it to his ear.

77

Dunstable
JACK

I watched Joanne lean over Elaine, trying to get her as comfortable as possible.

'I'll ring an ambulance,' I said.

'No,' struggled Elaine. 'Don't – I'll be okay.'

'Don't be stupid,' Jo said. 'Look at you!' Joanne looked up at me with concern and nodded. I dialled nine nine nine, but before I got the chance to press CALL, my phone rang. A number I didn't recognise.

I put it to my ear. 'Hello?'

'Mr Jack Haynes, what a lovely little surprise,' said the voice.

'Who's – who's this?' I asked, my hand starting to shake.

'You know who this is.'

'Alexander Hunt?' I asked.

'Got it in one. Congratulations.'

Joanne glared up at me with wide eyes. I could see the fear filling them.

'Where's Lucy?'

'Straight to the point – I respect that,' he said. 'She's in the back of a van. Her wrists are bound. Her mouth is gagged – and she looks lovely.'

'Listen… this isn't a game!' I screamed at him, stepping backward and making my way out into the hallway. Joanne's mouth opened in surprise at my words, which I regretted saying immediately. He had my daughter for Christ's sake. I planted my palm on the top of my head waiting for a reaction. 'You touch one fucking hair on her head,' I added, 'and I'll—'

'You'll what? You'll do what?' His voice was calm. My threat meant absolutely nothing to him.

'Listen, you're making a mistake here,' I explained. 'We've done nothing to you. Why are you doing this?'

'If your daughter wasn't a nosey little bitch, we wouldn't be in this situation.'

I realised I'd left Jo in the living room with Elaine and found myself almost near the kitchen. I turned, the phone pressed hard against my head. In the living room, Elaine was still on the floor, the left side of her face had taken a massive blow. I'm no doctor, but it could be a broken jaw. The way her cheek was slashed told us whoever punched her was wearing a large ring. At this point, I didn't consider she didn't know about Mark. I needed to find Lucy – that's priority number one.

'Where's Lucy?' I shouted.

'I've told you – she's in a van, tied up.'

'Where's the van?' I said, allowing anger to infiltrate my voice. Beads of sweat formed on my forehead and my back was soaked. I hear footsteps near. Jo hurried past me towards the kitchen.

'I'll tell you when the time is right,' said Hunt.

'No,' I said, firmly. 'You'll tell me now.' I couldn't help but make small circles in the hallway. I couldn't stand still. Jo passed me a wet cloth and a glass of water, disappearing back into the living room.

He didn't reply.

'You hear me?' I yelled.

'Keep calm, Mr Haynes.' He then laughed down the phone at me. Clamping my eyes shut, I could feel my skin getting hot, my face burning. There was literally nothing I could do.

'What do you want?' I asked him, finally opening my eyes, zoning in down the narrow hallway towards the dark kitchen.

'I want you to go to your house,' he told me.

'Why?'

'There's a package waiting on your doorstep.'

In silence, I froze.

All I could hear was the loud beating in my chest.

'You'll love what's inside.' Hunt laughed hysterically. 'Remember Jack, no police. If I see the police, Lucy dies.'

78

Dunstable
JACK

I felt sick to the pit of my stomach, butterflies flitting around relentlessly. The feeling of dizziness swooped down and shook me. My legs started to wobble. I lunged for the hand-rail, grabbed the bannister to steady myself for a moment, trying to compose myself to regain some stability. I still smelt the hanging scent of bacon and fat from the kitchen and managed to stop myself from vomiting on their carpet.

I closed my eyes, forced myself to take a few deep breaths. I opened them and placed my phone back into my pocket. In the living room, I heard Elaine groaning in pain. Joanne told her things would be okay, but her tone suggested otherwise, lacking any real conviction.

I appeared at the living room door, stared at the scene before me. What have we got ourselves into? Joanne turned to me and winces with sad eyes, telling me she wasn't in a good way. The side of her face was bulging more now, but the flow of blood from her wounds had stopped. Her eye was almost closed.

'What – what did he want?' Elaine struggled to ask.

Joanne and I looked down at her.

'Save your energy, Elaine,' I said to her softly. 'I'm ringing an ambulance. You need help.'

Joanne turned to her, and nodded firmly, agreeing it was a good idea.

'No!' she tried to bellow, but it comes out as a weak, muffled cry.

I sighed hopelessly towards Joanne. We all know Elaine is stubborn, but I was surprised at this. Her resilience and defiance were admirable.

'What does he want?' she asked, her words finally making sense.

'He said he has Lucy tied up in the back of a van.'

Joanne gasped and threw a palm to her open mouth.

'And he said there's a package on our doorstep he wants me to see.'

'Help me up,' Elaine demanded, 'please.'

I waited a few seconds wondering how to do it, but I finally nodded and lowered myself down. Joanne helped me, and together, we slowly got her up. She winced in pain, but we managed to place her down as comfortably as possible onto the sofa.

I picked up the drink of water that Joanne brought from the kitchen. 'Here, have some water.'

'Let us call an ambulance, El?' pleaded Joanne. 'You're in a bad way.'

Elaine shook her head defiantly. 'I'll sort it myself. Don't – don't worry about me. You go home and see what the package is. Then go get Lucy.'

I admired the strength of the words, considering it looked like she had been hit by a train, then another train.

'Where's Mark?' she asked after I moved the glass of water away from her mouth.

Over the next few minutes, I told her what had happened to Mark. She watched me carefully, absorbing the story, showing no expression throughout, no emotion at all. Her eyes were as cold as stone. There were no tears, no reactions, no desperate cries of anger.

'I'm so sorry, Elaine.' I took her weak hand, squeezed it a little. She gave me a small sympathetic smile.

'Go see what the package is,' she said. 'I'll sort myself out, okay. Go on.'

79

Dunstable
JACK

I felt terrible leaving Elaine on the sofa in the state she was in. But, we needed to get Lucy. She was in danger.

In the car, Joanne told me she was ringing an ambulance and put her phone to her ear. She gave the operator the address, then told the person at the end of the line that they needed to be quick. Joanne put her phone down and started to cry.

'Hey, come on, Jo,' I said softly. 'We'll get her back.' She could hear the lacking conviction in my voice. I looked back on the road feeling hopeless. I couldn't even reassure my wife that things would be okay. My daughter was tied up in the back of a van all alone guarded by thugs. My throat felt like it was beginning to close. I couldn't get enough air. I swallowed, gulping down some air.

Toddington

We sat in silence until we reached our house. I pulled the fob from my pocket to open the gates but, as we approached, we saw they were already open. The small box containing the mechanism barely hung from the left column, damaged, with thick, loose wires draping down to the floor.

'Fuck,' I said, letting out a sigh.

We passed through the open gates, followed the snaking gravel towards the front door. The familiar sight of home offered no comfort. No safety anymore. No reassurance of anything.

I noticed the box sitting on the doorstep in the shadows. A medium-sized cardboard box. The lid was folded closed.

Joanne waited in the car as I get out and stepped down onto the gravel. I nervously padded towards the doorstep under the blaring sun, the small stones crunching under my feet as I disappear into the shadows and stopped before the box. My heart tried to rip through my chest as it pounds relentlessly off my ribcage. Bending over, I pulled the top of the box open and gasped loudly.

My eyes widened.

My whole body froze.

My heart stopped.

The contents of the box sickened me. I fell to the right, landed hard on my knee. I heard frantic footsteps behind me, Joanne rushing from the car, asking me what was wrong. I wiped my mouth with the back of my trembling palm, but I couldn't speak. I couldn't physically say anything.

Joanne leaned forward to have a look inside. She staggered back, and let out a harrowing, blood-curdling scream.

80

Toddington
JACK

The bottom of the box contained a head full of bright, long blonde hair, curled up carefully around the bottom of the box. In the middle, there was the necklace Lucy was wearing earlier, neatly positioned within the shape of the hair. Inside the small space of the necklace, there was a long tooth. Clotted lumps of blood stuck to its huge root.

My face grew hot. I couldn't comprehend what he had done to her. My precious Lucy. Shaved off her hair and pulled out one of her teeth. I shook the thought of picturing how he actually did it creep into my mind.

My stomach flipped and I doubled over.

Joanne was behind me, sitting on the gravel with her head buried in between her knees, sobbing uncontrollably. I managed to climb to my feet, feeling like my whole world was shattered. An empty, gaping hole left open in my life. My brother was dead. My daughter had been tortured and was now with Hunt.

I peered over the box again, noticed something I missed. I leaned down, doing my best to ignore the hair and the bloody tooth, and saw a slip of paper at the base of the box. I picked it out carefully, stood up, and read it.

It said: *Call me.*

Next to the words, there was a smiley face.

I let out a scream of my own which rattled the morning air, causing Joanne to stop crying and glare up at me.

'I'm going to fucking kill him, Jo.'

I pulled my phone from my pocket and rang him. I couldn't keep still, stomping around the gravel waiting for him to answer. Each ring shot through my tense body.

'Ahh, Mr Haynes, how —'

'I'm going to fucking kill you, Hunt.'

Hunt didn't reply, absorbing the seriousness in my voice. My breathing was hard and fast, my chest bulging in and out. 'Do you fucking hear me?'

'Oh, I hear you loud and clear, Jack,' he said, a tinge of humour filling his voice. 'Strange, though isn't, it?'

'What's fucking strange?' I snapped.

'That you're the one making threats. I have your daughter tied up in the back of a van. The floor of the van is cold and hard, full of old rusty nails. She has tape around her mouth. She has pissed herself. She has no hair. She has a tooth missing. She looks silly if you ask me.'

'Hunt, you're dead!' I screamed down the phone at him, kicking a boot full of gravel against the side of the house in the process. The tiny stones crashed against brickwork and then fell abruptly. Joanne flinched to cover herself and yelped.

He laughed at me for a long time and I struggled to contain my rage. I felt like I was on fire. His laughing finally stopped.

'What do you want from me?' I asked.

'It was quite simple, Jack,' he replied, 'I want my Lorraine! Bring me her. And you could have your daughter back.'

81

Toddington
JACK

Hunt told me to look on the other side of the note I found inside the box. I turned it over to see a small map of where he wanted to meet us. From where Lucy had described Carl had taken the photos, it appeared to be the same spot.

'What does he want?' Jo asked, finding her feet.

I glanced up at her with sad, hopeless eyes, noticing the tears running down her red cheeks. 'He wants you, Jo. He wants to trade you for Lucy.'

Joanne let out a loud wail and threw her palms to her puffy, wet face. I put my arms around her and pulled her close to me. I didn't say anything for a long time and waited until she'd stopped sobbing. Finally, when she stopped shaking, she sniffed loudly and backed away.

'Right, okay,' she said as she wipes her eyes and cheeks. 'Come on, let's do it.' I could hear her determination, despite the situation we were in.

'Jo, we—'

'Jack, we have no choice,' she said, cutting me off. 'You've seen what he's capable of - he'll kill her.' She dropped her face onto my shoulder and I feel the tears soak into my t-shirt.

Her words shattered me.

What am I going to do?

I couldn't even believe it. Meet some gangster and hand my wife over to get my daughter back. They were both mine. Why the fuck was this happening? If I ring the police, Lucy will die. If I didn't meet him, then Lucy will die. If I met him and handed over Jo then get Lucy back, Jo may die, or worst-case scenario, we all might die. I had nothing left to give. On the whole, I had no choice.

I let my emotions take over and I started to cry, allowing my face to fall onto Joanne's shoulder. It wasn't long before my face was drenched in the taste of my own salty tears. She raised her arms and rubbed my back softly, to comfort me.

'Come on, Jack. Let's go get our daughter,' Jo said, giving me one final rub before edging away.

I leaned back, apologised for the damp patch on her shoulder and nodded. I took a breath, made my way back to the driver's seat of the Volvo, pulled the door closed, and got inside. I felt broken.

I turned the engine on, hearing a song play on the radio. Without thinking, I punched the button with a hard, angry fist, my hand crashing into the plastic with a loud, dull thud. The sound from the speakers cut off and the plastic twisty knob snapped off near Jo's feet. I put the gear in first, ignoring Joanne's stare, and guided the car towards the end of the drive. We took a right and accelerated along Park road.

We drove for a few minutes before I slowed down, turned left into a narrow dirt road. The suspension was tested by the uneven surface, filled with raised bumps and awkward potholes. The car bobbed side to side as if it floated on water. A few hundred metres in, Joanne put her hand to her mouth.

'I'm gonna be sick,' she said, quickly opening the door.

'Jo!'

I slowed down and came to a halt. She leaned out and vomited, hitting the inside leather of the passenger door with the yellowy-brown liquid. I leaned over and rubbed her back. She pulled herself back in and dropped into the seat, letting out a painful, heavy sigh. Her face was red. Her bloodshot eyes looked at me. I saw the hopelessness in her sunken eyes and it was nothing short of heartbreaking.

'You okay?' I asked, already knowing the answer.

She shook her head slowly and her eyes filled up. Tears fell down her face. Obviously, she was not okay. I put the gear in first and edged forward, keeping the speed low, watching the area around us, expecting to see them at any moment. After a quarter of a mile, the small narrow track expanded into an open grassy area where I decided to stop. I applied the handbrake and switched off the engine.

Everything around us became dead silent. I could hear the pounding of my heart alongside the hum of nearby machinery. I noticed Joanne's breathing was shallow, her chest rising and falling fast, her eyes flitting left and right, wearily searching for Hunt and Lucy.

There was a cluster of trees to the right, partially blocking the rays from the bright, rising sun, casting long thin shadows on the grass in front of us. I looked out onto the field through the windscreen.

'We'll be okay, won't we?' Jo whispered.

I turned towards her. I grabbed her right hand and squeezed it lovingly. 'Yeah,' I lied. 'We'll fix this.'

She forced a smile. It broke my heart that she didn't believe me. She knew, as well as I did, that this was the end. What possible good outcome could come from this? There wasn't one, I knew that. I continued to hold her hand for a few minutes as the hopeless silence filled the car. It was the most intense moment I'd ever shared with her. The feel of her soft hand, the way she used the tips of her fingers to run slowly up and down my palm.

'Where is he?' said Jo.

I squeezed her hand tightly. 'This is where the map said.'

I wanted to tell her how much I loved her. How much I'd appreciated what she had done over the years. How much of a fantastic mother she had been and still is. But I couldn't. I couldn't bring myself to let the words come out of my mouth. It would feel like I'd already given up hope of getting us out of this crazy situation.

Jo forced her lips together, staring at the sunshine through the windscreen.

'I hope Lucy is okay,' she whispered.

Holding back the tears, I watched a couple of birds flutter away from a treetop in the distance. 'She'll – she'll be fine,' I barely managed. 'If she's anything like you, anyway.'

I suddenly felt trapped, as if the shell of the car was closing in on me. The gentle wind blowing through the smashed windows at the back of the car had died down. The smell of urine on my jogging bottoms was becoming embarrassing now – I should have changed them whilst we were at home. Thick, rancid waves of it lingered up in the warm air. I knew Joanne could smell it too. Needing some air, I quickly unbuckled my seat belt, opened the door, climbed down into the warmth of the mild summer breeze, and move slowly away from the car. Joanne stays inside, sunk into the seat where she was comfortable, watching me – I felt her tired, emotional eyes on me as I rounded the front of the car.

I gazed out onto the large field, then further, absorbing the view of the distance. Gently sloping hills, crop fields, farmer's barns, and a cloudless, bright, blue horizon. I summoned a deep breath and exhaled heavily, finding myself feeling a little calmer, my heart rate steadying. I welcomed the warm breeze on my skin and the scorching sun beat down on me.

I'm infuriated with Hunt. What he had done to Lucy was unthinkable. My body rattled at the thought of him. I didn't know how I'd react when I saw her with no hair and a tooth missing – I didn't know what I'd do. I knew I couldn't go all guns blazing because he'd kill me. I wouldn't get any-where near him. Probably a bullet to my head.

My appreciation of the landscape ended abruptly when I heard something behind me.

A quiet hum of a motor.

The whirring noise of the tyres on the dirt.

The sounds gradually increased as something ap-proached, closing the distance on the back of the Volvo. Jo-anne watched me closely as I turned one-hundred and eighty degrees and moved to the side of the car, staring down the narrow dirt road we'd driven down minutes be-fore. I saw the car. A brand-new Bentley GT Continental. Black, polished, the paintwork dazzling in the sun. Behind the car was a van, also black – presumably the same van Stuart and Derek were in when they came to our house. The sound of the engines became louder as they draw nearer. My breathing quickened.

I had no idea what to expect as the Bentley gently rocked on the uneven track towards me. I saw a driver wearing a hat, both hands on the wheel, a blank expression on his thin, white face.

Joanne turned her head, looked out the broken rear win-dow, and started to tremble at the sight of the approaching vehicles. She turned her head at me and glared, desperate for a solution, desperate for me to tell her that things were going to be okay.

The Bentley entered the open grassy area and stopped about twenty metres behind the Volvo, the idling engine vi-brating the ground below my feet. The van stopped a few metres behind it, but I kept my eyes on the car. Suddenly, both engines shut down, and the hush of anticipation whis-pered in the air.

The driver of the car leaned to his right slowly, as if he had all the time in the world, and opened his door then climbed out. He didn't look in my direction, nor acknowledge my presence, which angered me. He casually moved around the front of the car and opened the passenger side rear door.

Behind the black car, both doors of the van opened. Two men stepped out, both dressed in black leather, both large, tall, and bloody intimidating. They stood for a moment and gave me a cold, hard stare. An awful feeling hit me like a wave.

What if Lucy wasn't here?

What if this was a set-up? A trap to kill me and grab Joanne?

I should've called the police. I should've phoned DCI Clarke. I had his card at the house. Why on earth did I think I could handle this?

'C'mon Lucy,' I whispered to myself. 'Where are you?'

The loud creek of the rear van doors opening rippled through the air.

A large man, maybe 6 foot four stepped into my view and gave me a menacing stare. He held his palm out towards the rear of the van and nodded, giving someone permission to open the door.

'Lucy,' I whispered in hope.

My heart bled at the sight of her.

I choked on a pocket of air when I saw her shaven bald head and the tape wrapped around her mouth. She let out a muffled cry when she saw me.

Behind me, in the Volvo, I heard Joanne cry uncontrollably.

I stared at the big man who had his gigantic hand around Lucy's arm, pinning her close to him as she shuffled and tried to wriggle free. I screamed so loudly that Lucy froze.

They all did and stared at me.

Then I did something totally out of character. Something inside of me erupted.

82

Woodland, Toddington
JACK

My feet pounded on the grass as dashed forward towards the back of the van. My tight fists zipped through the warm air. I kept my eyes on Lucy as I sprinted toward them. The large man holding her said something to one of the men nearby and edged Lucy away from him.

The large man then gave me a challenging grin before he dipped his shoulder and started toward me. He was moving very quickly.

I didn't really have a plan. I was just so furious at what had happened to Lucy that I wanted her back and would do anything to make that happen

As I drew nearer, I realised I'd underestimated his size. He was absolutely huge. Lucy was a few steps behind him, being held close by another thug. I needed to get her away from these men. Lucy nervously watched me in fear, wondering what I would do.

I heard a concerned Joanne scream my name somewhere behind me, but I ignored her and continued to gallop forward. The man was a few metres away now, and I dipped my right shoulder low to brace for the collision. He managed to get even lower and barged his thick shoulder into my thighs so hard, it flipped me over him and I crashed to the floor, landing hard on my back. I let out a cry. It genuinely felt like my back could be broken.

I was disorientated. Felt like I'd been hit by a train. My whole body ached and my head pounded in jolts of agony. I opened my eyes and watched the man who'd flipped me, walking casually towards the rear of the van.

I heard a car door slam, followed by a wave of laughter. How humiliating. From my right, I heard dull footsteps approach me on the grass. I straightened my head, looked up to the sky, and waited. There was nothing I could do.

'A valiant effort, Mr Haynes,' a voice said. 'Good effort indeed.'

As I tilted my head towards the sound, I winced at the pain I felt. A small, wide-shouldered man stepped into my line of vision. He was wearing a long brown coat, his head was nearly bald, his face tanned, covered in hard, rough skin. He let out a crooked smile.

'Nice to finally meet you, Jack,' Hunt said.

'I wish I could say the same,' I replied.

83

Woodland, Toddington
JACK

I felt the strength of two men hauling me up from the floor. My back felt like a jigsaw where the pieces weren't quite together.

'Where do you want him?' one of them said.

'Bring him to the woods,' Hunt demanded.

I attempted to shake them off me, but I was dizzy, my legs were unstable, and even if I tried, they were simply too strong. They led me towards a cluster of trees, almost carrying me, holding me up by my arms. Somewhere behind me, I heard Joanne scream, then heard Lucy wail elsewhere. My head shot around, but I couldn't see them. My eyes were out of focus. I experienced a jolt of anger and thrashed at the man to my right, managing to throw a fist into the side of his face, but I misjudged it completely, the skin of my knuckles skimming his cheek, and the momentum of my feeble effort throwing me hard to the ground. The side of my face slammed down into the solid ground with a thud that rattled my skull. Then I felt a sharp, horrendous pain in my side. One of the men kicked me hard and fast with what felt like the toe of his boot.

I cried out in agony. Then spent a few moments nursing the severe pain in my ribs. My body jerked suddenly as I was pulled up to my feet again. My lungs were desperate for a decent breath because the kick knocked the wind out of me like you wouldn't believe.

To my left, Joanne screamed.

I looked over, feeling helpless. She kicked and flayed her arms at the man standing behind her in an attempt to break free from his thick arms wrapped around her waist, but it was pointless. He carried her like a weightless doll towards the cluster of trees.

The light above faded, blocked by the high umbrella of leaves. The temperature dipped in the shade and I blinked several times to allow my eyes to adjust. I needed to find my bearings, needed to come up with a plan. The men were still on either side of me. I felt like my right arm may snap at the elbow if he bent it any further. I winced in pain as they finally dropped me to the floor. I rolled onto my back and finally breathed.

'Get on the fucking floor,' a coarse voice said to my left.

I cocked my head, watched Lucy being carried by the same man who hauled me over his shoulder moments ago. His arms looked huge around her small, young frame as he carried her towards me. The big man leaned forward and opened his arms out, letting gravity pull Lucy to the floor with a sickening thud. She cried out in pain and, for a second, I thought she had broken her back. She didn't move for a few moments.

'Lucy?' I shouted. My heart bled again when I saw the pain on her face. There was sadness in her teary eyes. 'You okay?' I asked her quietly. She gave me a small nod, then I turned to the big man. 'I'm going to fucking kill you. You know that, don't you?'

He gave me the biggest grin I'd ever seen, tipping his large head back and laughing hysterically up into the shade of the trees.

I sat up a little, looked around frantically for Joanne. I couldn't see her. The two men who carried me were here, as well as the bigger man who brought Lucy, but no one else.

'Where's – where's Mum?' Lucy asked.

'I – I don't—'

'She's in the van like you were,' the biggest man said, cutting me off.

'Let her fucking go!' I ordered him. 'She's done nothing. None of us have. This is fucking wrong.' Saliva cascaded out my mouth onto the dry mud below.

For his size, the big man moved quickly. Within a second, he was on top of me, his left hand wrapped around my throat like a vice. He swung his right arm back, and I flinched.

'Phil!' a voice shouted from my right. 'Calm down.'

Phil froze, released his grip slowly, his eyes burning into me. He backed off and jumped up to his feet. 'Sorry, boss. This Haynes guy is giving me shit,' he explained, taking a few steps back.

Hunt padded over, his shoes quietly crunching on the dried leaves. He stood a metre away, glaring down at me, his hands pushed into the pockets of his long brown coat. I felt my heart beat faster as I stared into the eyes of the monster that was responsible for all of this. For ruining my fucking life.

'Where is Joanne? Where is my fucking wife?' I shouted at him, my body shuddering with anger.

'You know,' he said softly, 'for a little guy, you seem so angry.'

'Little man syndrome,' Phil added. Then they shared a smile.

'Where's my mum?' Lucy asked, her voice quiet and sheepish.

He turned his head to her. 'She's coming with me. This was our plan. Your father chose to trade you for your mother. Not a bad deal I don't think, do you?'

Lucy frowned hard at me. I looked in her direction, caught her eye for a second. She couldn't believe what I'd done. 'You should've phoned the police, Dad!' she said. Maybe she was right. Maybe I should have. 'Now we're going to die.'

I cocked my head back up at Hunt. 'You have what you want. Let us go.'

My words lingered in the warm air. He smiled. A distance hum of an agricultural tractor sang from several fields away but, apart from that, all I could hear was my short, shallow breaths and a buzzing inside my head.

'I wish it was that easy,' he said, apologetically.

Hunt pulled the side of his jacket from his hip to reveal his gun. I didn't know what type of gun it was. It was black and metal, and that's all I cared about.

Using his right hand, he pulled it out.

Lucy let out a gasp and cowered to the floor, looking away from the gun nestled in his hand.

'Both of you,' he said, 'on your knees. Face that way.' His finger pointed behind us. Lucy moved. Maybe she had accepted her fate already. I rose to my knees and turned one-hundred and eighty degrees. I looked over the fields. They were the greenest fields I'd ever seen. The sky was bluer than I'd ever seen it. For a moment, I reached a height of clarity as the world paused in one high definitive still shot only for me to see.

Suddenly, I blinked several times, and I lost my focus. Footsteps grew loud behind us. I felt the vibration through the ground. My senses sharpened, hearing the mechanical clicking sound of the gun being loaded.

I stared into the distance, then decided to close my eyes.

Who was going to be first?

Me?

Lucy?

Moments passed, so I opened my eyes, angled my head towards my daughter. She met my gaze with her bright, blue eyes, causing emotions I'd never experienced before. As this was the end, I wanted to tell her how sorry I was for not being the perfect dad to her.

I loved her so much.

I heard Hunt take a step closer, then the material of his coat move as he raised his arm, presumably with the gun at the end of it, pointing at the back of our heads.

This was it.

This was the end.

'I love you, Lucy.'

She mumbled something through her bound mouth.

I clamped my eyes shut, found myself falling back into a nice warm bed, my head on a pillow, glancing across to a younger-looking Joanne. She was happy and giddy, holding a newborn baby in her arms, who was making the sweetest noises I'd ever heard. She whispered to me, 'I think we should call her Lucy.' I smiled at her.

Abruptly, the thought was ripped away from me. The sound of a gunshot exploded in the air.

84

Woodland, Toddington
JACK

I shuddered violently and squeezed my eyes tighter. My heart beat so fast. I sensed my blood surge around my body like it was on fire.

Next to me, I heard a loud thud, felt the vibration tingle in my right knee, the type you'd expect a dead weight to cause when it hit the floor.

'Oh, God,' I whispered. 'Oh, shit, shit.'

Lucy.

The bastard had killed Lucy first, so I could suffer.

I kept my eyes clamped shut. Rapid, shallow pants made my body vibrate. I suddenly become hot, as if lava was about to seep out of me at any second. My head was fuzzy, my body electric, as if I was floating up into the sky.

'Oh, God, Lucy, I love you,' I said. 'I'm so sorry.'

Silence then whispered in the air for what seemed like forever. I couldn't open my eyes. I couldn't turn my head to look at her, I couldn't face it.

Just get it over with.

Kill me, now.

I anticipated what dying would feel like. What would happen when—

Another gunshot rippled through the air, echoing from tree to tree, dispersing into the distance. I shuddered and let out a shriek. For a moment, I thought I'm dead, that everything has gone black. Waiting for the moment I realised I wasn't me anymore, the—

Another gunshot. I winced again and cowered.

'Dad?' a voice said near me.

I opened my eyes quickly, jerked my head to the right.

Lucy.

Oh my God, she was alive.

There was another shot – we both flinched and dived forward onto the floor. Lucy let out a helpless wail. I hit my forehead on hard mud and it rattled me for a moment. I opened my eyes, looked right at Lucy, watching the tears stream down her face.

'Get up now!' a voice screamed behind us. 'Now. Now!'

I rolled over to see Hunt standing over us. A frantic look lined his usually calm eyes. 'Get the fuck up now!' The end of the gun was inches from my face. The small black bullet hole appeared huge at close range.

I shuffled slowly and, as I climbed to my feet, I saw three bodies around us. Hunt's men. Phil, Stuart, and Derek. All dead. Blood slowly circled them.

'In the van now!' he screamed at me, the gun pointing at my face. I raised my palms quickly and nodded, taking a half step back.

He leaned over, grabbed Lucy up off the floor, and pulled her close. He was rough with her, turning her towards the van with the gun to her bald temple. He wrapped his left forearm around her neck and under her throat, pinning her close with her head back against his chest. I saw the pain and fear in her face as she watched me with wide, helpless eyes.

'Hey, what the—'

'Shut the fuck up!' he screamed in panic, eagerly moving towards the van, Lucy held tight up against his body. I followed them.

Another gunshot went off.

I heard the whistle of the passing bullet, smashing into one of the nearby trees, a small area of the tree bark shooting off in all directions. I ducked.

'In the van!' he shouted at Lucy. I heard the panic and fear and desperation in his voice.

This wasn't his plan.

Someone had taken his men out in the flick of a switch. The thing that scared him the most was that he didn't know who. I glanced around us quickly, but all I saw were trees and grass.

'You're hurting me,' Lucy cried.

'Shut the fuck up,' he told her, forcing her towards the van.

'It's okay, Lucy. Do as he says,' I shout, trying to keep the situation calm.

Hunt kept Lucy close, so if the shooter was in front, they'd hit her first. At the van's rear, he edged Lucy out the way and opened the door. Joanne let out a wail through her taped mouth. Hunt hauled Lucy inside. She bounced off the hard floor with a thud, crying in pain, and, after he closed the door, he turned to me.

'In the van – you drive.'

I raised my surrendering palms once again and made my way to the driver's side. Glancing around, I couldn't see anyone or anything. I opened the door and climbed in, found the keys swinging gently in the ignition slot. I turned the engine on, feeling the van shudder to life.

'Listen,' I said, 'just let us—'

'Fucking be quiet!' He hit me hard in the temple with the gun. 'Go to your house,' he told me. I nodded and put the gear in first. My hands were shaking. A sudden stab of intense pain reached my temple.

'Come on, Haynes!'

As I manoeuvred around the rear of the shiny Bentley, I watched him as he leaned back into his seat. Could I lean over, overpower him? Take the gun off him?

I hesitated.

'C'mon, Jack!'

'Our house?' I said, stalling whatever situation this was becoming.

'Yes – drive.' Hunt aimed the gun at my side, towards my hip. 'I'm losing patience, Jack Haynes. Fucking drive.'

I drove the van at a steady fifteen miles an hour as we rocked side to side down the dirt road, trying to avoid the potholes. I noticed Hunt glanced around him, trying to spot the shooter.

'Faster, Jack!' he shouted at me, slamming the gun off the dashboard. I flinched and glanced toward the damage he had caused.

I reached Park Road, edge out, took a right then moved through the gears slowly. Within a few minutes, we reached our house. I turned left, followed the gravel around to the front of the house. I applied the handbrake and sat back nervously.

'Turn off the engine and give me the keys,' he said. His tone had relaxed a little. It was clear he was feeling in control again. I did as he asked. 'Now, get out of the car and wait on your doorstep.'

I frown at him. 'I—'

'Just fucking do it.'

'Okay – okay.'

'Hey,' he said, grabbing my attention. 'Try anything here and you all die. Do you understand?'

I nodded, opened the door, got out, then slowly walked over the gravel towards the front door. I stopped on the step and turned around. The passenger door opens and he stepped out, then disappeared to the back of the van. From where I stood, I partially saw the rear doors swing open and heard a scream, then a loud shuffle.

Then silence.

Lucy and Joanne appeared at the side of the van and were pushed towards me, their feet crunching lightly on the gravel below. Tears streamed down both of their faces. It broke my heart.

Hunt was behind them, pointing the gun in our direction. 'Open the door and give me the keys back when it's open.'

I pulled the keys from my left pocket and did as he asked. I allowed Joanne inside the house first, then helped Lucy up, then followed her inside. I didn't want him in our house. Once I was inside, I quickly pulled the door—

Hunt's palm slapped the door and his boot kicked the base, stopping me. 'Don't even think about it, you, stupid man.'

Our faces were inches away from each other. I stared at him, looking into his big, brown eyes. 'Go on, inside,' he ordered me, pushing the tip of the gun into my stomach. I backed off and allowed room for him to enter. He closed the door and locked it, then put the keys into his pocket.

'Ooo, nice house, Mr Haynes. Very nice.'

'What do you want, Hunt?' I said, shielding my wife and daughter from him. 'Just take what you want, okay?'

He laughed at me. 'You think I want your money? Your fucking ornaments?' He shook his head. Lucy and Joanne huddled closer and tucked themselves behind me. 'Get upstairs, now! Go on!' he screamed.

I turned, pushed Lucy towards the stairs first, then Joanne. I follow, keeping them away from him. We climbed the stairs.

'To your bedroom, the one at the front,' he told us.

He walked into the bedroom and closed the door. 'Give me your phones.'

I pulled mine from my pocket and threw it on the bed.

'Theirs, too,' he said, nodding towards Joanne and Lucy. Their hands were still bound by rope, so I dug my hands inside their pockets, plucked them out, and dropped them onto the bed. He leaned forward, grabbed them, and put them inside his brown coat.

We were standing against the window, backed into a corner. The gun was down by his side and a smile suddenly found his old face.

'Lorraine, come with me.'

Joanne shook her head, mumbled something through the tape. He moved forward to the foot of the bed but I held out a solid palm as if I possessed some magical authority over the gun in his hand.

'She's not going anywhere with you – she isn't yours, Hunt. She's my wife,' I explained.

He raised his arm and pointed the gun at the wall behind us and fired it. The sound echoed in the bedroom and we all flinched in panic. Pieces of plaster and brickwork fell onto the carpet near our feet. Lucy and Joanne both cowered to the floor and cried through her taped mouth.

'Lorraine. In the bathroom now.'

Joanne didn't move. She didn't look at him.

'Lorraine,' Hunt shouted. 'The next bullet is for Lucy. In the bathroom now.'

Joanne slowly rose to her feet and reluctantly moved towards him. I stepped in front of her, blocking her movement. 'She's not going anywhere with you, Hunt,' I said, defiantly.

'Jack, I'll shoot you in the fuckin face. Move now,' he told me. I didn't move. I held my ground. Anger grew in his face and he sighed. 'Okay, your call.' He angled the gun towards me and, out of nowhere, I forced myself at him, darting across the carpet.

He fired the gun at my head but I ducked, hearing the hiss of the bullet whizz by my ear, which smashed into the wall behind with another dull thud. I saw him fluster as I got close and I threw my arms at him, hoping to connect in some way but, for an older guy, he moved well. He leaned to the left and hit me in the face with a punch so hard, it feels like a sledgehammer.

I dropped to the floor.

I didn't remember anything after that.

85

Toddington
JACK

My eyes flicked open. I wondered if I was dreaming for a moment until I saw Lucy's worried face looking down at me. She was shaking me and telling me to get up. She'd ripped the tape off away her from her mouth.

I realised I was on the bedroom carpet, laying on my back. I heard muffled screams coming from the bathroom. It was Joanne. Her desperate cries for help seeping through the closed door.

I found my feet slowly and felt the horrendous pain on my face from where Hunt had punched me. Touching it, it felt tender and bruised already.

'Dad – Mam's in the bathroom with him!' Lucy told me quickly. I untied her sore, bruised wrists.

Another scream rippled from the en-suite.

What the fuck was he doing to her in there?

Without thinking, I charged at the en-suite door, jumping at it with my right shoulder. The door gave way, folding in, the lock ripping away from the door frame. I fell onto the en-suite tiled floor awkwardly, my weight landing awkwardly on my wrist.

I glanced up. Joanne was backed into the corner inside the shower tray, naked, trying to cover herself up. Hunt was standing in front of her, his left hand grabbing at her breasts. He turned quickly in my direction.

In a rage, I jumped up from the floor. 'You fucking —'

'Hey, hey!' he shouted. 'Steady now, Jack.' He'd kept the gun in his left hand the whole time and pointed it at me, inches away from my face, right between my eyes. 'Don't be silly.'

A phone rang inside his pocket.

He stood there for a moment, his eyes glued to mine, deciding whether to answer it or not. The ringtone continued to echo in the small en-suite until he let out a sigh and, whilst keeping the gun on me, pulled his phone from an inside coat pocket to see who the caller was.

'Fuck,' he whispered.

Behind him, Joanne was sat in the corner of the shower, curled up in a ball, weeping in pain and embarrassment. I flicked my attention back to Hunt, who answered the phone.

'Listen, I can't speak right now, Red, I'm busy,' he said.

'I need to see you, Alexander,' Red informed him.

'Listen,' he began, I'm busy —'

'I don't give a fuck if you're busy,' she screamed down the phone. 'I need to see you now!'

Hunt's eyes changed like he'd been summoned by his master.

'Wait on,' Hunt sighed. He turned back to Joanne. 'Don't you go anywhere, dear.'

He pushed past me and left the en-suite.

I lowered myself to her. 'Oh, Jo,' I said, helping her up. Lucy appeared at the door, tears rolling down her face. The house fell quiet for a moment and a wave of relief washed over me.

Had he gone?

I helped Joanne out and helped her put her clothes back on. I stepped into the bedroom, went over to the door, and peered out into the landing. Hunt stood at the top of the stairs, his right hand supporting the phone pressed against his head, the gun nestled in his left hand, gently tapping against his thigh. I edged the door closed and told Lucy and Joanne to go over near the window. I went to the bed, leaned down to grip the wooden frame, then started to pull it across the carpet towards the door. If I could shut him out—

Loud footsteps echoed on the landing before the door opened.

'Sorry about that, guys,' Hunt explained, putting his phone back into his pocket. He laughed. 'What do you think you're doing?' He shook his head at my attempt to pull the bed towards the door. 'You're making me feel unwelcome here, Jack. Go on, over there.' He pointed the gun towards the window where Joanne and Lucy were already standing. 'I need to take a very important call, so you guys just wait here. If you try and move that bed again, I'll kill Lucy first.' Hunt smiled at us. 'I'll be right outside this door, okay?'

He turned to leave, then paused, cranking his head back towards us. 'This will all be over soon, I promise.'

Hunt closed the bedroom door gently, and I heard fading footsteps disappear into silence.

'Where's he gone?' asked Lucy, clutching my hand tightly.

86

Toddington

Dark Red was standing on the slanted grass verge a few hundred metres from the Haynes house. She turned to the man next to her, who was tall, slim, and athletic. His name was Todd. Ex-special forces.

He asked, 'Are you okay?'

'I've already said I am.'

'Okay, okay.' He looked forward again at the big house in the distance.

'Are we ready?' she asked him.

Todd lifted the walky-talky to his mouth, pressed firmly down on the small button on the side, and said, 'Are we ready?' He released his finger and they heard a short cackle.

'Yes, boss. In position. Snipe one and two are ready. Three is almost ready.' Todd and Red waited patiently. Then they heard, 'Yes, three is in position – ready on your call.'

Todd glanced at Red, making sure she had heard the same he had. She nodded. 'Tell them I'm ready.'

Before he spoke into the walkie-talkie, Todd said to her; 'You don't have to do this, boss. That's what we're here for.'

Red slowly angled her head towards him. 'I know. But I need to do this. Not just for the Haynes, but for me.'

Todd gave her a compassionate nod, then leaned into the walkie-talkie.

Red took a second to watch the Haynes house, then took a deep breath. 'Good luck,' she said to Todd, leaving him on the hillside as she made her way down the steady, grassy decline. She could see the black van parked in front of the house near the door as she stepped through a patch of boggy grass before reaching the low wooden fence. She stepped over it, walked out onto Park Road, and through the open gates of the Haynes property towards their front door.

JACK

'Are you okay, Joanne?' I said, softly.

Still sitting against the wall under the window, I glanced down at her in my arms. She slowly nodded, but her body still trembled. Lucy was on the other side of her, holding her close. The bedroom door was still closed, Hunt hadn't returned yet.

'Where is he?' Lucy asked me, quietly.

'I don't know,' I said.

In the silence of our bedroom, I heard a noise downstairs. Heavy, panicked footsteps. The way they echoed on the wooden floor sounds like he was in the study – what was he doing in the study? Ahh, it made sense. He was watching the cameras. He'd be able to see if anyone comes to the house – specifically the people who killed his men moments ago.

I felt Jo's head move as she glanced up. I looked into her sad, teary eyes. I admired her resilience. What she'd been through - what she and Lucy had both been through - was awful. I made eye contact with Lucy, who gave me a blank, sad stare.

'You okay, Luce?'

She nodded and tucked her head back into Jo's shoulder. I heard something outside. Footsteps on the gravel.

'Hey,' I said, 'let me up a second.'

Joanne leaned to her right while I moved from under her, climbed to my feet, and stared out the window.

'What the..?'

Jo frowned at me. 'What is it, Jack?'

'Why… why is she here?' I said. 'Look – come look. Here.'

Joanne and Lucy both got up fast. We all looked out, watched the woman slowly walk over the gravel towards the front door.

'What the hell is *she* doing here?' gasped Lucy.

87

Toddington

Hunt scowled at one of the screens in the study, tapping his right shoe on the hard, wooden floor. Someone was there, approaching the front door. It was a woman, slowly moving across the gravel. It looked like she was in pain, moving awkwardly, nursing something in her side. Her hip maybe.

It was Red.

Hunt watched her appear at the camera above the front door. She glanced up and smiled at him through the screen, as if she knew he'd be watching her.

Seeing her face through the camera screen made his heart skip a beat. A ball of air got stuck in his throat.

'Here we go,' he muttered to himself, squeezing the gun tight in his hand. He turned around and headed for the front door. The hallway was soundless. He stopped, cocked his head. Upstairs, he heard nothing. The Haynes were doing as they'd been told.

He gave a heavy sigh as he reached the front door, took a few breaths to steady himself in the cool silence. It was the first time he had ever met Red. He had heard the stories about her, about how no one had ever crossed her and gotten away with it. Then suddenly, he felt a jolt of anger towards the woman standing on the other side of it, for taking cuts from his dealings in the past. He felt hot in his long, brown coat, his body sweating underneath, his heart beating loudly in his thick, padded chest.

He gave himself a mental shake to get himself into character, reached forward, and pulled the door open.

The hallway flooded with light. He squinted at the woman down on the gravel. She was not tall, nor small, not thin, or fat. She was very average.

'Red.'

'Alexander,' she said. 'What a pleasure this is.' Her words were ice cold and calm.

Hunt's reminded of the phone calls with her. By her voice, it was definitely her. 'What – what happened to your face?'

She ignored his question and stepped closer —

'Ahhh, that'll do,' said Hunt, throwing his gun out in front of him, halting her movement. 'That's close enough.'

She froze to the spot, keeping her dark eyes on him.

'I unfortunately had an accident earlier,' she explained. 'I don't always look like this.'

'Shame when that happens to good people, isn't it?' he said, with a grin.

'Put down the gun, Alex,' she told him. Her words were soft, calm, and collected. She showed no cause for concern, no fear of what may happen if Hunt pulled the trigger. He could sense her power and authority, and it chilled him to the bone. She was that confident in herself.

And God knew, she did.

Hunt scowled at her. 'So… what happens now?'

Before Red spoke, she saw a red dot appear on Hunt, quavering an inch or two on the centre of his chest, coming from the laser of a gun resting on the sloping hill over two-hundred metres away.

'I think that would give you enough motivation to lower that gun of yours,' she said to Hunt, nodding towards his chest. He looked down, noticed the bright red pea-like dot hover and dance.

'What's to stop me from killing you?' Hunt asked.

'I guess I don't have an answer to that. But if you do decide to do that, you know, that within a second, you'll be joining me on the ground. So… your call, Mr Hunt?'

'Okay.' He held the gun for a few seconds longer until he finally lowered it by his side. 'You know, it's a shame.'

'What's that, Alexander?'

'That we've had to meet like this. Under different circumstances, maybe it could have been different.'

'Well, Alexander, I must say, I'm flattered. Now before you get too excited, drop the gun.' She pointed towards the floor. 'Go on, down there.'

Hunt squinted his eyes in thought, his mind searching for an alternative scenario. Maybe if he shot her, he'd have enough time to throw himself back into the house, dodging the sniper in the distance, and close the door quickly. Then he'd go upstairs, and kill Jack, Lucy, and Joanne. Get this over and done with.

He squinted down at her, his dark eyes glistening in the sun. A wide smile found his thin lips. 'Nothing fazes you, does it?' he said.

She shook her head. 'Last chance, Alexander.'

'You're not the one with the power here, Red,' he said, then laughed.

She nodded in understanding, knowing what needed to be done. She raised her left hand in the air beside her face, and clenched it into a fist leaving only her index finger pointing to the sky.

'What the fu—'

The bullet hit the brickwork left of the door, just above the tip of her finger. Hunt flinched in panic, throwing himself to the left.

Although in severe pain, she quickly plucked the knife from the back of her trousers with her right hand, took a step forward, and, bringing her arm round, stabbed the blade into the side of his thick neck. The blade went deep, slicing through his skin like a knife through warm butter. She then twisted it fast.

Hunt staggered back, gasping uncontrollably, his back colliding into the door frame. He dropped the gun, and hysterically, threw both hands up to his throat but the heavy blood cascaded through them. His eyes widened as he fell onto his back through the open door onto the floor of the hallway.

As Hunt let out his last gurgle, Red watched his body go limp, his blood-filled hands finally letting go of his throat. She saw the crimson liquid surround the wooden floor around his head and smiled widely.

From her pocket, she plucked her phone out, tapped a few buttons, then put it to her ear.

'Yes, boss,' Todd answered, standing on the sloping hill.

'As you can see, it's done,' she told him. 'Get someone to clean this up ASAP.'

'Consider it done.'

'No traces left. Remember.'

'We know the drill, boss.'

Red put the phone back into her pocket and sighed. Inside the house, she heard whispers upstairs.

Jack, Joanne, and Lucy.

The remaining members of her family.

Elaine stepped over Hunt and, leaving leaves the door open for her men to come and clean up, disappeared into the shadows of the house.

88

Toddington
JACK

There was a loud thud outside and we all jumped.

'What was that?' Lucy gasped. Her hand was wrapped around my forearm. We were still looking out the window but couldn't see Elaine anymore – the position of the front door didn't allow it. It sounded like something hard against the brickwork of the house. I felt the short, sharp vibration rip up through the outer shell, along the joists below us.

'He's going to kill her,' Jo said, her voice filled with worry. 'He's going to kill Elaine!'

I absorbed her words, knowing there could be some truth to them. I went to speak but a series of muffled thuds kept me quiet, coming from somewhere downstairs.

'Dad?' Lucy wept.

I didn't say anything, instead, I cocked my head towards the door to listen. It fell silent for a long time and I knew we couldn't just sit here waiting. I knew I needed to do something. I turned away from the window and —

'Dad?' Lucy said. 'Where are you going?'

'I'm – I'm going to sneak out onto the landing, see what's happening.'

'No, Jack, please,' Joanne pleaded. 'Stay with us.'

'No, I have to. He's going to kill her – you two, get in there.' They followed my gaze towards the en-suite and nodded their understanding.

'Okay, I'll be straight back.'

I edged the bedroom door open soundlessly and crept out onto the landing. Quietly, I leaned over the bannister. I heard muffled voices then it went quiet. Then there were footsteps coming along the hall, towards the stairs. I backed away and opened the door of the bedroom next to ours and stepped inside. I stopped and thought hard, my eyes darting around the room at anything I could potentially use as a weapon. When he came back up, I could use the weapon to attack him from behind, and gain an advantage in our situation. Looking around the bedroom, the only suitable object was the metal curtain pole that was fixed above the window. As quickly as I could, I reached up on my tiptoes, pushed the pole upwards over the shape of the hooks, and lowered it down. I tipped the pole vertically, allowing both curtains to slide off onto the floor.

I went back to the door, closed it, leaving a gap of six inches, then hid behind it. Hopefully, he'd realise it wasn't open when he left our bedroom, and when he comes in to investigate, that's when I'd take him out.

I heard footsteps on the stairs, growing louder. I brought the pole high above my right shoulder and waited. The footsteps stopped outside the bedroom door.

I heard light, shallow breathing on the other side of the door.

Then it slowly opened.

89

Toddington
Jack

My hands were tight around the metal pole above my head. My breathing was light and fast. Sweat soaked my t-shirt and lined my hot face. I tried to keep as still as possible as the door opened further.

I heard him enter the room, the floorboards creaking under his weight.

I squeezed the pole and readied myself for a swing.

'Jack?'

I blinked a few times. The voice sounded familiar.

'Jack?' the voice said again.

'Elaine?' I whispered.

'Yes, Jack. It's me.'

I loosened my grip on the pole and sighed in relief. The door opened further. Her swollen face appeared around the edge of the door. 'What happened – did you see him?' I asked quickly.

She frowned. 'See who?'

'Hunt,' I said, lowering the improvised weapon. 'He went downstairs. He, he —'

Elaine raised a gentle palm and placed it on my chest. 'Jack, there's no one here. I've checked the whole house looking for you. There's just us.' I looked deep into her eyes for a moment and saw the confidence in them.

'What are you doing here?' I asked her.

'I'm making sure my family is okay.' She lowered her hand on my forearm, forcing a thin smile. 'Where's Lucy and Jo?'

'Bedroom.'

In the bedroom, I shouted to Lucy and Jo. They stepped out from the en-suite and, when they saw Elaine, they went over to her and hugged her tightly.

'Careful,' she whispered into Lucy's ear.

'I'm just glad you're okay,' Lucy gasped.

'Where's Hunt?' Joanne said, looking past her out onto the hallway.

'There's no one here, love,' Elaine reassured her. I watched Elaine hug Joanne. Her frail battered body comforted my wife as if Joanne was the one who'd been violently attacked, not her.

I had to check the house, had to see if Hunt was still here. He hadn't just vanished surely.

'Where are you going?' Elaine asked me on my way out of the bedroom.

'I need to check the house - he was here ten minutes ago.'

I left them in the bedroom, cautiously padded downstairs. As I reached the bottom, I saw the front door was closed. On the other side of it, I could hear low, quick voices and, for a second, I hesitated. My heart beat like a drum. I didn't see anyone through the distorted glass of the door, and the voices seemed to fade into a comforting silence. I shook my head, wondering if I'd imagined it.

I went to the door and pulled it open.

Out on the gravel, Hunt's black van had gone. I breathed deeply and realised Elaine had been right – there was just us here. A tired smile found my face as I dipped my head to the floor, releasing the stress in my neck. As I did, I saw something on the gravel. I focused, lowered down to my knees, and frowned.

'What's that?'

A small pool of blood.

'What are you doing, Jack?' someone said behind me.

I flinched and turned quickly to see Elaine standing there.

'Jesus, Elaine… you scared me.'

She leaned down. 'Come on,' she said, 'let's get you back inside.' She helped me up, wrapped her arm around my shoulder, led me back into the house, and closed the door.

90

FRIDAY
Toddington

Two days later, Lucy was lying on her bed in the attic, peering at her phone. The balcony doors were open. They swayed gently against the afternoon breeze. It was just after three in the afternoon. Her morning had been filled with film-watching and social media scrolling.

Jack and Joanne were downstairs.

Jack had taken the rest of the week off work, after speaking with the bank's director, who actually showed unexpected sympathy and told him to take as long as he needed.

Yesterday, all three of them watched him spend a few hours looking over the security footage from the day before.

They watched Elaine walking up to the house, across the gravel, until she reached the front door. The camera blacked out for a total of thirty-four minutes with no audio attached to the blank screen. Then it flicked back on, showing two police cars turn up at the house. Jack phoned Vision Security, who checked the footage from the storage files at HQ. All they could do was apologise, saying the thirty-four minutes of their recorded footage was also gone – there were ongoing updates across the network at the time, so there could've been interference. They credited Jack's account and told him the following month would be free of charge.

The rest of yesterday was spent in the company of Elaine. She'd seen a doctor about her injuries and had been prescribed some painkillers, explaining that only time would heal the bruising. Luckily, no bones had been broken.

They had visited a funeral director in Luton. Lucy didn't want to go, but Jack and Joanne weren't letting her out of their sight. Understandable really – to their knowledge, Hunt was still out there. On their way back, Lucy glanced across the rear of the car towards her Auntie. She really admired Elaine. Her strength and courage were admirable, her ability to be strong considering what'd happened to Mark.

Lucy rolled onto her front and scanned the messages on social media.

Are you okay?

Omg! What happened?

Babe… you have been through so much…

It was endless. But it made her feel loved.

Her phone beeped. A text from Harry: *Hi Lucy, I can't believe what you've been through. I can't believe it. It's like you were in a mad film or something! I put some pics on my page, if you wana have a look. Hope you're holding up okay. Lv, H x*

Interestingly, the message made Lucy smile.

She replied, thanking him for the message, and told him she was doing okay. She messaged him more about photography and started to feel more comfortable with him.

Just as 'Harry' had planned.

At 8 p.m., Lucy sat down in the living room next to Joanne. She smiled and looked up at the television.

Her phone beeped in her pocket, so she plucked it out.

Another text from Harry.

I really shouldn't tell you this, but… we're in trouble. My dad has done something stupid at work. He had stolen some money. What do I do?! I'm scared people will find out and he'll go to prison.

Lucy frowned at the message from Harry and stood up, stepping around Joanne.

'Where you going?' asked Joanne.

'Just getting a drink, won't be long.'

'Don't be. The film is starting soon,' Joanne said.

Lucy walked along the hallway towards the kitchen, confused at the text from Harry. She was also feeling vulnerable, like her dad's secret might get him into trouble, too. In Harry, she found some common ground and messaged him back: *what happened? x*

In Harry's reply, *he* said his dad needed money and made the mistake of stealing some from the cash register. Lucy then told him not to worry about it. And that these things happened. That things could be kept quiet if nobody knew about them.

'Lucy?' Joanne shouted from the living room.

Lucy looked up. 'Two seconds, Mum.'

Harry replied asking her what she meant.

Lucy, feeling weak and exhausted, replied: *my dad made a mistake a while ago. He did something similar. No one knows about it…it was in the past so it's forgotten about.*

This past week had been a rollercoaster ride that she'd never forget. She put her phone in her pocket, made a drink, and returned to the living room.

The message came through on 'Harry's' phone.

The woman behind the screen smiled, leaned back in her chair, and sighed heavily. That was all she needed. Months of be-friending Jack's daughter had all boiled down to this moment. A moment of clarity. A moment when all of her suspicions had been confirmed.

Jack *had* robbed the bank.

With a smile on her face, Jack's PA, Debra, put down her phone and clapped her hands.

91

SUNDAY
Toddington
JACK

Four days had passed since the incident with Hunt. It felt like forever. We'd barely left the house, apart from the visit to the funeral director about Mark. I'd never have thought the next funeral I'd be going to would be that of my brother. My Volvo had been taken away to be fixed and we'd been given a new XC60 for the time being.

The police watched the house for three days, providing a car which parked up at the side of the house, near the broken gates.

Hunt hadn't been found yet. He was still out, still a threat. But after three days of watching the house, the police left, explaining they couldn't stay there forever.

They'd checked the property of Alexander Hunt in Hemel Hempstead, but there was no sign of him. It was like he'd vanished like a ghost. Joanne told the police about the murder of the Hembridge Bank CEOs, which had given them more motivation to locate his whereabouts.

I missed Mark more than words could describe. At the time I didn't realise but I wished I saw more of him. I'd taken him for granted and felt bad. He'd only lived ten minutes away for Christ's sake.

You didn't seem to miss something until it was gone, until it was taken from you. You took something for granted until the day it was no longer there, it shatters you. It's how life works.

I'd spoken to Elaine every day, telling her if there was anything she needed, to let us know. Whether it was out of kindness or being stubborn, she told me the same and thanked me. Elaine seemed to be handling the whole thing very well. She was a strong woman, no doubt about it.

The thought of going back to work next week, dealing with all the politics and stress of the bank, overwhelmed me. I pondered a thought that rattled in my head. I stood up, left the study, and went to see Joanne in the kitchen.

'Hey,' I said.

She turned her head, smiling.

'I've been thinking.'

'About?' She returned her focus to chopping the carrots on the worktop.

'We should move away.'

She frowned. 'Out of town?'

'I mean abroad. Leave all this behind us, start afresh. Elaine seems to be coping well. I can't stand the thought of going back to the bank, putting up with the pressure anymore. We could move to Spain, see out the rest of our days in the sun in the Costa Blanca.' I paused. 'Lucy won't finish her course, but we've got enough money to do it.'

Joanne placed the knife down by the half-chopped carrots. She was about to open her mouth to say something when there was a loud series of knocks at the front door.

'I'll get it,' I said, turning and making my way down the hallway to the door. I unlocked it and pulled it open. Bright sunlight shone down on the faces of DCI Clarke and DS Horton.

'Detectives, I – we weren't expecting you,' I said, confused. I realised they must be following up on what'd happened. 'Things are okay here.' I gave them a smile.

But they didn't return one.

'What's this regarding?' I asked.

'We have information that leads us to believe that you are the man responsible for the robbery at Hembridge bank six months ago,' Clarke said.

I stared at them both with a blank expression, feeling my stomach twist in knots.

'Please, sir, come with us. We need to ask you a few questions at the station.' DS Horton took my arm and led me to their car.

92

Police Station
JACK

Sitting alone in the hot interview room, I felt claustrophobic in the small space, as if the walls were creeping in every few minutes. I stared down at the half-filled cup of cold coffee on the table, trying to calm myself down but my heart beat too fast.

The door opened. Clarke and Horton entered the room.

'Would you like a lawyer?' Clarke said, sitting down on a chair opposite me.

I shook my head. 'No, I don't need one.'

'You sure?' Horton added, taking the seat next to him.

I nodded.

'So,' Clarke began, 'Hembridge Bank was robbed six months ago. Just over a million pounds. You remember this?'

'Of course, I remember,' I said. 'It was one of the biggest robberies in the bank's history.'

'Sounds like theirs pride in your voice,' Horton said, smiling.

'Why are we here – what evidence points to me being responsible?'

'We'll discuss that later. First, we want to hear your side of the story,' Clarke said.

'You know my side of the story. I was in Greece with my wife and Daughter. The police got statements from every employee at the bank – I was included in that list.'

'Well… that's what your statement said, didn't it?' Horton added.

I edged back and let out a long sigh. 'I was hoping it wouldn't come to this.'

'Come to what?' asked Clarke, intrigued.

I exhaled heavily then leaned forward. 'I had my suspicions, but I didn't want to say. I didn't want to get him into trouble.'

'Go on,' Clarke said, frowning.

I told them about the ex-financial director, Keith. About catching him messing around with clients' bank accounts, transferring money back and forth to buy stocks and shares. I explained to them that Keith's wife had cancer and only had months to live. I told them Keith pleaded with me not to say anything. He told me he needed the upcoming bonus to get out of debt and that his pension fund had fallen through.

'He was in a mess,' I continued. 'I didn't know what to do. I knew morally, that turning a blind eye, was wrong.' I dipped my head for effect. 'But he'd been good to me. He was a good friend, a friend I couldn't turn my back on.' I shook my head. 'Maybe the bonus wasn't enough for him, I don't know.'

The detectives mulled over my words carefully.

I coughed. 'I don't know where your information is coming from, but I can honestly say I had nothing to do with it.' I tried and think of anyone in the bank who may have set this in motion. Then it came to me that there was one name: Debra. 'My PA has been a little difficult over the past few months too. I shouldn't be saying this but she told me she loved me. She had asked me to leave Joanne for her. Don't get me wrong, she's a nice lady but I'm happily married. She couldn't seem to let it go. Since then, she's been off with me, being awkward, not really carrying her PA role out properly. Getting sloppy with paperwork and appointments. I feel sorry for her, but I let her get on with it. I don't like seeing people out of work.' I shrugged. 'But she does need to change.'

Clarke gave me an understanding nod, then glanced at Horton thoughtfully. 'Okay. Well, thanks for your time. We'll look into Keith – I remember speaking with him not so long back. We'll have a word with him.'

'You can't,' I said.

Clarke's eyes narrowed. 'Why – if he's the man responsible for this, the —'

'He's dead. His wife died of cancer, then he died a month after from a broken heart.'

The detectives let me go. They didn't have any concrete evidence to hold me. I told them about Debra because I feel she was the only one who would do something as malicious as this.

93

WEDNESDAY
Toddington

Four letters dropped through the letterbox just after ten. Jo-anne paused the television, got up from the sofa, and picked them up from the mat at the front door. Above her, she heard a hum of music seep out of the open door up to Lucy's room. Jack was currently out doing the weekly shop. Jo would normally go, but Jack offered this time.

From the four envelopes in her hand, she noticed three of them were addressed to Jack Haynes. But the last one was for her, addressed to Joanne Haynes. She didn't recognise the handwriting on the front of the white envelope but, frowning, turned it over and pulled the flap open. It was a typed letter on printed, A4 plain paper. There was a logo on the back of the paper with the Hembridge bank logo.

It read:

Dear Joanne,
I'm sorry to tell you this, but your Husband Jack is a cheat. We've been seeing each other for a few months. I can't lie to you anymore. I know it's wrong and, morally, it isn't fair on your family. Thought you needed to know.
Sorry again,
Debra (Jack's PA)

The words on the paper hit Joanne like a sledgehammer. She was stunned. She staggered back a few steps, her back colliding with the doorframe of the living room. She put her right hand to her open mouth and re-read it over and over, focusing on the word 'cheat'. She dropped the letter by her side, slowly moved to the living room in a daze, and sat down on the sofa.

Her eyes filled up and she cried quietly into her palms, her body rocking back and forth. After a few minutes, she wiped her eyes and the tears were gone, replaced with dark hatred.

'No one does this to me,' she said.

94

Toddington
JACK

I unpacked the shopping in the kitchen and turned towards the door when hurried footsteps enter.

Her face was focused, her eyes frowning likethere was something on her mind.

'Hey, Luce.'

'Hi, Dad.' She went straight to the fridge, opened it, and grabbed a yoghurt.

'What's up? You look a little angry?'

'Uni work – trying to work something out,' she explained.

'You seen mum? I've been calling her for a few minutes now.'

She frowned and shook her head. 'She was in the living room earlier - hold on.' Lucy padded down the hallway, then peered into the living room. She backed out and looked my way. 'No, she's not there now.'

I smiled, continued putting the tinned food and fruit away, humming to myself joyfully. When I finished with the food, I made a coffee, sat down at the kitchen table with my tablet. The ideal time to catch up on some reading. Before it all kicked off a few weeks ago, I was reading a thriller by Linwood Barclay. Strangely enough, one of the girls at work had started writing books, and we got talking. Turned out she was nearly finished with her first book. She told me a rough outline about it – it sounded intriguing. She told me her favourite writer was Mark Edwards.

My eyes found page two-hundred and six as I sipped coffee.

I reached the end of the chapter and put it down. I finished my coffee and left the kitchen, leaving the tablet and the empty mug on the circular table.

'Joanne?' I shouted, my voice ripping through the silent house.

As I climbed up to the landing, I heard Lucy talking on the phone to someone, her voice squeezing through the small gap at the bottom of her stairs. Probably a friend, I figured. I walked towards the landing to our bedroom.

'Jo, you in here?' I said, quietly.

The bedroom was empty and soundless. A dull light fell in through the two windows. It wasn't as bright as yesterday, the sun masked by a thin film of hanging clouds. It was cooler, too. Chances of a light shower were expected this afternoon. I glanced at my wrist to see the time.

My eyes narrowed.

My watch wasn't there.

I scowled down at my wrist, then remembered I never actually put it on this morning. I must have left it in my bedside drawer last night. I smiled and gave my head a shake. I pulled open the top drawer, my hand lowered down but I couldn't see it.

It wasn't there, either.

'Where is it?' I asked myself, opening the middle and bottom drawers, the frustration of my voice disturbing the grey silence of the bedroom. I straightened my back, glanced around the room. I couldn't see it. I checked in the en-suite to see if I'd put it on the shelf below the mirror. It wasn't there either.

I stepped into the through-room and opened my wardrobe door, looking along the top shelf. I didn't know why it would be in here, but I checked anyway, my fingers moving objects out the way, reminding me I needed to organise it better. I slid the door closed, turned, and padded over to Joanne's side. I slid her dark brown door across, the familiar smell of her perfume seeped out. I ran my hand along the top shelf, across a variety of shoes until I felt something oddly familiar.

I grabbed the item and pulled it down.

It was the small leather box I'd found up in the attic a few weeks ago. The one I couldn't open. The one I asked Lucy and Joanne if they had seen. I vividly remember Joanne saying she hadn't. I left the bedroom with the box and went back downstairs. The house was still silent. In the kitchen, I pulled the cutlery drawer open and pulled out a large flat-headed screwdriver that was tucked down the side of the cutlery tray.

I took a seat at the table and sighed.

Maybe Lucy had shown Joanne the box and she'd put it in her wardrobe, not thinking much into it. And when I'd asked her, she'd forgotten. Easy mistake to make, considering what had been going on recently.

I placed the box in front of me on the table and picked up the screwdriver. I needed to know what was in the box. I tipped the box on its side and dug the tip of the screwdriver into the small gap next to the lock. I push down hard and twisted quickly.

The lock split in two and the box opened suddenly. The contents made a racket as they spilled out onto the wooden table.

I glared at them, not understanding what was before me.

I picked up a pocket watch, held it in my hands. It was old, the gold coating was scratched and rounded. I placed it down and noticed more watches. All wrist watches. Inside the bottom of the box, I saw folded newspaper clippings. I pulled them out carefully and unfolded them one by one.

'I – I don't understand,' I said.

I glanced down at the watches and froze.

'How is that possible?' I muttered.

One of the watches was mine. The one I'd just been looking for upstairs.

95

1975
Luton

The little girl cowered into her big brother's arms in the corner of his bedroom. The sounds coming from the room next door were horrible. Their mother screamed in pain as their father banged her head off the bed frame. The loud thuds vibrated through the thin walls.

Three days ago, her brother was brave. He'd challenged his father when he had seen him hit his mother. Enough was enough, he thought. He charged into their bedroom and jumped on his father's back. His father swung him round and threw him onto the floor. The boy landed on his back, cracking his head on the hard, un-carpeted floor.

His father peered over him and smiled. 'Big and tough are you now – getting a big boy are you now?'

The monster then stamped on his stomach three times, causing so much horrific pain, he wailed helplessly as the little body flayed in agony. His mother hadn't even moved. She was scared stiff in the corner of the room, her eyes watching the horror unfold.

The little girl had heard what had happened and had hidden under the bed.

In recent times, he'd started hitting them, too.

The girl's body shuddered in his little arms.

'Shh, please, Shh,' he begged her. He was terrified that if their father heard her crying, he'd come in and they'd be next. The girl's sobbing got quiet as they held each other.

It was late. The house was dark and quiet. Everyone was asleep. But not her. She could hear a constant dripping sound coming from a leaking tap in the small bathroom at the end of the hall. She looked across the room, watched her brother sleeping silently. She had been sleeping in his room over the past few months – she was too scared to stay in a room by herself. Reaching down and grabbing something from under her bed, she silently climbed out, her small bare feet cold on the uneven wooden floor.

She pulled the bedroom door open and looked out onto the dark, small, narrow landing. Her parent's door was closed. Stopping for a second in the silence of the house, she felt her little heart thumping. She put her small hand on the door handle, pushed down, and edged the door open.

She could see them in the bed. Her father with his big arms wrapped around her mother, as if trapping her in, not letting her getaway.

After a deep breath, she entered. Her small feet light on the floor, as she made her way around to her father's side. Dim light from a nearby streetlamp seeped in through the window. At her father's side, she watched him for a long time.

Steadying herself, she raised the knife above him and, taking one last breath, she lunged forward and stabbed it into the back of his neck.

She lifted it out and did it again. Over and over and over and over.

Her mother wriggled and woke, turned on the bedside lamp. A soft light erupted in the room. There was blood everywhere. The bed was soaked. Her husband's face is unrecognisable, a pile of mangled flesh. She let out a blood-curdling scream which rattled the whole house.

She looked beyond him at her daughter holding the knife standing behind him.

'Oh, Lorraine,' she said, 'what have you done?'

96

Police Station

DCI Clarke appeared at the open door of the canteen, seeing DS Horton casually making coffee near the sink.

'Here, now!' Clarke shouted, waving his palms frantically. Horton looked up at the sound of Clarke's voice and sensed the panic. 'Come on, James, we haven't got all day.'

Horton nodded firmly in understanding, leaving the spoon whirling in the hot cup of coffee, then turned and headed for the door. He followed his superior through the corridors, where they received strange looks from others, wondering why they were rushing. Clarke threw his office door open, rounded his desk, and sat down with the energetic thud. Horton took the seat next to him, wondering what was so urgent.

'Have a look at this,' Clarke muttered. Horton thought he seemed fidgety, unsure of himself. The cool, calm, collective manner had left his superior. 'It's the footage,' Clarke said, 'from the place next door to the club in Milton Keynes.'

'You watched it yet?'

'Just watch!' Clarke snapped, raising a silencing palm.

Horton nodded and did what his superior asked. Clarke pressed the play button on the screen.

On the camera timeline, at 12.59 a.m., they saw the front of the taxi come into view and stop. It then edged forward a few metres and stopped for a minute. The camera picked up a clear side shot of the taxi, sitting there in the darkness, the engine idling. They saw the faint familiar outline of the driver they'd spoken with, Manual Corr, sitting patiently, turning his head every few seconds to watch the people pass by the taxi.

'Watch this,' Clarke said, pointing.

Horton focused hard, squinting over the top of his glasses.

The woman entered the camera shot from the left. She opened the rear passenger door, leaned in, and spoke to Peter Lewes. After a few seconds, she lowered in and closed the door. The taxi moved forward, disappeared to the right of the screen out of view. Clarke used the mouse to drag the video back to the shot of the woman, standing by the open door, then he paused it.

They stared at the side shot of the woman.

Dark hair, attractive face. Slim figure, large breasts.

'You recognise her?' Clarke asked Horton.

He nodded firmly. 'It's Joanne Haynes. Without a doubt.'

'I think so, too,' Clarke said, standing up. 'Come on, let's go see her!'

Toddington
JACK

I sat in silence at the kitchen table, glaring down at the contents of the box with wide eyes, wondering why my missing watch was locked up in this old box.

I froze. I couldn't actually move, as if I was stuck to the chair. I couldn't take my eyes off the watches in front of me. Shaking my head, I clamped my eyes shut – I didn't understand. My breathing had become faster, shallow breaths in and out, in and out. My skin started to get hot. I could feel my cheeks glowing. I suddenly felt the walls were closing in, so I jumped up, went to the sink, and leaned over. My stomach was twisted and I felt something climbing up my throat.

Inhaling a deep breath, I steadied myself, leaning against the worktop, and focused out onto the fields. The skies above were darker than before. Spots of rain landed and clung to the window in front of me.

Who do these watches belong to?

Why was the box hidden upstairs in the cupboard of Lucy's room?

Why had Joanne hidden it in her wardrobe and denied even seeing it?

My head was fuzzy with a million questions.

I went back to the table, picked up the box, the watches and the newspaper clippings and took them into the study, and placed them down carefully on my desk. I told myself there must be a logical reason for this. I fired up the computer and waited, the whirring hum breaking the ghastly silence.

Placing each of the watches in a neat line, I picked out the newspaper clippings and laid them out to the right. I signed into the computer and opened the internet. The first newspaper clipping was titled: Double CEO murder at Hembridge Bank.

My heart missed a beat and my eyes narrowed in confusion. I read the article carefully, reminded myself of the familiar story. Then I typed 'CEO Hembridge bank murders' into the search engine and read the first website that came up. Holding my breath, I scanned over the words in front of me:

'I'm deeply heartbroken by what has happened to my husband, and I will never forgive the person who did this to him. Worst of all, my daughter had saved up a lot of money to buy her Dad the special watch he was wearing that day. The watch is missing. It was stolen from him, like he was stolen from us.'

Below her quote, there was a picture of the watch.

I felt icy fingers crawl up my spine as I looked down at the watch to the far left of the desk. It was the exact same watch.

This couldn't be true.

It couldn't be.

Hunt killed the men with a knife and stole their briefcases. Joanne was terrified. She told me how it had happened.

The next clipping was the murder of Andy Butler. The article read he was a father of four and happily married. His body was found in an alley in London, his throat slashed. I put the article down and typed 'Andy Butler' into Google and pressed ENTER. I read over a couple of articles with a fast-beating heart. One link took me to a website of unsolved crimes. I clicked it, tapping my foot quickly off the floor as I waited impatiently for it to open up. There was a short story about Andy Butler, telling me what had happened to him. It said the killer was never found. I read over the words 'Crime Unsolved'.

'Fuck,' I muttered to myself.

I picked up the next newspaper article.

As I started reading the words, I threw a hand to my mouth in horror. It was a story close to home. It was our friend, Peter Lewes, the husband of Joanne's best friend, Alison. As I knew, he was found murdered in the park near his home, with fatal stab wounds to his stomach. Again, the case was never solved.

I leaned over the side of the desk chair and took deep breaths. After a while, I sat upright. Further down the article, there was a statement from Alison. My heart bled as I read it when she mentioned the blue-faced Omega watch that she'd bought him for his fortieth birthday, stating that he was wearing it that night, but it was missing when his body was found.

I glanced down at the desk. There was the blue-faced Omega watch.

I felt dizzy, physically feeling the life being sucked out of me. My head was spinning and became weightless. I glared down at the watches before me, my eyes fixed on my own watch.

'Why is my watch here?' I whispered in confusion.

I froze when I heard them.

Quiet, fast footsteps behind me.

I turned my head, seeing a large metal object inches away from my face. It happened too fast.

And then everything went black.

98

Toddington
JACK

'Wakey, wakey,' a muffled voice said.

My head was heavy like there was a weight on top of it.

'Hey, Jack,' the voice said, 'wake up.'

I flinched, trying to lift my head up slowly from my chest. The headache behind my eyes was a constant, pounding drum and, as I began to wake up, my left temple burned like hell. I flicked open my eyes, but I couldn't focus. Everything was blurry. It was like looking through an obscured window of a bathroom.

I didn't know where I was.

Letting out an inaudible muffle, I heard laughter somewhere in front of me. I tried shaking it away, but the laughter grew louder and I wouldn't if I was imagining it. Then I realised it was a familiar laugh.

I blinked several times and tried to move forward, but I couldn't. I was stuck to the chair. I attempted to move my legs, but they didn't work either. I felt something sharp wrapped around my body. I tried again, but something stopped me: rope. I was tied to a chair.

As my eyes flickered into focus, I saw a figure in front of me, standing still.

'That's it – that's good, Jack,' the voice said again.

It was Joanne's voice.

After I blinked, my vision returned. Joanne stood in the centre of the study; a knife nestled in the hand by her side. Her smile was from ear to ear.

'Jo – I don't…' I began to say.

She padded forward, leaned closer. 'What is it, Jack?'

I took a breath. 'I don't understand, Jo.'

'I don't expect you to, dear,' she said. 'It's just the way it is.'

I couldn't believe I was about to say it: 'Did you kill them?'

She nodded. 'I did,' she said, calmly.

'All of them – the newspaper clippings, the watches...'

She nodded again, and a proud grin lined her face.

The rope was digging into my stomach. I tried to use my feet as leverage to push myself higher on the chair, so the rope wasn't as tight, but my feet weren't touching the floor. She'd tied them to the base of the chair. 'Why, Jo?' I gasped. 'Why?'

'Because they were all cheating bastards. And I simply don't tolerate it.'

Her words lingered in the air.

'Okay, Jack. I shall explain,' she said as if reading my mind. 'Let me start from the beginning.'

99

M1, Luton

DCI Clarke and DS Horton motored up the M1, flashing the blues and twos, approaching one hundred miles an hour in the fast lane. Cars moved over to make way for them. The rain started to thicken now, the conditions for driving becoming deadly. The road was saturated and only getting worse.

'It's her, isn't it?' Horton said, glancing at Clarke for a moment.

'Yup.' Clarke watched the road carefully, edging off the accelerator for a moment to wait for the driver of a van to realise they were behind them. They probably didn't see them in the heavy drizzle.

'C'mon, move!' Horton screamed, waving a frantic hand out in front of him towards the van. The van finally shifted over and they passed it.

When Clarke saw the sign for the turn-off for Junction twelve, they moved over to the left lane and went up the ramp towards Toddington.

100

Toddington
JACK

Joanne glared down at me with a smile, tapping the knife off her thigh. 'The first person I ever killed was my father. Oh, God, he was awful, Jack.'

'Your father?' I frowned at her.

'Yes,' she said with a nod. 'My father. I was only eight at the time. He was a horrible bastard, Jack. He really was. Oh, you didn't know, did you?'

She stepped back and broke out into a hysterical laugh. For a second, I hoped Lucy would come downstairs. Jo noticed me looking at the closed door.

'Don't you worry, Jack, Lucy isn't here. I've sent her out to the cinema with her friends. I told her you were busy with work stuff in here while you were unconscious. She never questioned it, because that's all you fucking do nowadays, isn't it?' She paused to catch her breath. 'Anyway, my parents aren't my real parents, Jack. They adopted me when I was thirteen. I lived on the streets, you know, before that. Each day was a fight to stay alive. But I learned a lot. I became wise. I killed my father because he was a cheating bastard who treat my mother worse than I could even describe.'

I shuffled. 'How – how did—'

'How did I do it?' she said. 'I crept into their room one night and stabbed him eight times in the neck with the biggest knife I could find in the kitchen. You should have seen the blood, Jack. Jesus. I stole his old pocket watch as a souvenir before I left.' She paused again to smile. 'My next trick was the CEOs.' She forced her lips together for a moment. 'You see, you guys believed the story about Hunt, didn't you? The one where he had this idea about robbing the CEOs? Well, it wasn't his idea. It was mine.'

Her words sent a shiver down my body.

'I used to wander the streets, Jack. To look for men who were bad. Look for men who treated their wives in a way that I couldn't tolerate. I found out if they were married, and had their own little lives at home with kids. Playing happy families. Then one night, I watched them through the window of a bar. They were talking to two blonde-haired women. Let's just say it wasn't long before they got in a taxi and went somewhere private.'

I breathed heavily, listening to her.

'That's when I mentioned it to Hunt, and by God, he didn't take much persuading, that nutjob. When he got out of the car in the car park behind the back of the bank, I didn't stay in the car.'

'You never?'

She shook her head. 'I got out. Hunt had them backed into a corner held at knife point. I pretended to be an innocent bystander and went over to Hunt and took the knife off him. I then approached the CEOs and stabbed them both.' She smiled. 'Then I took their watches.

'Back in the car, Hunt was screaming at me for what I'd done, saying I didn't have to kill them. He told me I was stupid. And that's when I snapped. I sliced the side of his face and we drove off the road and crashed.'

'Jesus,' I whispered.

She nodded. 'I know, crazy, isn't it? That's when I went into a coma and blah blah blah.'

'What about Andy Butler?' I asked, my voice quavering at the monster before me.

'I saw him on a night out. One of my friends knew him. He was married, had kids, you know. I pulled him that night – it was so easy, Jack. I took him down an alley and slit his throat. He gurgled up blood as you've never seen.' She hunched over into a terrifying giggle.

'What – what about Peter Lewes? My God, your best friend's husband.'

'Well, you see,' she began, 'Peter told me many times he liked me over the years. I loved Alison, as you know, and I ignored him for years. Then I got sick of it. I had to find out if he'd actually cheat on her. I wasn't accepting it, Jack. I wasn't letting him do that to my best friend – not a fucking chance. The night he died, I left the club, didn't I – I don't know if you remember… we were at Popworld? He told Alison he was leaving, and I told you I had a headache. I got in the taxi with him.'

I waited, my heart beating so fast.

'Then I told the driver to pull over because I felt sick.' A grin formed on her face. 'We got out near the park. I told him I'd fancied him for years and I wanted him. Then I suggested we go deeper into the park.'

My stomach twisted at the thought of it. Her psychotic manipulation led my friend into it.

'As he lifted his top off, I pulled the knife from my handbag and stabbed him more times than I can remember. I left him to bleed out and flagged a taxi down on the main road.'

I stared at her. I didn't believe what she was saying. I shuddered in my chair with anger.

'I've tied an extra special knot in that, Jack. You're not going anywhere.'

'What about Henry?' I shouted. 'The big man who came around…'

'Oh, Henry, he was a strapping gentleman, wasn't he?' She pouted her full lips at me. 'The plan was the same. I'd seen him a few times at the gym and we got talking. I found out he had a wife and three kids. He played into my hands, Jack. I would've killed him in our bedroom if needs be.'

'So…?' I said.

'And now you're wondering why you're sitting where you are? Why your watch is in the little magical keepsake box?'

I gave her a cautious nod.

'I received a letter from your PA, Debra, who informed me about your little seedy affair, Jack. What can I say – I'm disappointed in you. You have everything you need right here, in this fucking house. Don't you?'

I bowed my head and stared at the floor.

'I can't accept it, Jack,' she continued. 'You also have to die – the world will be better off without men like you. Who thinks they can go around, doing as they please? It doesn't work like that.'

She took a step closer to me. I tensed, watching the knife in her hand.

Outside, I heard the faint sound of a police siren grow louder as the seconds ticked by. My heart beat quicker, a glimmer of hope rising within me.

Joanne smiled. 'They're too late, Jack. No one's going to save you.'

She took a step toward me with the knife in her hand.

101

Toddington

Clarke threw the driver's door open after he brought the car to a halt outside the Haynes' house. He jumped out quickly and dashed towards the front door. Horton wasn't far behind him. Clarke pushed down on the handle, but it was locked.

'Bastard!' he shouted. He then gave six heavy knocks, his knuckles colliding with the thick glass. 'C'mon, c'mon,' he muttered.

'No one is coming, boss,' Horton said, after a lengthy silence.

Clarke sighed. 'Get the ram, go on, get…'

Horton shifted across the gravel towards the back of the Astra, opened the boot, and grabbed the battering ram. He ran over with it as fast as he could.

'Go on, go on,' Clarke shouted, taking a step back, making room for him.

Horton stood sideways to the door, swung back the ram, and brought it down as hard as he could. The door smashed inwards, metal and plastic splintering everywhere. He dropped the ram on the doorstep and headed inside, closely followed by Clarke.

'Hello?' Horton shouted in the silence of the house, unclipping the baton from his belt.

They stopped at the base of the stairs and listened, batons steady in their hands. To their left, the door to the study was closed. The silence was interrupted by a loud scream coming from inside the study.

Clarke darted left, opening the door.

The screaming was so loud, they winced.

Joanne Haynes was down on the floor, laying on her back shuddering in agony, a volcano of blood coming from a severe stab wound to her stomach. Blood surrounded her, pooling on the floor.

'Help me,' she shouted in between the screams. 'Help me.'

To their left, Jack Haynes was standing a few metres away from her, the knife on the floor by his feet. He had his palms pressed on the top of his head, his face in absolute terror.

Clarke stepped towards Jack. 'Freeze! Keep your hands where I could see them. Turn around, turn around, keep your hands where they are, Jack—'

'Hey, this isn't what it looks like!' Jack pleaded.

'Do not move!' Clarke screamed, kicking the knife away. It slid quickly across the floor, coming to rest against the skirting board underneath the desk. Clarke brought Jack's hands down behind his back and cuffed him. 'On your knees!'

Jack lowered to the floor and yelped.

Clarke turned to Horton. 'Ring an ambulance, James!'

Horton plucked his phone from his pocket and made the call. He ended the call by telling them to hurry up. Horton stayed with Joanne, pressing down on her stomach to suppress the heavy bleeding.

'You're safe now,' he told her.

'Thank God, thank you, thank you,' she panted under her breath.

'Hey – don't talk, just relax.'

In the hallway, Clarke man handled Jack through the open doorway, across the gravel, and put him in the back of the police car. He read him his rights and slammed the door shut.

Jack dipped his head and started to cry.

102

Police Station
JACK

I was in a cell for an hour before they brought me into the interview room. I took a seat next to my lawyer. Clarke and Horton sat across from me, scowling at me as if I was a piece of shit. They turned on the recorder, said who they were, what time it was, the date, and who they were speaking to. They also mentioned the lawyer's name, Jamie Crane.

They didn't offer me a cup of coffee this time.

Over the course of an hour, I explained everything to them. About Joanne. The names of the people she'd killed. How their deaths were unsolved. I relayed exactly the same story as she told me when I was tied to the desk chair a few hours before. I told them when we heard the sirens, she came at me with the knife but, instead of using it on me, she cut the ropes and pulled me up, she then pushed me away towards the French doors. Then she stabbed herself in the stomach and fell to the ground, started screaming just before they arrived.

They held me in a cell overnight, until they checked the story.

The biggest giveaway that I never stabbed her was that my prints weren't found on the knife, funnily enough. It showed how often I did the cooking.

The next day, in the interview room, my lawyer built a solid case for me. He told the detectives there was no evidence to actually suggest that I had done anything wrong. They told me they'd check out the authenticity of my statement, to make sure the facts were true about the men she had killed.

They were.

I had no part in the things she had done in the past, nor was I responsible for stabbing her in her stomach.

Joanne Haynes was sentenced to life

I was set free, not guilty of being associated with the awful crimes that were kept secret for years.

Rot in there, Joanne, fucking rot in there.

103

(One week after Joanne's arrest)
Toddington
JACK

Lucy cried in her room constantly. She couldn't believe the things her mother had done. To be honest, I couldn't – it was horrible. I walked around all day feeling sick about it. Everything in the house reminded me of her. I wanted to either vomit or smash the place to pieces.

DCI Clarke and DS Horton came over yesterday to check on us. I told them I felt horrendous, which they said was to be expected. They told me to take it easy and keep my mind active. That things would get easier in time.

I hadn't been up long. It was just after 10 a.m. I just checked on Lucy – she was still asleep in her room. She had been spending a lot of time up there since her mother was arrested, most likely to cut herself off from everything or everyone. She mainly slept during the day, then she'd be up most of the night, not being able to sleep. I couldn't bring myself to start laying down rules this soon.

Both of our lives were shattered to pieces.

Two days ago, Alison Lewes came to the house. I didn't know what to say to her, instead, I cried into her arms, apologising that I hadn't seen how much of a monster Joanne was. She told me it wasn't my fault. She said she was heartbroken but she was happy she knew the truth. Glad she could let it go. I gave her back Peter's Omega watch, which brought a tear to her eye just before she left.

I went into the kitchen and made coffee. When the kettle boiled and clicked off, I realised how alone I really was. But I needed to be strong, I needed to stay strong for Lucy. I put a spoonful of coffee into an empty mug and dropped some milk in. I left the kitchen, went into the study, and slumped into the chair at my desk.

I spent most of the day catching up with work and reading a few chapters of Linwood Barclay's 'No Time For Goodbye' before I started to feel tired. I heard Lucy walking around upstairs and, glancing at the time in the corner of the desktop screen, It was 9.48 p.m. I placed the bookmark on page 343 and lowered the book down onto the surface of the desk, then yawned loudly.

I stood up and left the study, then heard Lucy coming down the stairs.

'Hey,' I said, waiting for her at the bottom.

She ignored me, turned, and headed toward the kitchen. I stopped and turned, watching her.

'Lucy?'

'Fuck off, Dad.'

I was taken aback. 'Excuse me?'

She stopped in the kitchen doorway and turned. 'Fuck. Off. Dad.'

I was frozen to the wooden floor at the base of the stairs, stunned by her words. She had been through so much over the past few weeks.

Witnessing a murder.

The thugs breaking in.

Losing her uncle.

Finding out her father was a thief.

And lastly, finding out her mother was a psychotic killer, who would now spend the rest of her life behind bars.

Taking a breath, I decided to let it go. Then I walked up the stairs. We'd talk about it tomorrow. I closed my bedroom door, padded across the carpet, and pulled the curtains across. Climbing into bed, I let out a yawn and, when my head hits the pillow, it was only a few minutes until I succumbed to sleep.

An hour before Lucy had come downstairs, she found it.

The letter.

It had come in today's post and Jack had taken it upstairs and left it on her desk. She hadn't even seen it during the hours she had spent up there.

'What's this?' she'd said, picking it up. She broke away the seal, pulled it out, and took a seat on the bed.

After she read it, she cried into her pillow, her whole body shaking with emotion. Finally, she wiped her eyes and made her way down the stairs where she saw her father waiting at the bottom.

He'd said 'Hi' and she told him to 'Fuck off'. She heard him climb the stairs and go into his bedroom.

Full of emotions, Lucy wiped her eyes once more. She left the kitchen and padded along the hallway slowly. At the base of the stairs, she took a left and calmly climbed them.

At the end of the landing, at her father's closed door, she stopped, looked down, and re-read the letter:

My Dear Lucy,

By now, you will know what I've done and how much of a monster I am. The things I've done in the past are inexcusable and I'm sorry I'm different from the person you always knew me to be.

You should know the things I did were for a reason. That reason is to stand up for what's right. To stand up to people who do us wrong.

Every one of them deserved what they got. They had a loving family and were married. We can't let these people do that to us, we have to stand up for what's right.

Your father has done the same. He had committed the same crime, Lucy. Sleeping with his PA at work. I can't forgive him, I can't. I loved him so much, God knew I did, but I'm not letting him do that to you and me – it isn't fair.

We deserve better than that, Lucy.

I failed in my attempt to kill your father, Lucy, which you now know. He deserves to die. No man should ever treat a woman that way, no man should ever treat his family that way.

I know I probably won't ever see you again. I accept that. I'll miss you more than words could say. It's hard but I accept that. But when you have morals, you need to live by them, you need to make a choice and stick with it. Forever.

Everything I've done was for you, Lucy. I love you so much.

Whatever you choose to do in your life, I want you to know that I'll always be proud of you.

Lots of love,
Your mother,
Joanne.

Tears filled the corners of her eyes, but she wiped them away with the back of her hand.

She dropped the letter from her mother onto the carpet and composed herself. She leaned forward and grabbed the handle of her father's bedroom door and opened it slowly.

She slowly stepped into the darkness with the knife in her hand.

The End.

C. J. Grayson

Acknowledgements

I personally would like to thank you, the reader, for taking the time to read my debut novel. I hope you enjoyed it as much as I did writing it.

After four years of working on it, and making countless changes to the plot and characters, I finally got there.

I would like to said a special thank you to my sister, Laura, who spent countless hours proof reading this – she has a lot going on in her life with full-time university and working as many hours as she could at a local café in between, so fitting in the time to do this, is massively appreciated. She picked up on things I hadn't even thought about, which I've made changes to. So, credit to her. She was finishing University next year with her degree. I know she'll do very well in life – I'm very proud of her.

Another special thank you goes to my mother-in-law, Judith, who also took the time to proofread this – she picked up on some mistakes I would never have picked up on (mistakes which could have been embarrassing). She also gave me an honest opinion of the book and we discussed a possible alternative ending – which I decided to use.

I would like to thank my Grandad, Arthur (a fellow writer who uses the pen name of A. K. Adams), for his guidance throughout this journey. He has given me food for thought along the way, in terms of the ideology of writing and the craft that goes into it.

A big thank you to other members of my family and my friended, who I'm sure, are sick of me shutting myself out from the world to write.

My biggest thank you goes to my wife, Becky. If not for her, you simply would not be reading this right now. She's an amazing wife and an amazing mother to our three boys.

For the four years of doing this, she has given me the time to write it, the time to change it, the time to edit it, and the time for me to be the person who I believe I am. A writer.

Thanks,
Chris.

About the Author

C. J. Grayson has self-published this debut novel after years of reading and writing. He had always had the passion from a young age and decided to put this novel together, battling through the joys – and, as many writers know, the struggles – of writing, editing, etc.

He did an apprenticeship in Pipefitting and has worked in Engineering and construction. He completed his HND in Mechanical Engineering and a Level 6 Diploma in Business Management.

He was born in 1989, lives in Darlington, in the North East of England. He had married to Becky, and has three boys.

He has published his 2nd novel (That Night: book 1 in DI Max Byrd and DI Orion Tanzy) and his 3rd (Never Came Home: book 2 in DI Max Byrd and DI Orion Tanzy) which are both based in his hometown of Darlington and include his new characters: DI Max Byrd and DI Orion Tanzy. They are a part of a series. He is currently writing the 3rd book (his 4th) in the series.

If you can spare a few minutes and enjoyed this book, he'd really appreciate some feedback on Amazon and / or Goodreads. Your thoughts and support are more valuable to him than you'll ever know. They keep him up till the early hours writing.

Keep up to date with his current work and updates regarding future novels through his website and following social profiles. You can also sign up to his Newsletter by going on www.cjgraysonauthor.com and filling in the very short form at the bottom of the page. You will get updates on progress, exclusive giveaways, and news before the rest of the world does, so feel free to sign up.

www.cjgraysonauthor.com

www.facebook.com/cjgraysonauthor/

www.goodreads.com/author/show/19642709.C_J_Grayson

www.instagram.com/cjgrayson_writer/

www.twitter.com/CJGrayson4

Thank you

Printed in Great Britain
by Amazon

43932452R00219